CHAPTER 141: MONSTER TRANCE

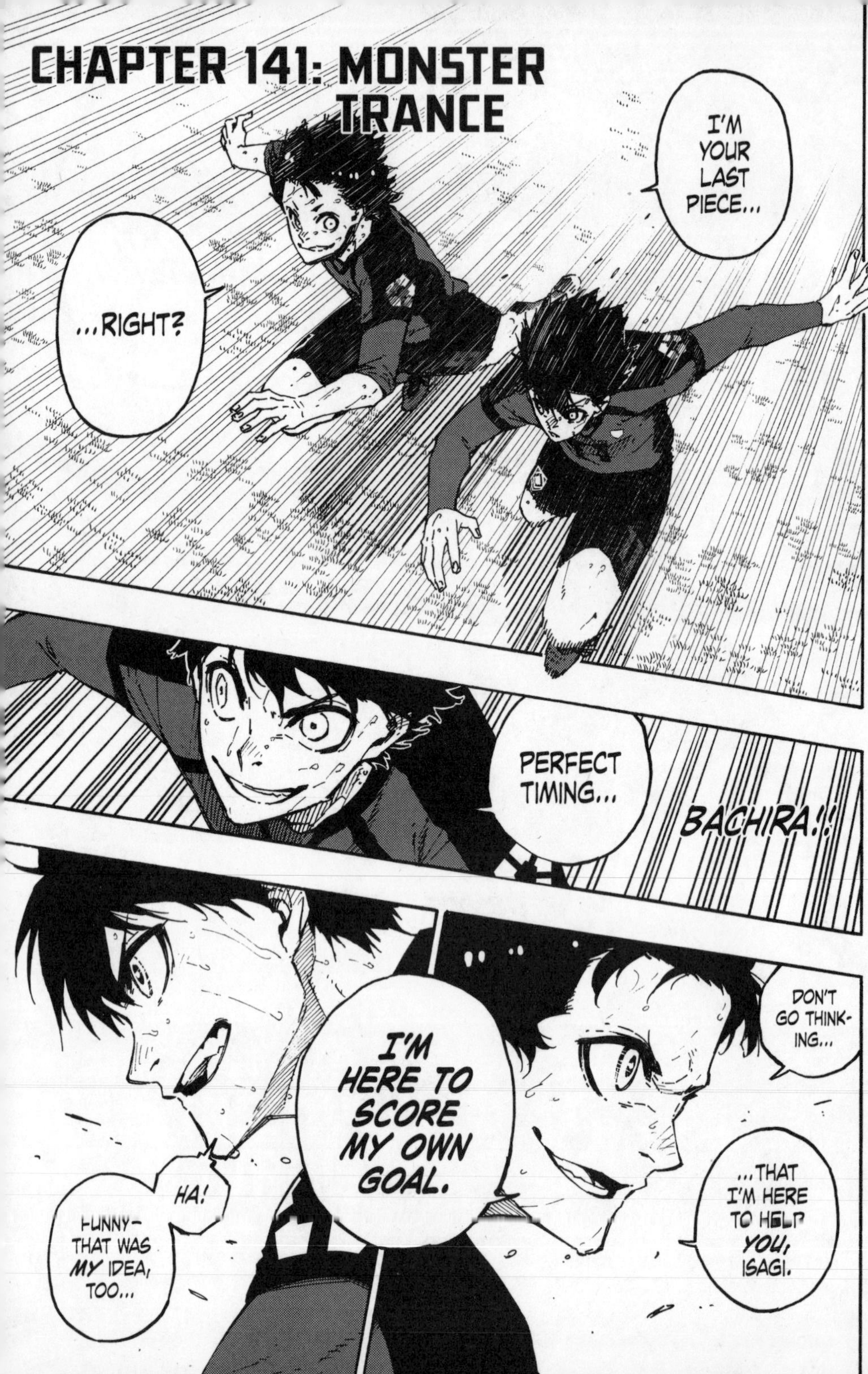
I'M YOUR LAST PIECE...
...RIGHT?
PERFECT TIMING...
BACHIRA!!
DON'T GO THINKING...
...THAT I'M HERE TO HELP *YOU*, ISAGI.
I'M HERE TO SCORE MY OWN GOAL.
HA!
FUNNY—THAT WAS *MY* IDEA, TOO...

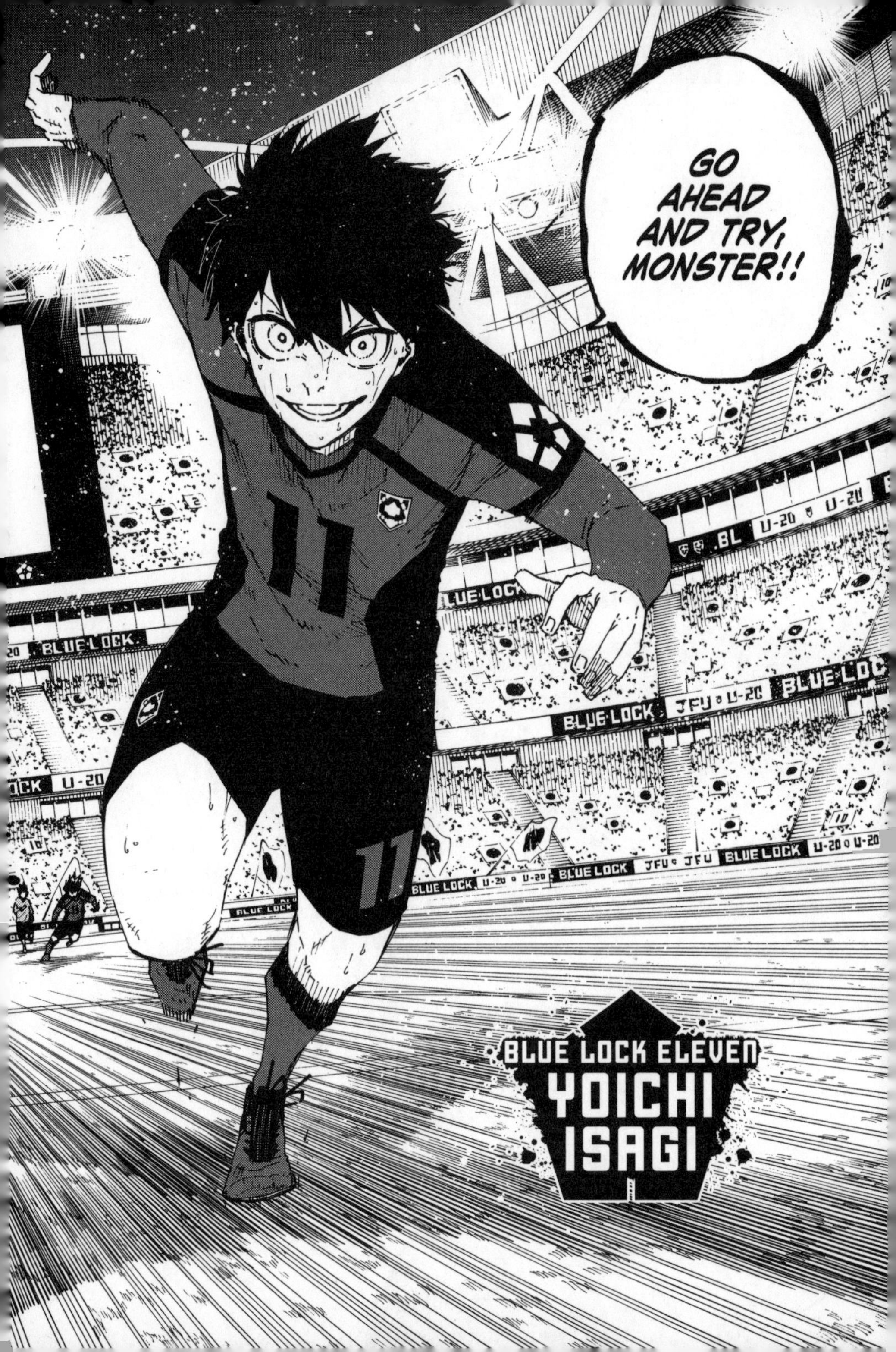
GO AHEAD AND TRY, MONSTER!!
BLUE LOCK ELEVEN
YOICHI ISAGI

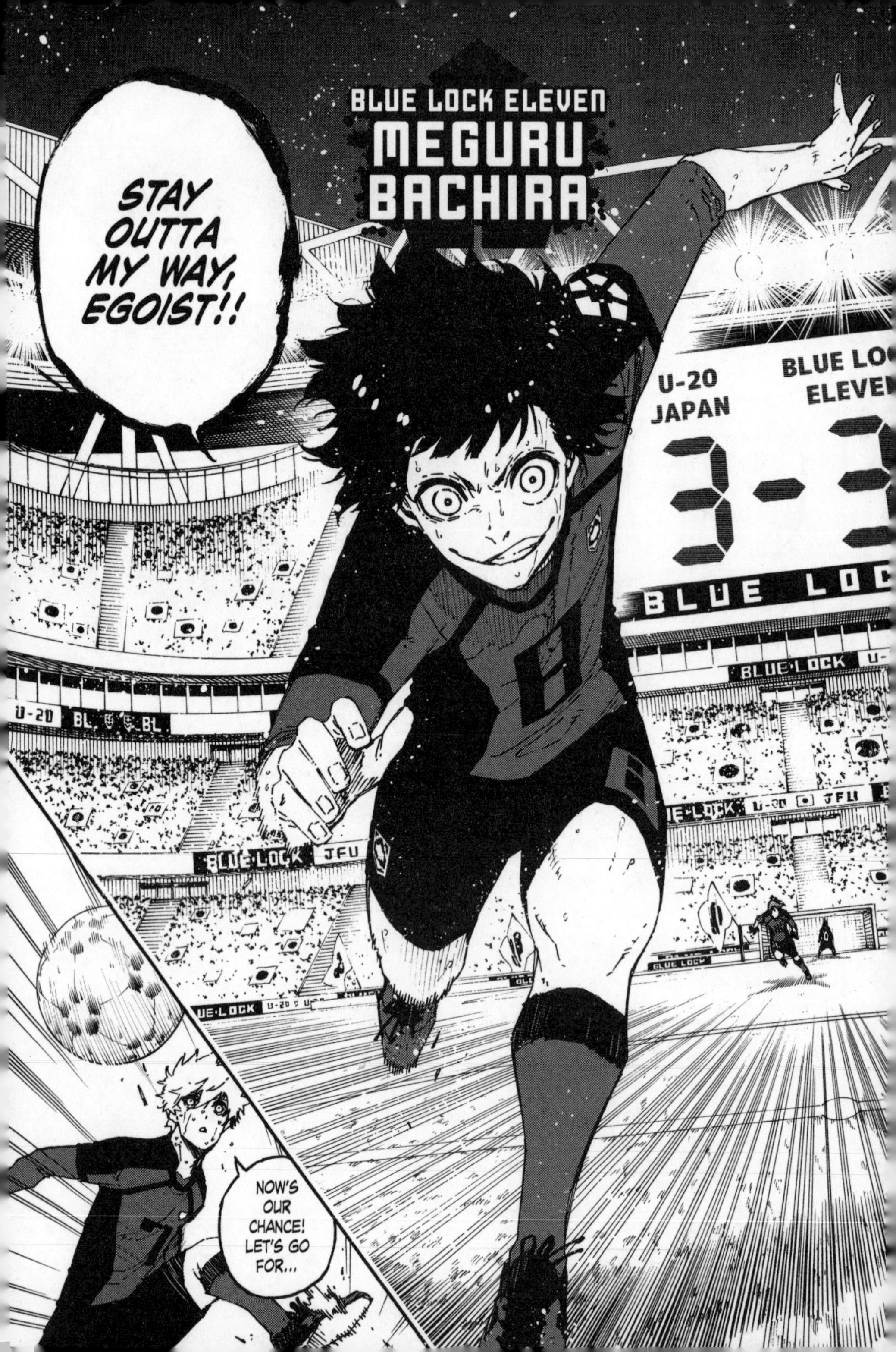
BLUE LOCK ELEVEN
MEGURU BACHIRA
STAY OUTTA MY WAY, EGOIST!!
U-20 JAPAN
3-3
NOW'S OUR CHANCE! LET'S GO FOR...

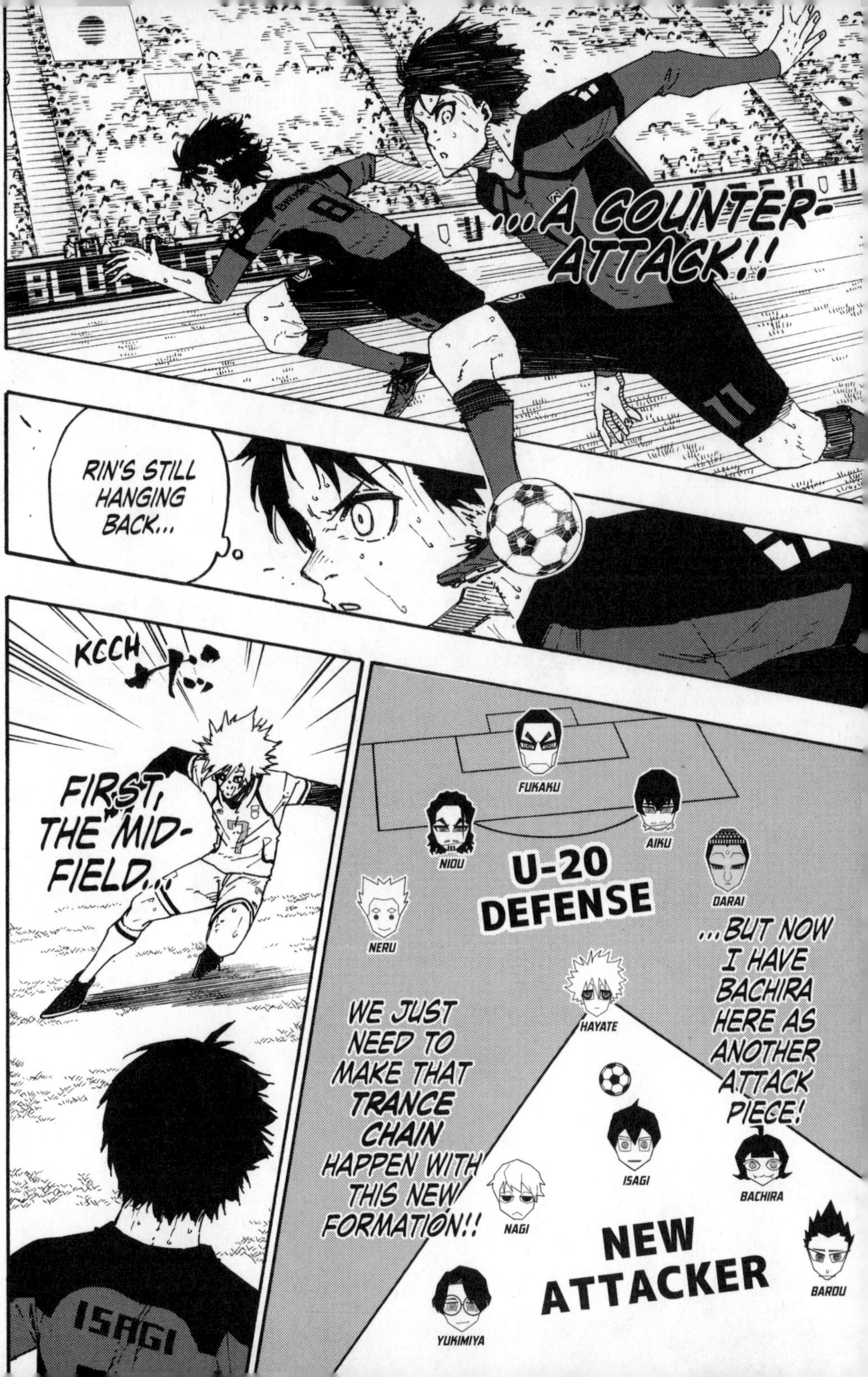
...A COUNTER-ATTACK!!
RIN'S STILL HANGING BACK...
FUKAKU
AIKU
NIOU
DARAI
U-20 DEFENSE
NERU
...BUT NOW I HAVE BACHIRA HERE AS ANOTHER ATTACK PIECE!
HAYATE
WE JUST NEED TO MAKE THAT TRANCE CHAIN HAPPEN WITH THIS NEW FORMATION!!
ISAGI
BACHIRA
NAGI
NEW ATTACKER
BAROU
YUKIMIYA
KCCH
FIRST, THE MIDFIELD...
ISAGI

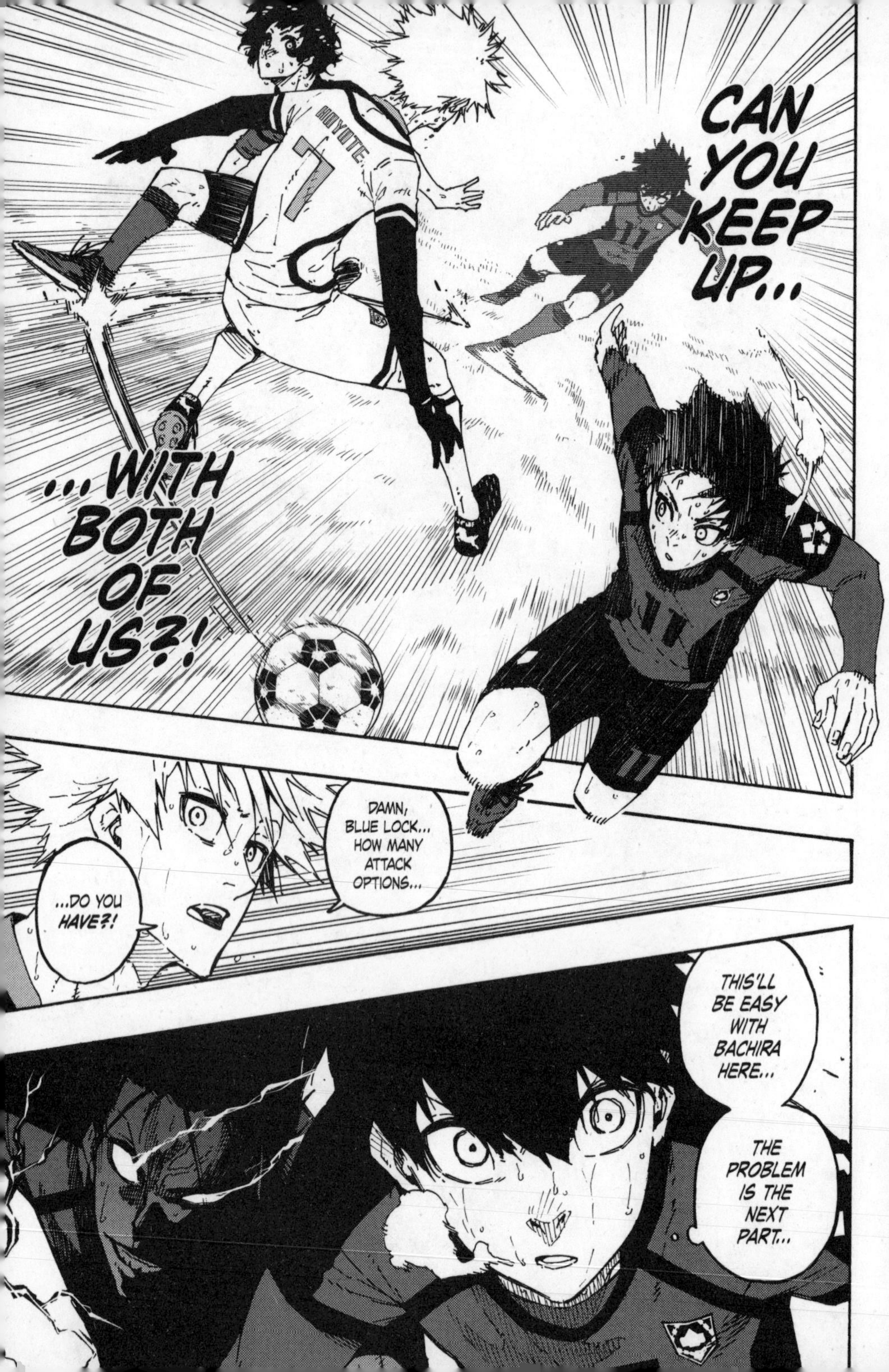
CAN YOU KEEP UP...
...WITH BOTH OF US?!
DAMN, BLUE LOCK... HOW MANY ATTACK OPTIONS...
...DO YOU HAVE?!
THIS'LL BE EASY WITH BACHIRA HERE...
THE PROBLEM IS THE NEXT PART...

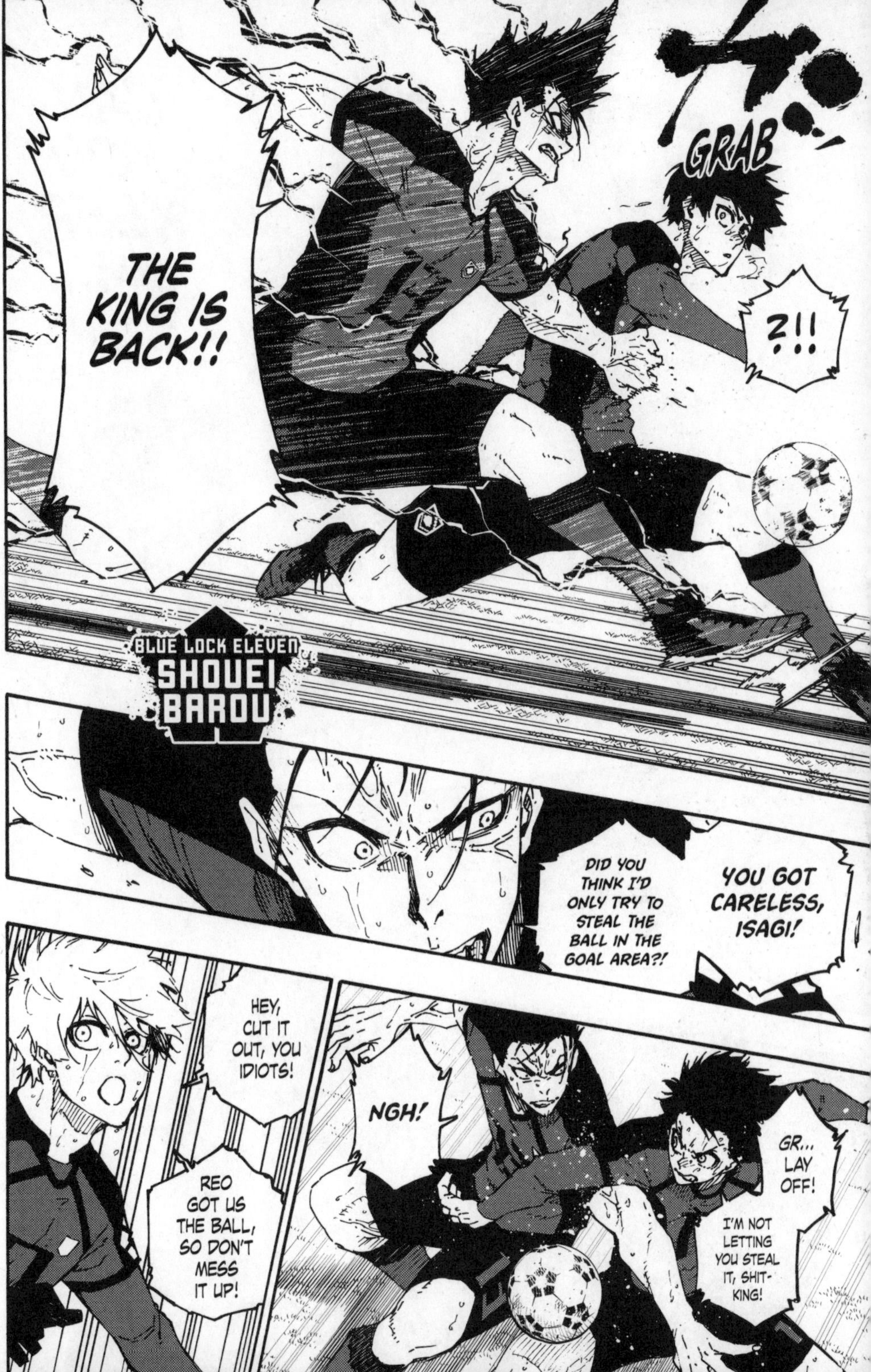
GRAB
?!!
THE KING IS BACK!!
BLUE LOCK ELEVEN
SHOUEI BAROU
YOU GOT CARELESS, ISAGI!
DID YOU THINK I'D ONLY TRY TO STEAL THE BALL IN THE GOAL AREA?!
GR... LAY OFF!
I'M NOT LETTING YOU STEAL IT, SHIT-KING!
NGH!
HEY, CUT IT OUT, YOU IDIOTS!
REO GOT US THE BALL, SO DON'T MESS IT UP!

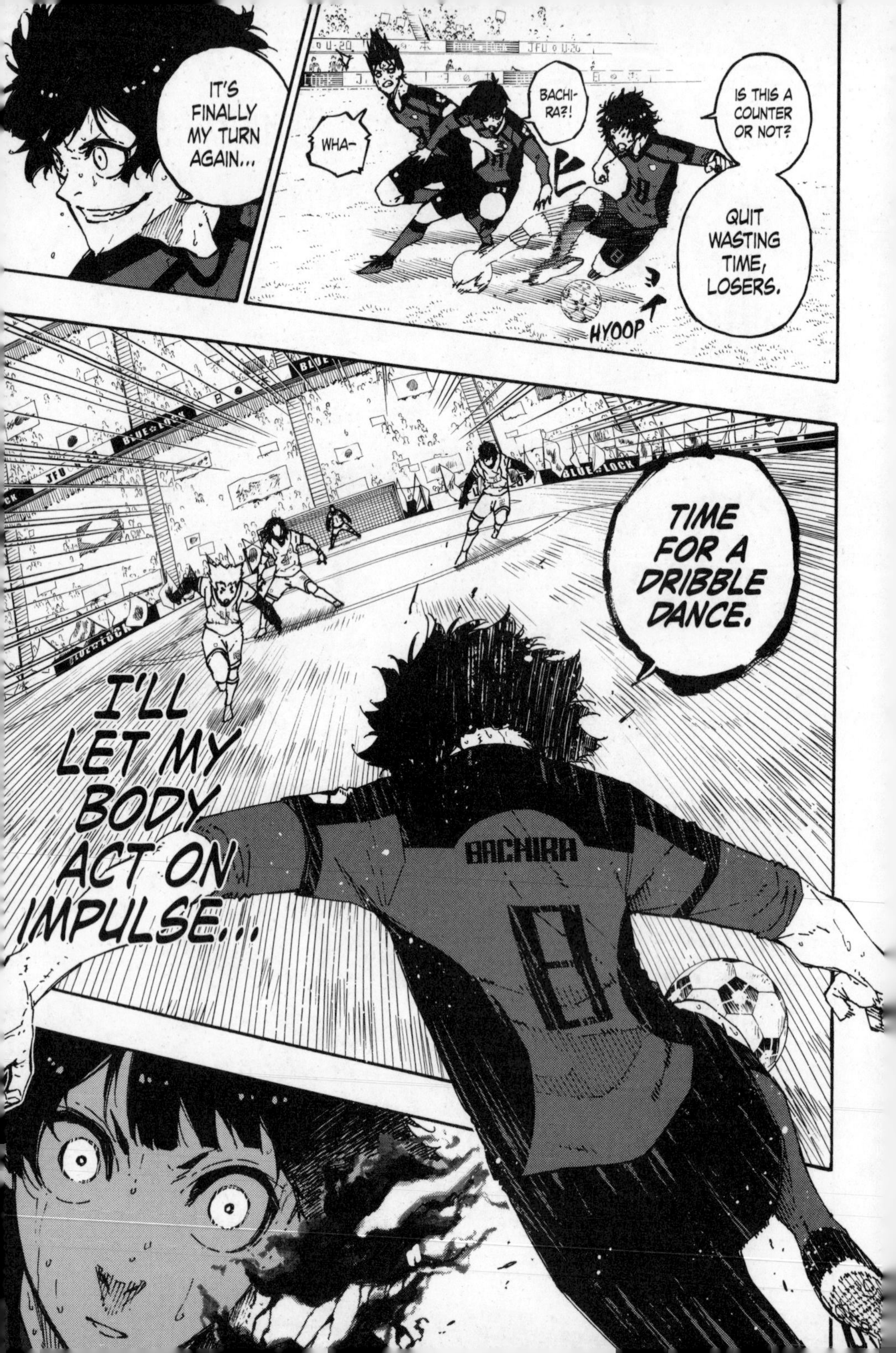
IS THIS A COUNTER OR NOT?
QUIT WASTING TIME, LOSERS.
BACHI-RA?!
WHA-
HYOOP
IT'S FINALLY MY TURN AGAIN...
TIME FOR A DRIBBLE DANCE.
I'LL LET MY BODY ACT ON IMPULSE...
BACHIRA

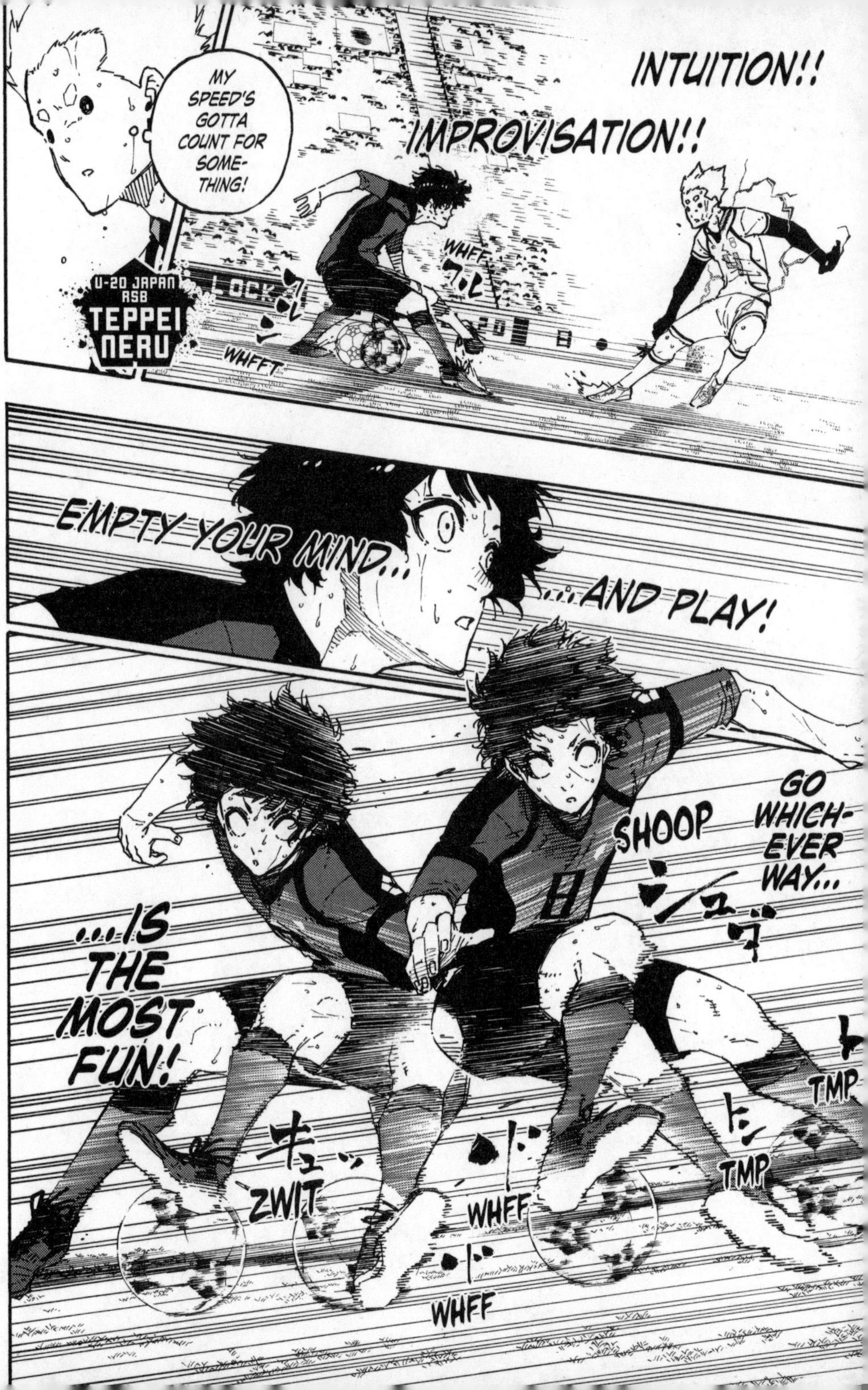
INTUITION!!
IMPROVISATION!!
MY SPEED'S GOTTA COUNT FOR SOME-THING!
U-20 JAPAN RSB TEPPEI NERU
WHFF
WHFFT
EMPTY YOUR MIND...
...AND PLAY!
GO WHICH-EVER WAY...
SHOOP
...IS THE MOST FUN!
TMP
TMP
WHFF
WHFF
ZWIT

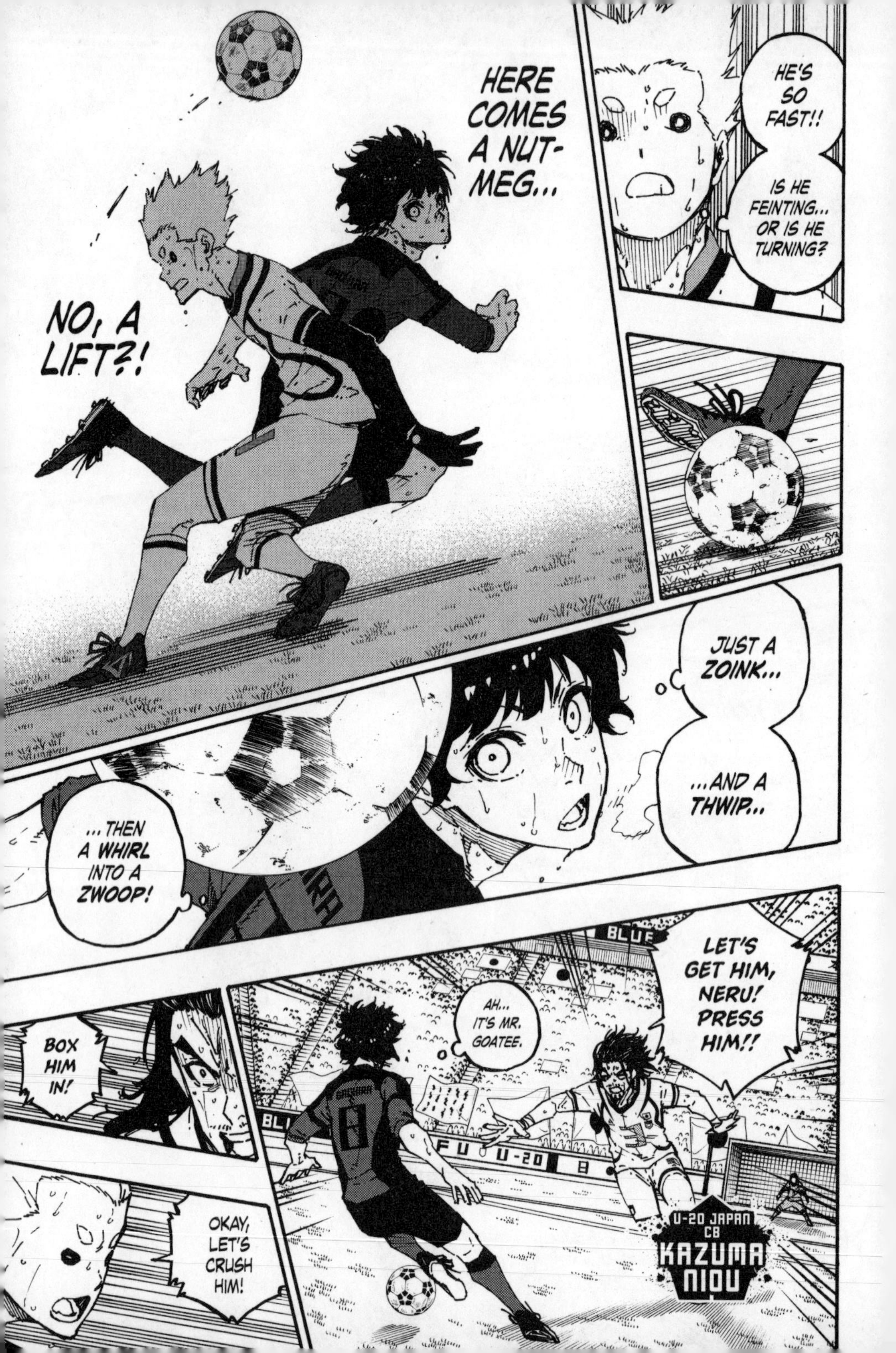
HE'S SO FAST!!
IS HE FEINTING... OR IS HE TURNING?
HERE COMES A NUT-MEG...
NO, A LIFT?!
JUST A ZOINK...
...AND A THWIP...
...THEN A WHIRL INTO A ZWOOP!
LET'S GET HIM, NERU! PRESS HIM!!
AH... IT'S MR. GOATEE.
U-20 JAPAN CB
KAZUMA NIOU
BOX HIM IN!
OKAY, LET'S CRUSH HIM!

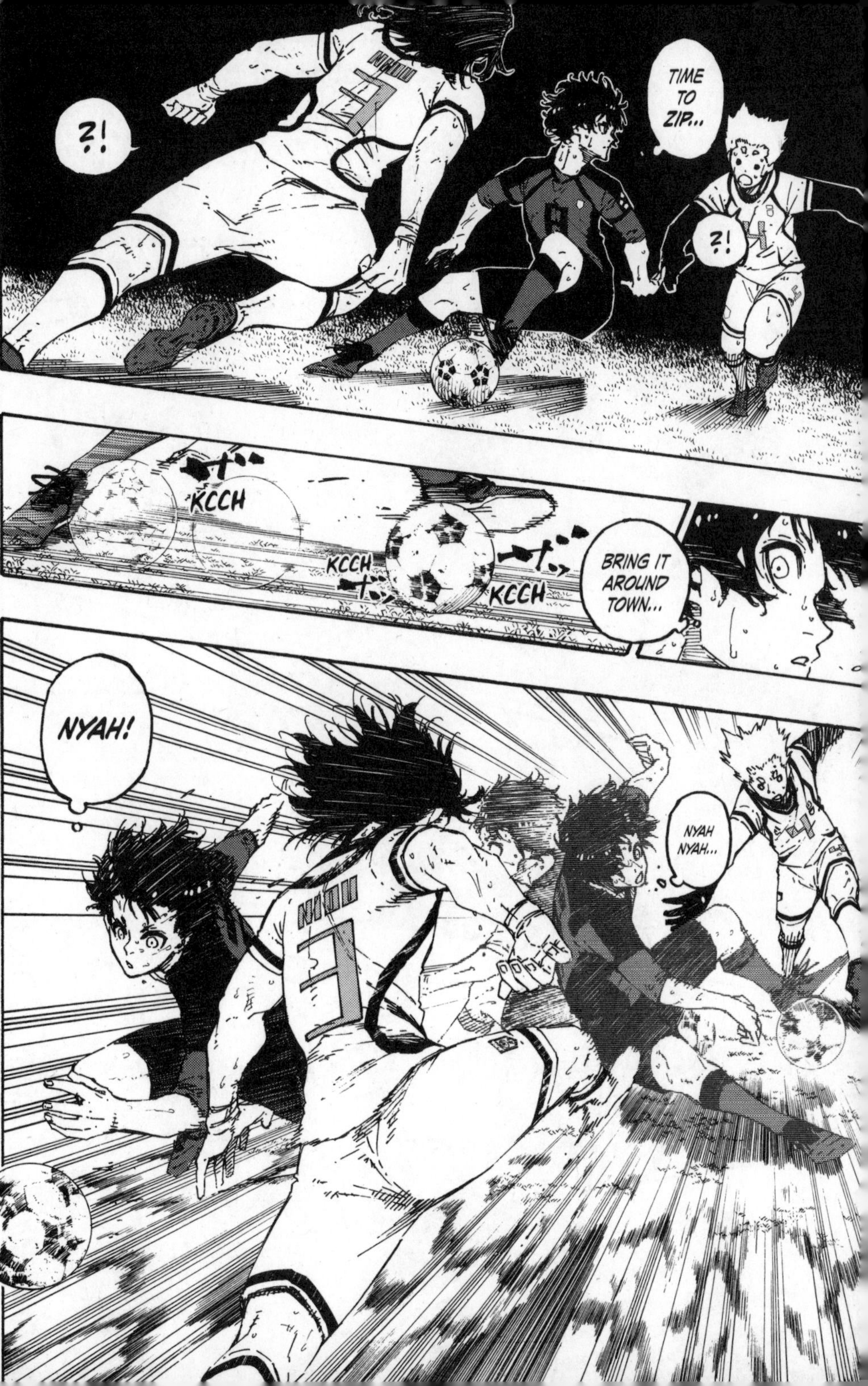
TIME TO ZIP...
?!
?!
BRING IT AROUND TOWN...
KCCH
KCCH
KCCH
NYAH NYAH...
NYAH!

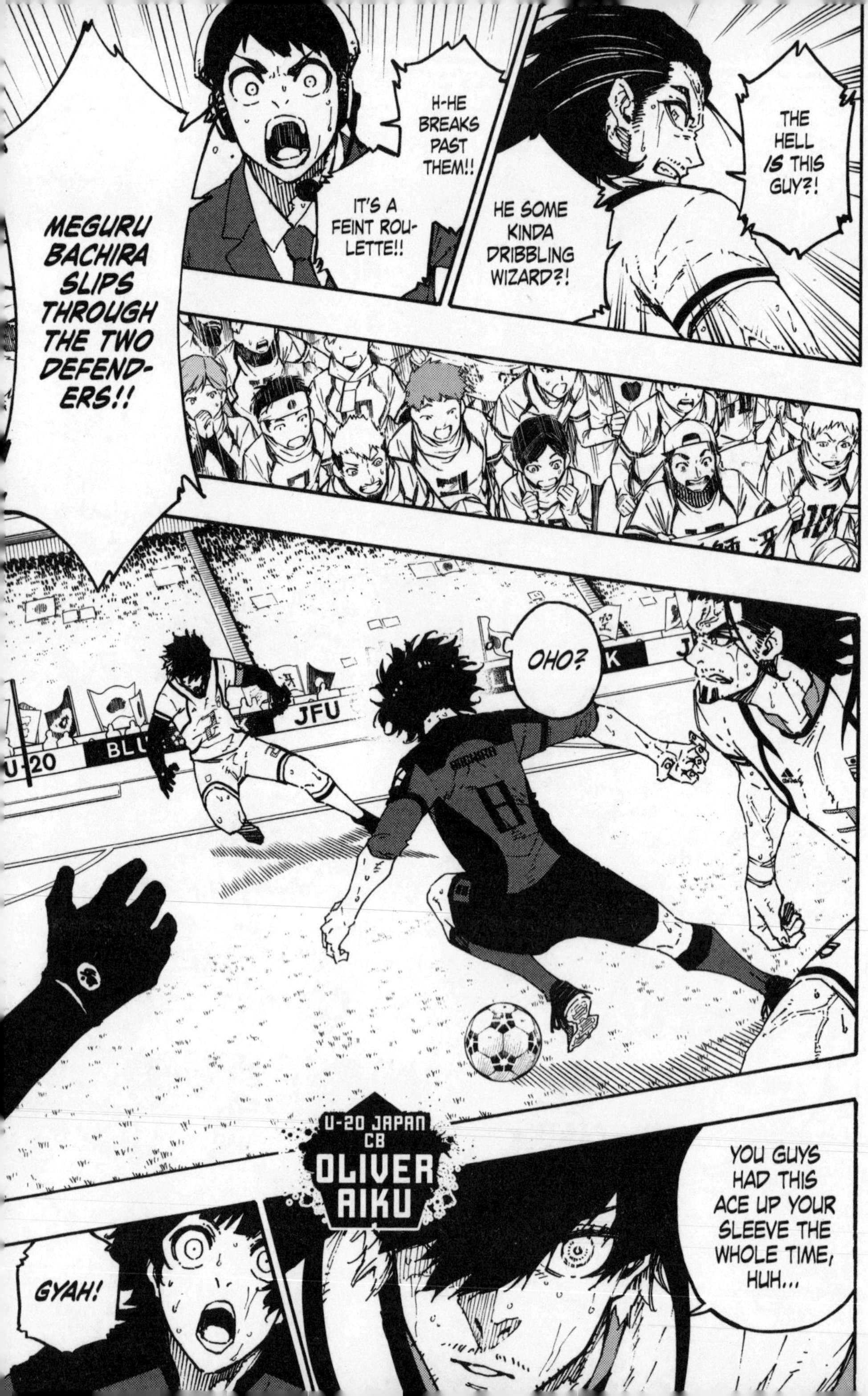
THE HELL IS THIS GUY?!
HE SOME KINDA DRIBBLING WIZARD?!
H-HE BREAKS PAST THEM!!
IT'S A FEINT ROULETTE!!
MEGURU BACHIRA SLIPS THROUGH THE TWO DEFENDERS!!
OHO?
JFU
U-20 JAPAN CB OLIVER AIKU
YOU GUYS HAD THIS ACE UP YOUR SLEEVE THE WHOLE TIME, HUH...
GYAH!

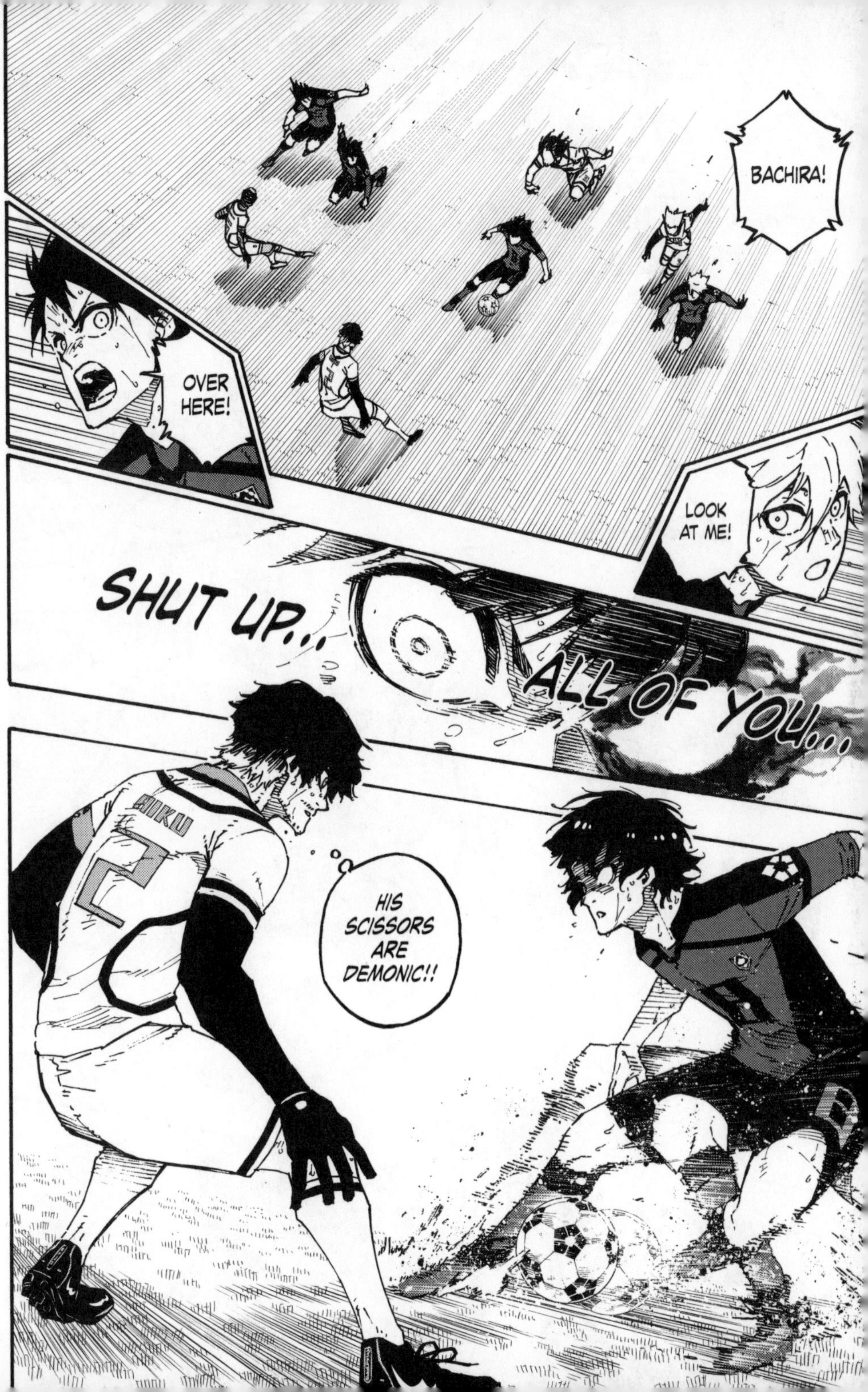
BACHIRA!
OVER HERE!
LOOK AT ME!
SHUT UP...
ALL OF YOU...
HIS SCISSORS ARE DEMONIC!!

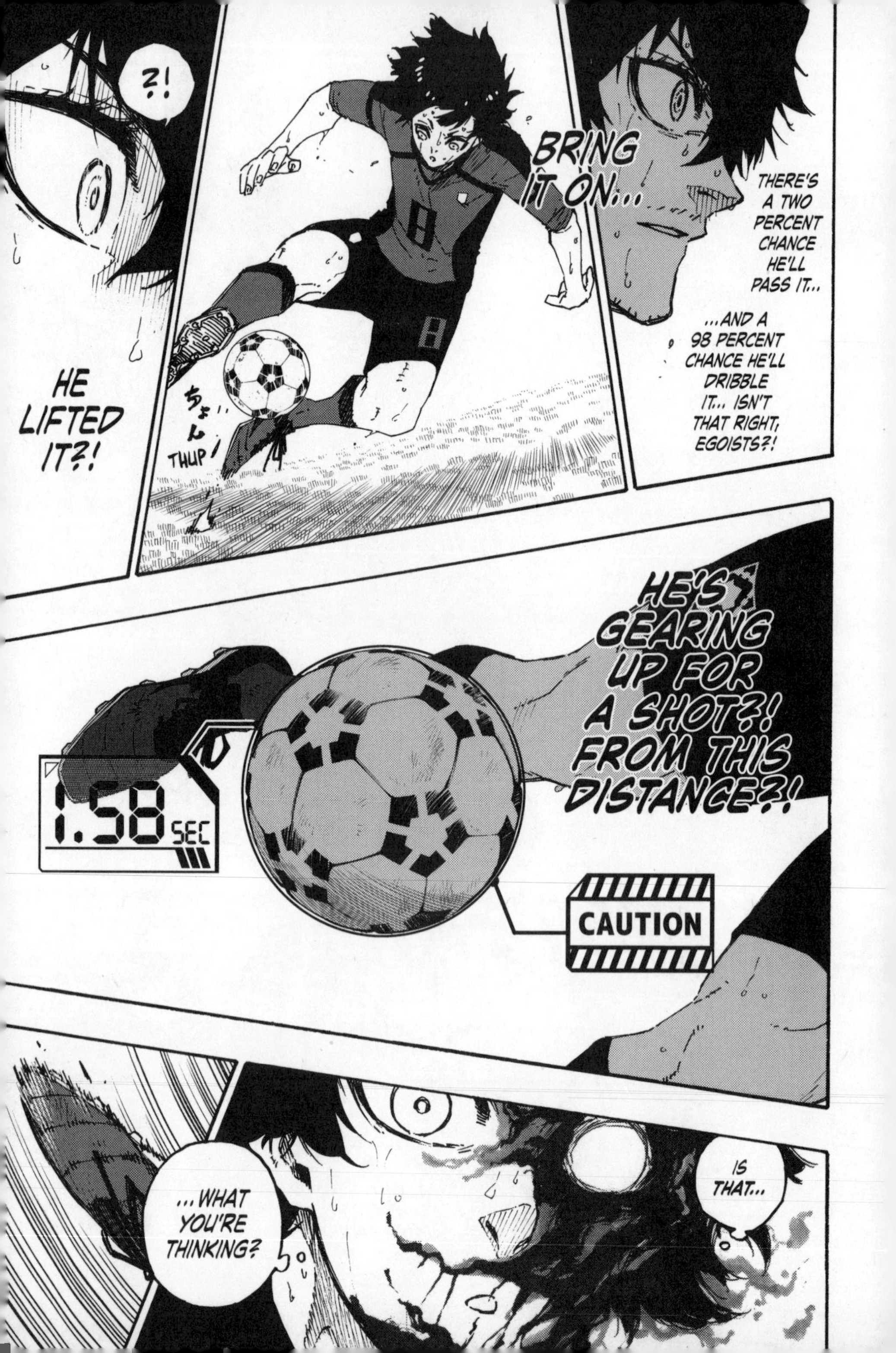
THERE'S A TWO PERCENT CHANCE HE'LL PASS IT...
...AND A 98 PERCENT CHANCE HE'LL DRIBBLE IT... ISN'T THAT RIGHT, EGOISTS?!
BRING IT ON...
ちょん
THUP
?!
HE LIFTED IT?!
HE'S GEARING UP FOR A SHOT?! FROM THIS DISTANCE?!
1.58 SEC
CAUTION
IS THAT...
...WHAT YOU'RE THINKING?

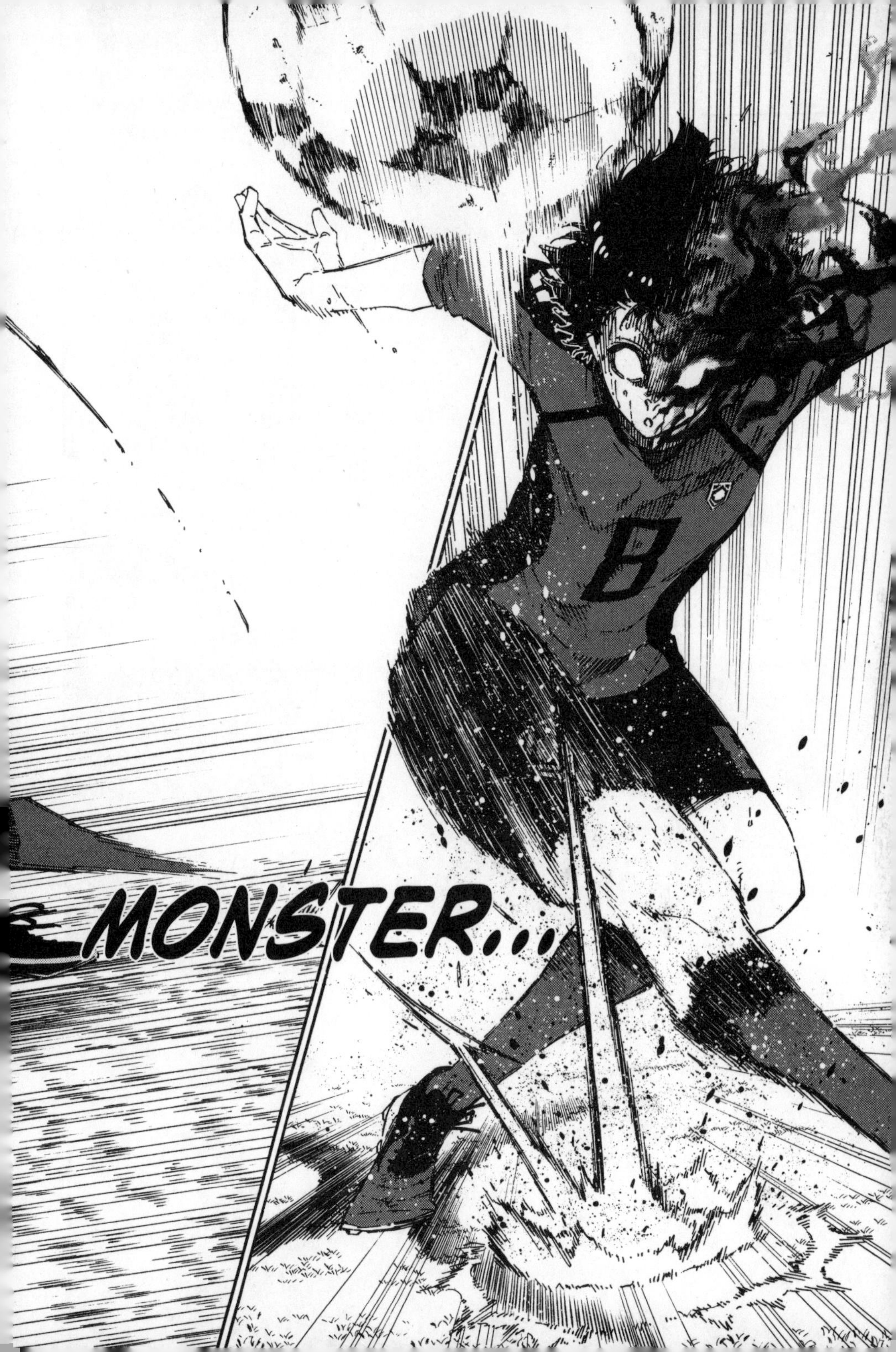
MONSTER...

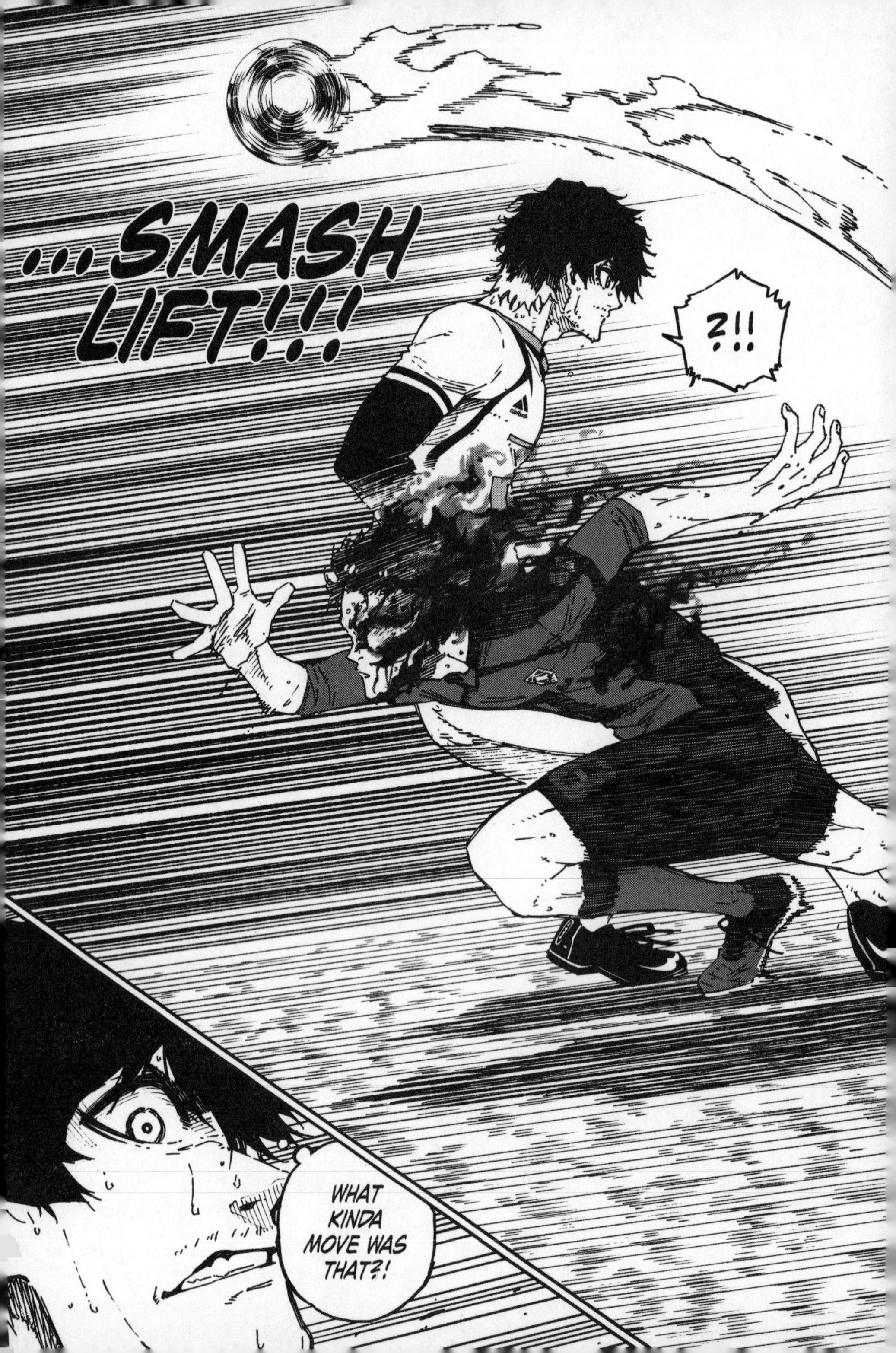
...SMASH LIFT!!!
?!!
WHAT KINDA MOVE WAS THAT?!

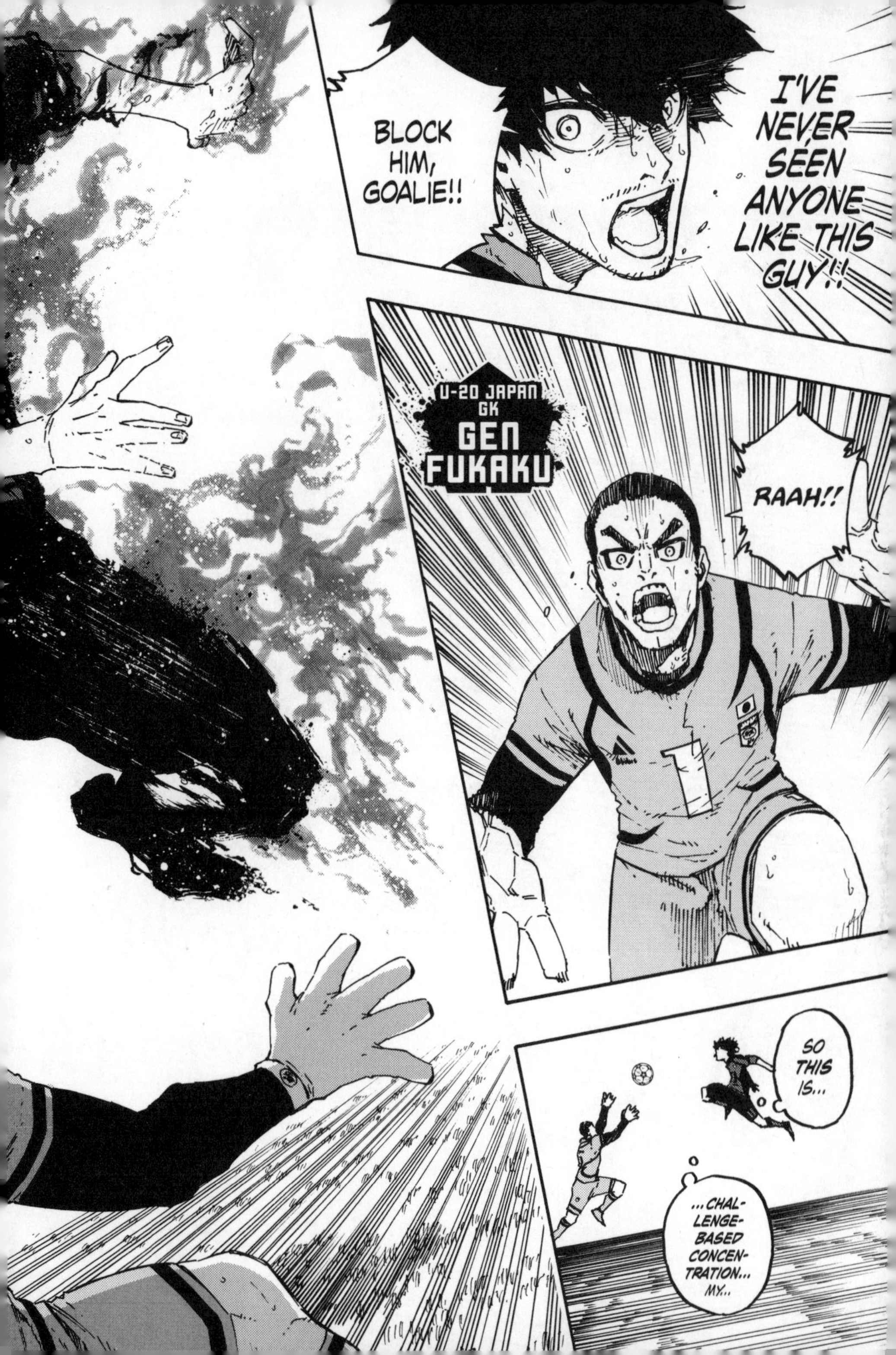
I'VE NEVER SEEN ANYONE LIKE THIS GUY!!
BLOCK HIM, GOALIE!!
RAAH!!
U-20 JAPAN GK
GEN FUKAKU
SO THIS IS...
...CHAL-LENGE-BASED CONCEN-TRATION... MY...

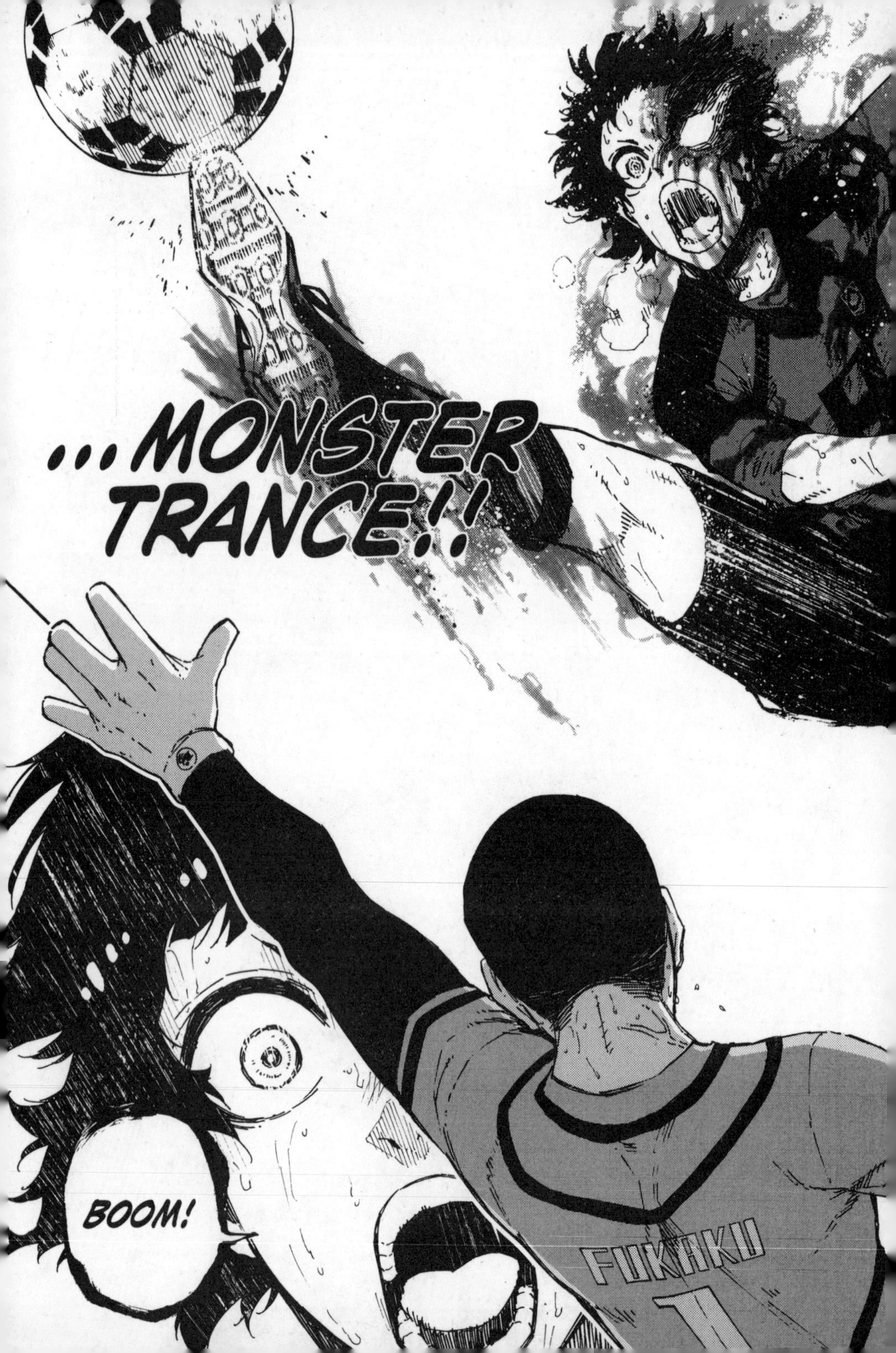
...MONSTER TRANCE!!
BOOM!
FUKAKU
1

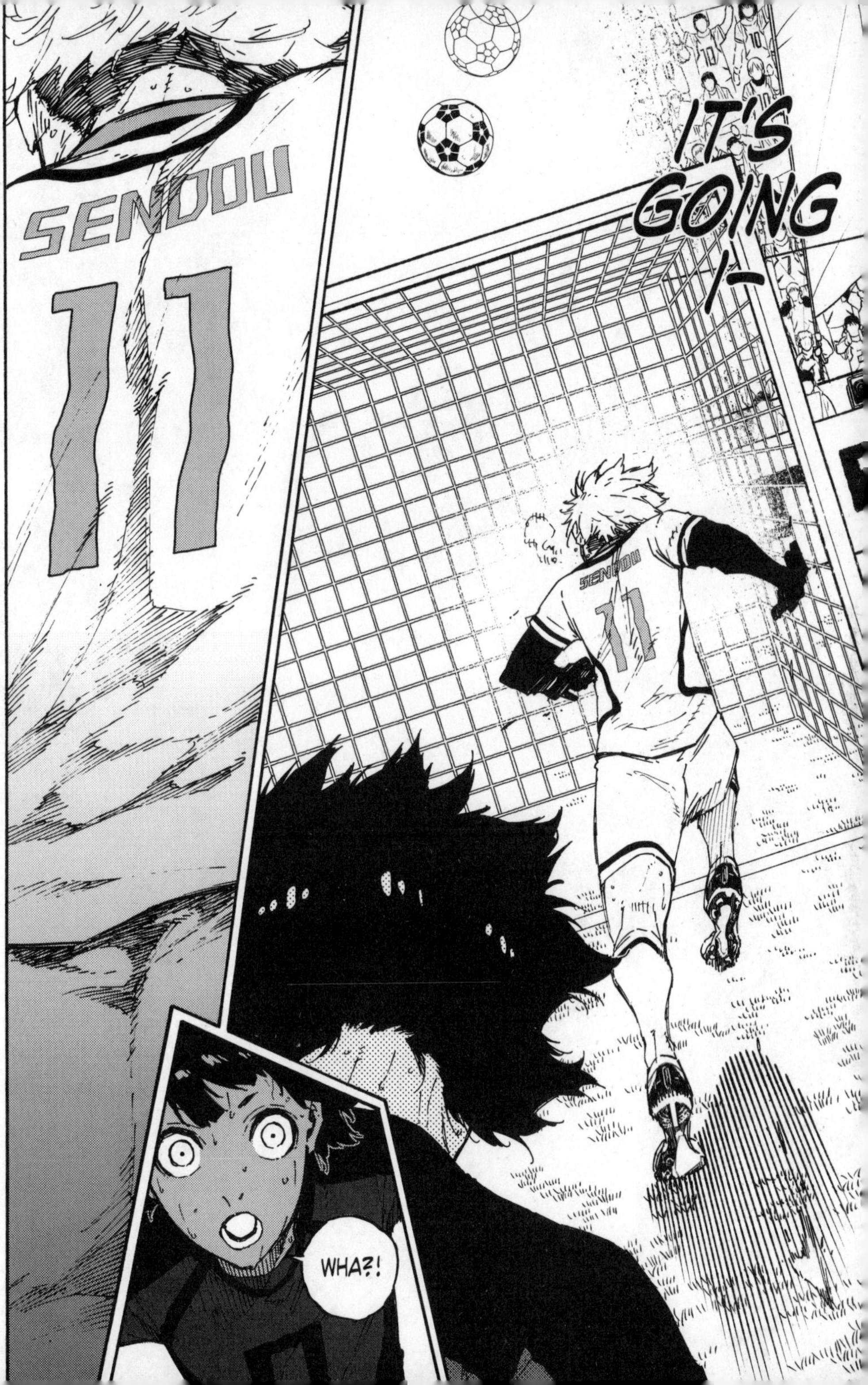
IT'S GOING I—
SENDOU
11
WHA?!

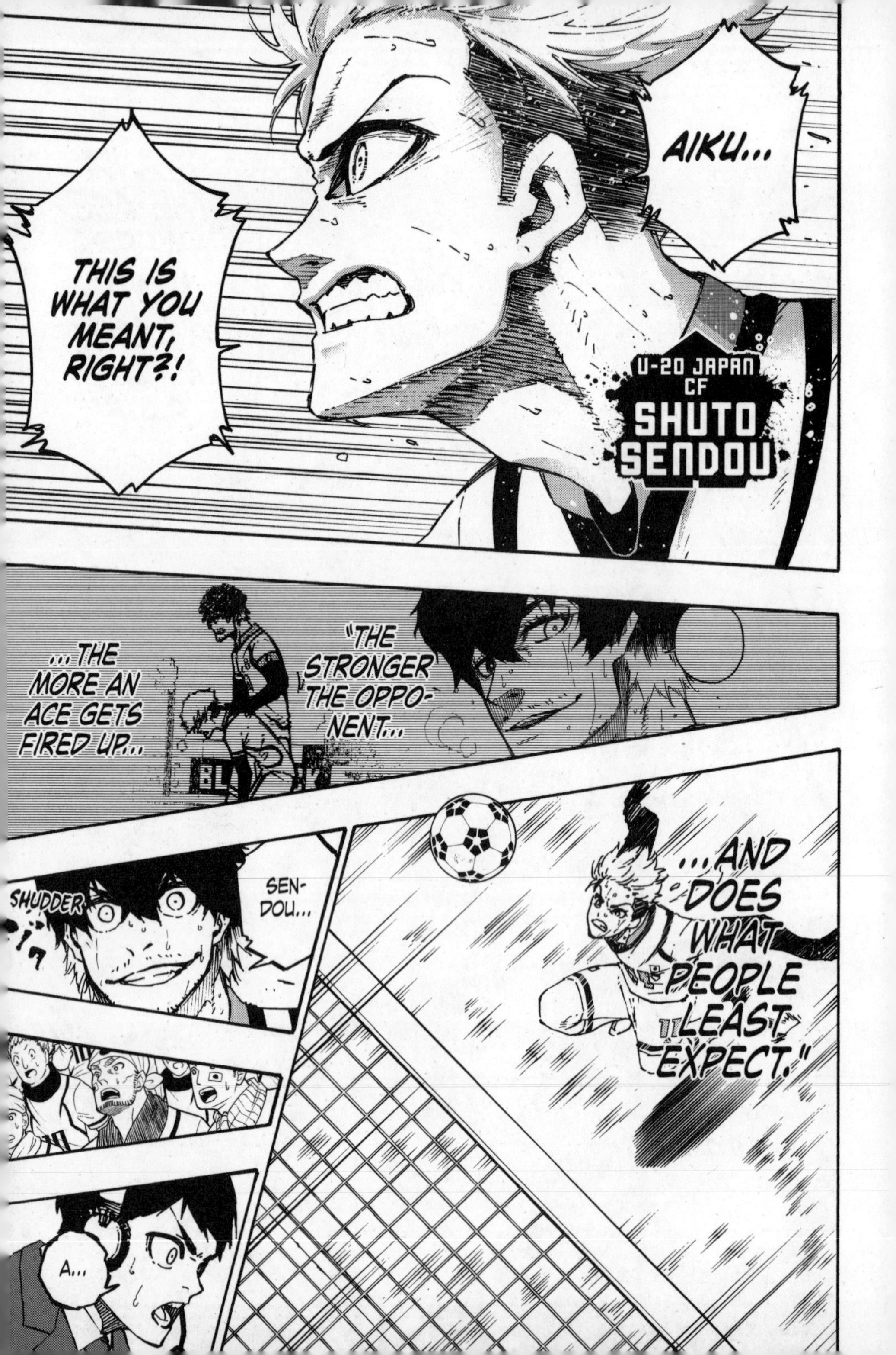
AIKU...
THIS IS WHAT YOU MEANT, RIGHT?!
U-20 JAPAN CF
SHUTO SENDOU
"THE STRONGER THE OPPO-NENT...
...THE MORE AN ACE GETS FIRED UP...
...AND DOES WHAT PEOPLE LEAST EXPECT."
SEN-DOU...
SHUDDER
A...

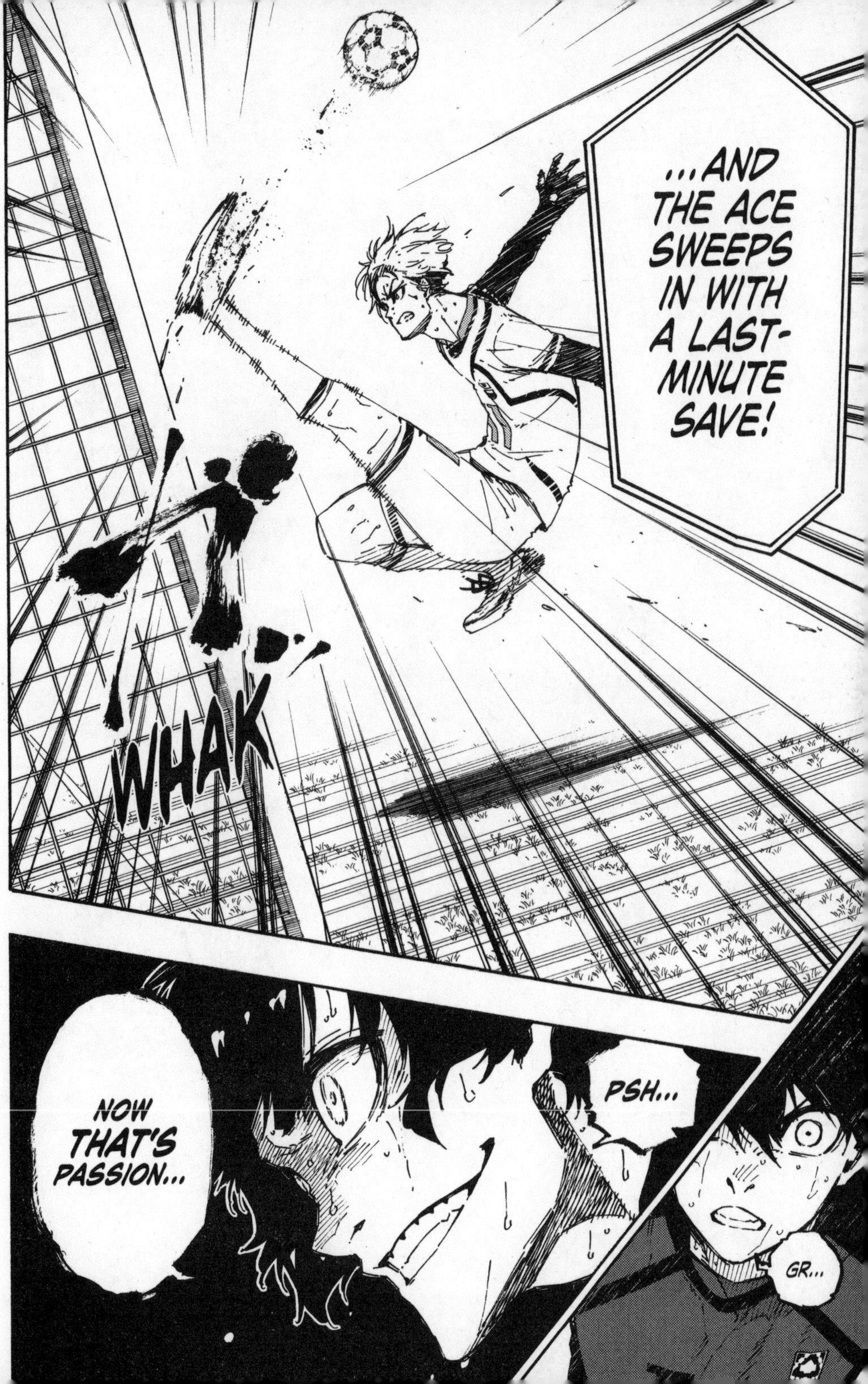
...AND THE ACE SWEEPS IN WITH A LAST-MINUTE SAVE!
WHAK
GR...
PSH...
NOW THAT'S PASSION...

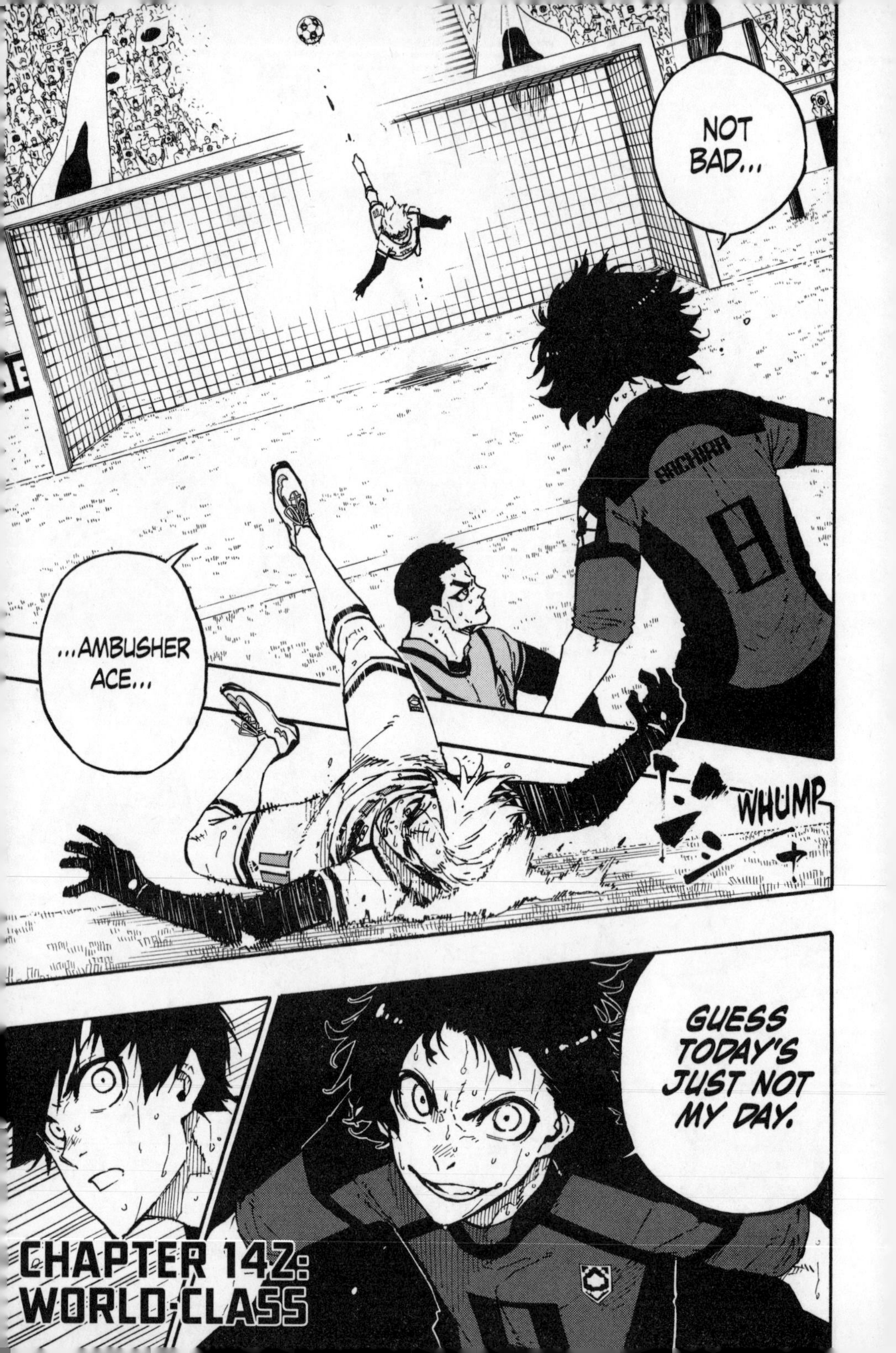
NOT BAD...
...AMBUSHER ACE...
WHUMP
GUESS TODAY'S JUST NOT MY DAY.

CHAPTER 142: WORLD-CLASS

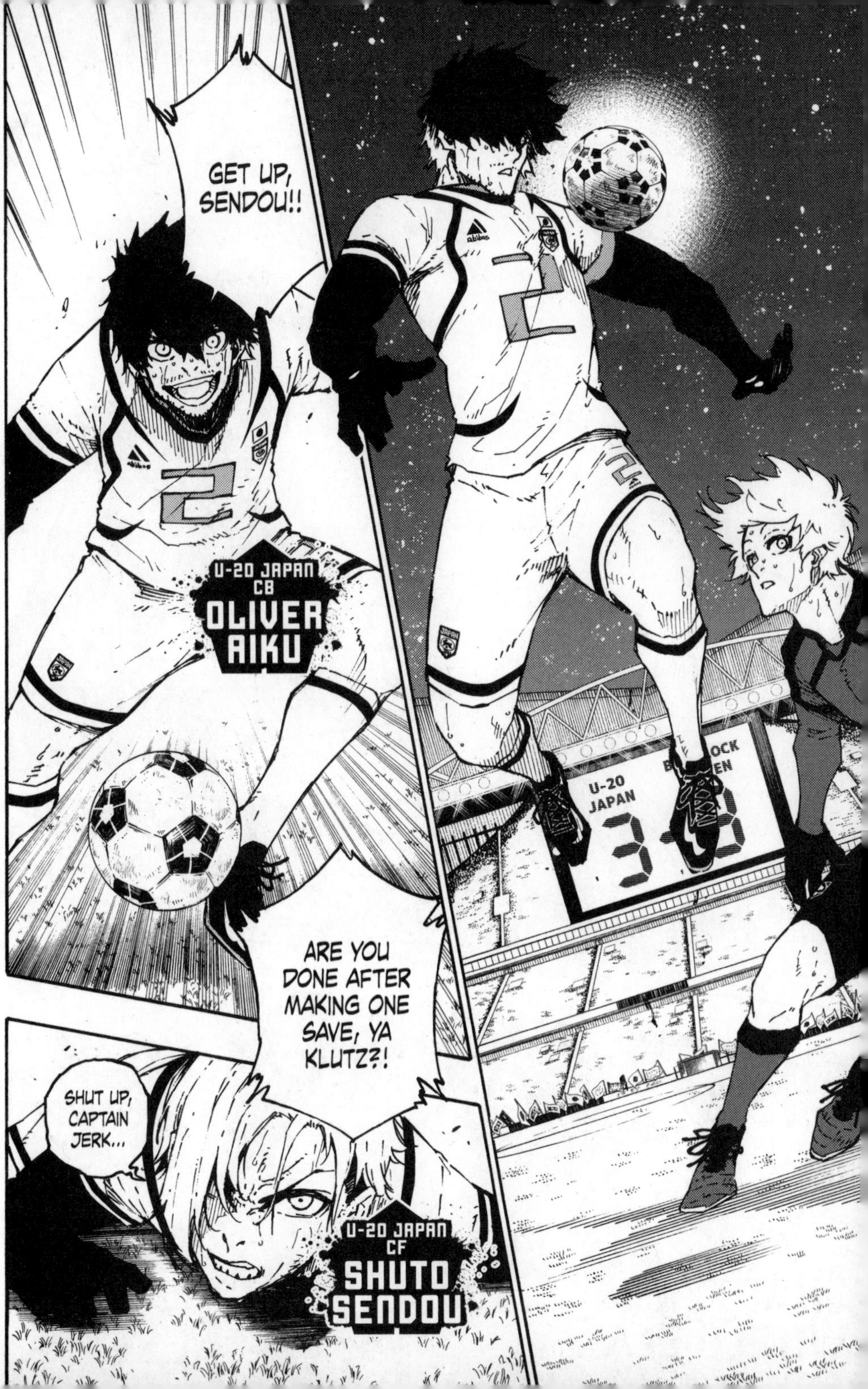
U-20
JAPAN
3
GET UP, SENDOU!!
U-20 JAPAN
CB
OLIVER
AIKU
ARE YOU DONE AFTER MAKING ONE SAVE, YA KLUTZ?!
SHUT UP, CAPTAIN JERK...
U-20 JAPAN
CF
SHUTO
SENDOU

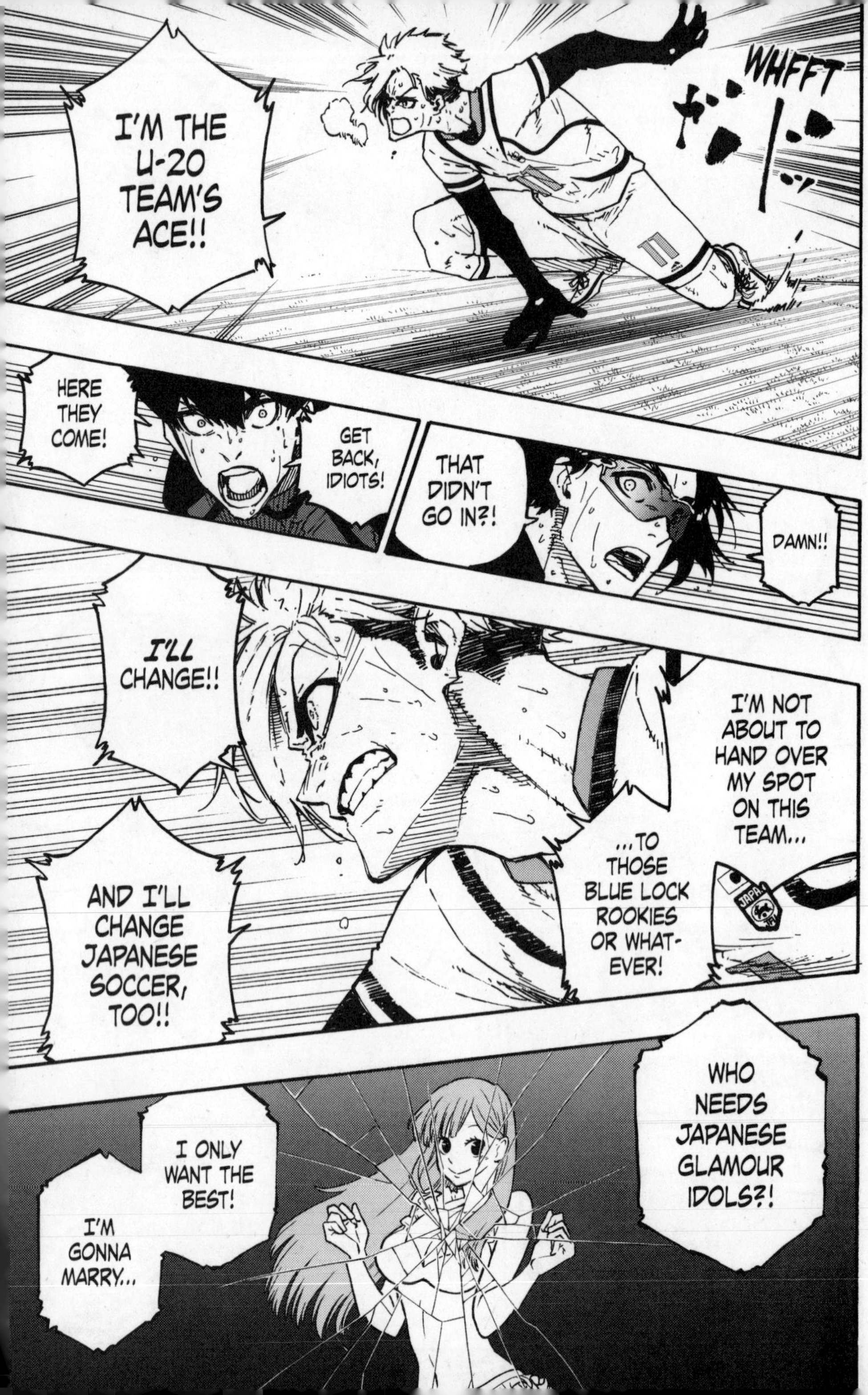
WHFFT
I'M THE U-20 TEAM'S ACE!!
DAMN!!
THAT DIDN'T GO IN?!
GET BACK, IDIOTS!
HERE THEY COME!
I'M NOT ABOUT TO HAND OVER MY SPOT ON THIS TEAM...
...TO THOSE BLUE LOCK ROOKIES OR WHATEVER!
I'LL CHANGE!!
AND I'LL CHANGE JAPANESE SOCCER, TOO!!
WHO NEEDS JAPANESE GLAMOUR IDOLS?!
I ONLY WANT THE BEST!
I'M GONNA MARRY...

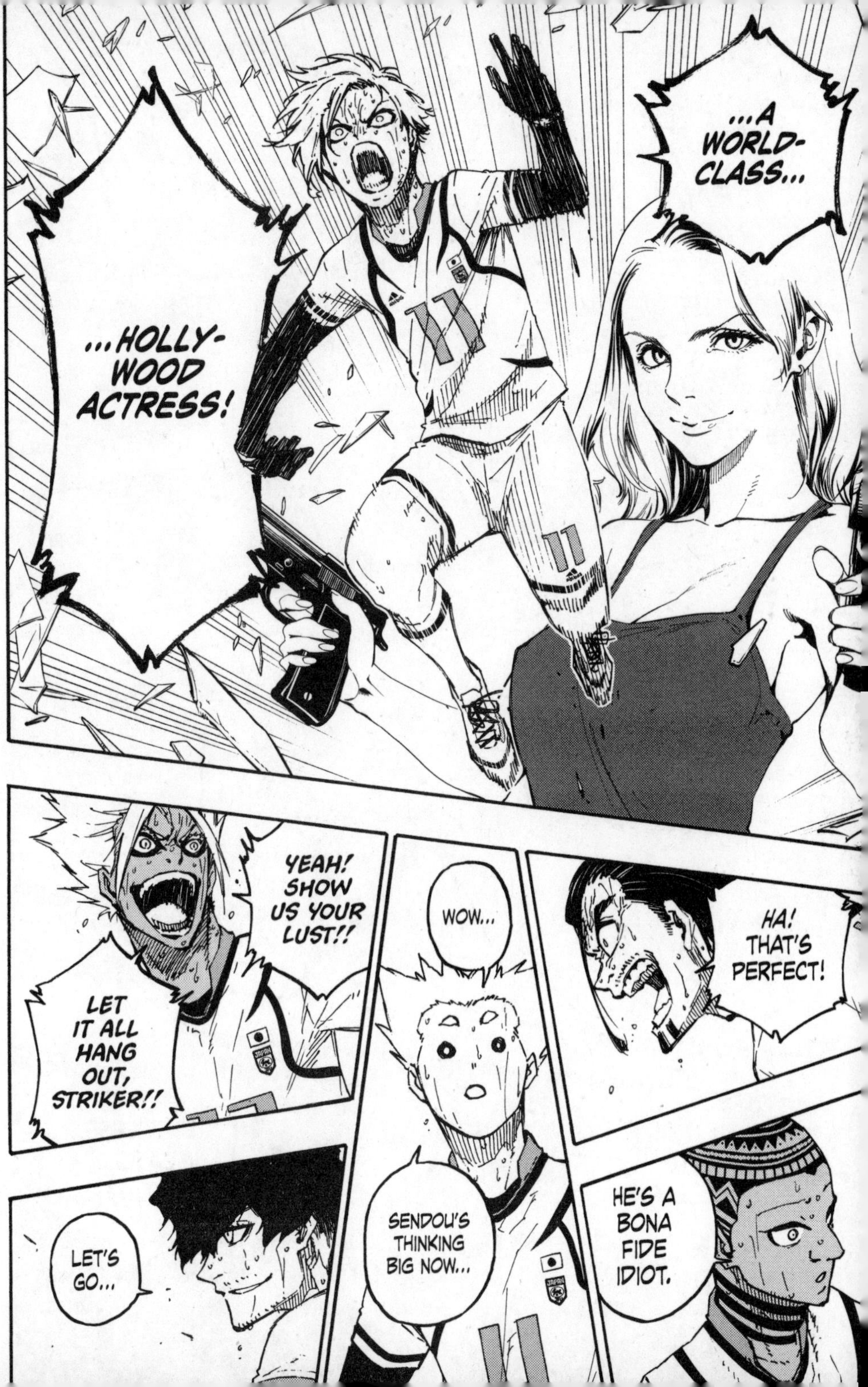
...A WORLD-CLASS...
...HOLLY-WOOD ACTRESS!
HA! THAT'S PERFECT!
HE'S A BONA FIDE IDIOT.
WOW...
SENDOU'S THINKING BIG NOW...
YEAH! SHOW US YOUR LUST!!
LET IT ALL HANG OUT, STRIKER!!
LET'S GO...

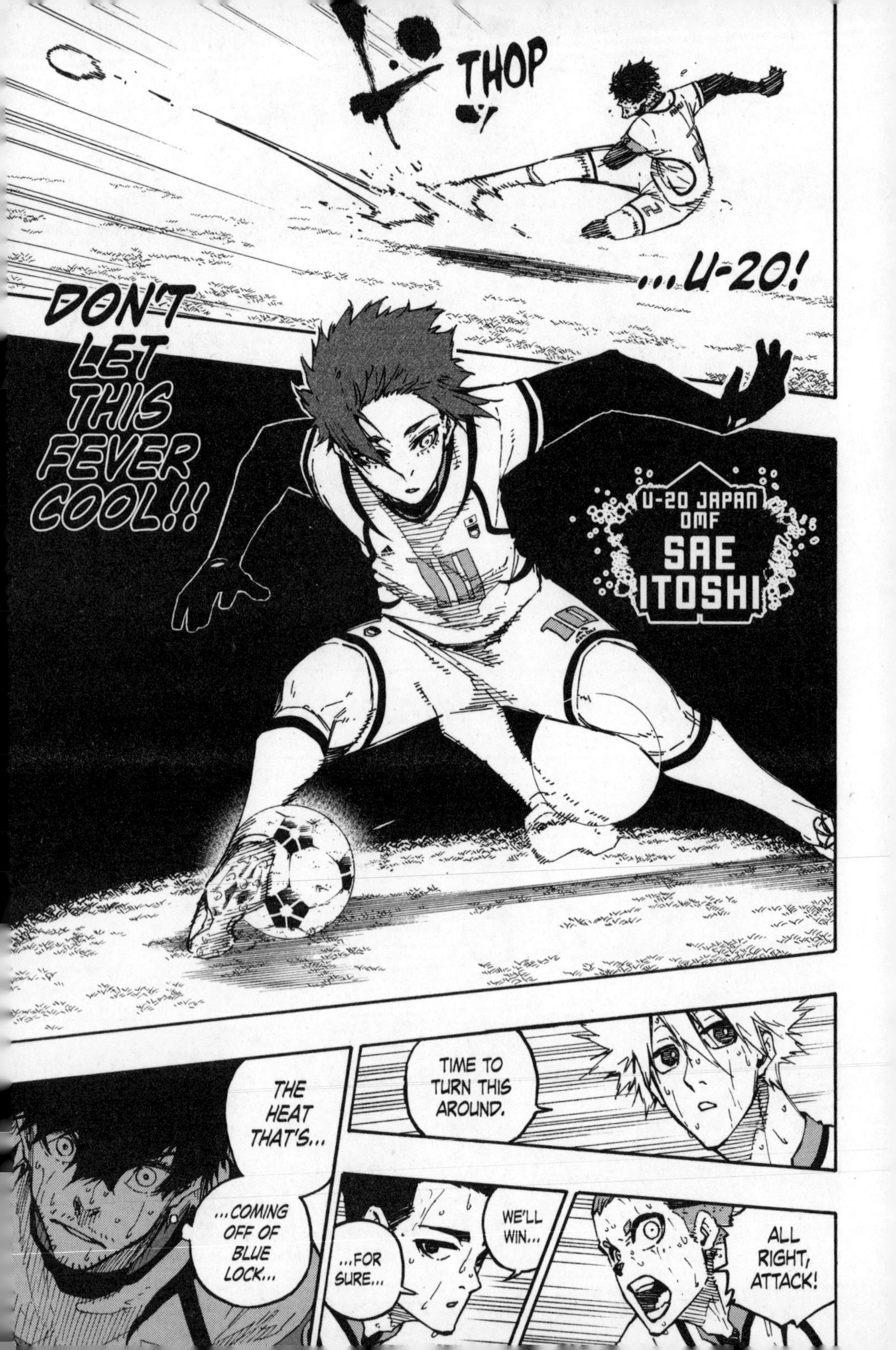
THOP
...U-20!
DON'T LET THIS FEVER COOL!!
U-20 JAPAN OMF SAE ITOSHI
TIME TO TURN THIS AROUND.
ALL RIGHT, ATTACK!
WE'LL WIN...
...FOR SURE...
THE HEAT THAT'S...
...COMING OFF OF BLUE LOCK...

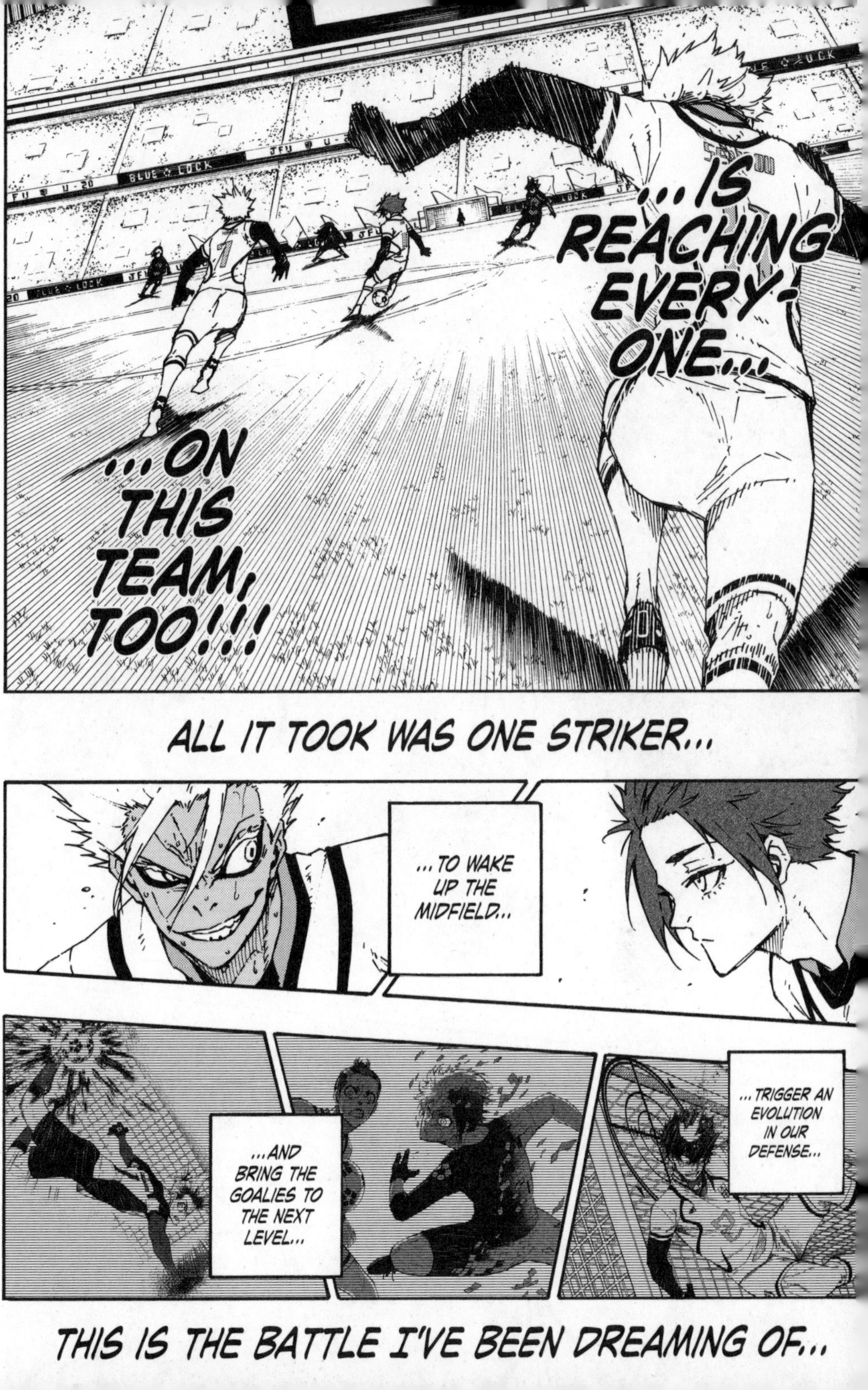
...IS REACHING EVERY-ONE...
...ON THIS TEAM, TOO!!!
ALL IT TOOK WAS ONE STRIKER...
...TO WAKE UP THE MIDFIELD...
...TRIGGER AN EVOLUTION IN OUR DEFENSE...
...AND BRING THE GOALIES TO THE NEXT LEVEL...
THIS IS THE BATTLE I'VE BEEN DREAMING OF...

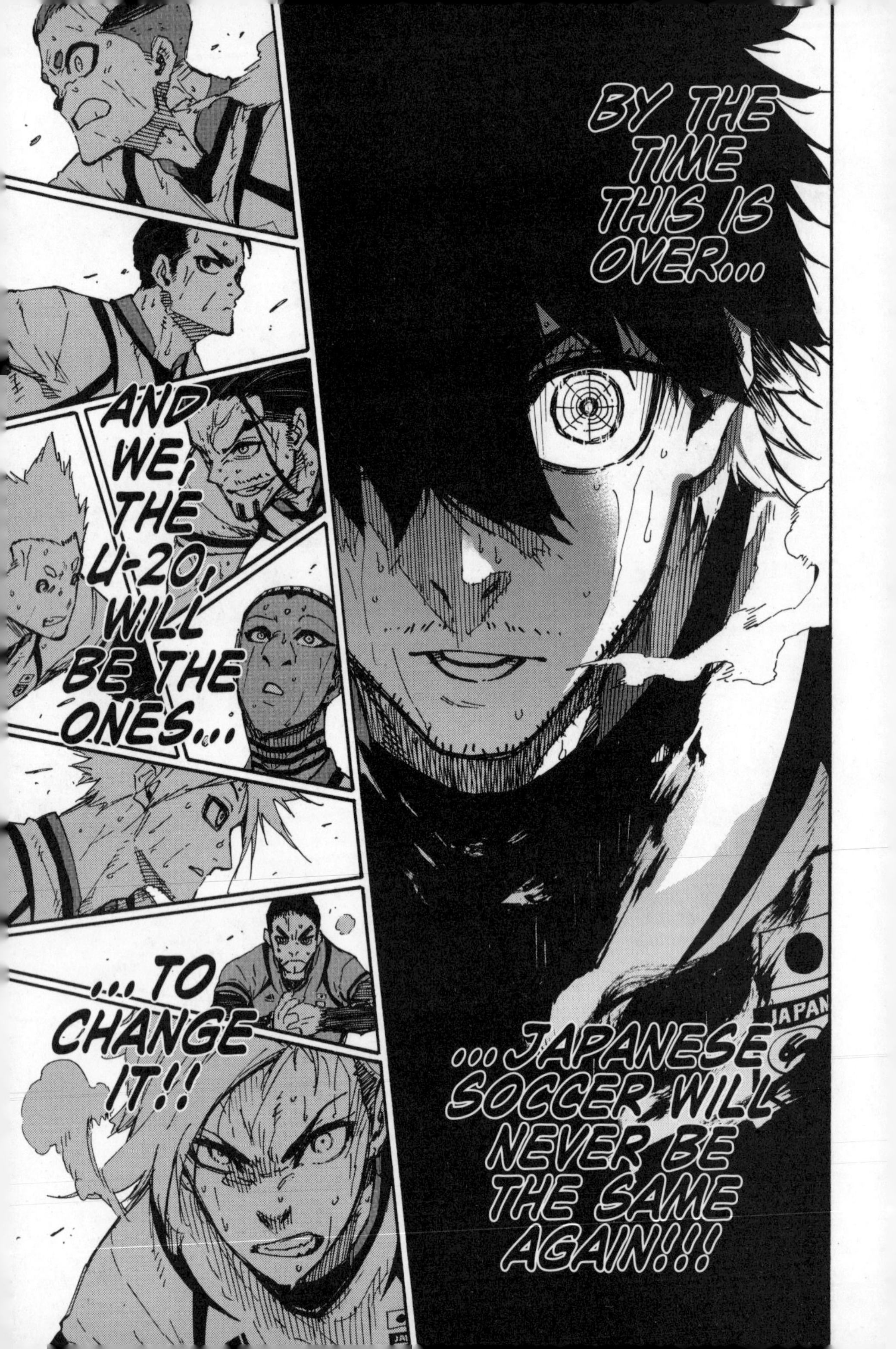
BY THE TIME THIS IS OVER...
...JAPANESE SOCCER WILL NEVER BE THE SAME AGAIN!!!
AND WE, THE U-20, WILL BE THE ONES...
...TO CHANGE IT!!

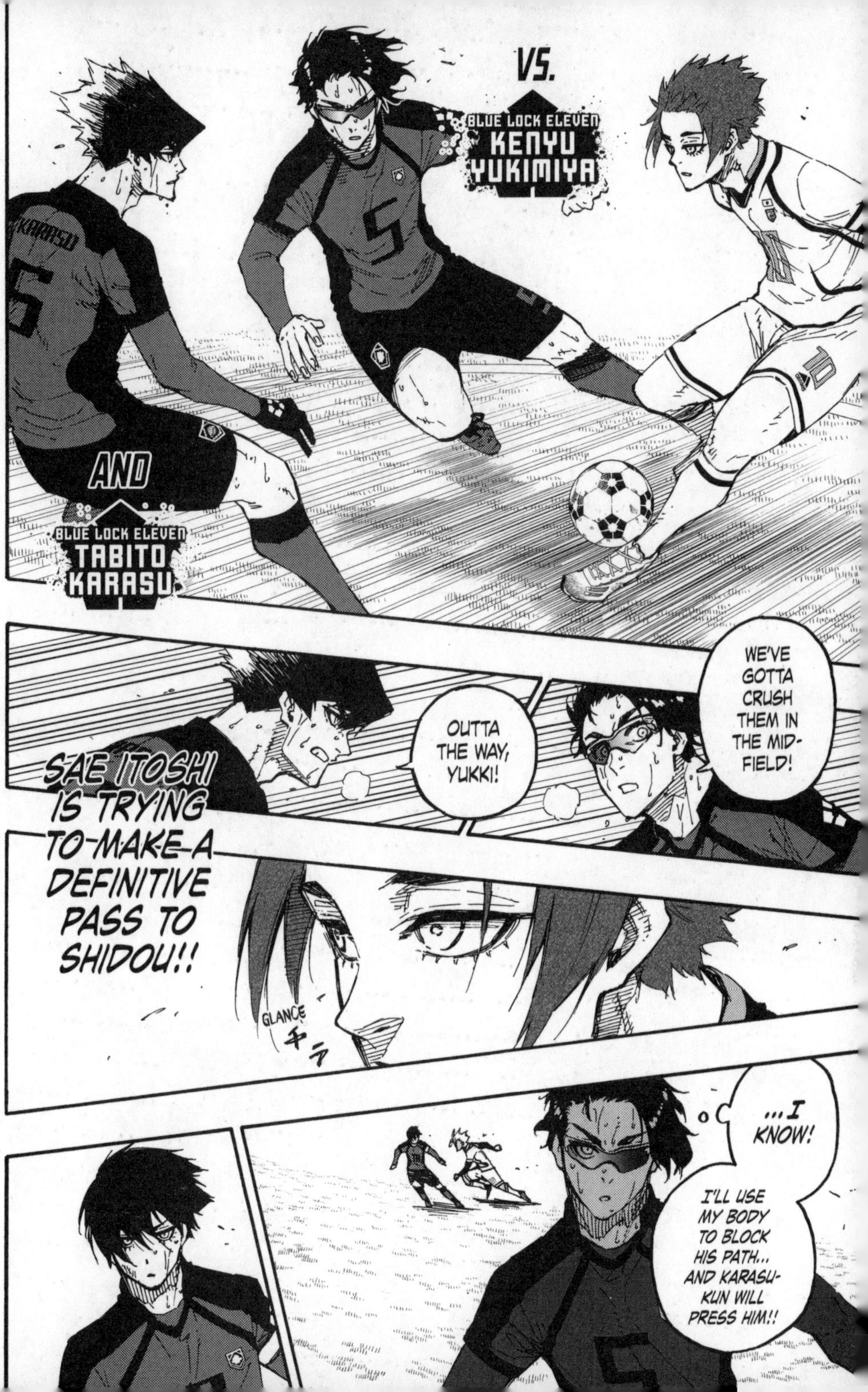
VS.
BLUE LOCK ELEVEN
KENYU YUKIMIYA
AND
BLUE LOCK ELEVEN
TABITO KARASU
WE'VE GOTTA CRUSH THEM IN THE MID-FIELD!
OUTTA THE WAY, YUKKI!
SAE ITOSHI IS TRYING TO MAKE A DEFINITIVE PASS TO SHIDOU!!
GLANCE
チラ
...I KNOW!
I'LL USE MY BODY TO BLOCK HIS PATH... AND KARASU-KUN WILL PRESS HIM!!

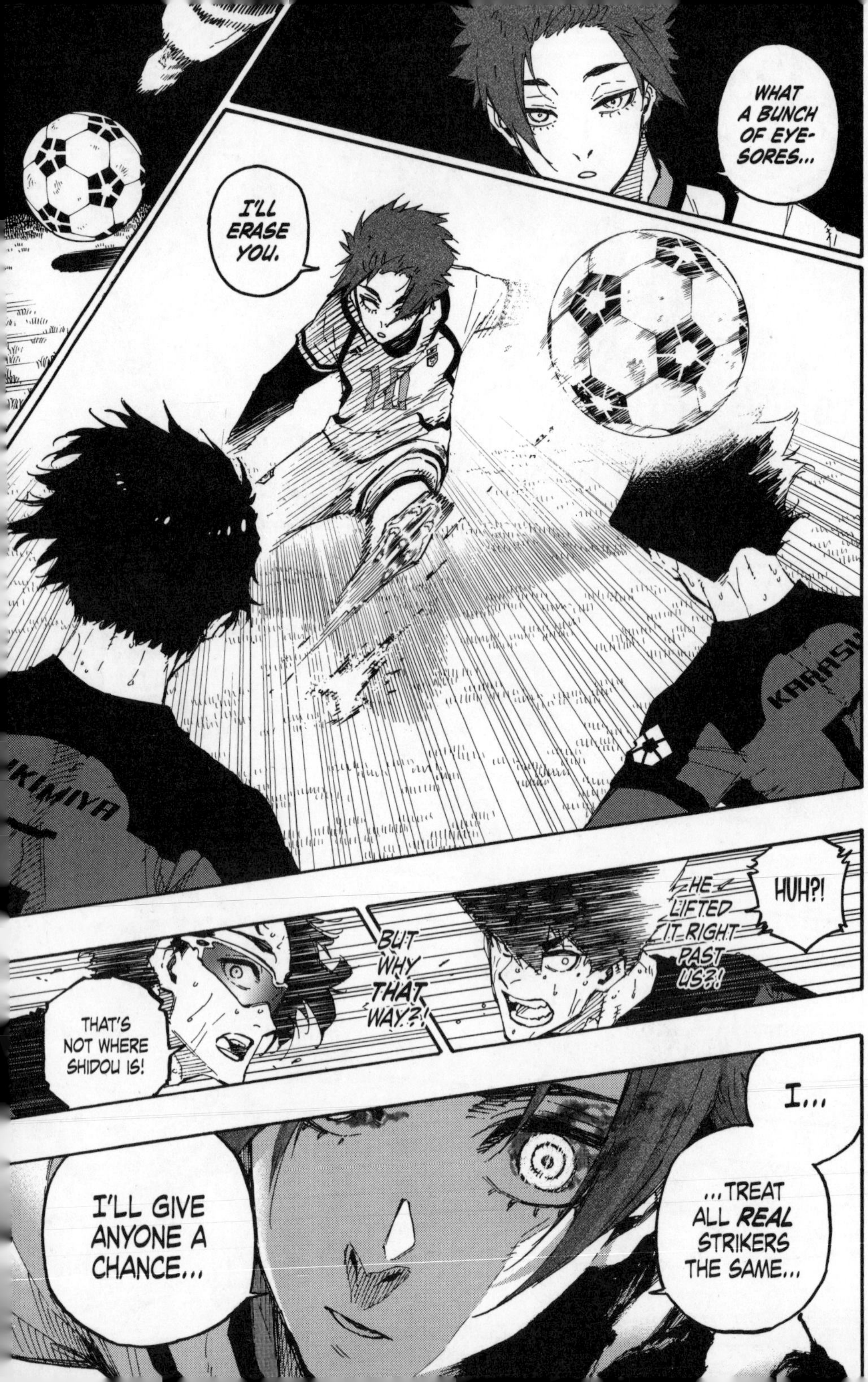
WHAT A BUNCH OF EYE-SORES...
I'LL ERASE YOU.
HUH?!
HE LIFTED IT RIGHT PAST US?!
BUT WHY THAT WAY?!
THAT'S NOT WHERE SHIDOU IS!
I...
...TREAT ALL REAL STRIKERS THE SAME...
I'LL GIVE ANYONE A CHANCE...

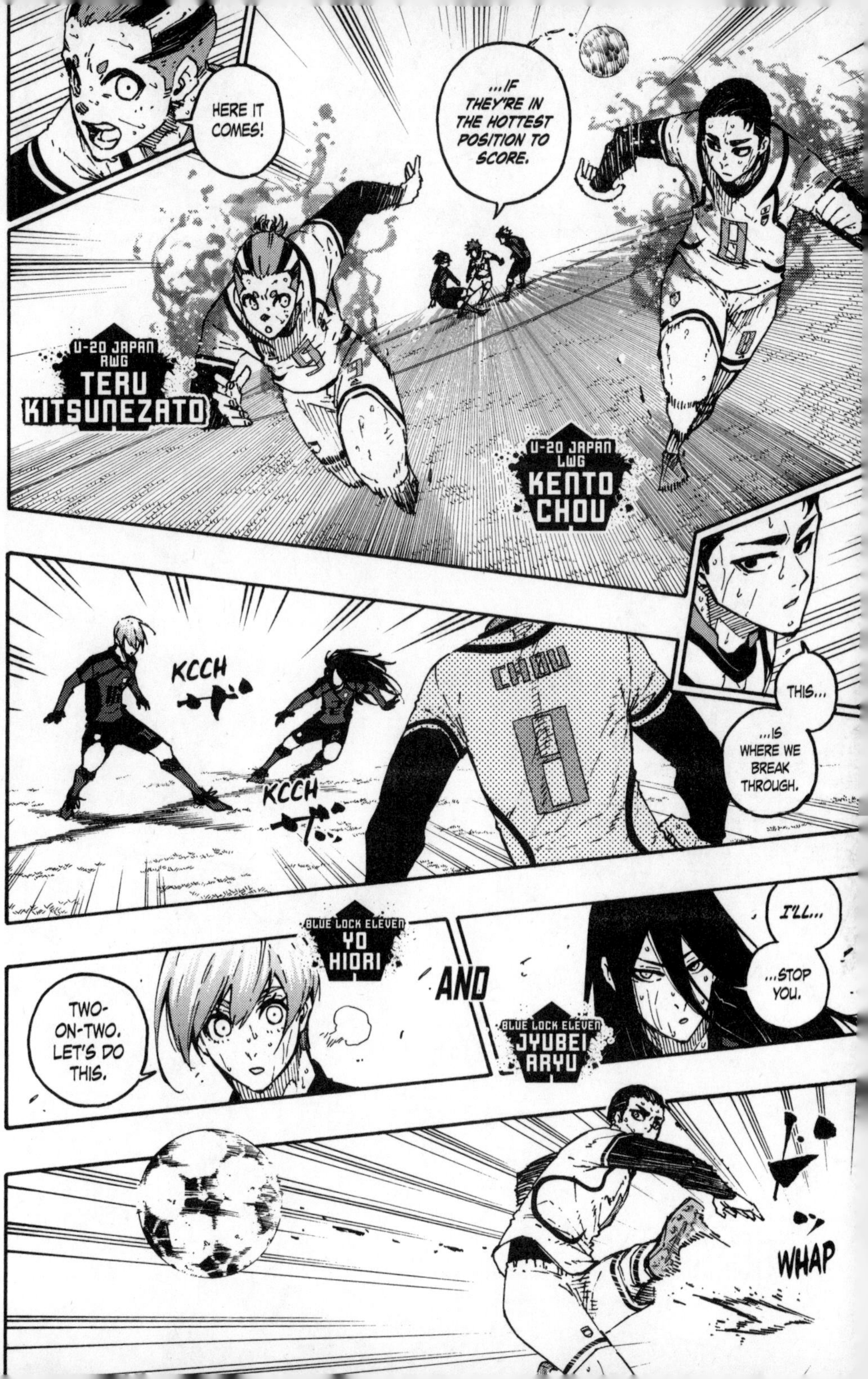
...IF THEY'RE IN THE HOTTEST POSITION TO SCORE.
HERE IT COMES!
U-20 JAPAN RWG TERU KITSUNEZATO
U-20 JAPAN LWG KENTO CHOU
THIS...
...IS WHERE WE BREAK THROUGH.
CHOU
KCCH
KCCH
I'LL...
...STOP YOU.
BLUE LOCK ELEVEN JYUBEI ARYU
AND
BLUE LOCK ELEVEN YO HIORI
TWO-ON-TWO. LET'S DO THIS.
WHAP

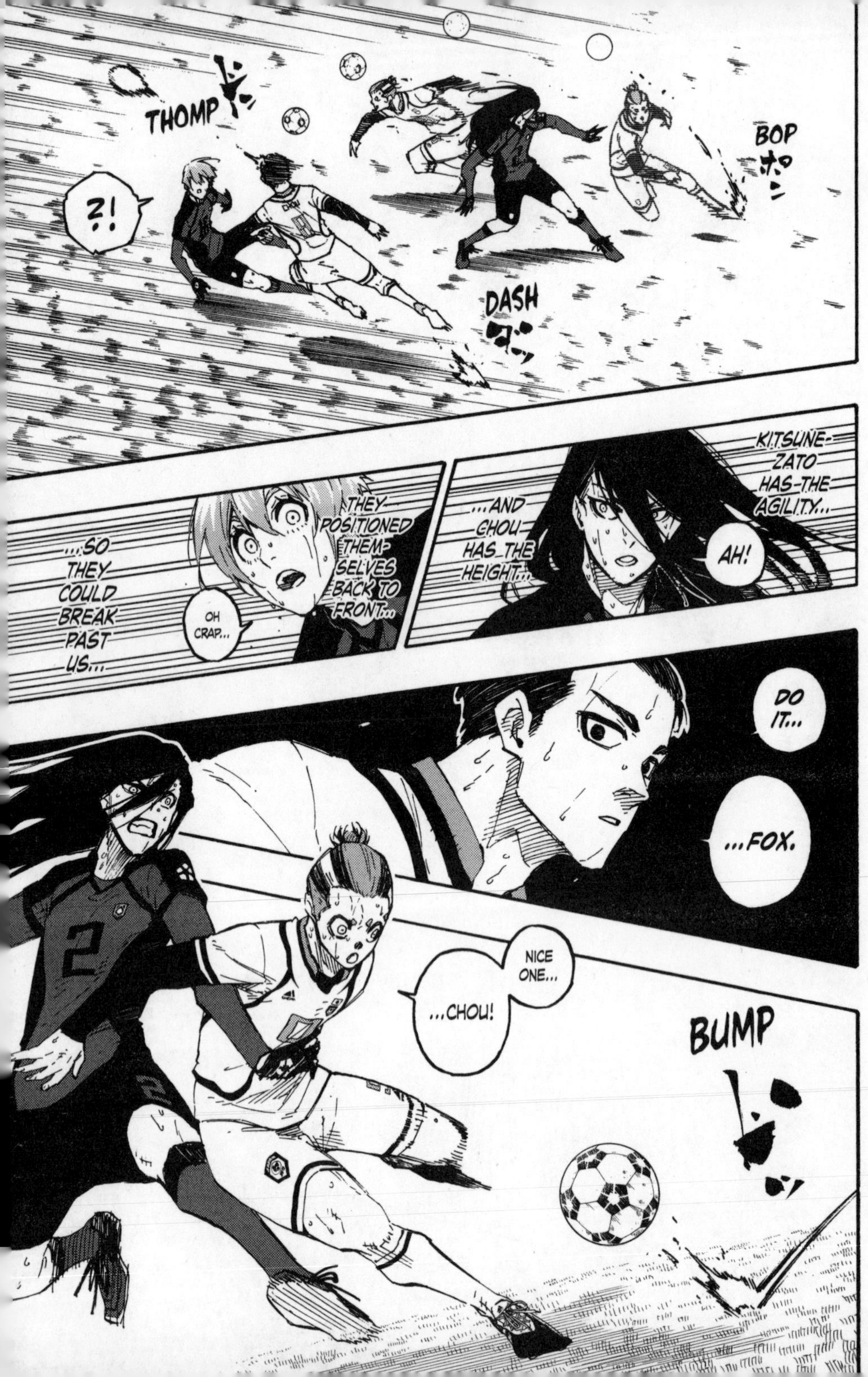
BOP
DASH
THOMP
?!
KITSUNE-ZATO HAS THE AGILITY...
AH!
...AND CHOU HAS THE HEIGHT...
THEY POSITIONED THEMSELVES BACK TO FRONT...
OH CRAP...
...SO THEY COULD BREAK PAST US...
DO IT...
...FOX.
BUMP
NICE ONE...
...CHOU!

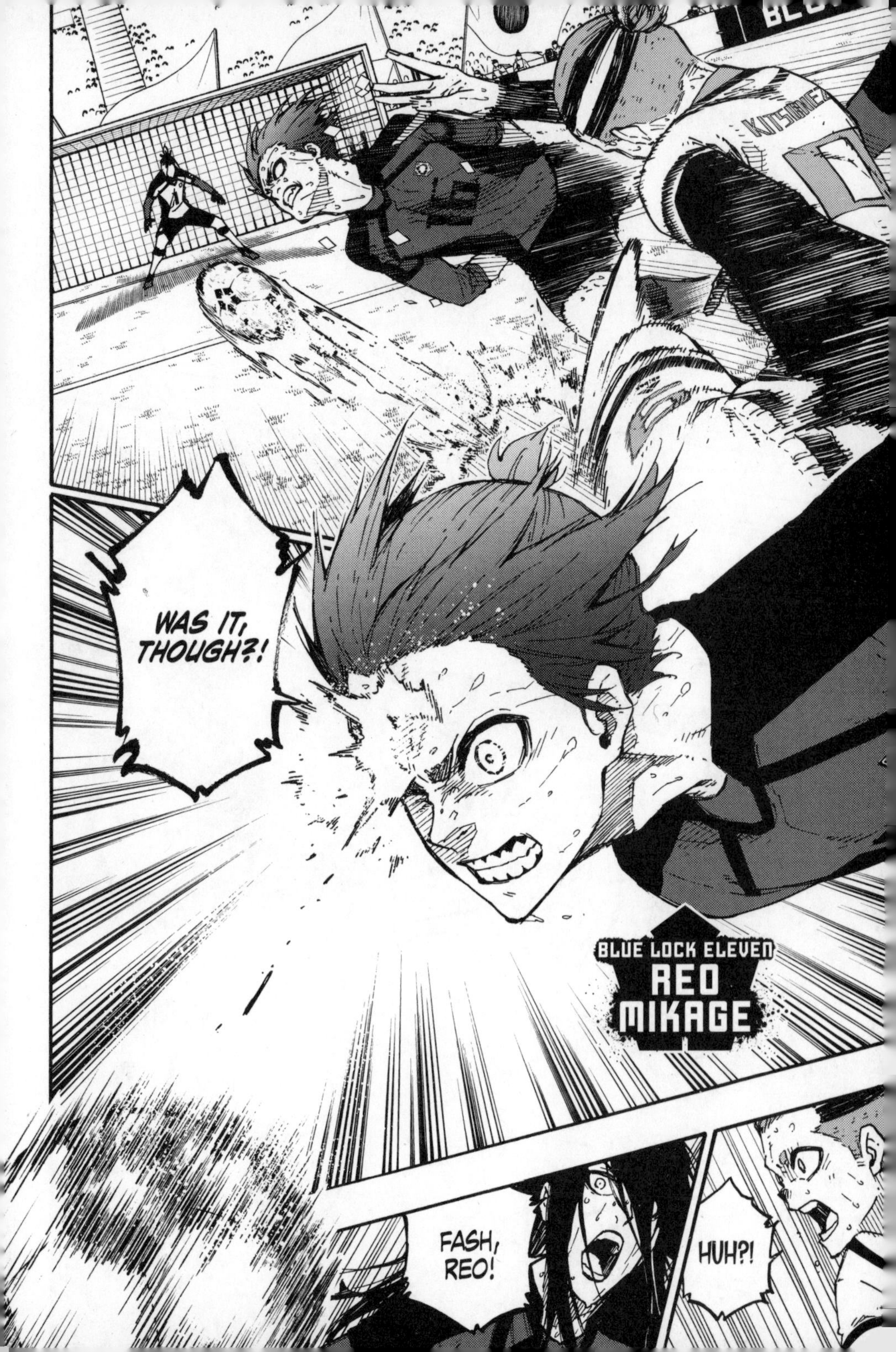
WAS IT, THOUGH?!
BLUE LOCK ELEVEN
REO MIKAGE
HUH?!
FASH, REO!

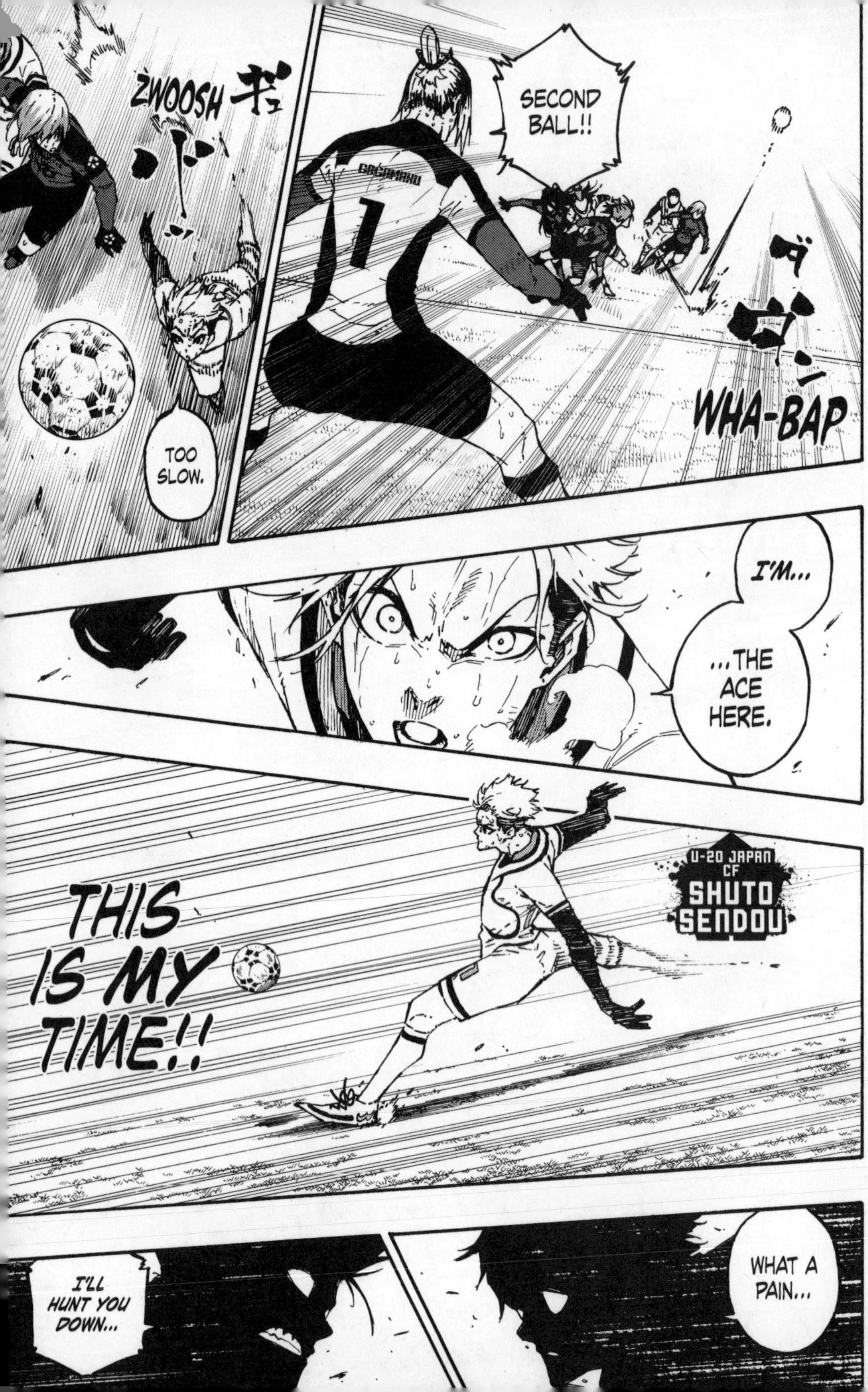
SECOND BALL!!
WHA-BAP
ZWOOSH
TOO SLOW.
I'M...
...THE ACE HERE.
U-20 JAPAN CF
SHUTO SENDOU
THIS IS MY TIME!!
WHAT A PAIN...
I'LL HUNT YOU DOWN...

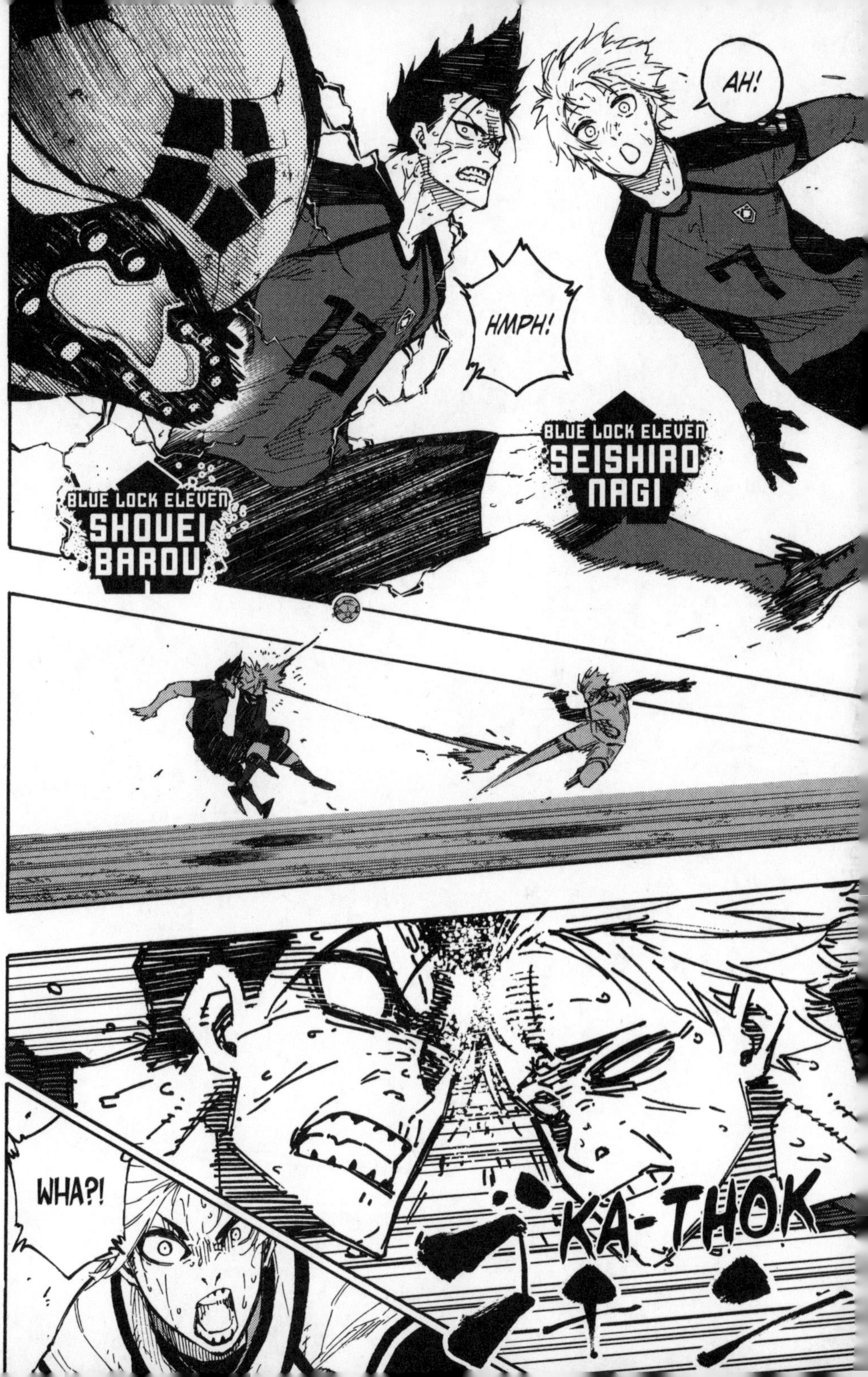
AH!
HMPH!
BLUE LOCK ELEVEN
SEISHIRO NAGI
BLUE LOCK ELEVEN
SHOUEI BAROU
KA-THOK
WHA?!

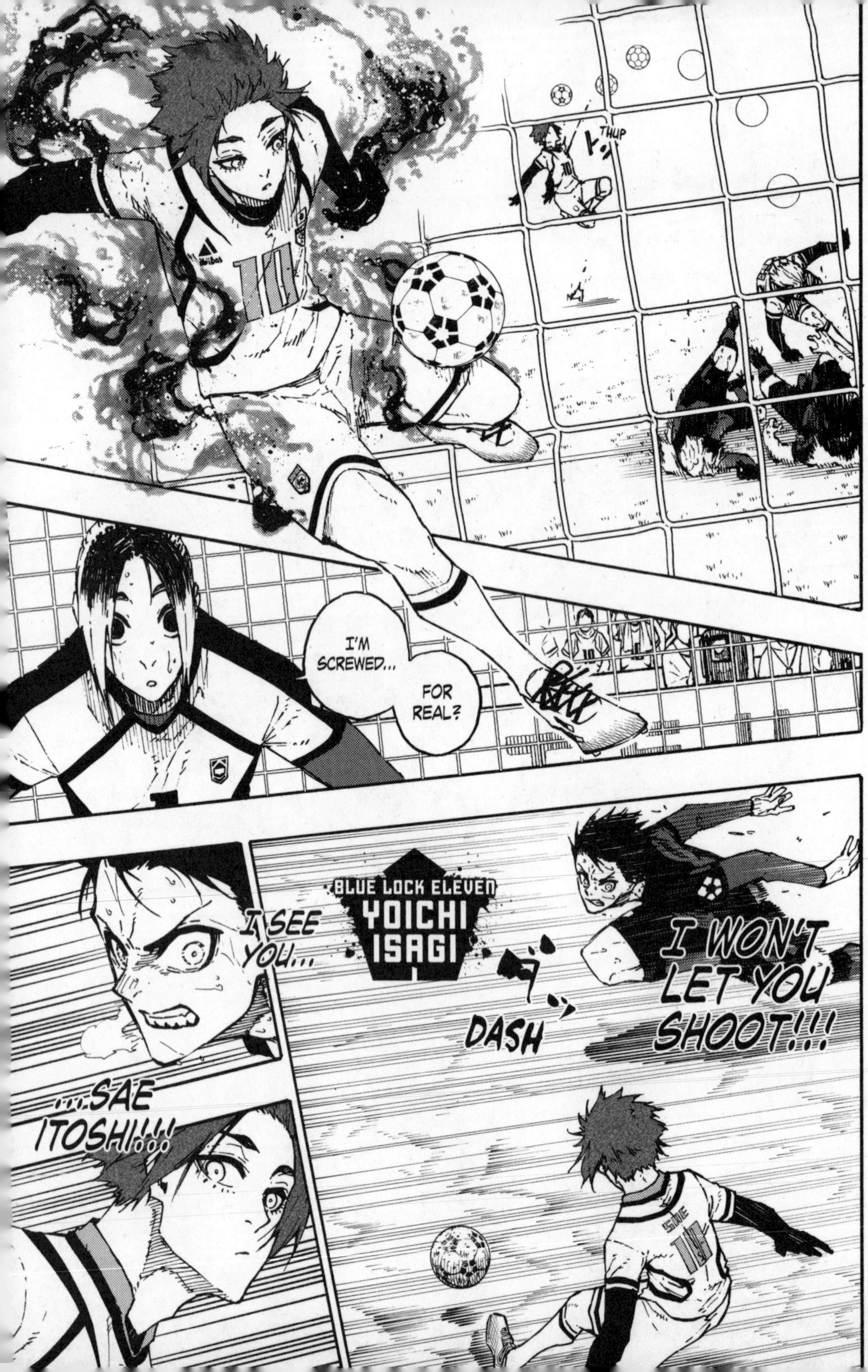
THUP
I'M SCREWED...
FOR REAL?
BLUE LOCK ELEVEN
YOICHI ISAGI
I WON'T LET YOU SHOOT!!!
DASH
I SEE YOU...
...SAE ITOSHI!!!

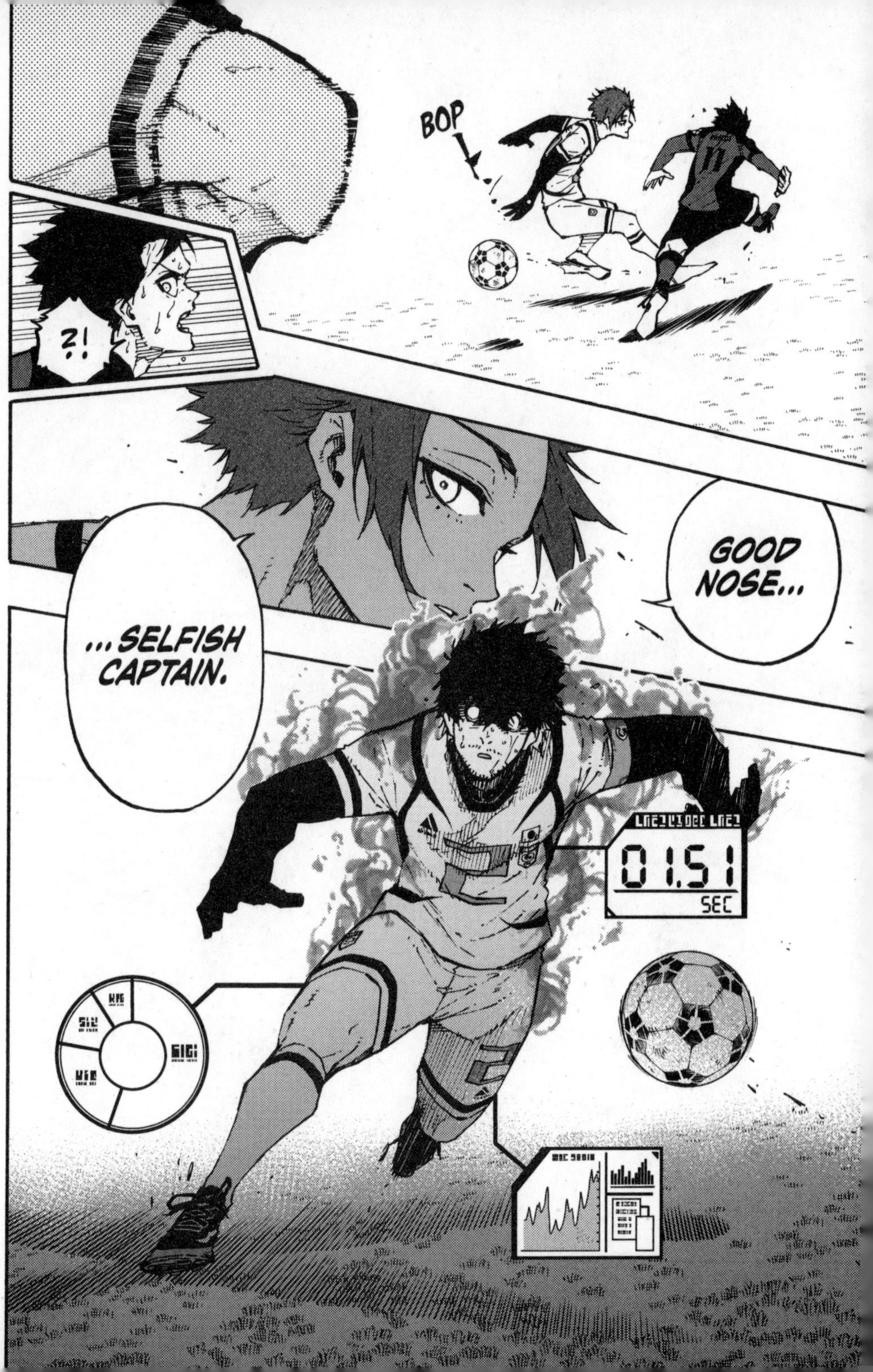
BOP
?!
GOOD NOSE...
...SELFISH CAPTAIN.
01.51
SEC

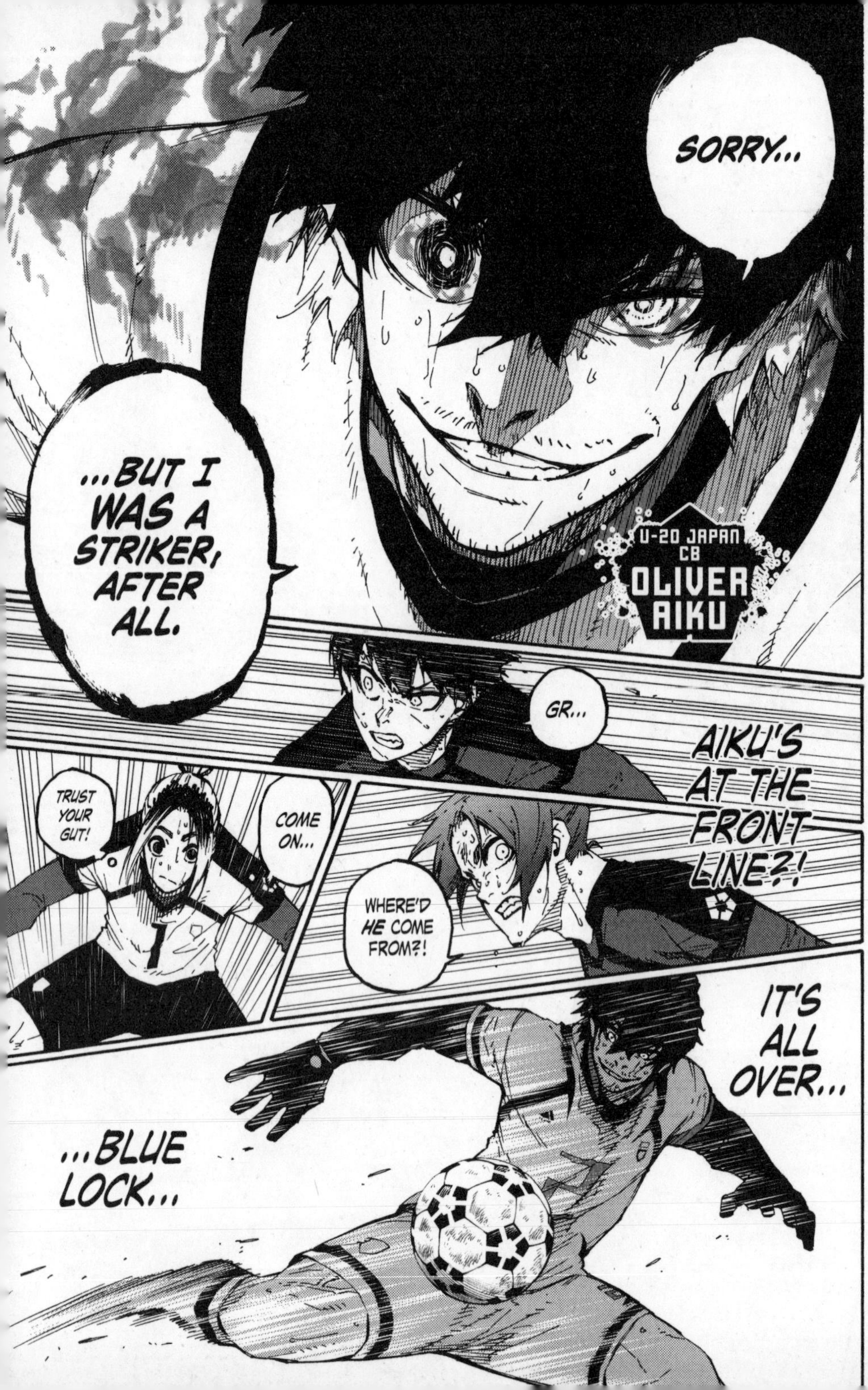
SORRY...
...BUT I WAS A STRIKER, AFTER ALL.
U-20 JAPAN CB
OLIVER AIKU
GR...
AIKU'S AT THE FRONT LINE?!
WHERE'D HE COME FROM?!
COME ON...
TRUST YOUR GUT!
IT'S ALL OVER...
...BLUE LOCK...

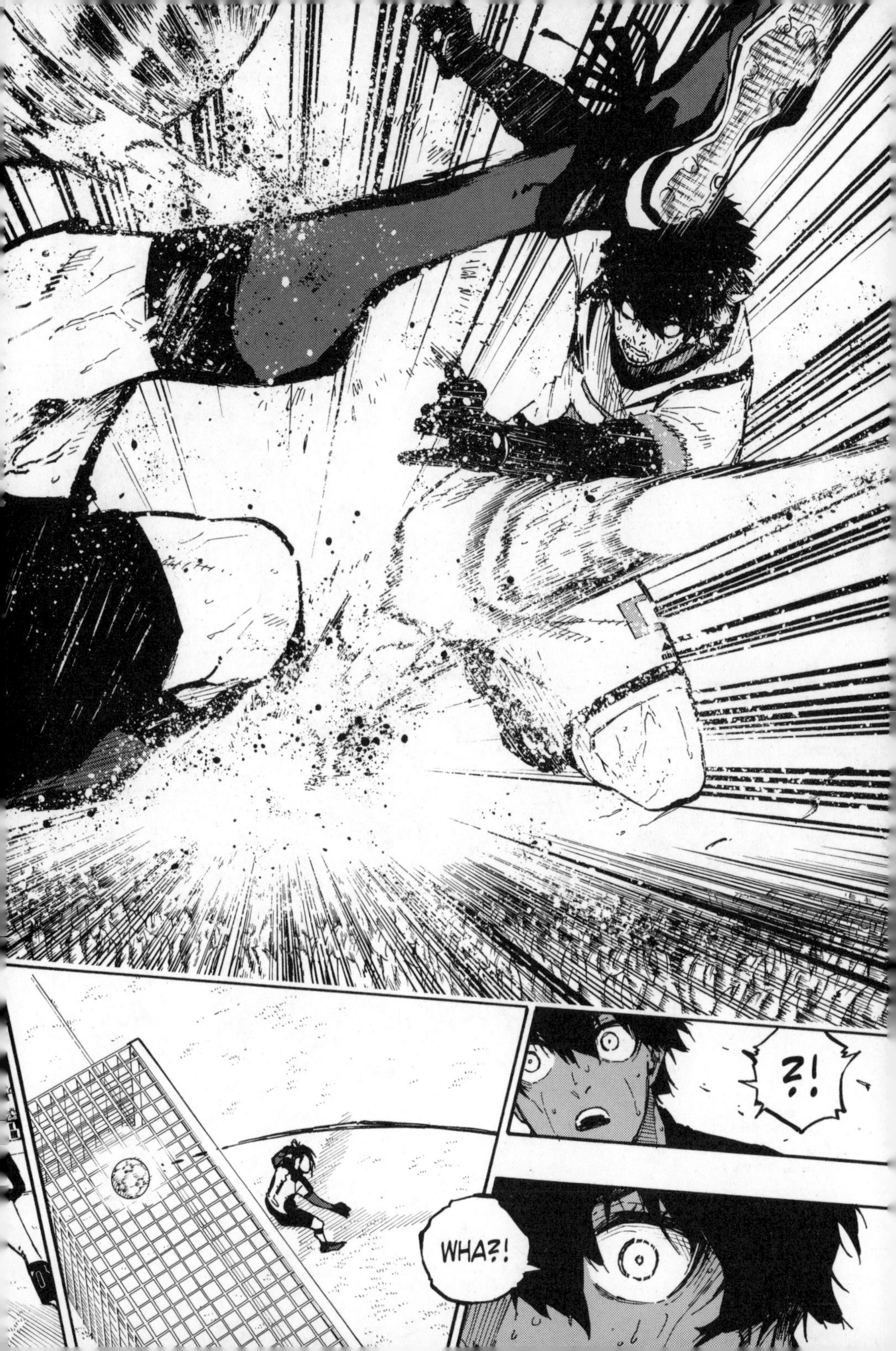
?!
WHA?!

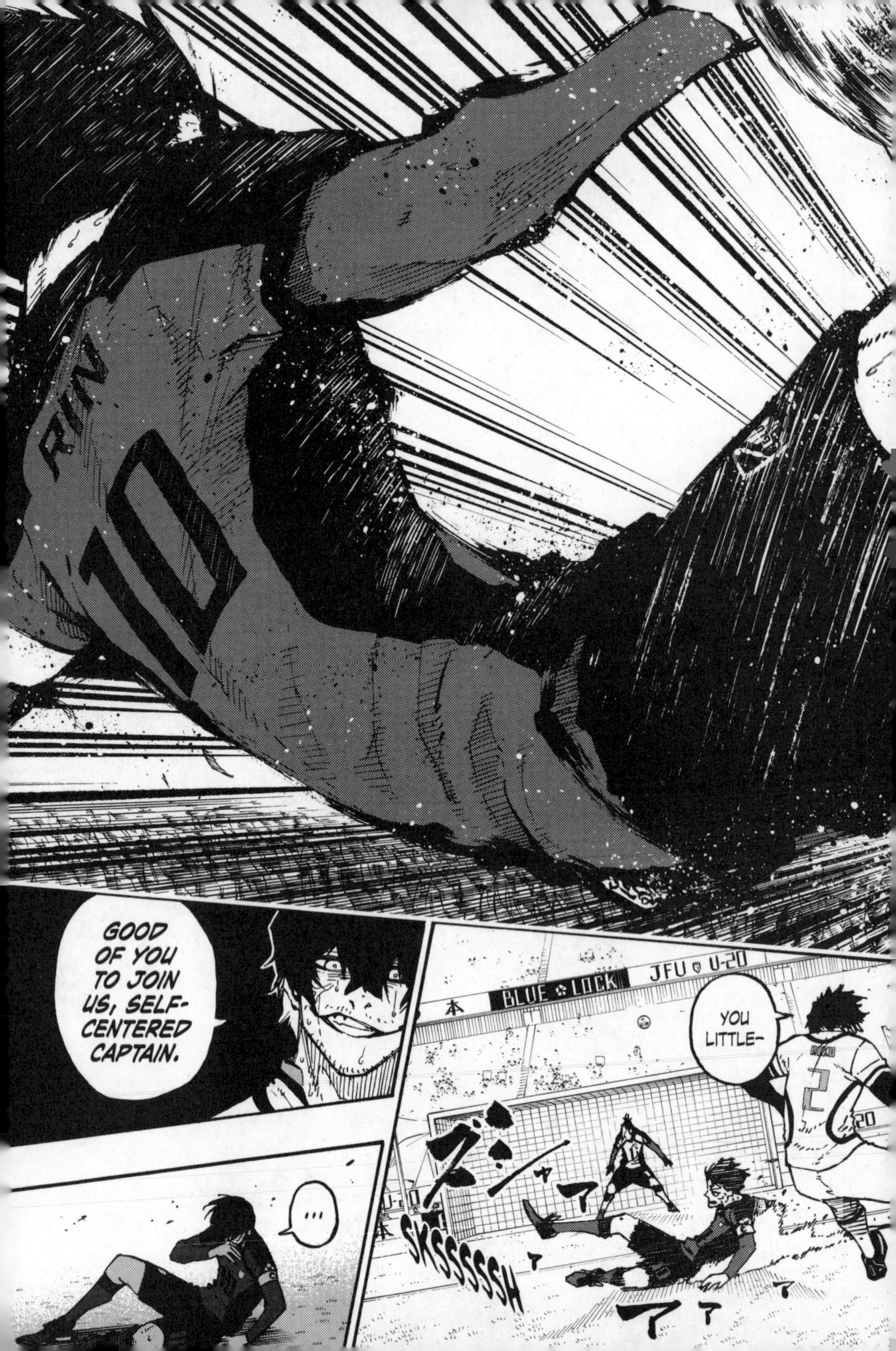
RIN
BLUE LOCK
JFU U-20
YOU LITTLE-
SKSSSSSSH
GOOD OF YOU TO JOIN US, SELF-CENTERED CAPTAIN.
...

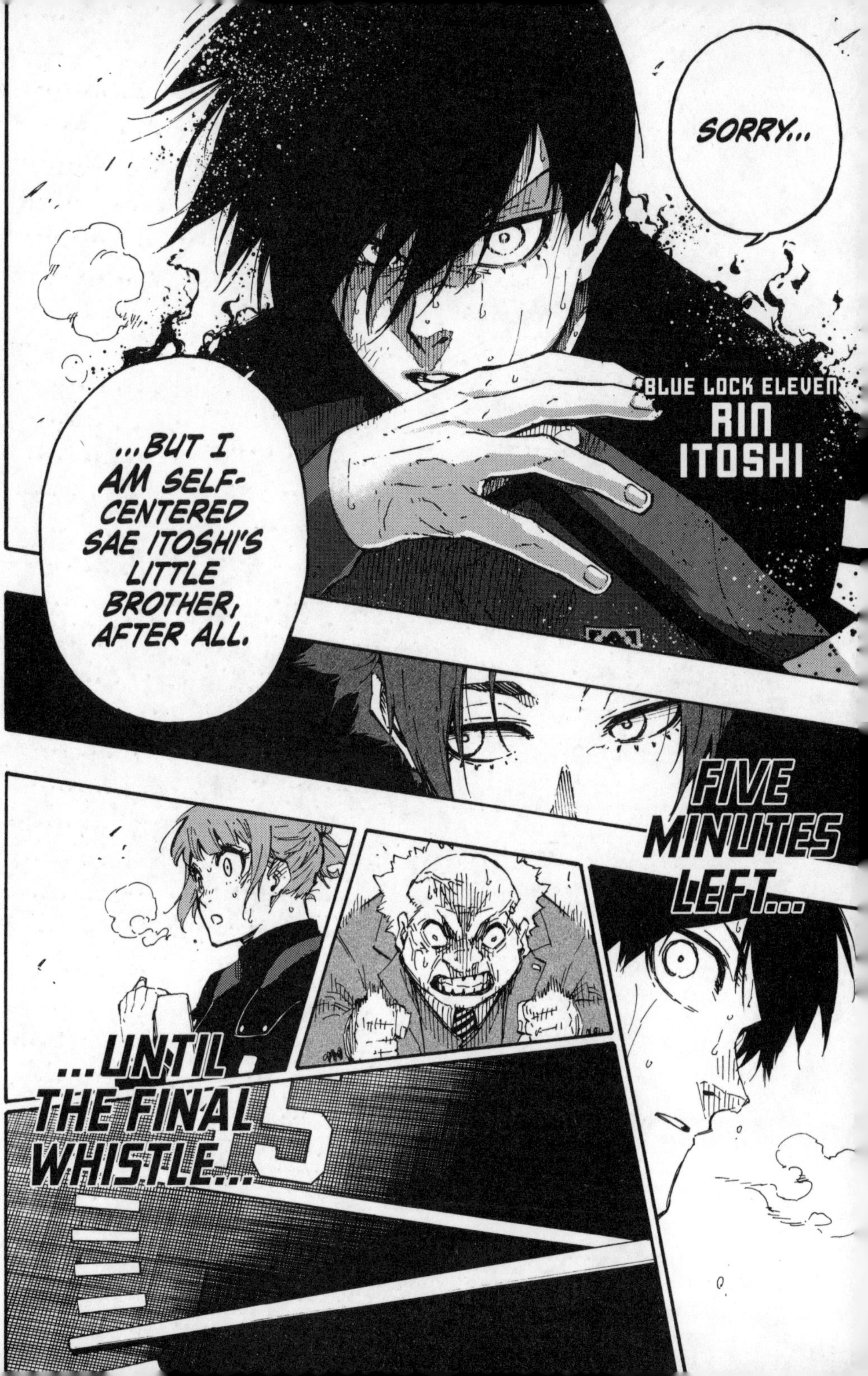

SORRY...
...BUT I AM SELF-CENTERED SAE ITOSHI'S LITTLE BROTHER, AFTER ALL.
BLUE LOCK ELEVEN RIN ITOSHI
FIVE MINUTES LEFT...
...UNTIL THE FINAL WHISTLE...

CHAPTER 143: NOT ALONE

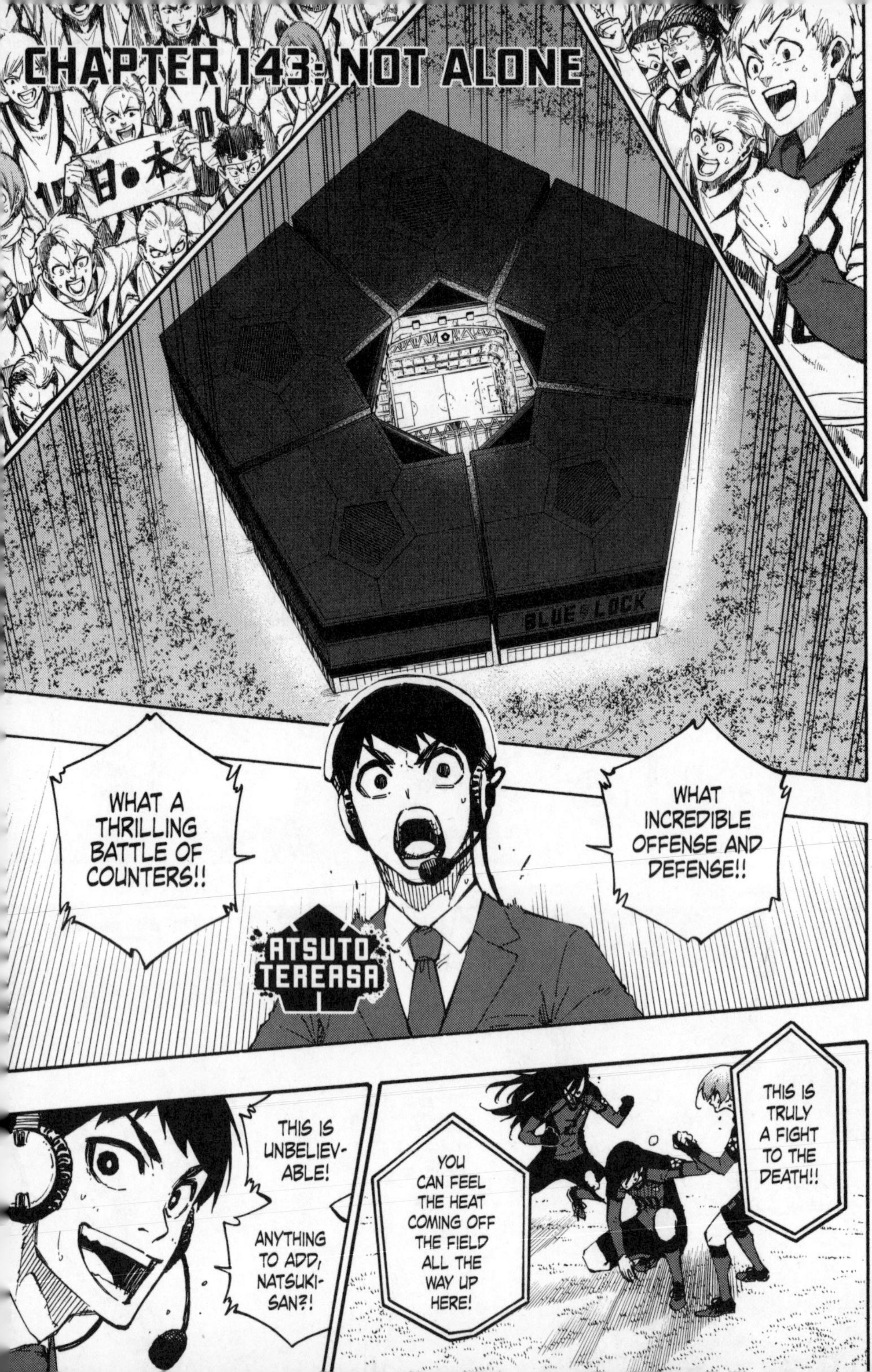
日本
BLUE LOCK
WHAT INCREDIBLE OFFENSE AND DEFENSE!!
WHAT A THRILLING BATTLE OF COUNTERS!!
ATSUTO TEREASA
THIS IS TRULY A FIGHT TO THE DEATH!!
YOU CAN FEEL THE HEAT COMING OFF THE FIELD ALL THE WAY UP HERE!
THIS IS UNBELIEVABLE!
ANYTHING TO ADD, NATSUKI-SAN?!

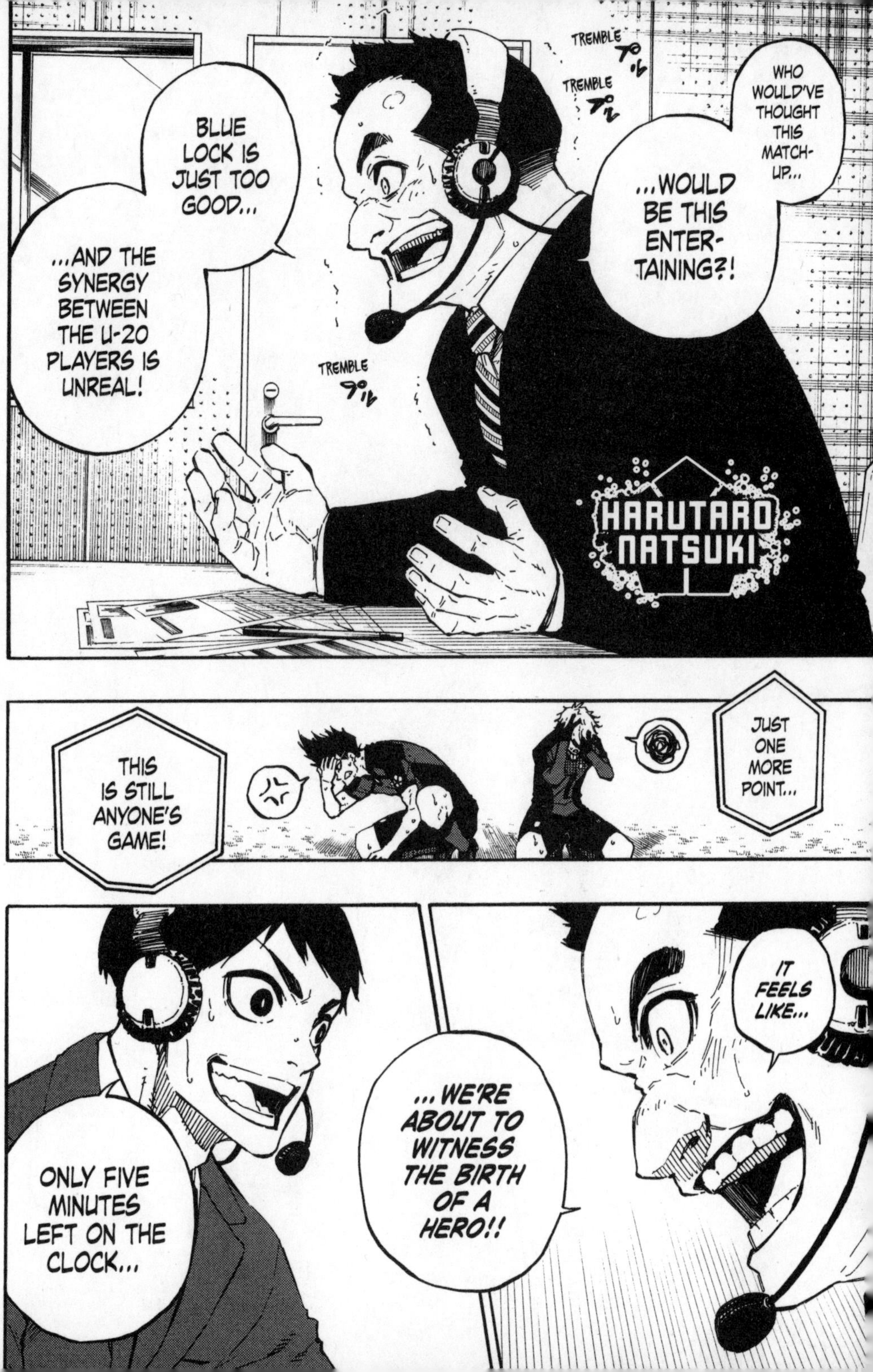
TREMBLE
TREMBLE
WHO WOULD'VE THOUGHT THIS MATCH-UP...
...WOULD BE THIS ENTERTAINING?!
BLUE LOCK IS JUST TOO GOOD...
...AND THE SYNERGY BETWEEN THE U-20 PLAYERS IS UNREAL!
TREMBLE
HARUTARO NATSUKI
JUST ONE MORE POINT...
THIS IS STILL ANYONE'S GAME!
IT FEELS LIKE...
...WE'RE ABOUT TO WITNESS THE BIRTH OF A HERO!!
ONLY FIVE MINUTES LEFT ON THE CLOCK...

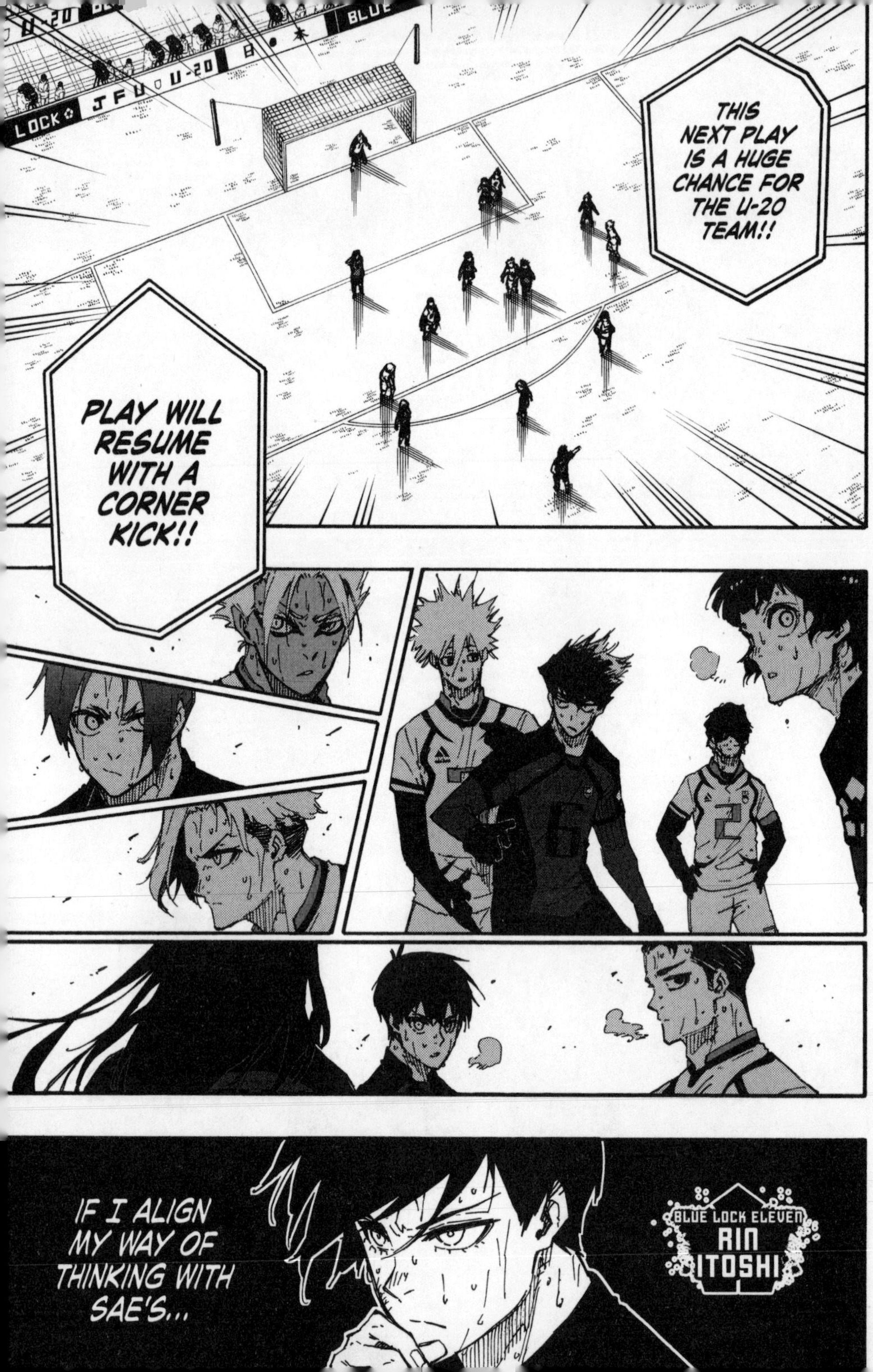
THIS NEXT PLAY IS A HUGE CHANCE FOR THE U-20 TEAM!!
PLAY WILL RESUME WITH A CORNER KICK!!
BLUE LOCK ELEVEN
RIN ITOSHI
IF I ALIGN MY WAY OF THINKING WITH SAE'S...

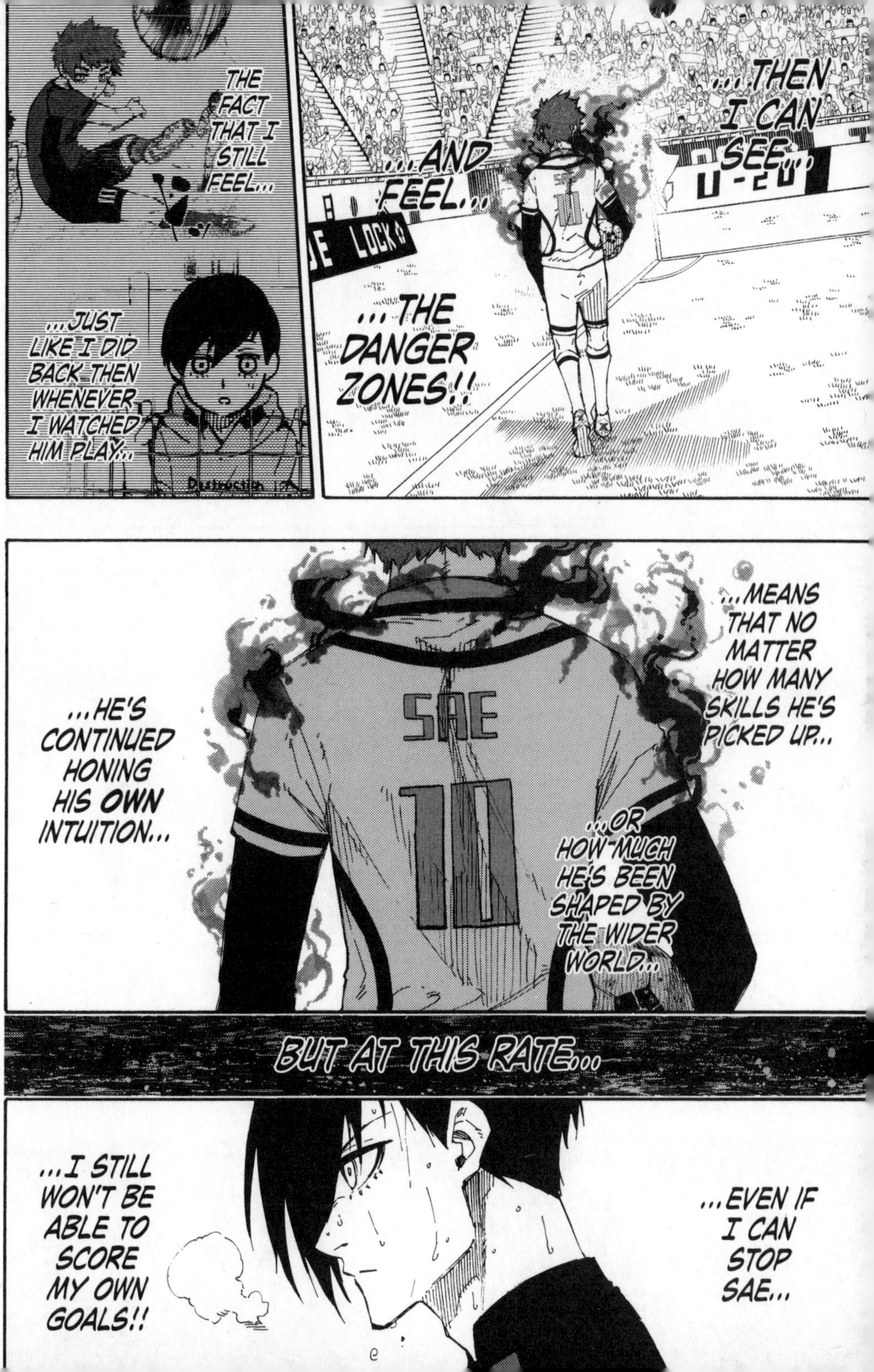
...THEN I CAN SEE...
...AND FEEL...
...THE DANGER ZONES!!
THE FACT THAT I STILL FEEL...
...JUST LIKE I DID BACK THEN WHENEVER I WATCHED HIM PLAY...
Destruction
...MEANS THAT NO MATTER HOW MANY SKILLS HE'S PICKED UP...
...OR HOW MUCH HE'S BEEN SHAPED BY THE WIDER WORLD...
...HE'S CONTINUED HONING HIS OWN INTUITION...
SAE
10
BUT AT THIS RATE...
...EVEN IF I CAN STOP SAE...
...I STILL WON'T BE ABLE TO SCORE MY OWN GOALS!!

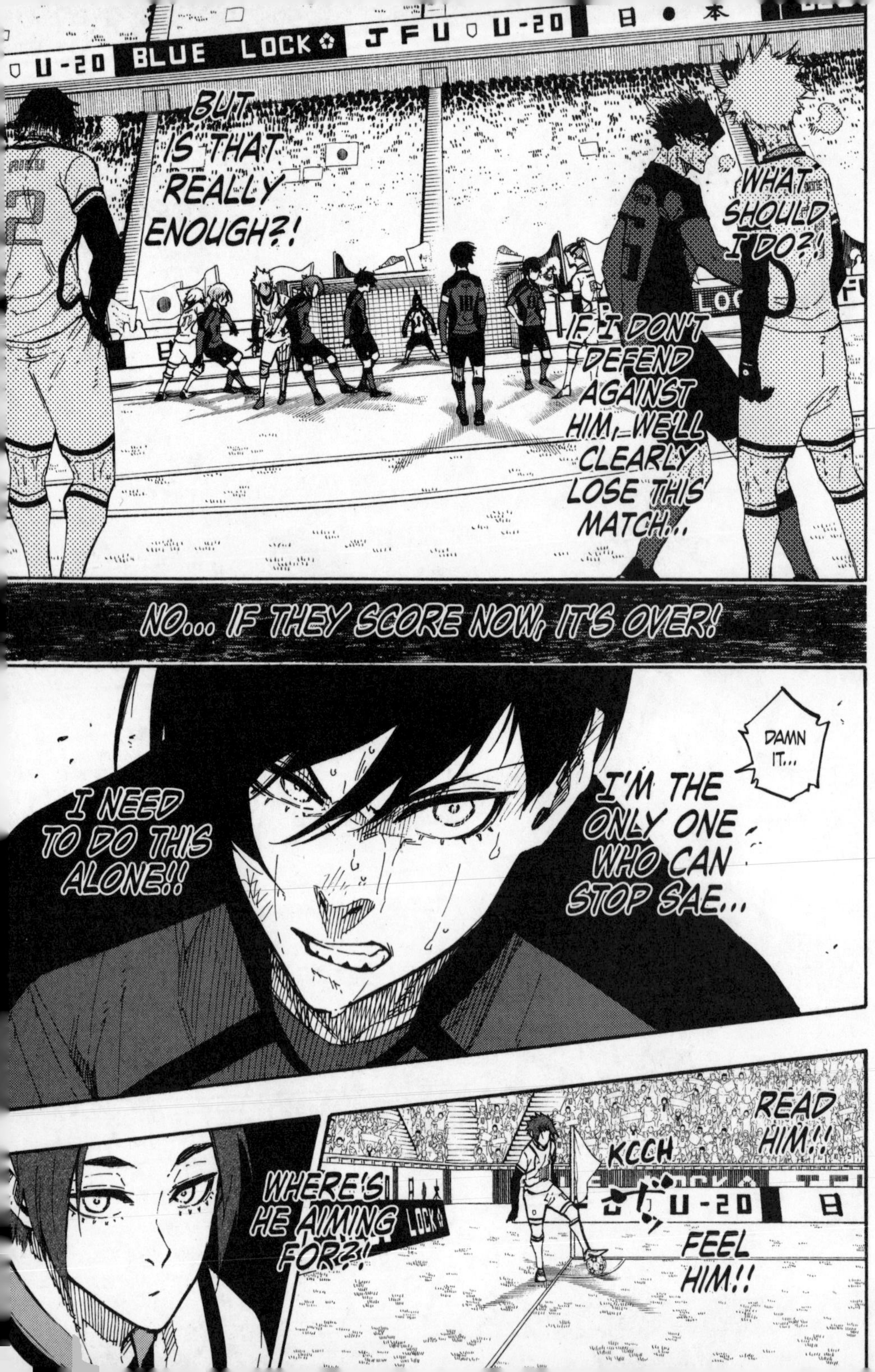
U-20 BLUE LOCK JFU U-20 日 本
WHAT SHOULD I DO?!
IF I DON'T DEFEND AGAINST HIM, WE'LL CLEARLY LOSE THIS MATCH...
BUT IS THAT REALLY ENOUGH?!
NO... IF THEY SCORE NOW, IT'S OVER!
DAMN IT...
I'M THE ONLY ONE WHO CAN STOP SAE...
I NEED TO DO THIS ALONE!!
READ HIM!!
KCCH
FEEL HIM!!
U-20
WHERE'S HE AIMING FOR?!

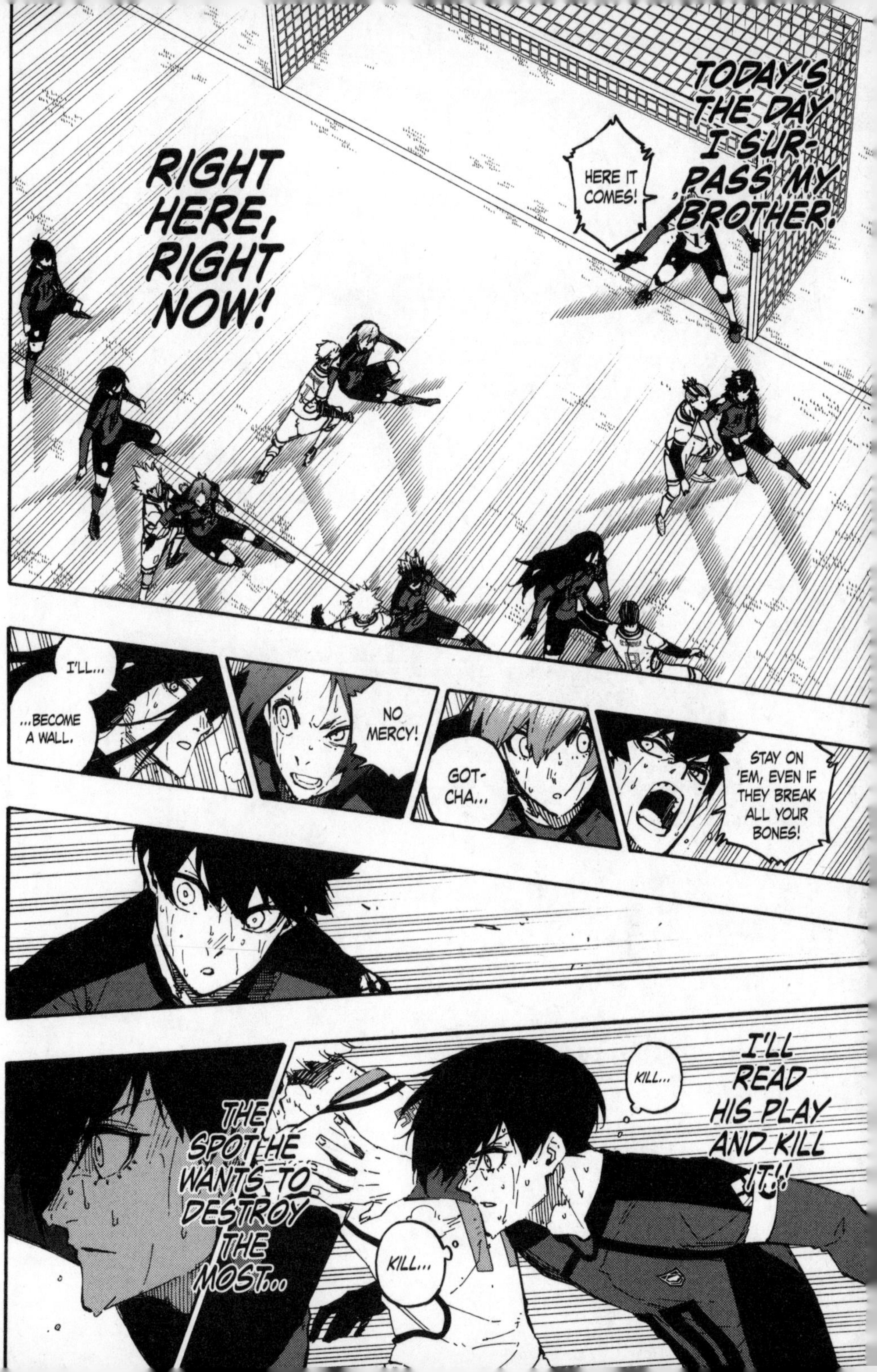
TODAY'S THE DAY I SUR-PASS MY BROTHER.
HERE IT COMES!
RIGHT HERE, RIGHT NOW!
STAY ON 'EM, EVEN IF THEY BREAK ALL YOUR BONES!
GOT-CHA...
NO MERCY!
I'LL...
...BECOME A WALL.
I'LL READ HIS PLAY AND KILL IT!!
KILL...
KILL...
THE SPOT HE WANTS TO DESTROY THE MOST...

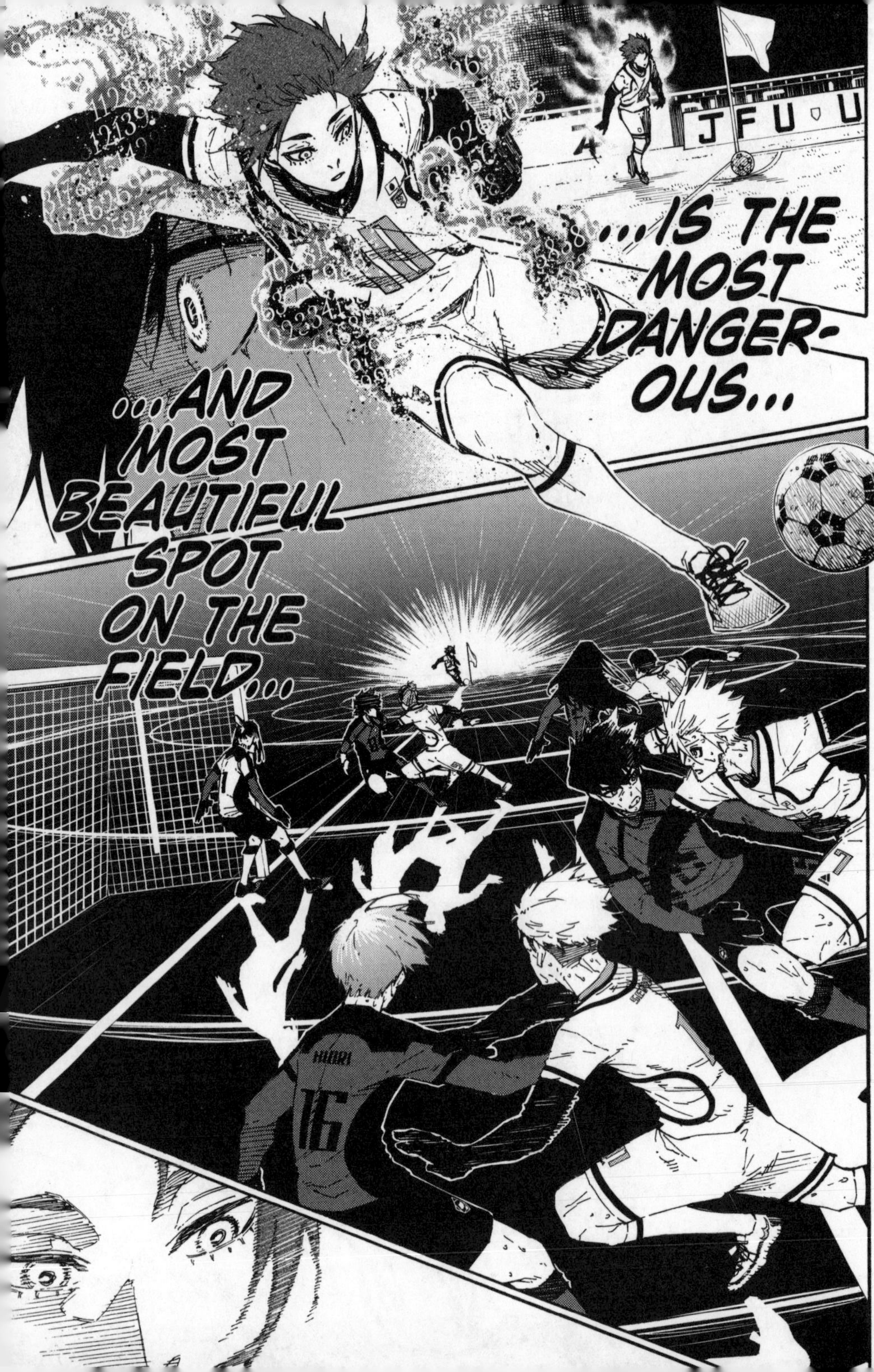
...IS THE MOST DANGER-OUS...
...AND MOST BEAUTIFUL SPOT ON THE FIELD...

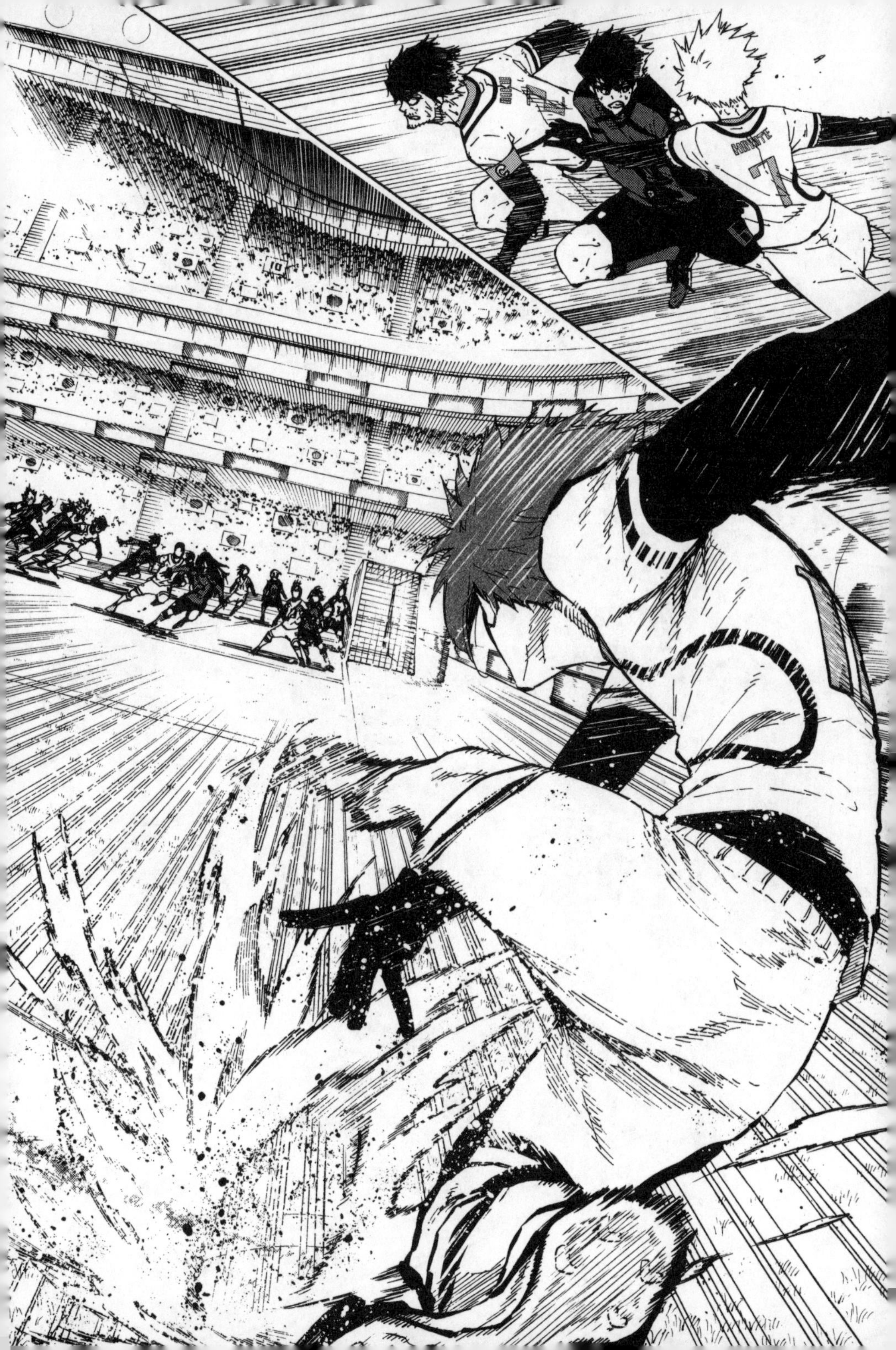

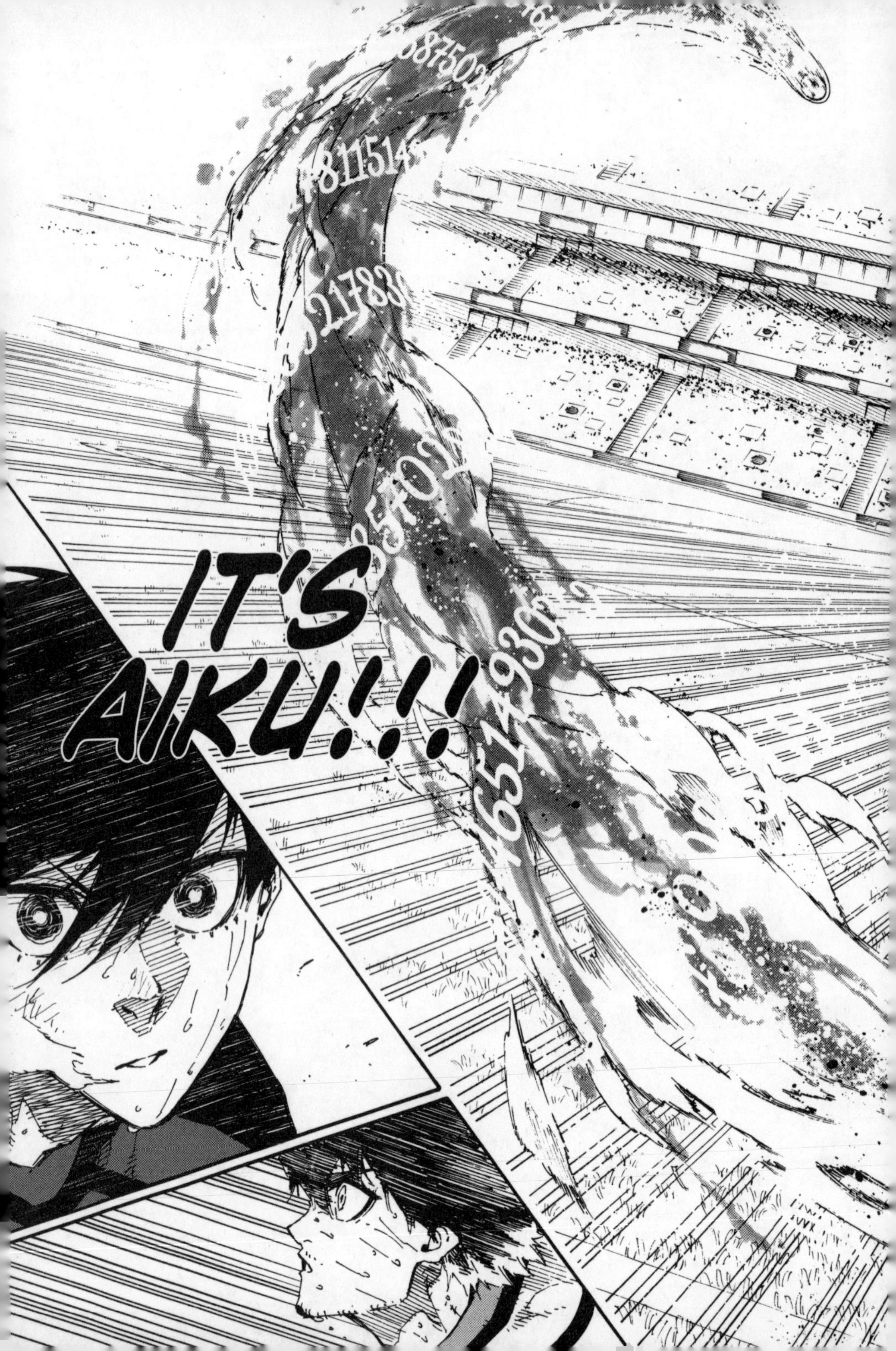
IT'S AIKU!!!

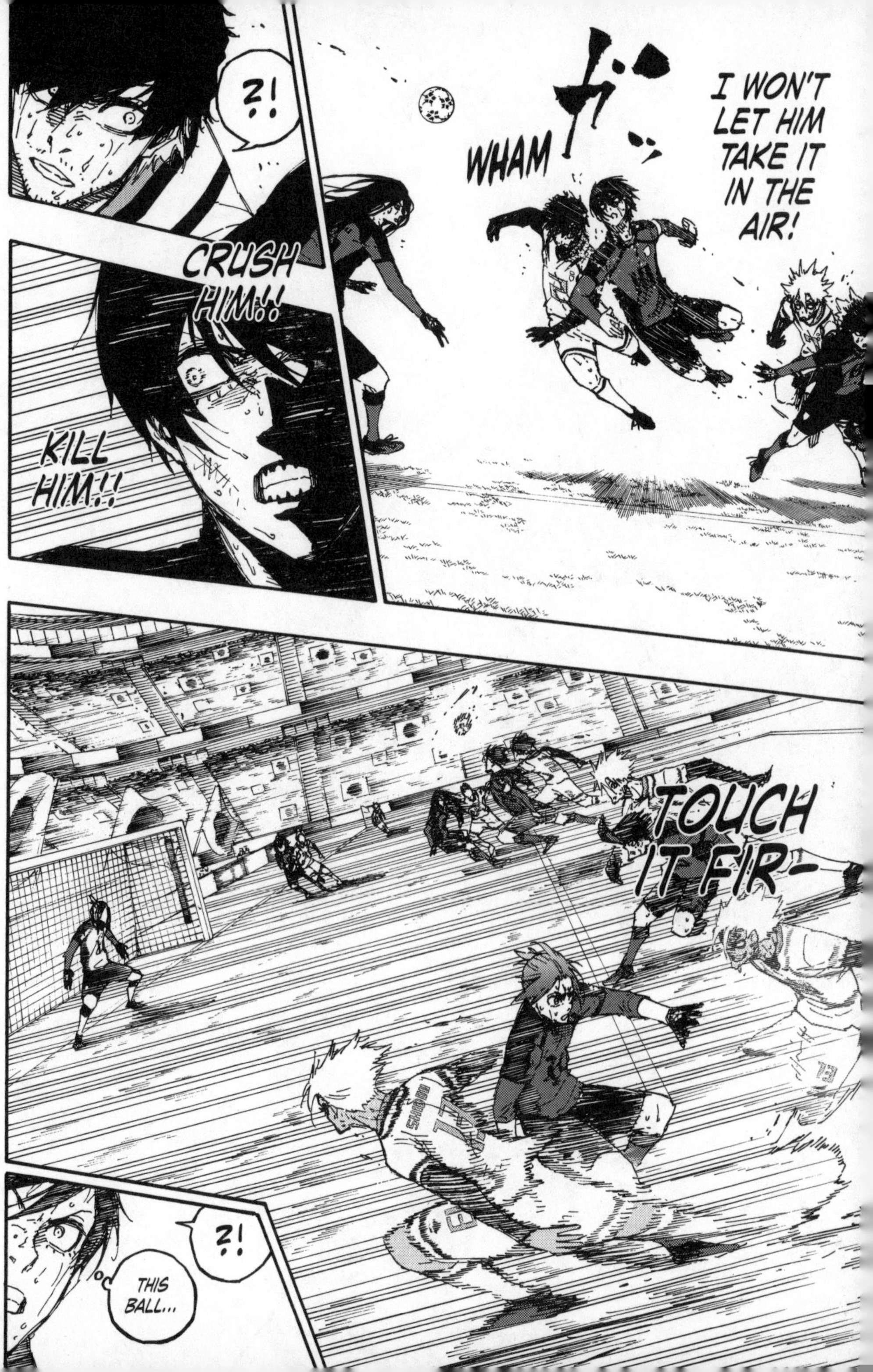

WHAM
I WON'T LET HIM TAKE IT IN THE AIR!
?!
CRUSH HIM!!
KILL HIM!!
TOUCH IT FIR-
?!
THIS BALL...

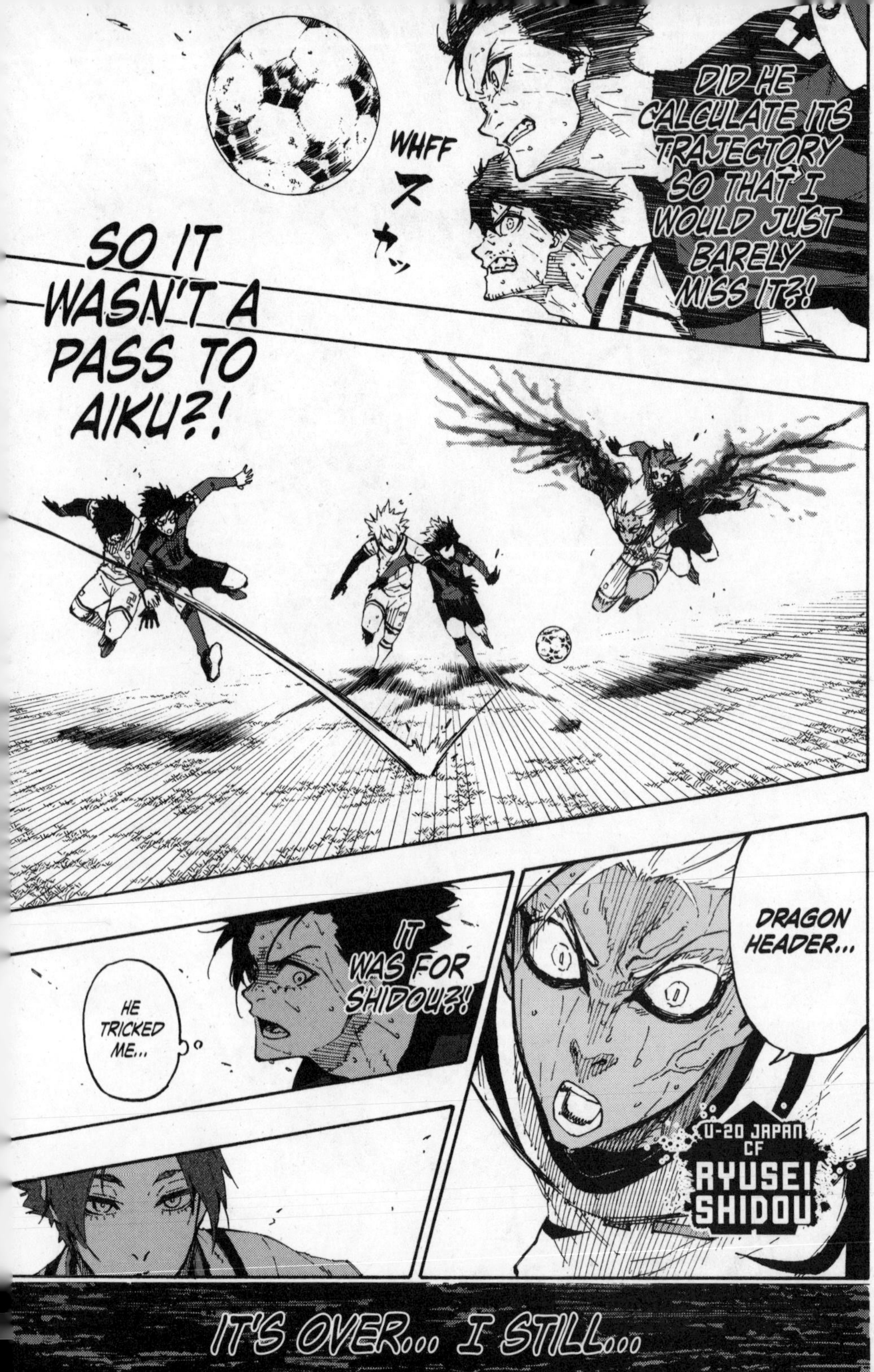
DID HE CALCULATE ITS TRAJECTORY SO THAT I WOULD JUST BARELY MISS IT?!
WHFF
スカッ
SO IT WASN'T A PASS TO AIKU?!
DRAGON HEADER...
U-20 JAPAN CF
RYUSEI SHIDOU
IT WAS FOR SHIDOU?!
HE TRICKED ME...
IT'S OVER... I STILL...

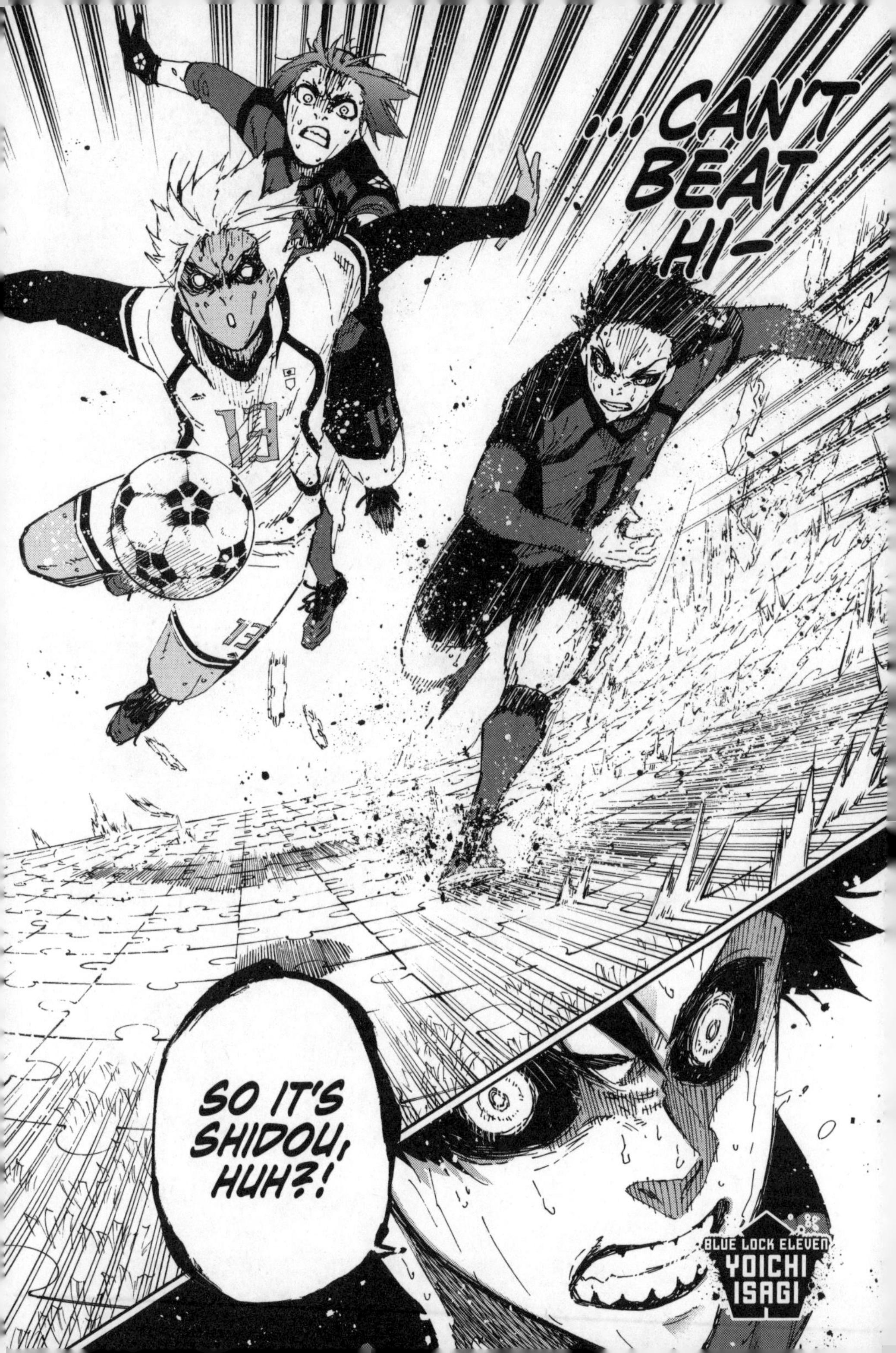
...CAN'T BEAT HI-
SO IT'S SHIDOU, HUH?!
BLUE LOCK ELEVEN
YOICHI ISAGI

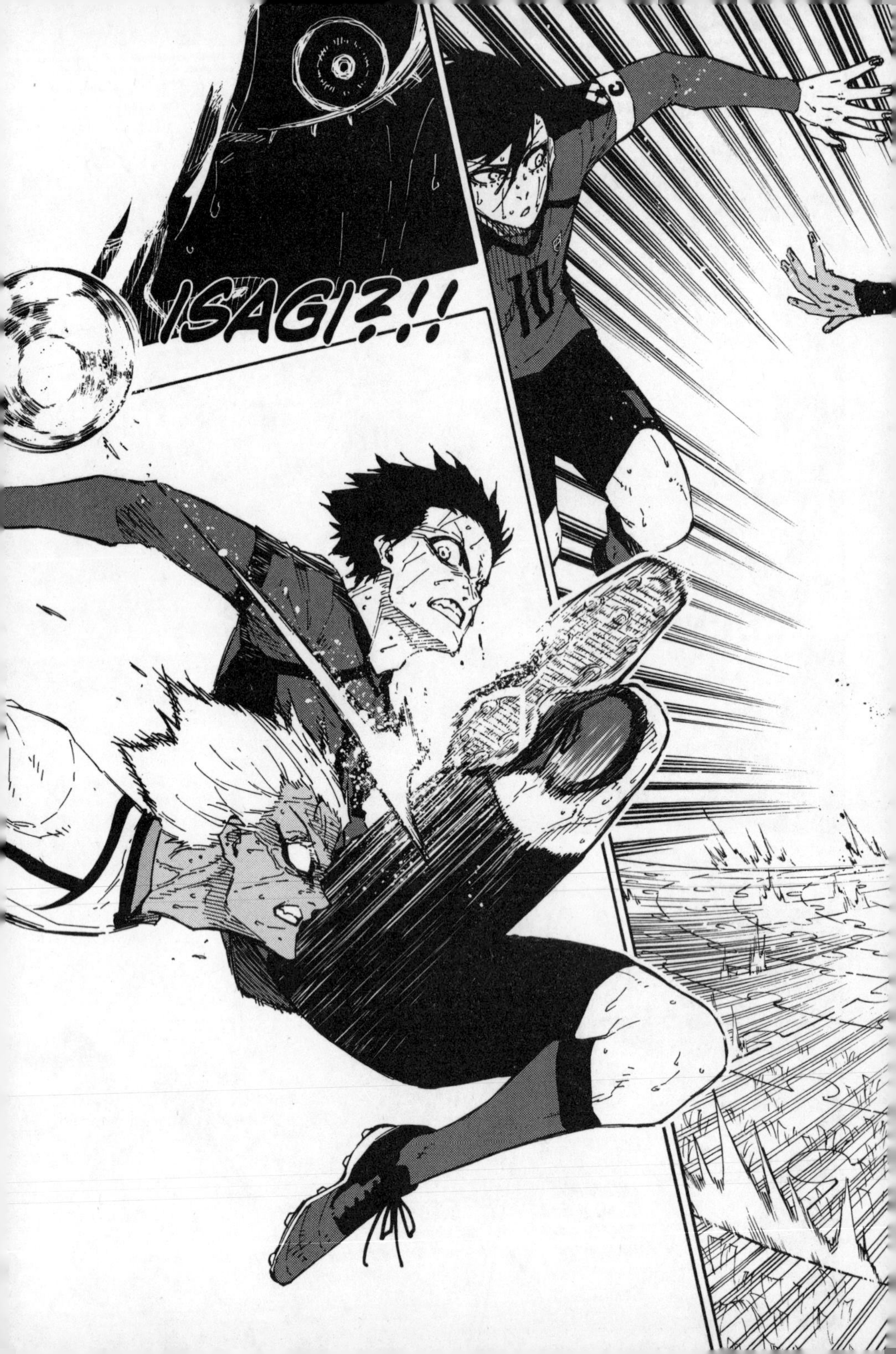
ISAGI?!!

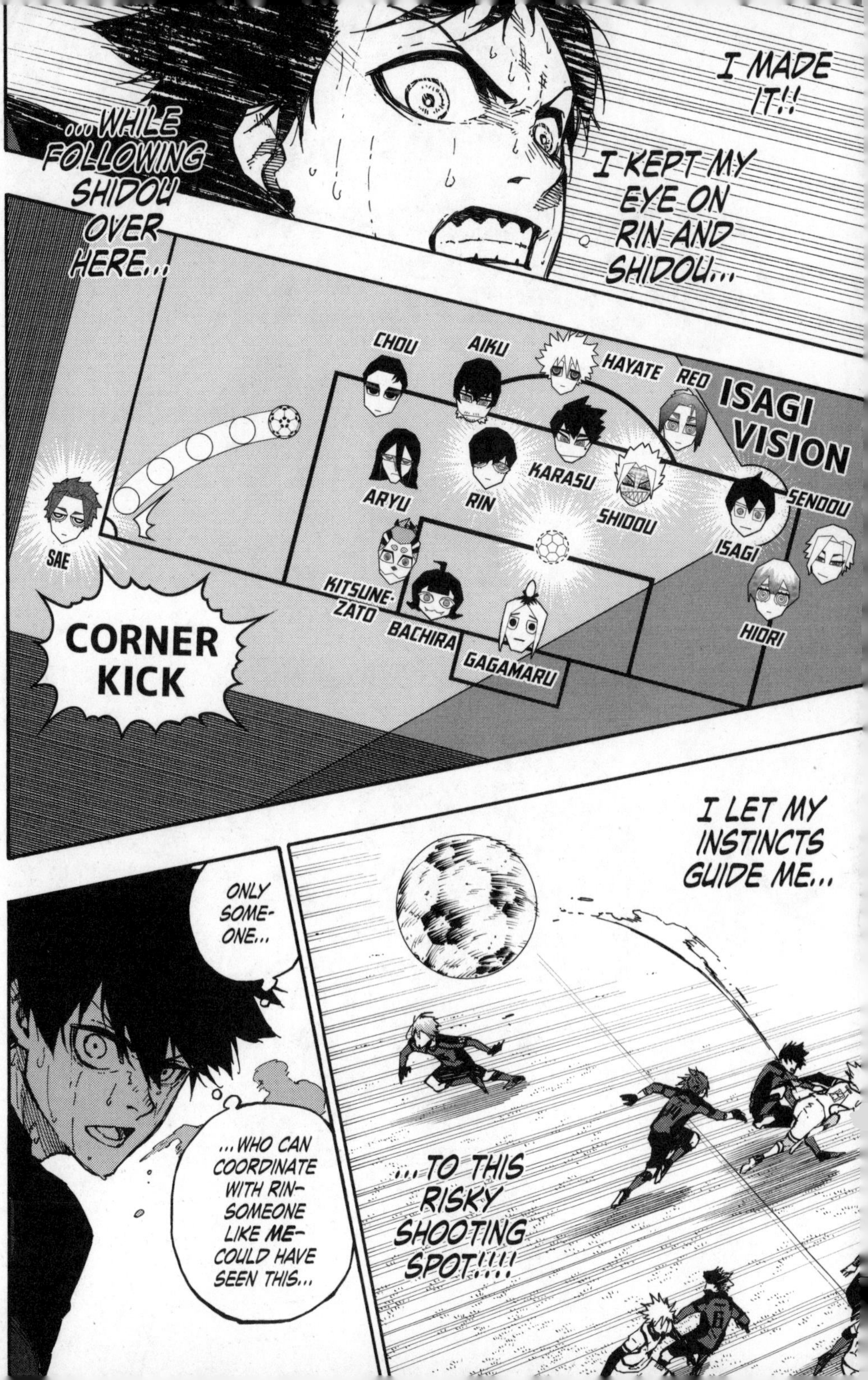
I MADE IT!!
I KEPT MY EYE ON RIN AND SHIDOU...
...WHILE FOLLOWING SHIDOU OVER HERE...
ISAGI VISION
CHOU
AIKU
HAYATE
REO
ARYU
RIN
KARASU
SHIDOU
SENDOU
SAE
ISAGI
KITSUNEZATO
BACHIRA
GAGAMARU
HIORI
CORNER KICK
I LET MY INSTINCTS GUIDE ME...
...TO THIS RISKY SHOOTING SPOT!!!!
ONLY SOMEONE...
...WHO CAN COORDINATE WITH RIN-SOMEONE LIKE ME-COULD HAVE SEEN THIS...

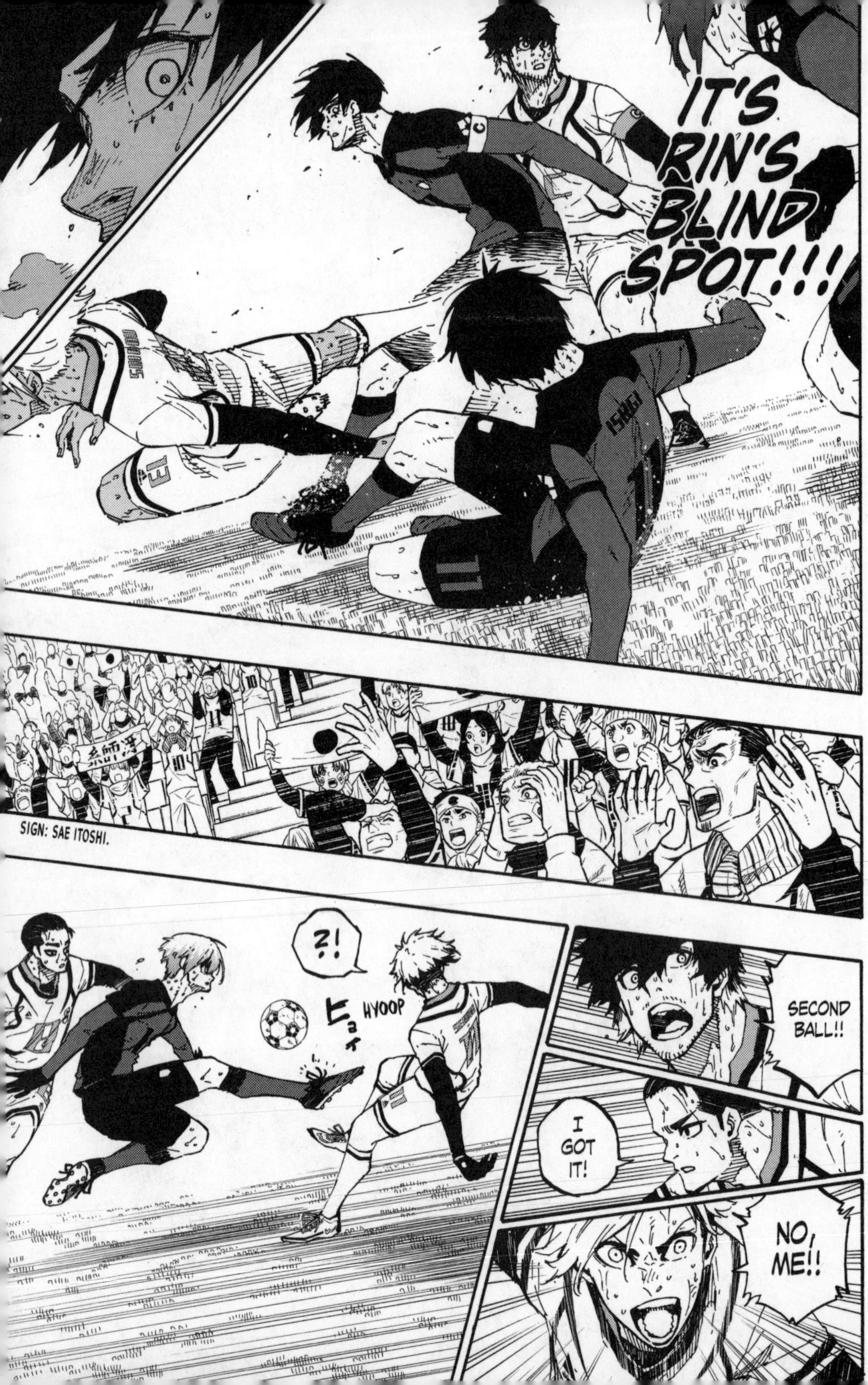
IT'S RIN'S BLIND SPOT!!!
SIGN: SAE ITOSHI.
SECOND BALL!!
I GOT IT!
NO, ME!!
?!
ヒョイ
HYOOP

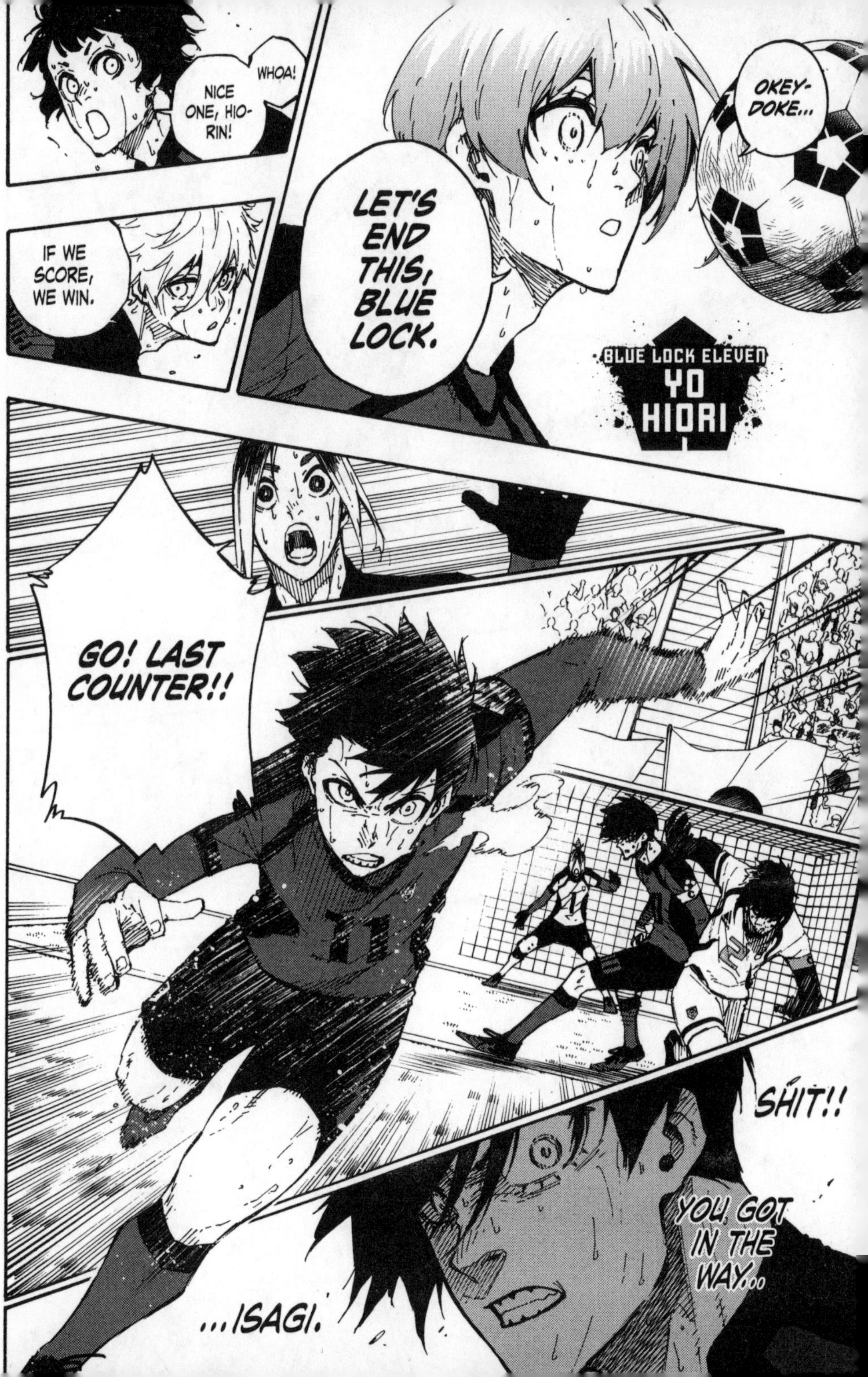
OKEY-DOKE...
LET'S END THIS, BLUE LOCK.
BLUE LOCK ELEVEN
YO HIORI
WHOA!
NICE ONE, HIO-RIN!
IF WE SCORE, WE WIN.
GO! LAST COUNTER!!
SHIT!!
YOU GOT IN THE WAY...
...ISAGI.

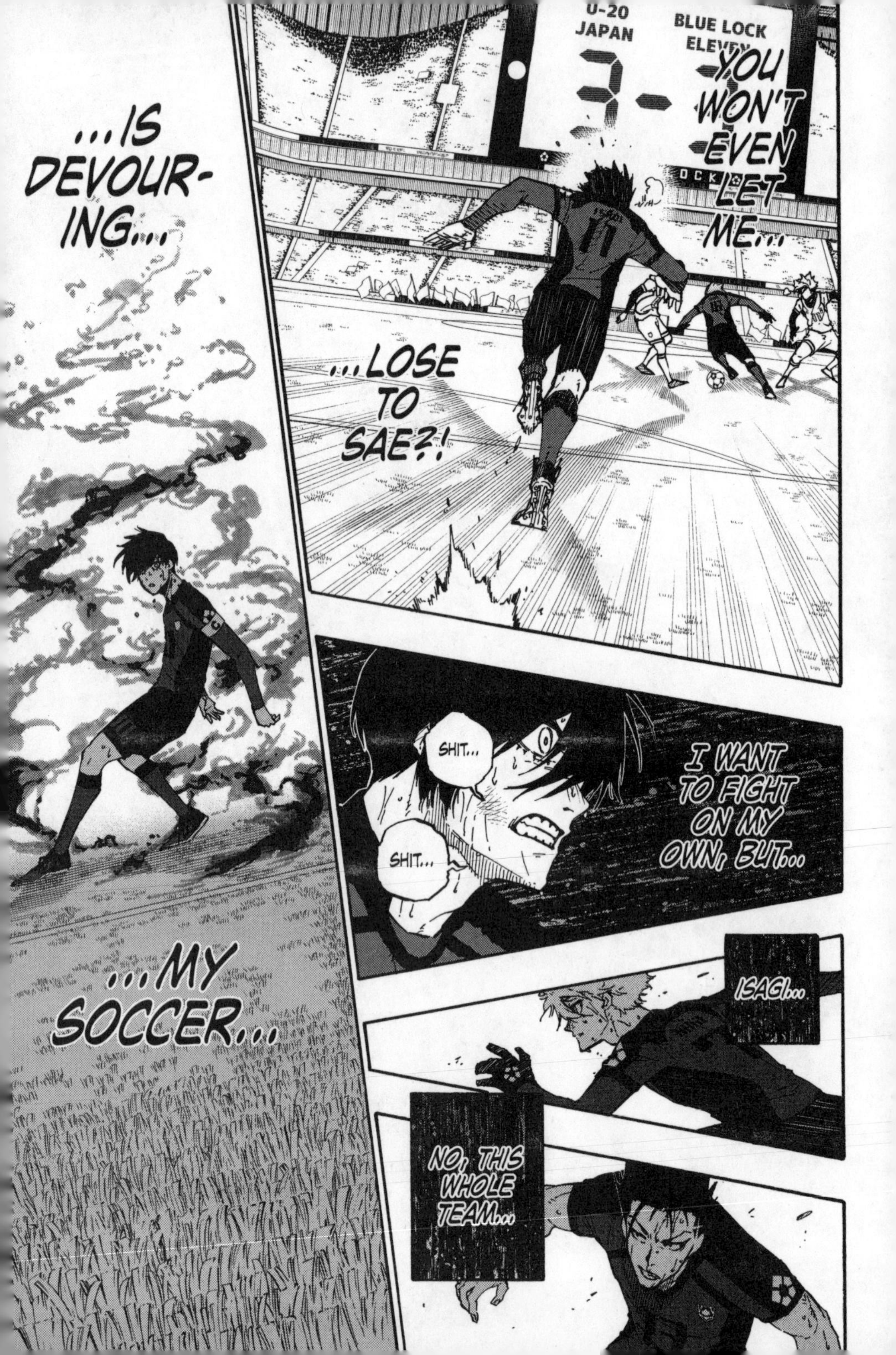
U-20 JAPAN
BLUE LOCK
YOU WON'T EVEN LET ME...
...LOSE TO SAE?!
SHIT...
SHIT...
I WANT TO FIGHT ON MY OWN, BUT...
ISAGI...
NO, THIS WHOLE TEAM...
...IS DEVOUR-ING...
...MY SOCCER...

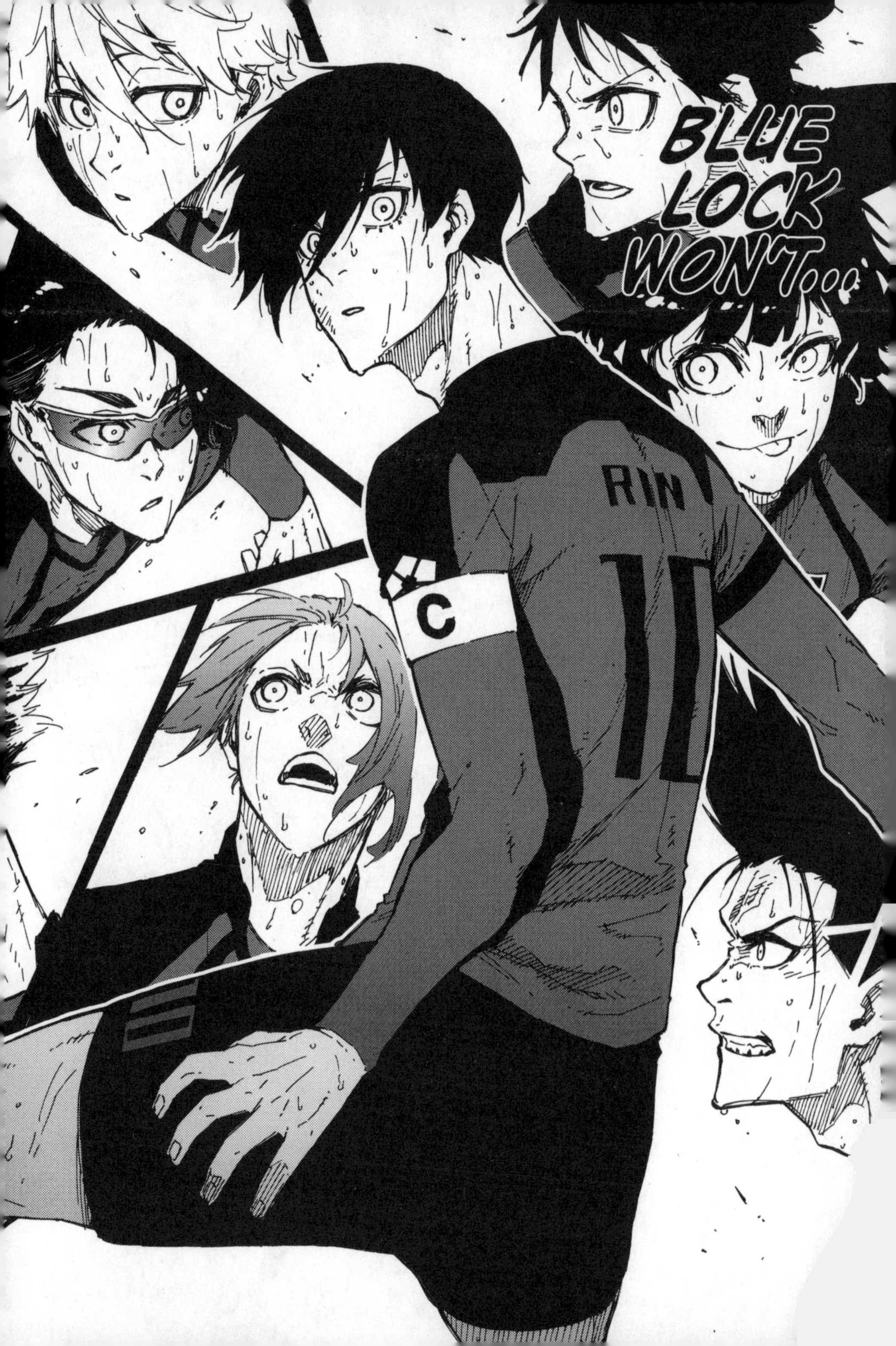
BLUE LOCK WON'T...
RIN
11
C

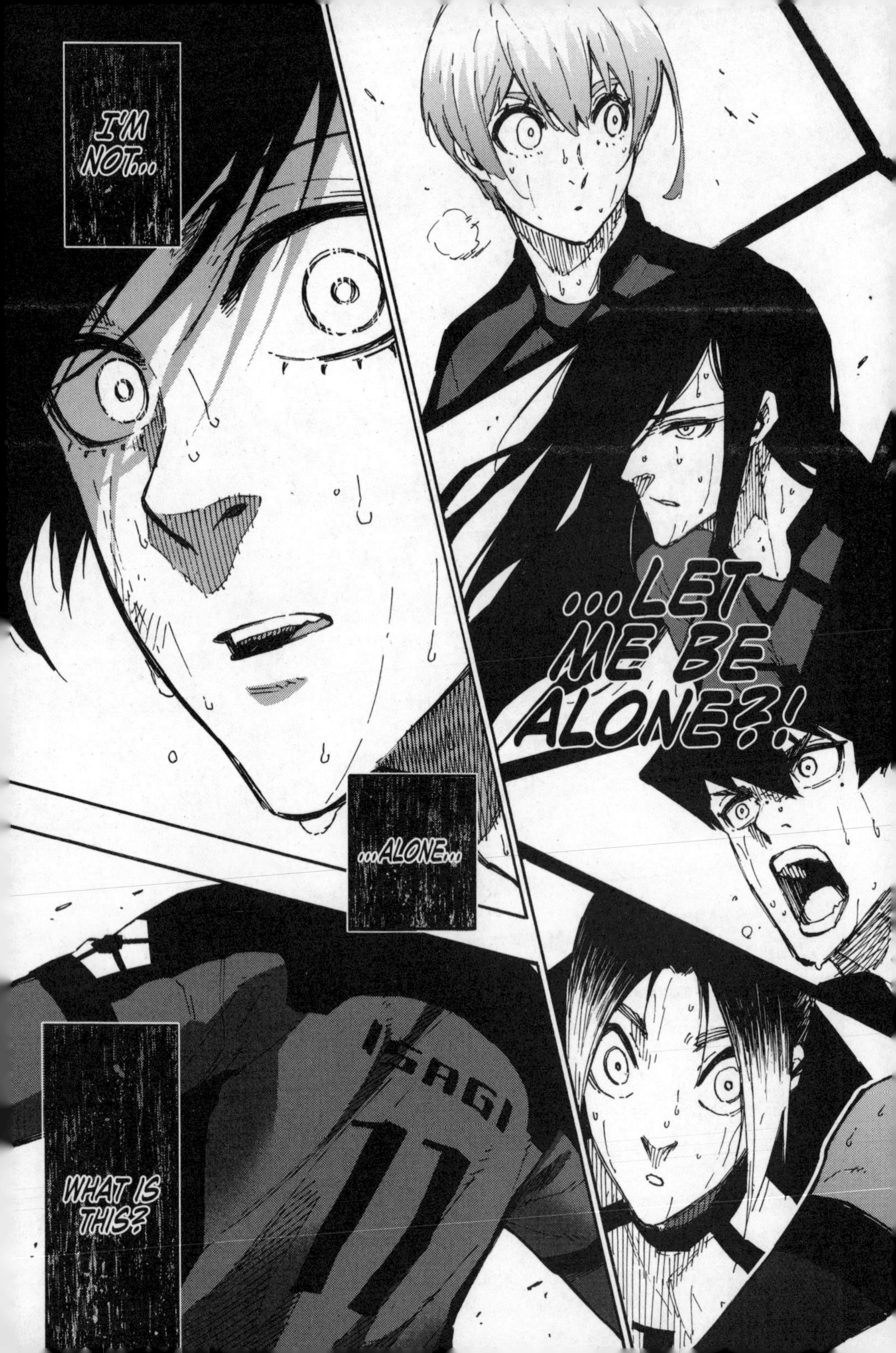

...LET ME BE ALONE?!
I'M NOT...
...ALONE...
ISAGI
11
WHAT IS THIS?

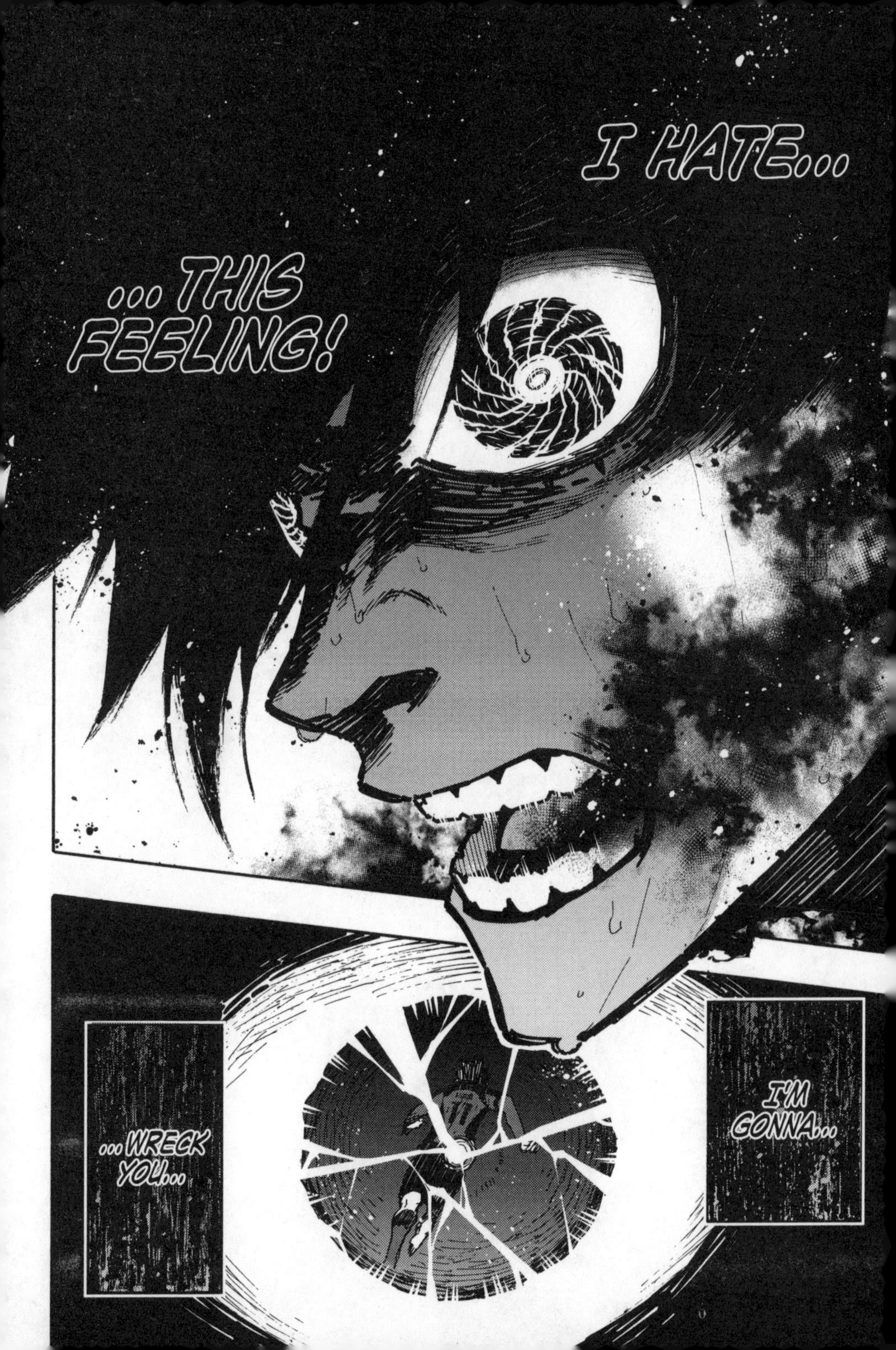
I HATE...
...THIS FEELING!
I'M GONNA...
...WRECK YOU...

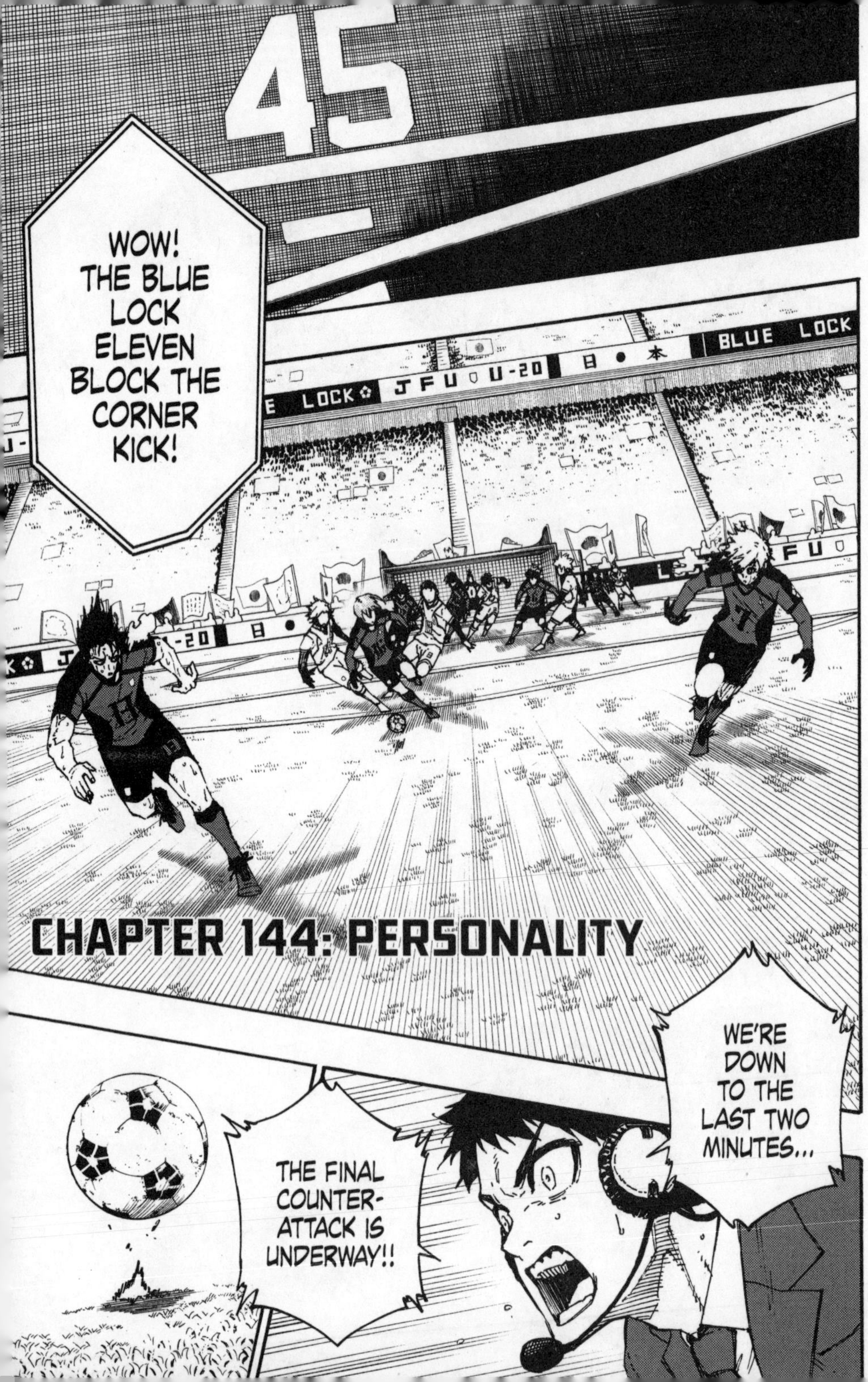
45
WOW! THE BLUE LOCK ELEVEN BLOCK THE CORNER KICK!
BLUE LOCK
JFU U-20 日●本
CHAPTER 144: PERSONALITY
WE'RE DOWN TO THE LAST TWO MINUTES...
THE FINAL COUNTER-ATTACK IS UNDERWAY!!

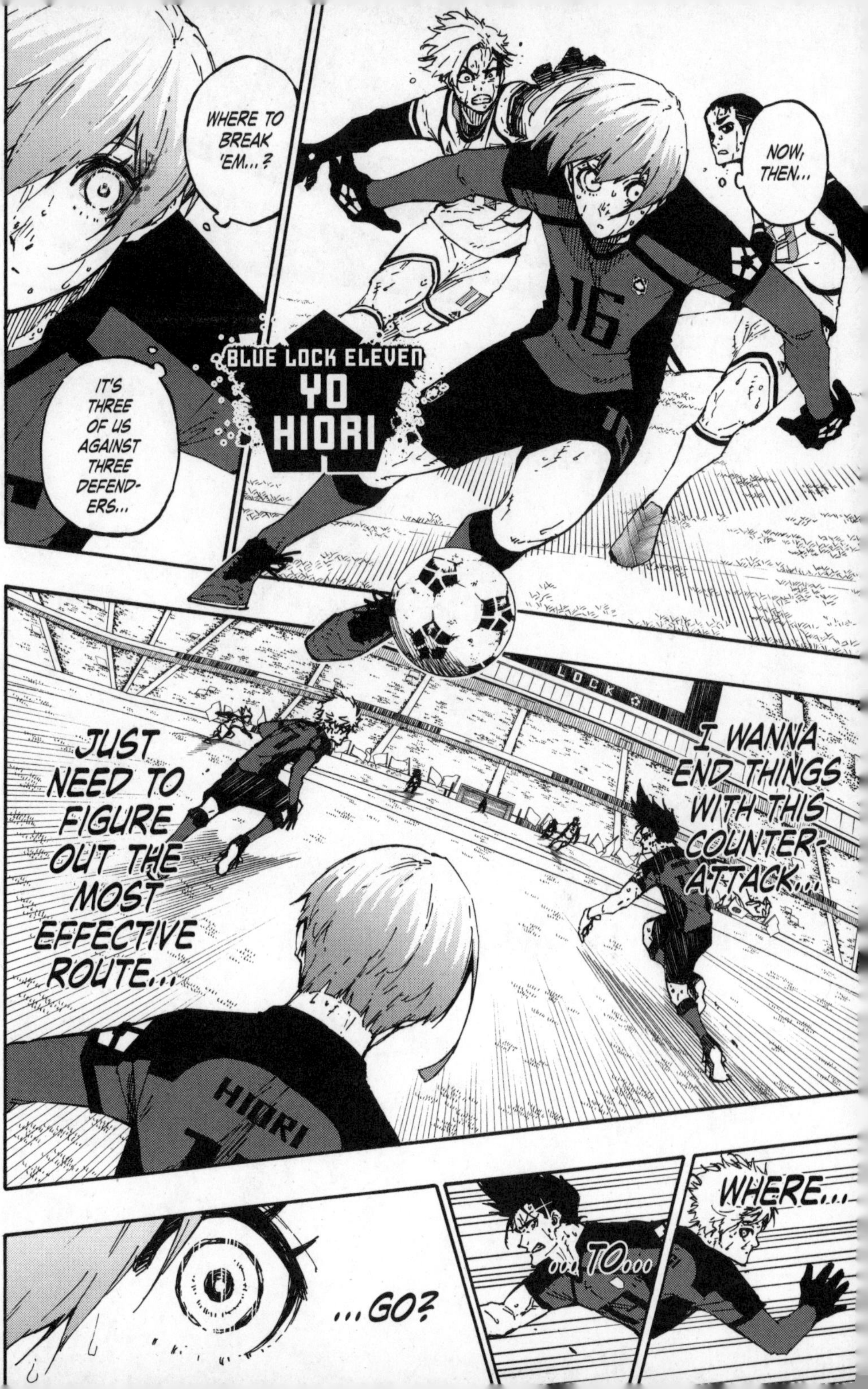
NOW, THEN...
BLUE LOCK ELEVEN
YO HIORI
WHERE TO BREAK 'EM...?
IT'S THREE OF US AGAINST THREE DEFENDERS...
LOCK
I WANNA END THINGS WITH THIS COUNTER-ATTACK...
JUST NEED TO FIGURE OUT THE MOST EFFECTIVE ROUTE...
HIORI
WHERE...
...TO...
...GO?

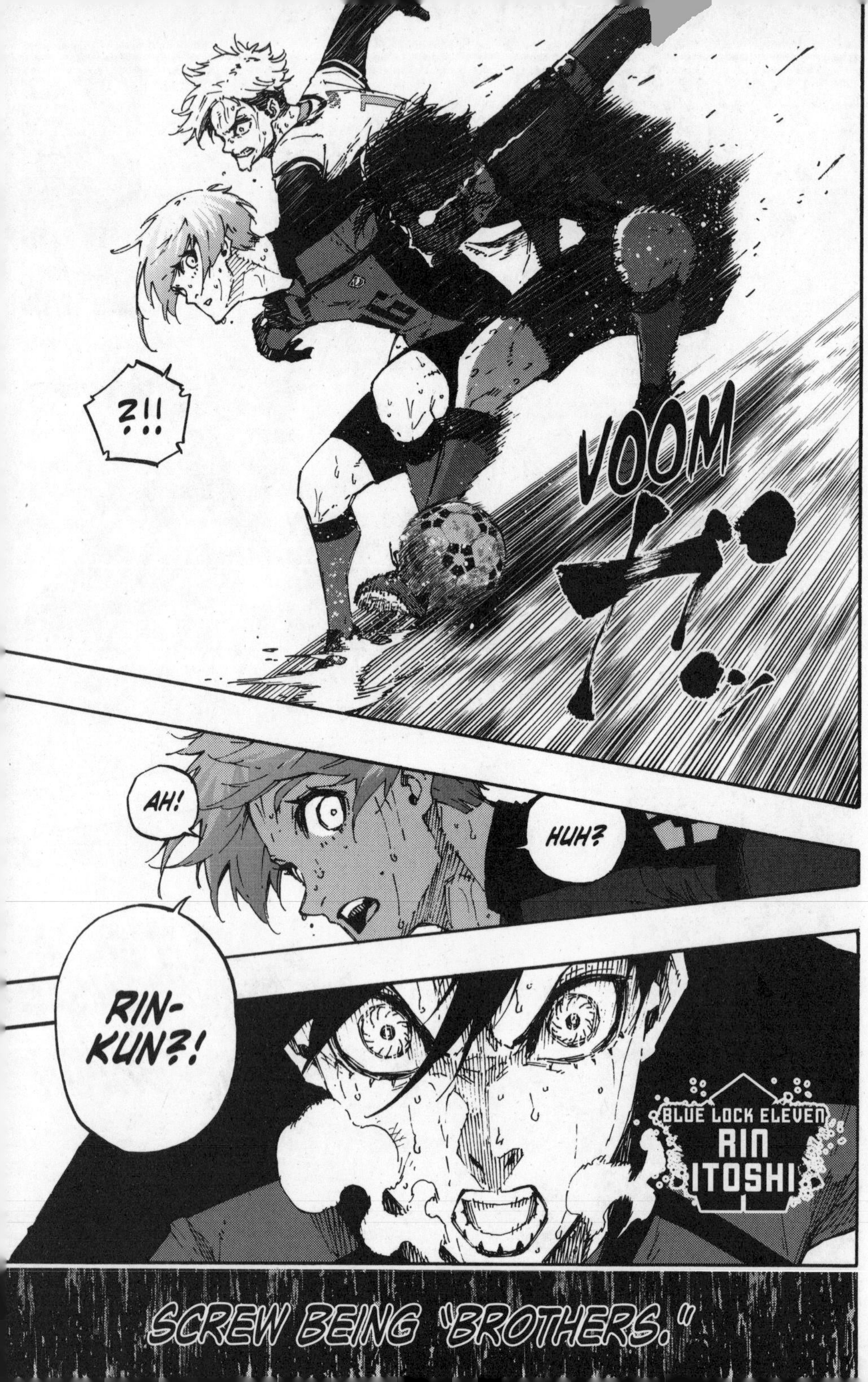
VOOM
?!!
HUH?
AH!
RIN-KUN?!
BLUE LOCK ELEVEN
RIN ITOSHI
SCREW BEING "BROTHERS."

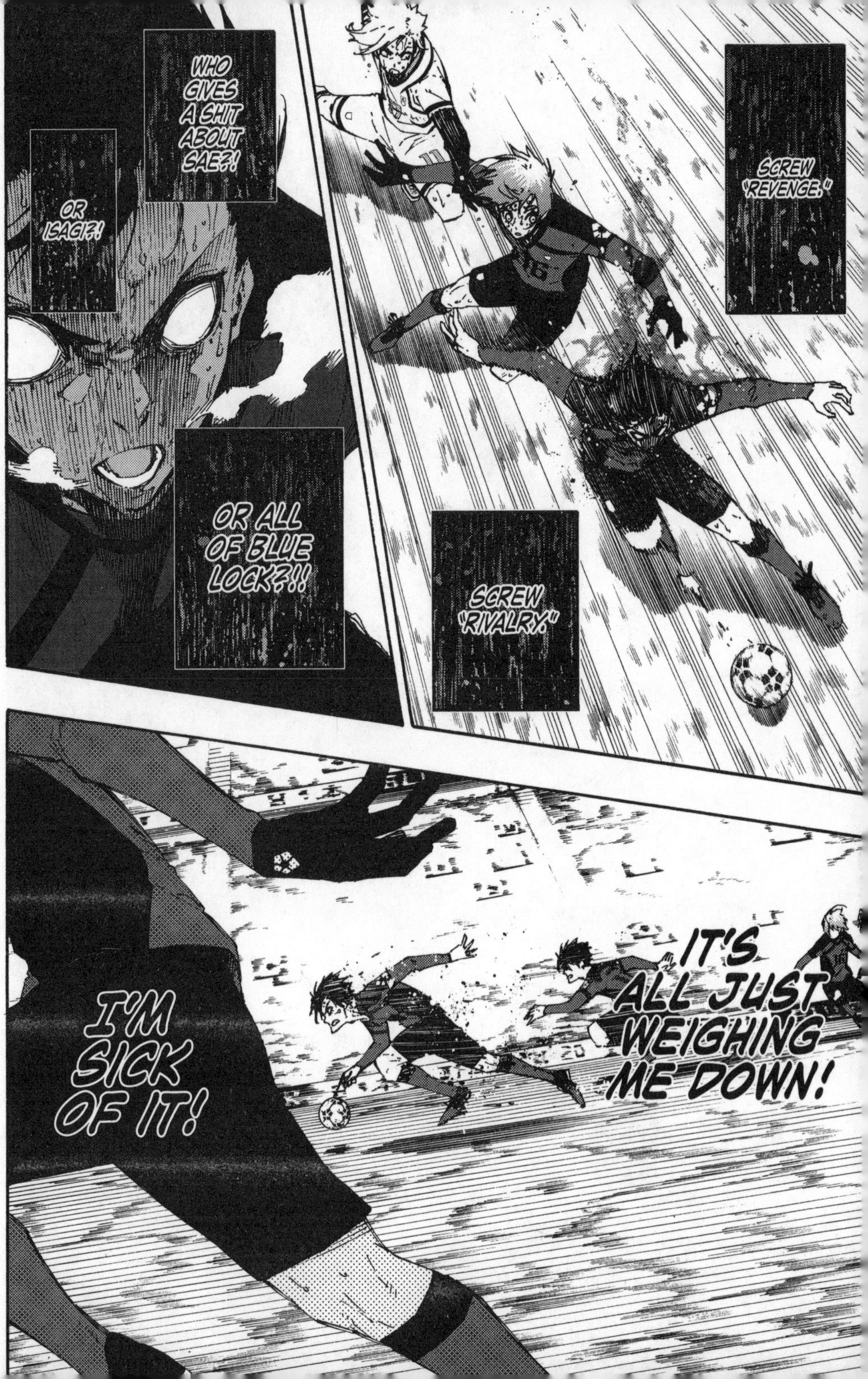

SCREW "REVENGE."
SCREW "RIVALRY."
WHO GIVES A SHIT ABOUT SAE?!
OR ISAGI?!
OR ALL OF BLUE LOCK?!!
IT'S ALL JUST WEIGHING ME DOWN!
I'M SICK OF IT!

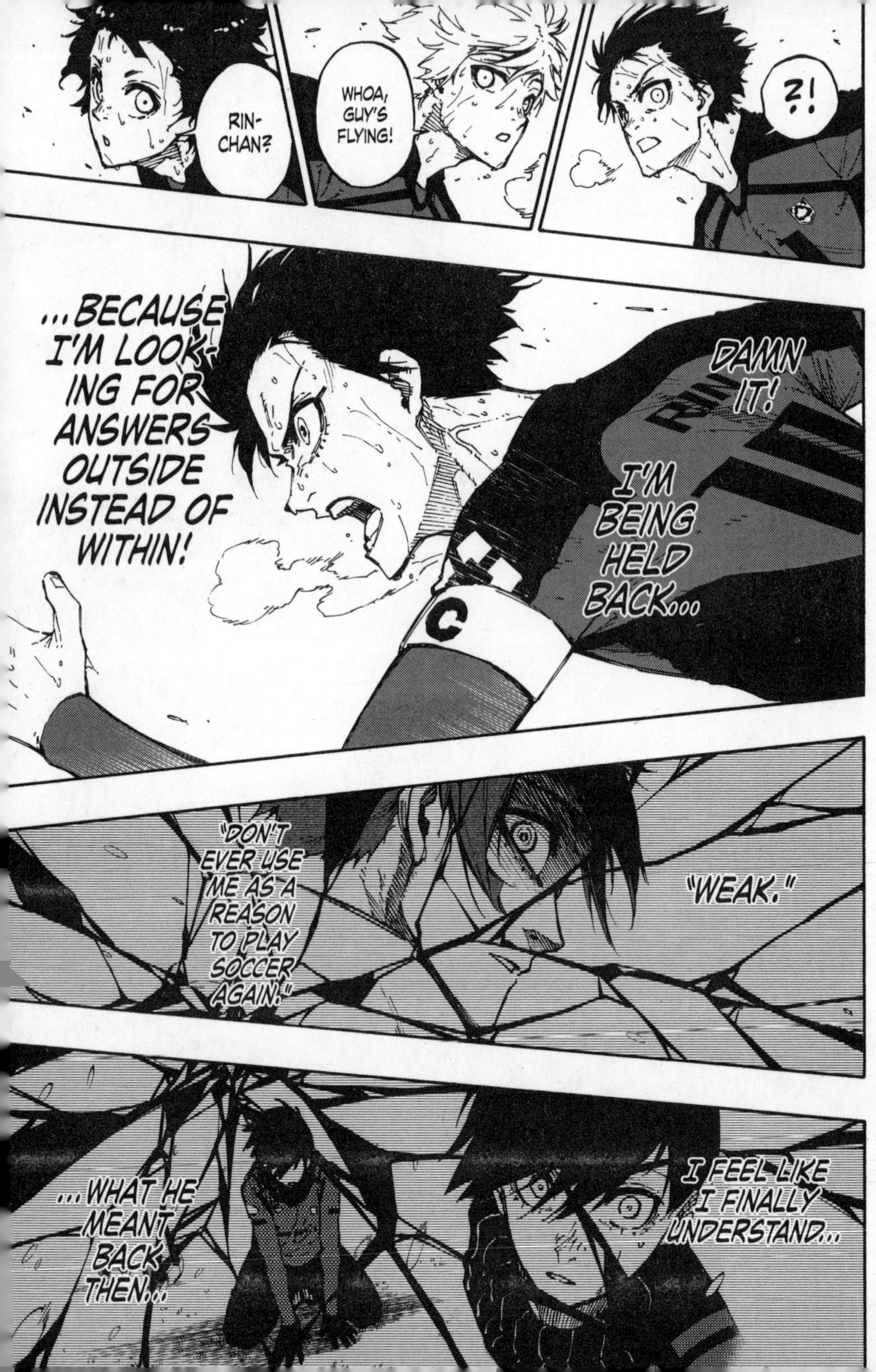
?!
WHOA, GUY'S FLYING!
RIN-CHAN?
DAMN IT!
I'M BEING HELD BACK...
...BECAUSE I'M LOOK-ING FOR ANSWERS OUTSIDE INSTEAD OF WITHIN!
"WEAK."
"DON'T EVER USE ME AS A REASON TO PLAY SOCCER AGAIN."
I FEEL LIKE I FINALLY UNDERSTAND...
...WHAT HE MEANT BACK THEN...

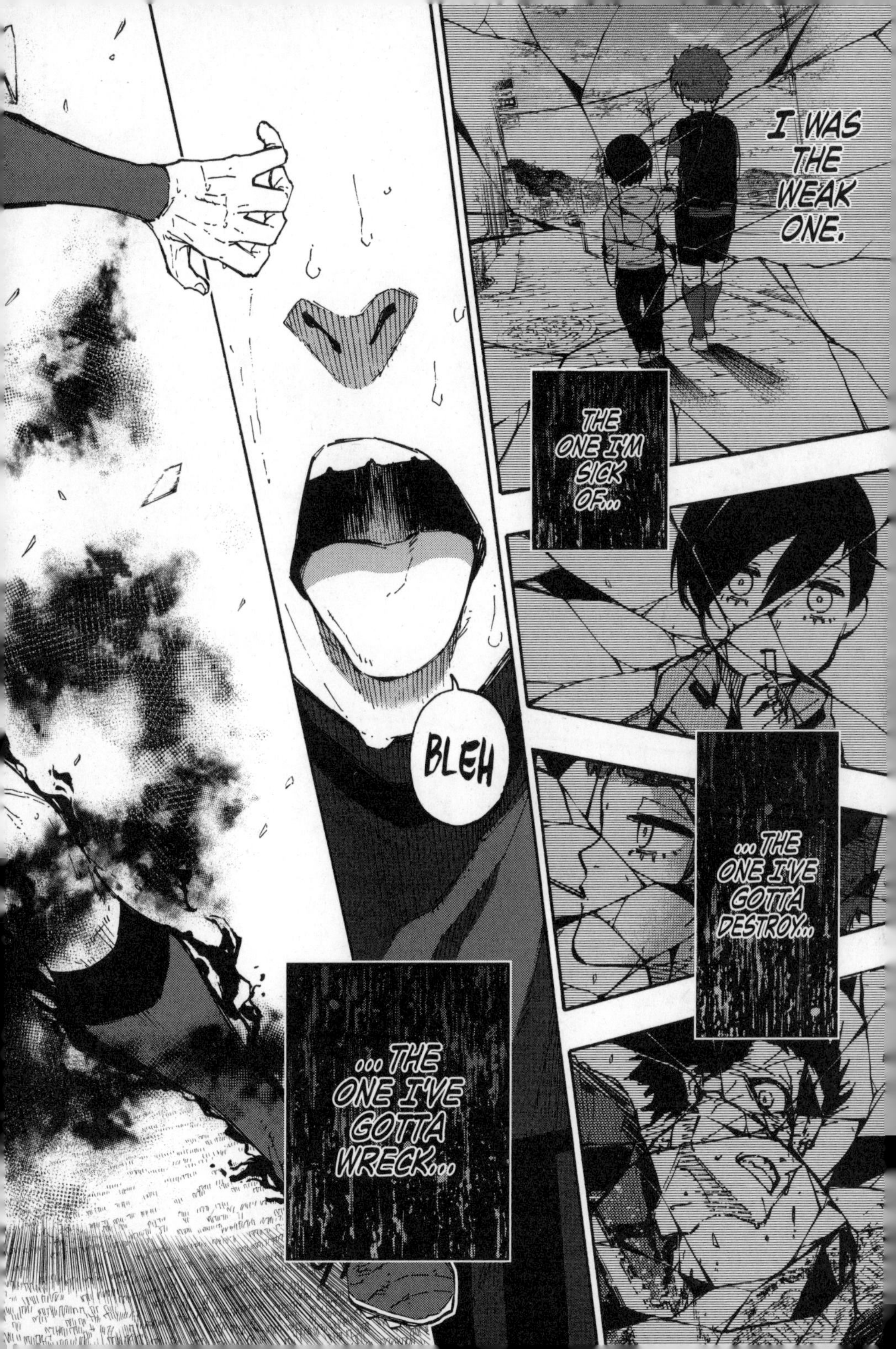
I WAS THE WEAK ONE.
THE ONE I'M SICK OF...
...THE ONE I'VE GOTTA DESTROY...
BLEH
...THE ONE I'VE GOTTA WRECK...

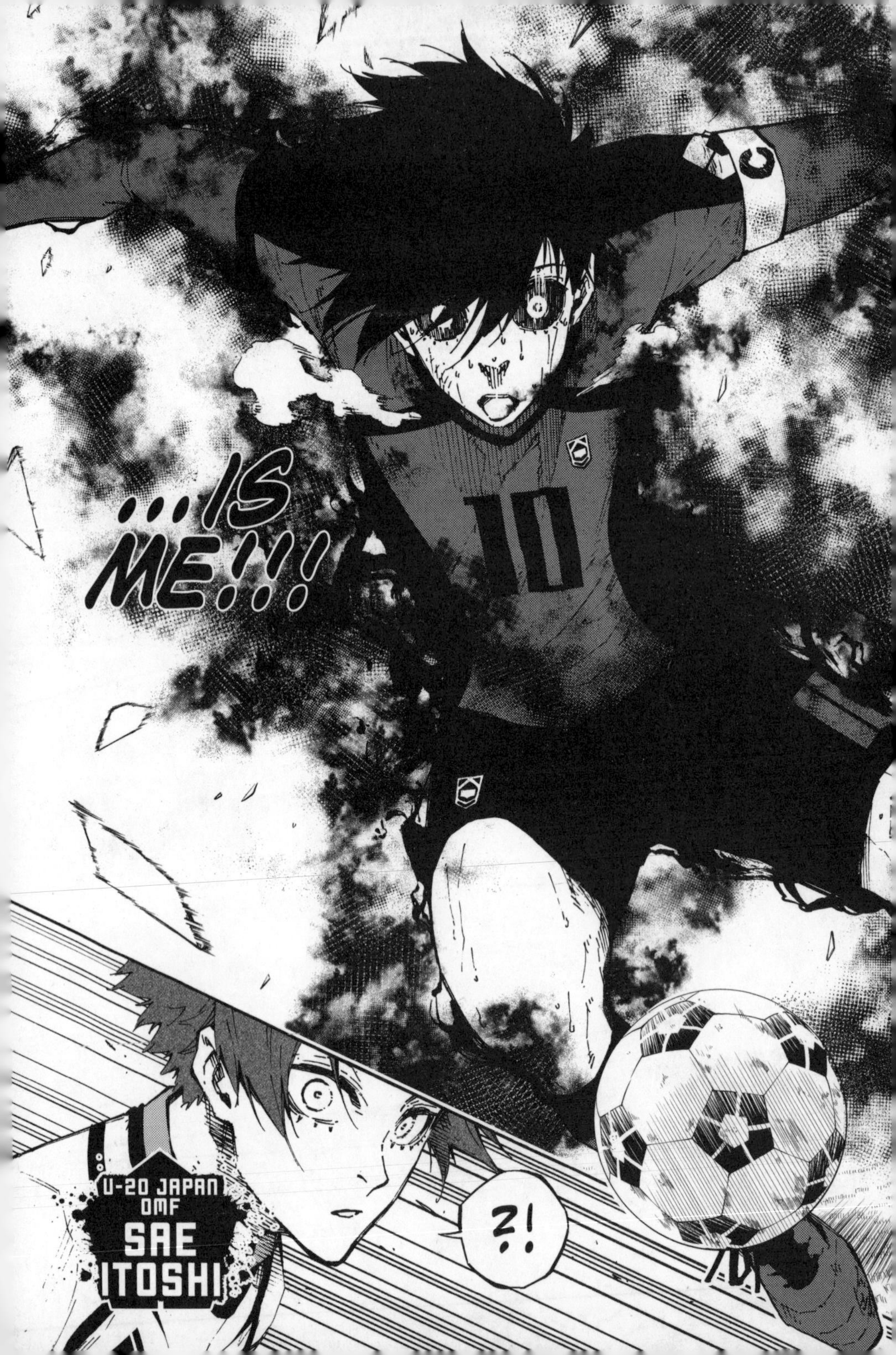
...IS ME!!!
U-20 JAPAN OMF SAE ITOSHI
?!

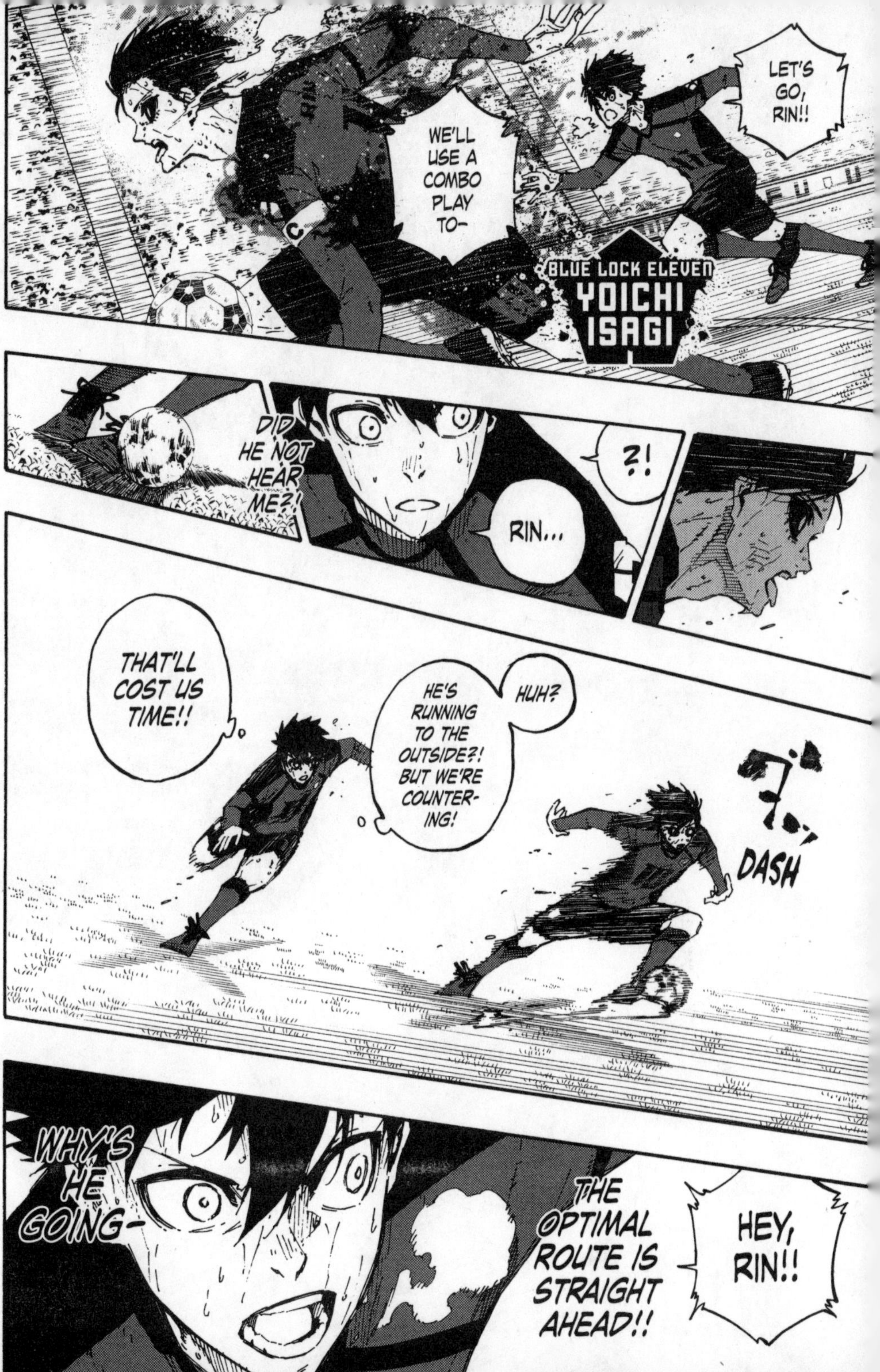
LET'S GO, RIN!!
WE'LL USE A COMBO PLAY TO-
BLUE LOCK ELEVEN
YOICHI ISAGI
?!
RIN...
DID HE NOT HEAR ME?!
DASH
HUH?
HE'S RUNNING TO THE OUTSIDE?! BUT WE'RE COUNTER-ING!
THAT'LL COST US TIME!!
HEY, RIN!!
THE OPTIMAL ROUTE IS STRAIGHT AHEAD!!
WHY'S HE GOING-

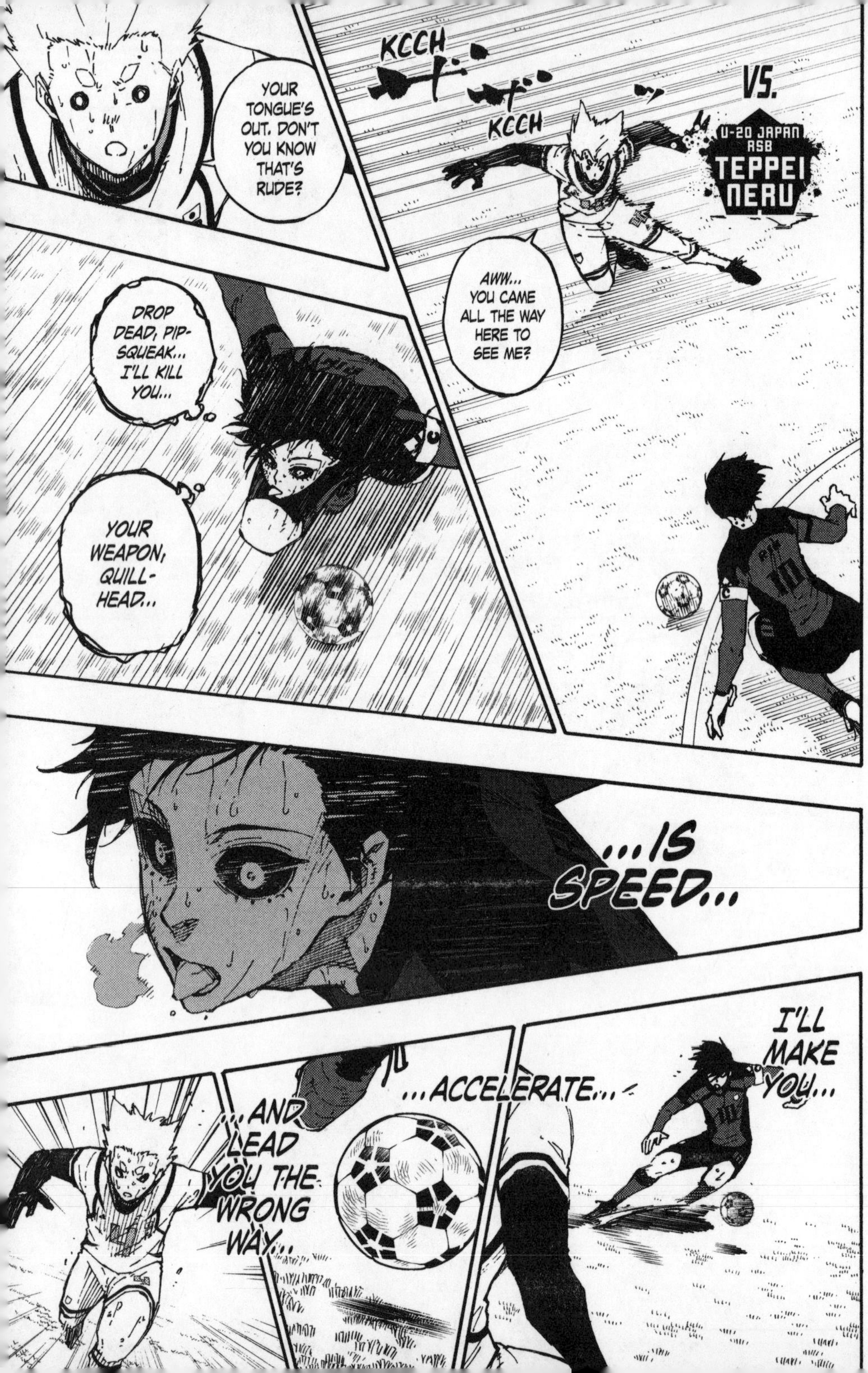
KCCH
KCCH
VS.
U-20 JAPAN RSB
TEPPEI NERU
AWW... YOU CAME ALL THE WAY HERE TO SEE ME?
YOUR TONGUE'S OUT. DON'T YOU KNOW THAT'S RUDE?
DROP DEAD, PIP-SQUEAK... I'LL KILL YOU...
YOUR WEAPON, QUILL-HEAD...
...IS SPEED...
I'LL MAKE YOU...
...ACCELERATE...
...AND LEAD YOU THE WRONG WAY...

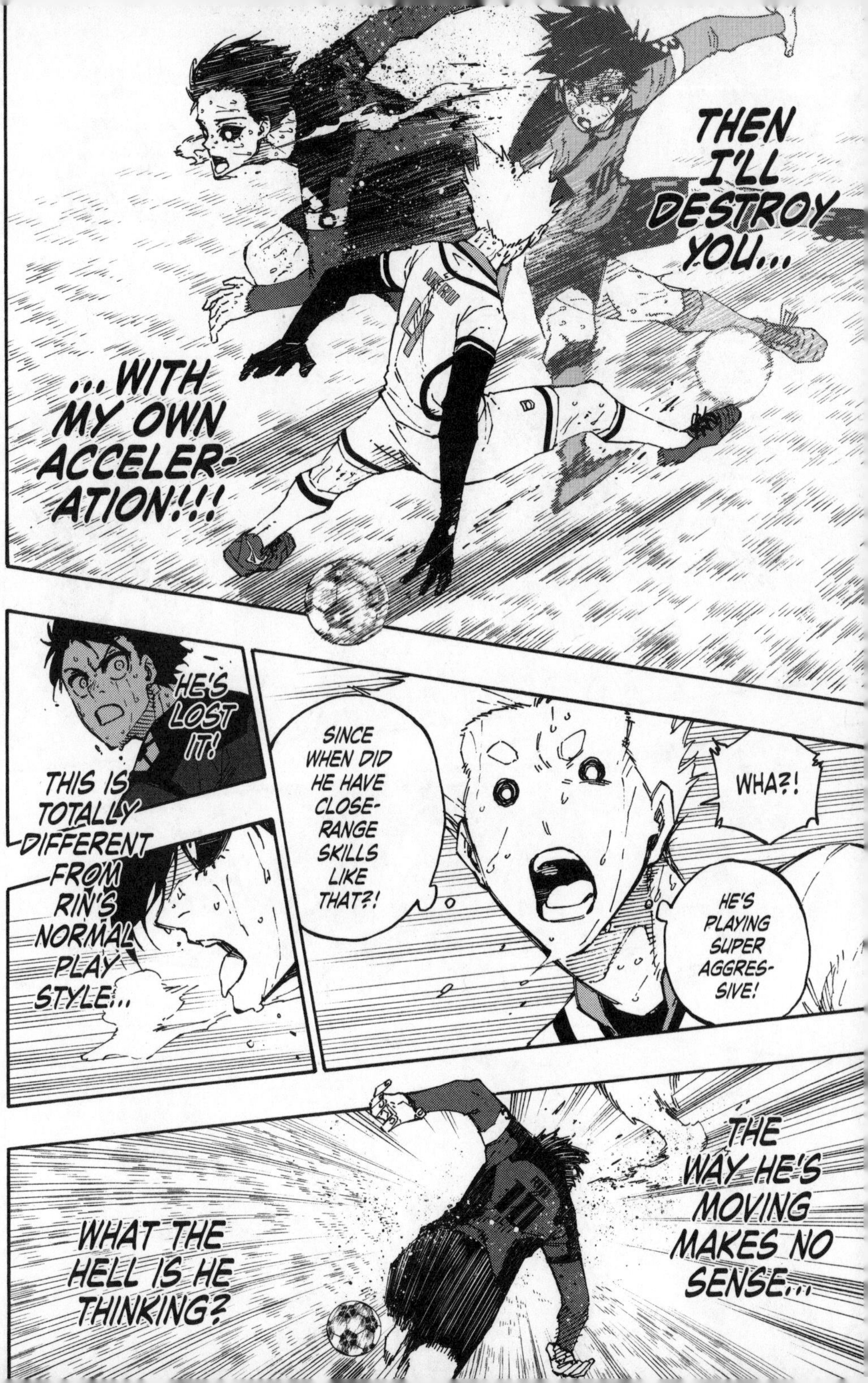
THEN I'LL DESTROY YOU...
...WITH MY OWN ACCELER-ATION!!!
WHA?!
HE'S PLAYING SUPER AGGRES-SIVE!
SINCE WHEN DID HE HAVE CLOSE-RANGE SKILLS LIKE THAT?!
HE'S LOST IT!
THIS IS TOTALLY DIFFERENT FROM RIN'S NORMAL PLAY STYLE...
THE WAY HE'S MOVING MAKES NO SENSE...
WHAT THE HELL IS HE THINKING?

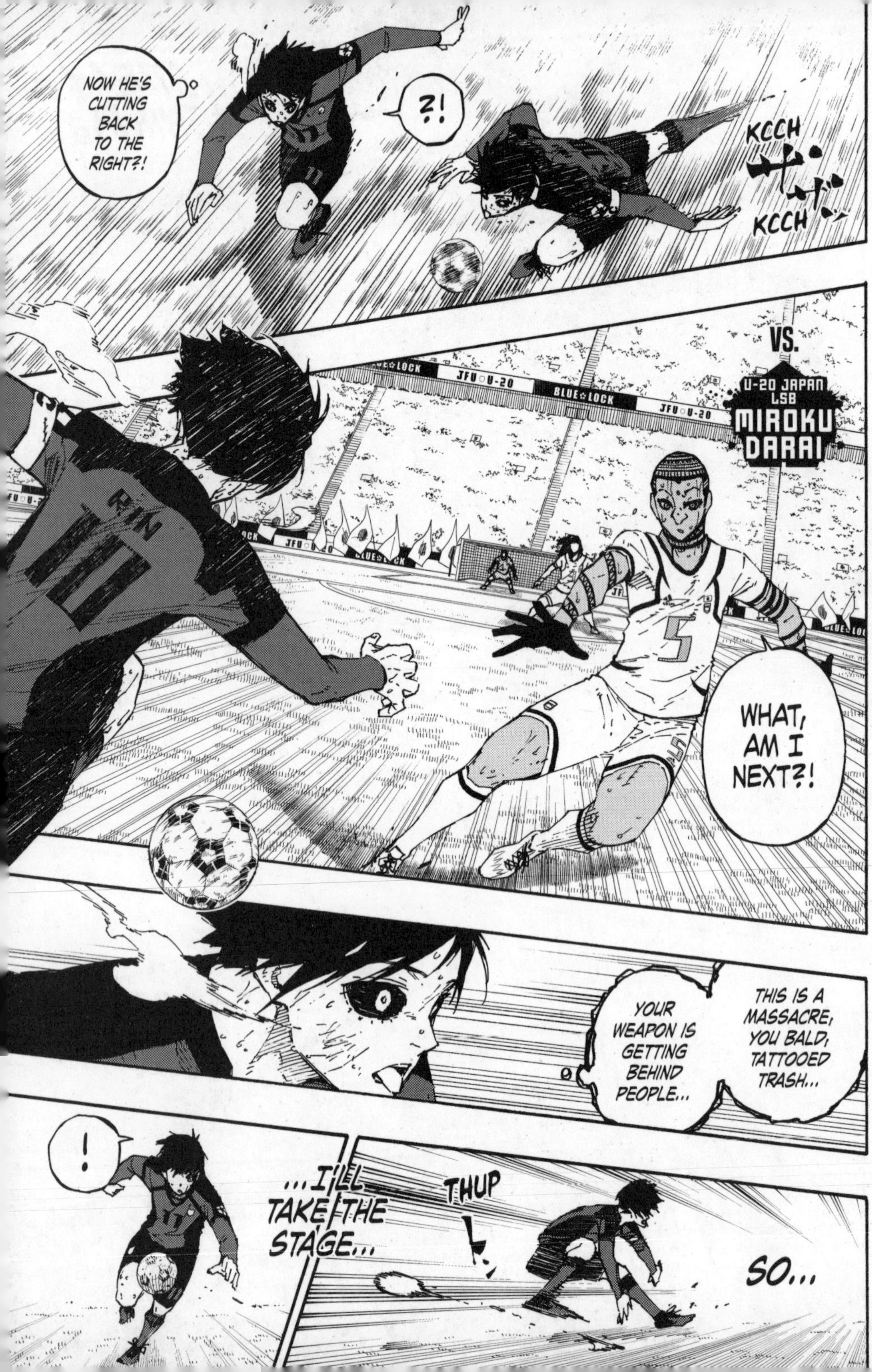
KCCH
KCCH
?!
NOW HE'S CUTTING BACK TO THE RIGHT?!
VS.
U-20 JAPAN LSB
MIROKU DARAI
WHAT, AM I NEXT?!
RIN
THIS IS A MASSACRE, YOU BALD, TATTOOED TRASH...
YOUR WEAPON IS GETTING BEHIND PEOPLE...
SO...
THUP
...I'LL TAKE THE STAGE...
!

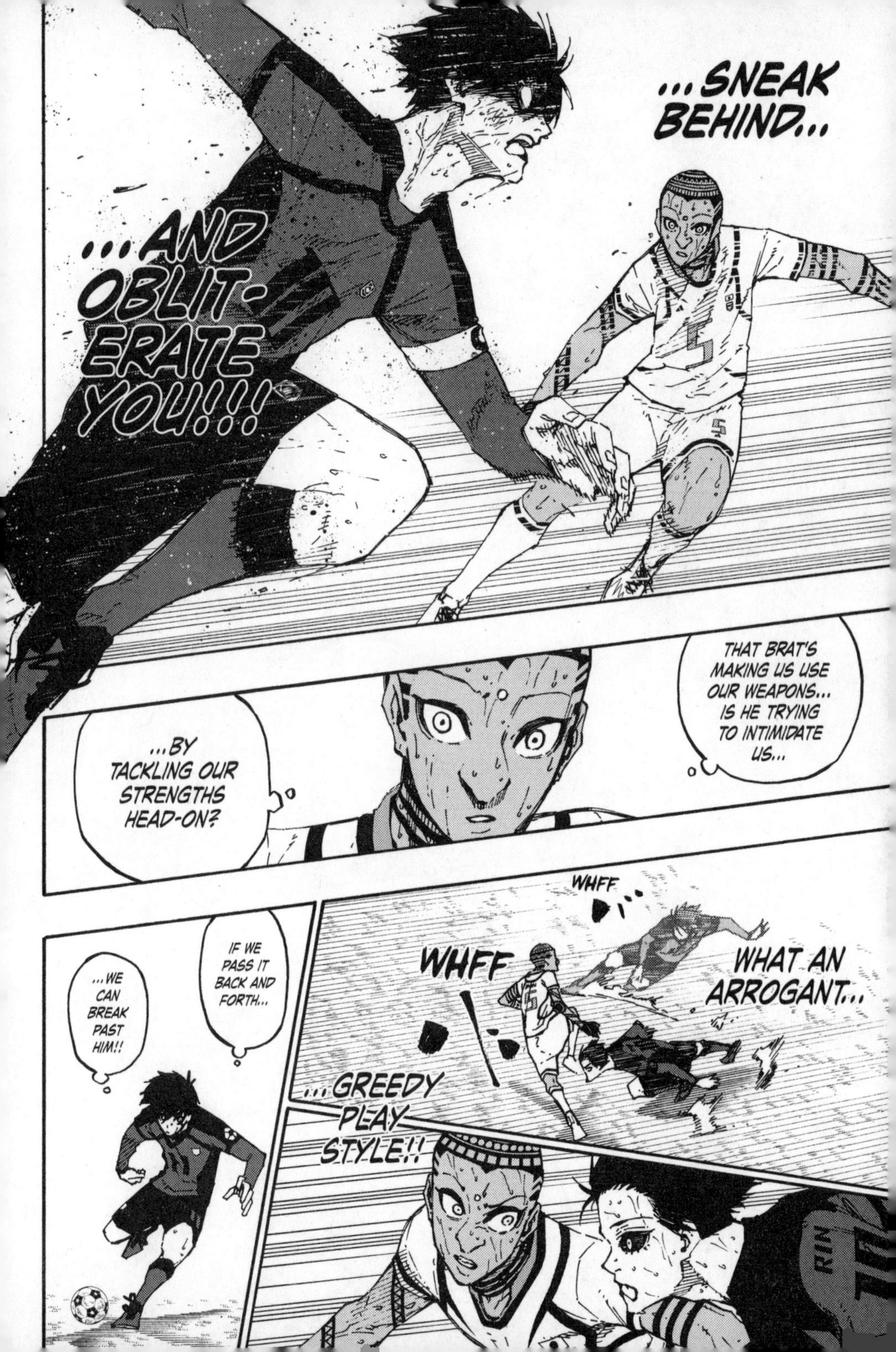
...SNEAK BEHIND...
...AND OBLIT-ERATE YOU!!!
THAT BRAT'S MAKING US USE OUR WEAPONS... IS HE TRYING TO INTIMIDATE US...
...BY TACKLING OUR STRENGTHS HEAD-ON?
WHFF
WHFF
WHAT AN ARROGANT...
...GREEDY PLAY STYLE!!
RIN
IF WE PASS IT BACK AND FORTH...
...WE CAN BREAK PAST HIM!!

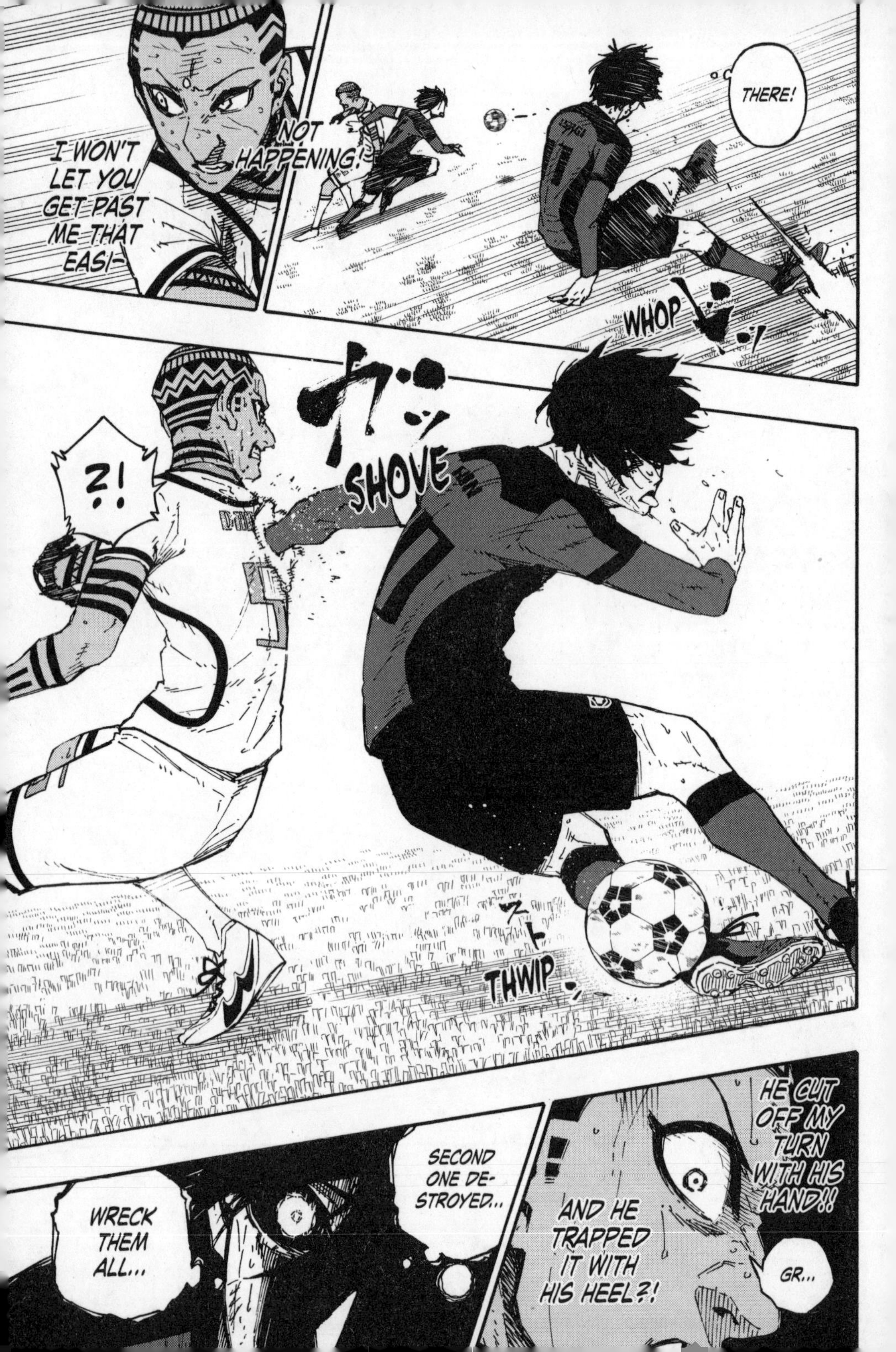
THERE!
WHOP
I WON'T LET YOU GET PAST ME THAT EASI-
NOT HAPPENING!
SHOVE
?!
THWIP
HE CUT OFF MY TURN WITH HIS HAND!!
AND HE TRAPPED IT WITH HIS HEEL?!
GR...
SECOND ONE DE-STROYED...
WRECK THEM ALL...

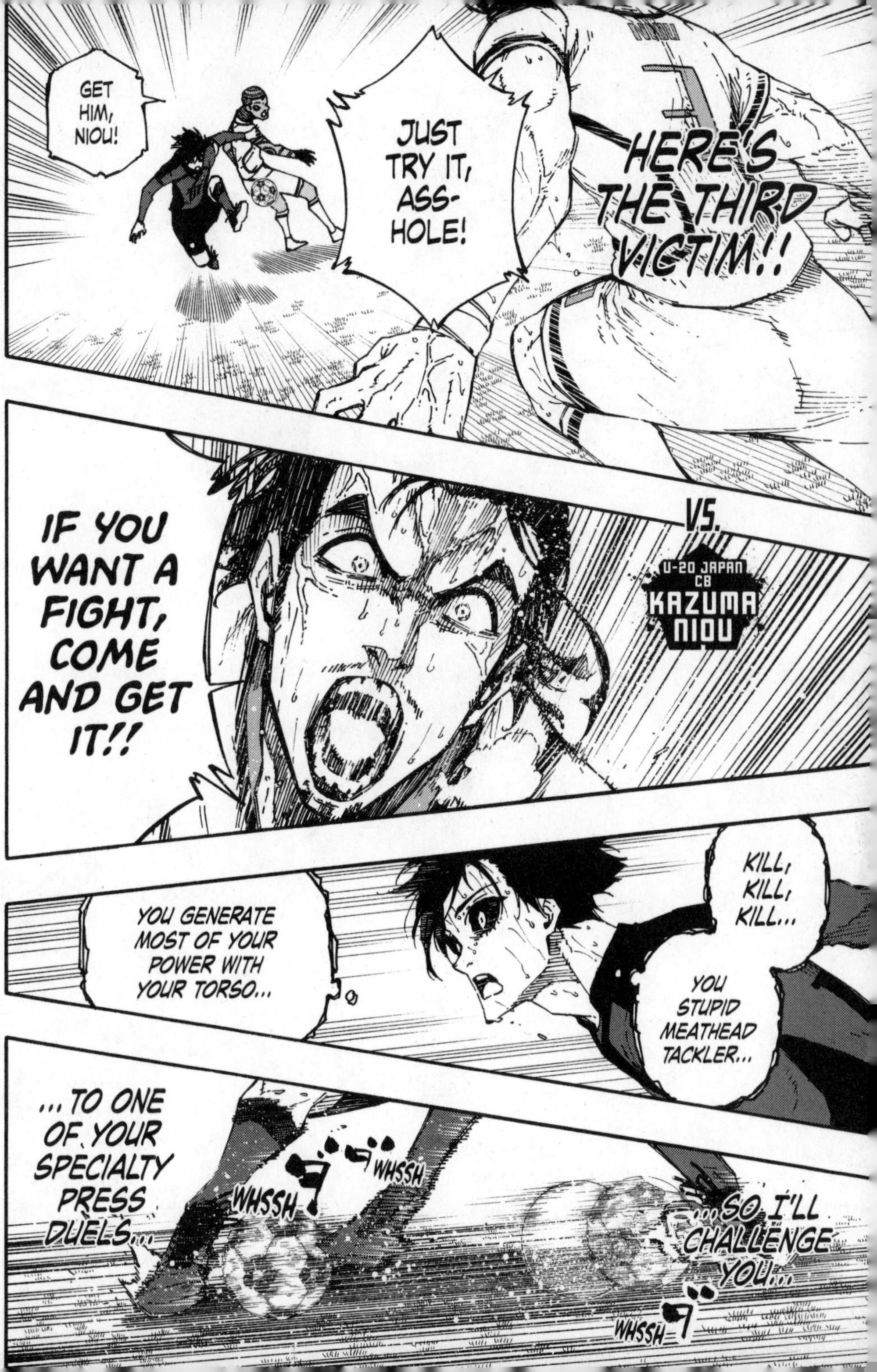
HERE'S THE THIRD VICTIM!!
JUST TRY IT, ASS-HOLE!
GET HIM, NIOU!
VS.
U-20 JAPAN CB
KAZUMA NIOU
IF YOU WANT A FIGHT, COME AND GET IT!!
KILL, KILL, KILL...
YOU STUPID MEATHEAD TACKLER...
YOU GENERATE MOST OF YOUR POWER WITH YOUR TORSO...
...SO I'LL CHALLENGE YOU...
WHSSH
WHSSH
WHSSH
...TO ONE OF YOUR SPECIALTY PRESS DUELS...

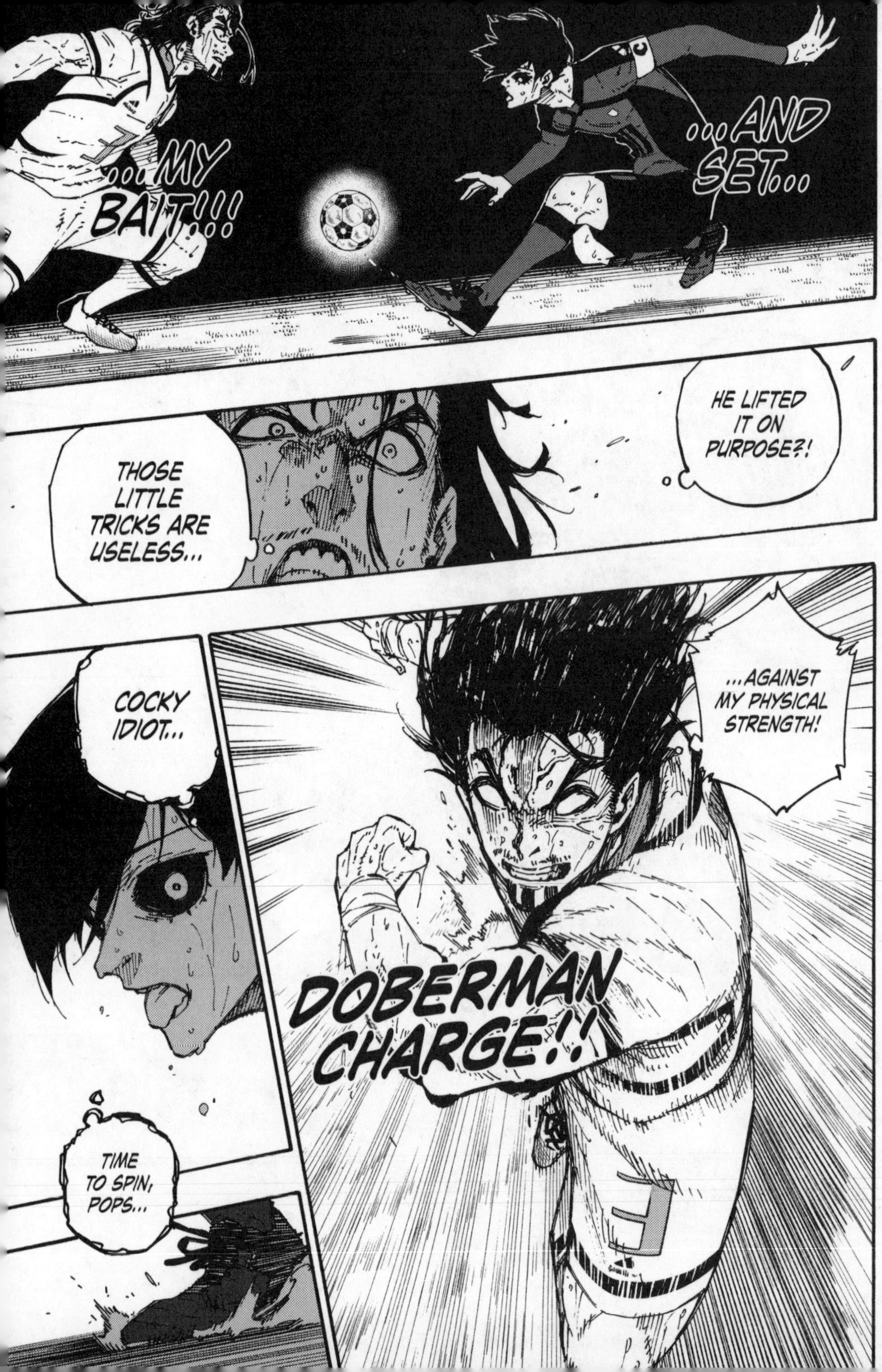
...AND SET...
...MY BAIT!!!
HE LIFTED IT ON PURPOSE?!
THOSE LITTLE TRICKS ARE USELESS...
...AGAINST MY PHYSICAL STRENGTH!
DOBERMAN CHARGE!!
COCKY IDIOT...
TIME TO SPIN, POPS...

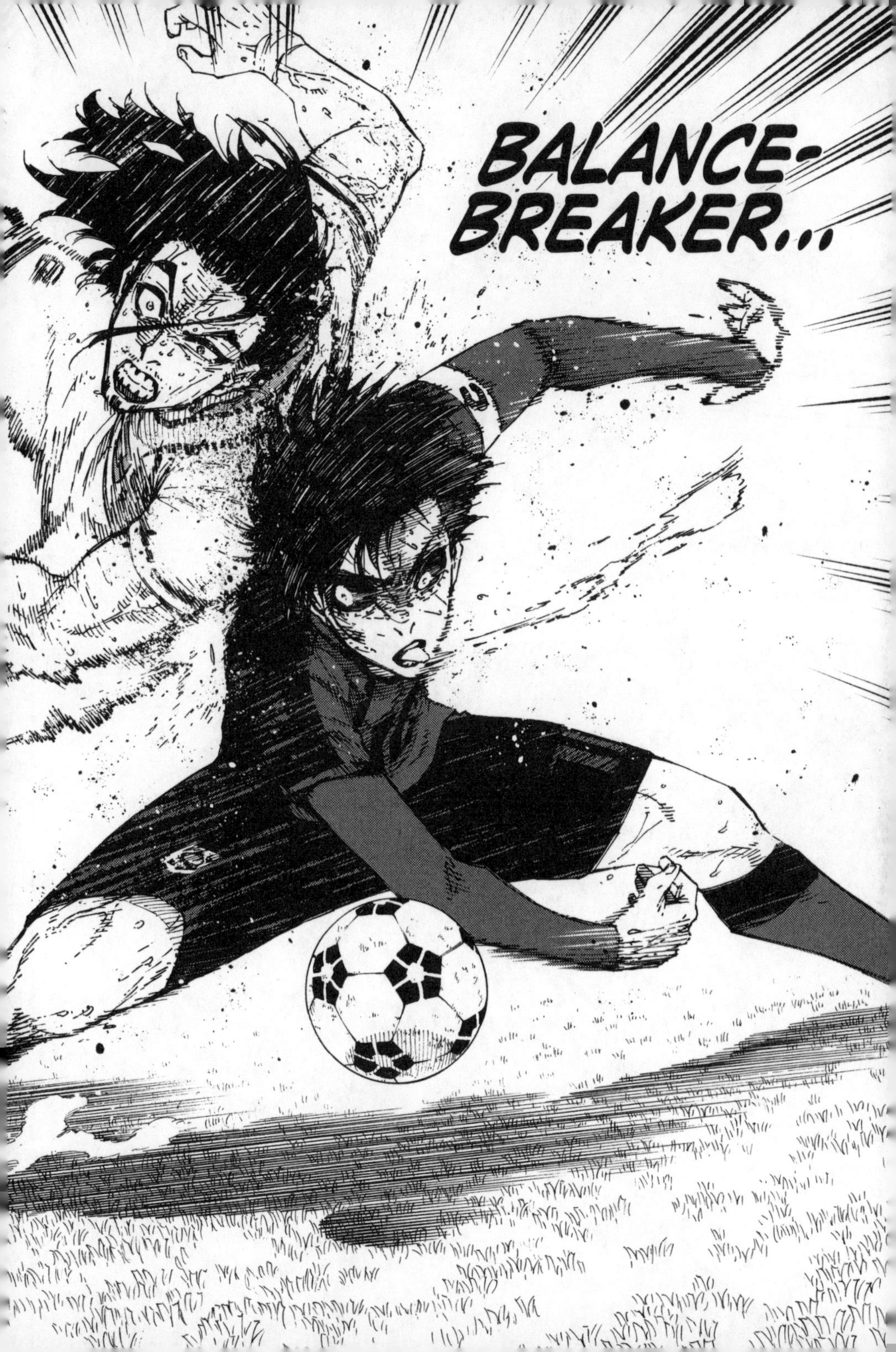
BALANCE-
BREAKER...

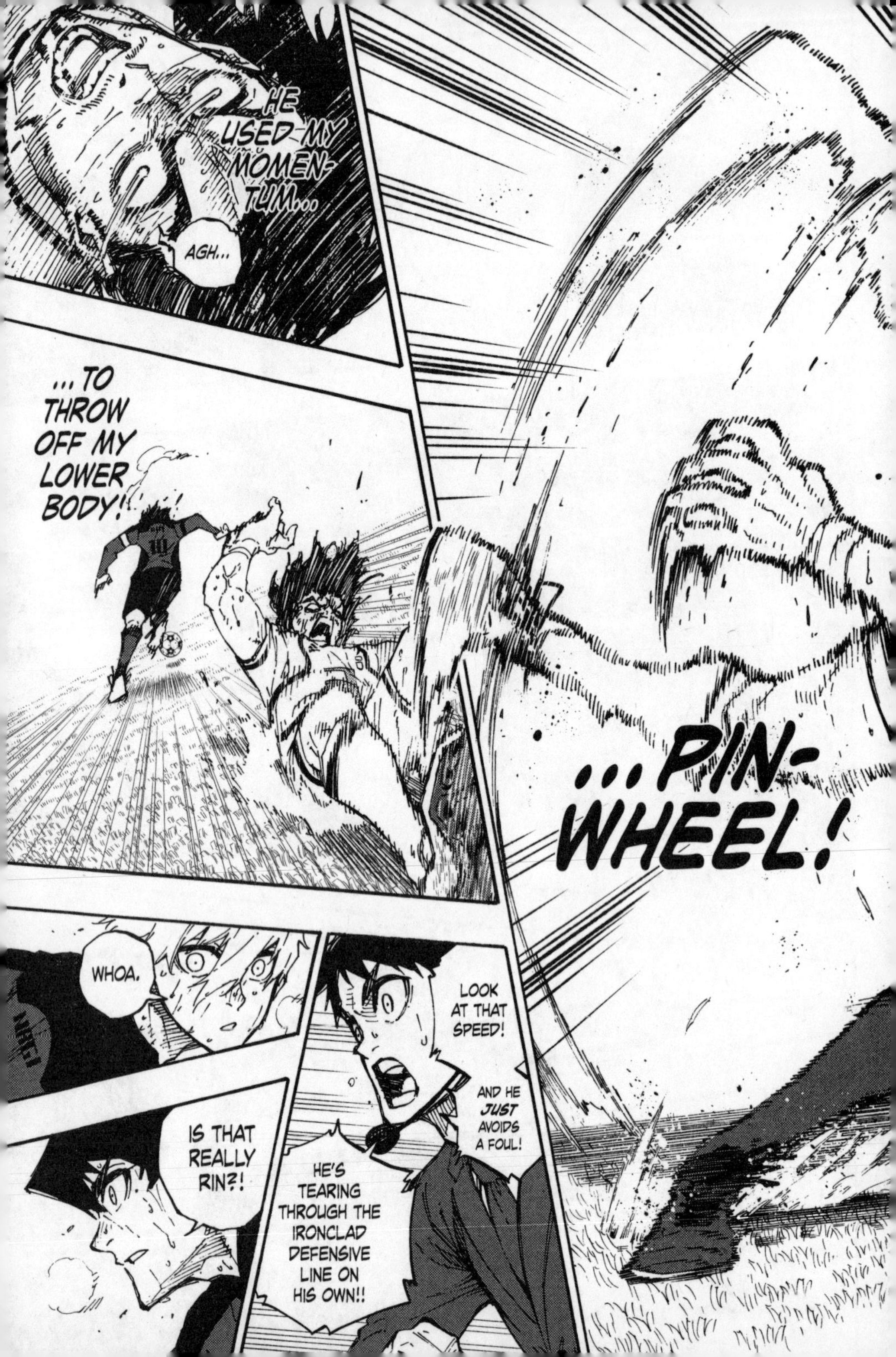
HE USED MY MOMENTUM...
AGH...
...TO THROW OFF MY LOWER BODY!
...PIN-WHEEL!
LOOK AT THAT SPEED!
AND HE *JUST* AVOIDS A FOUL!
HE'S TEARING THROUGH THE IRONCLAD DEFENSIVE LINE ON HIS OWN!!
WHOA.
IS THAT REALLY RIN?!

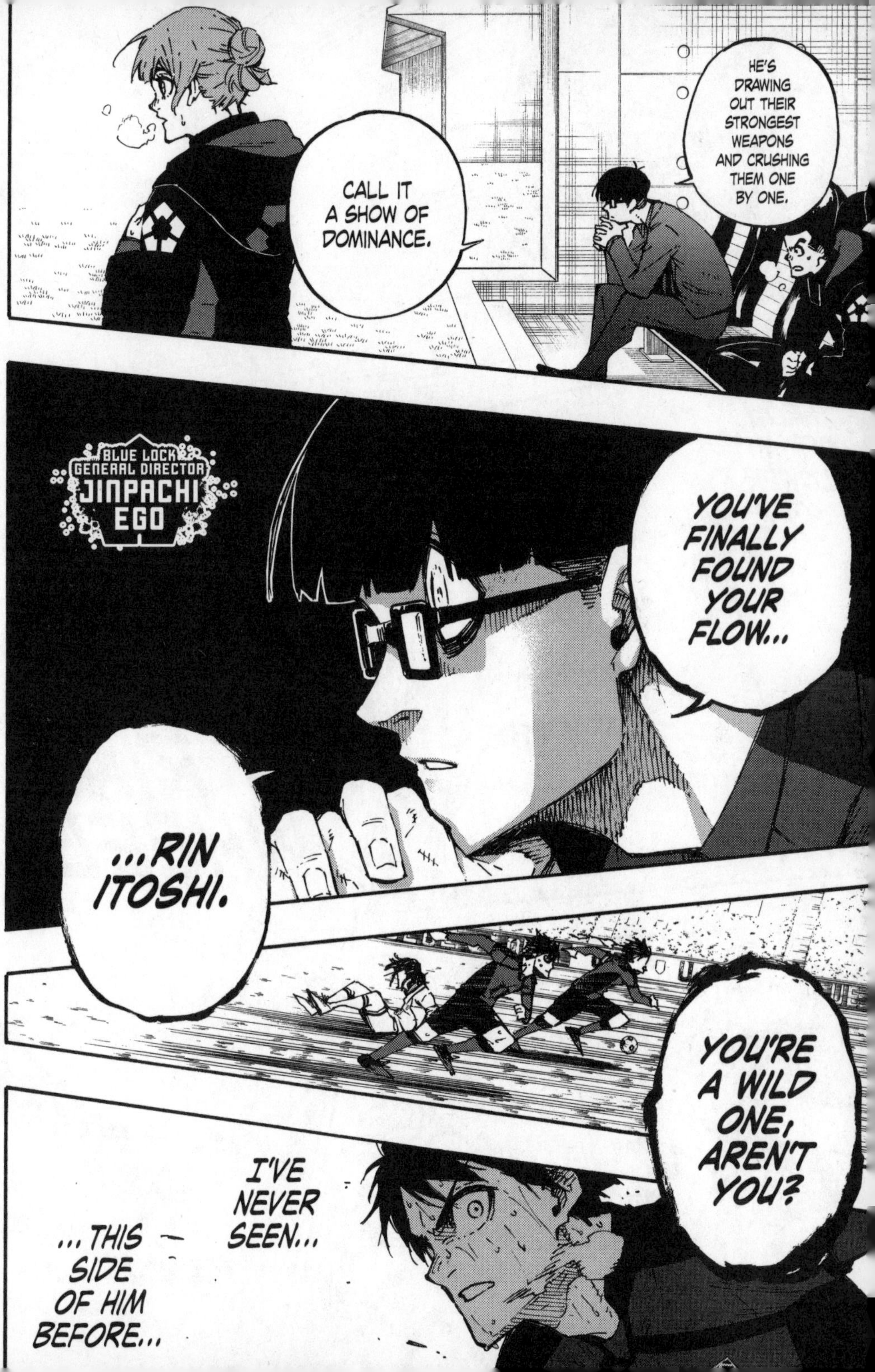
HE'S DRAWING OUT THEIR STRONGEST WEAPONS AND CRUSHING THEM ONE BY ONE.
CALL IT A SHOW OF DOMINANCE.
YOU'VE FINALLY FOUND YOUR FLOW...
BLUE LOCK GENERAL DIRECTOR JINPACHI EGO
...RIN ITOSHI.
YOU'RE A WILD ONE, AREN'T YOU?
I'VE NEVER SEEN...
...THIS SIDE OF HIM BEFORE...

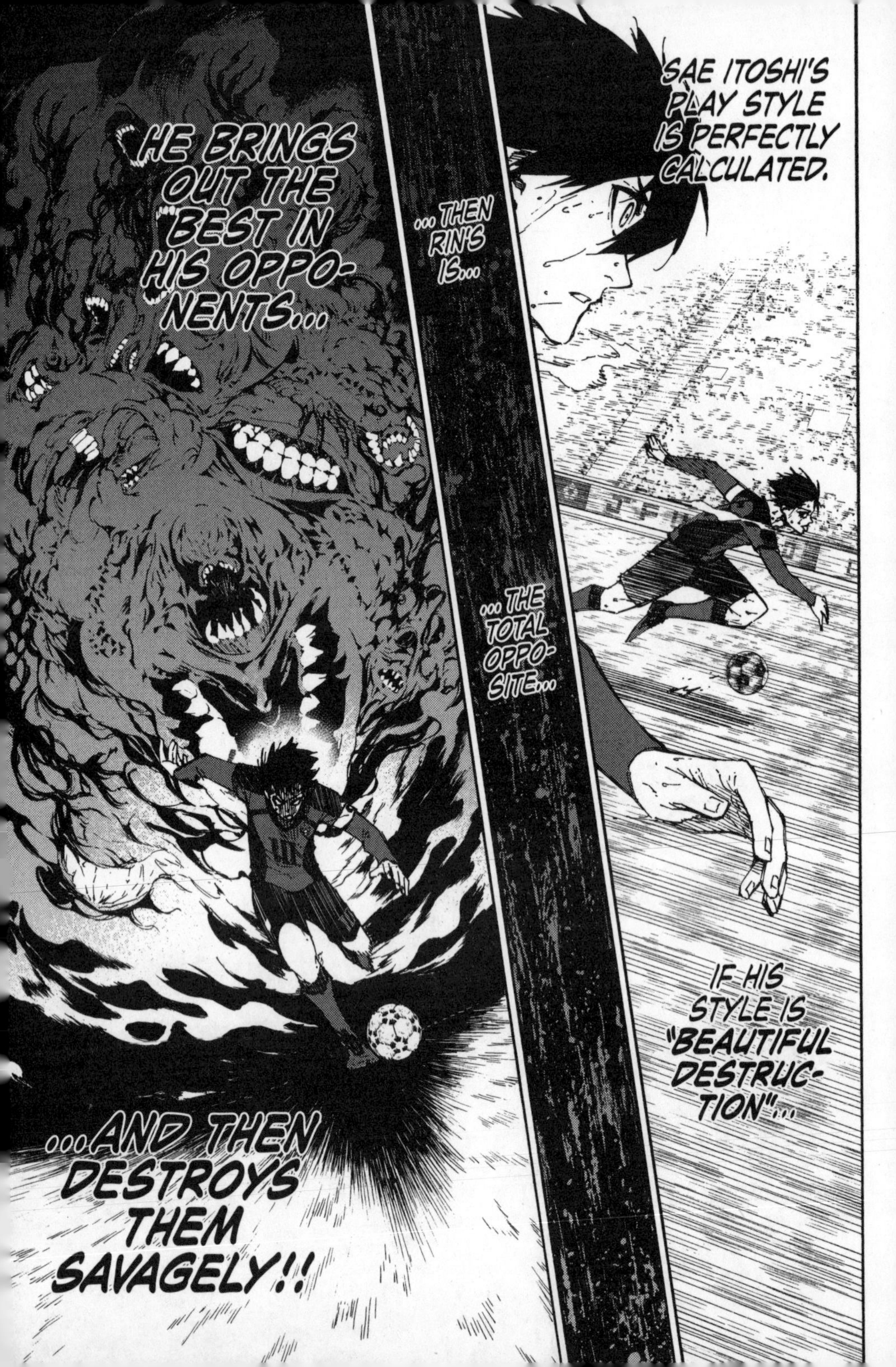
SAE ITOSHI'S PLAY STYLE IS PERFECTLY CALCULATED.
IF HIS STYLE IS "BEAUTIFUL DESTRUCTION"...
...THEN RIN'S IS...
...THE TOTAL OPPOSITE...
HE BRINGS OUT THE BEST IN HIS OPPONENTS...
...AND THEN DESTROYS THEM SAVAGELY!!

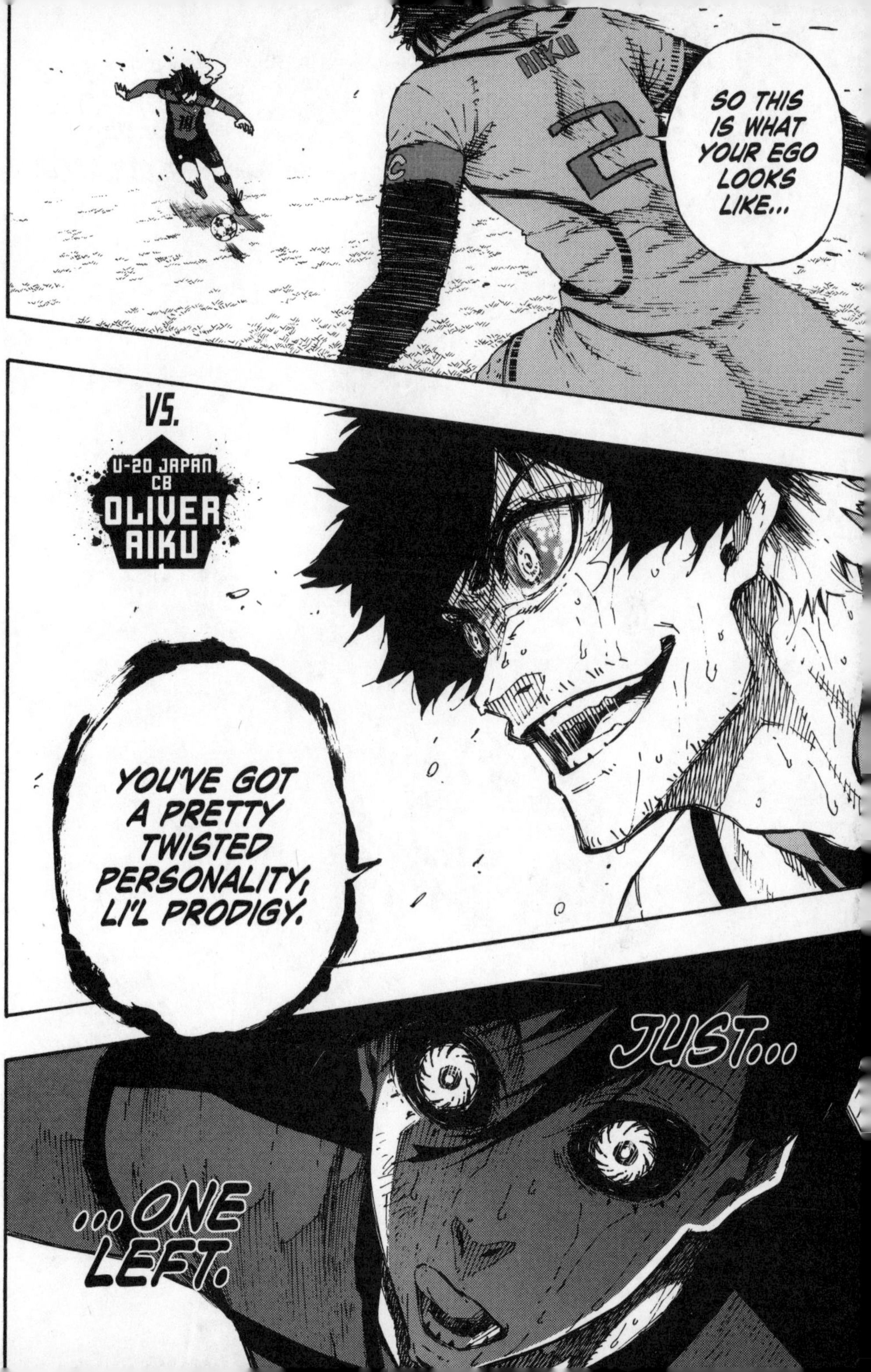
SO THIS IS WHAT YOUR EGO LOOKS LIKE...
VS.
U-20 JAPAN CB OLIVER AIKU
YOU'VE GOT A PRETTY TWISTED PERSONALITY, LI'L PRODIGY.
JUST...
...ONE LEFT.

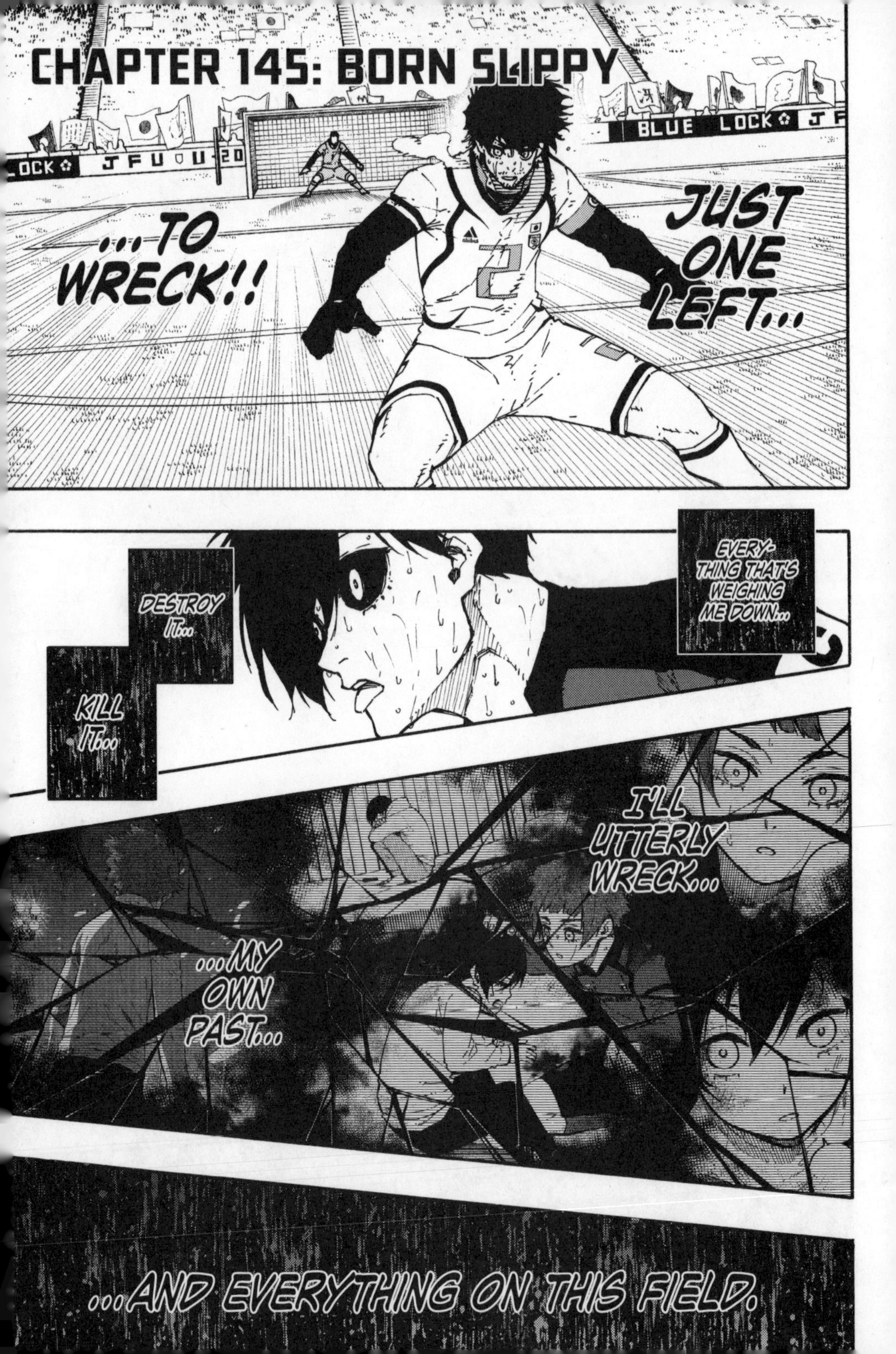
CHAPTER 145: BORN SLIPPY
BLUE LOCK
JFU U-20
JUST ONE LEFT...
...TO WRECK!!
EVERY-THING THAT'S WEIGHING ME DOWN...
DESTROY IT...
KILL IT...
I'LL UTTERLY WRECK...
...MY OWN PAST...
...AND EVERYTHING ON THIS FIELD.

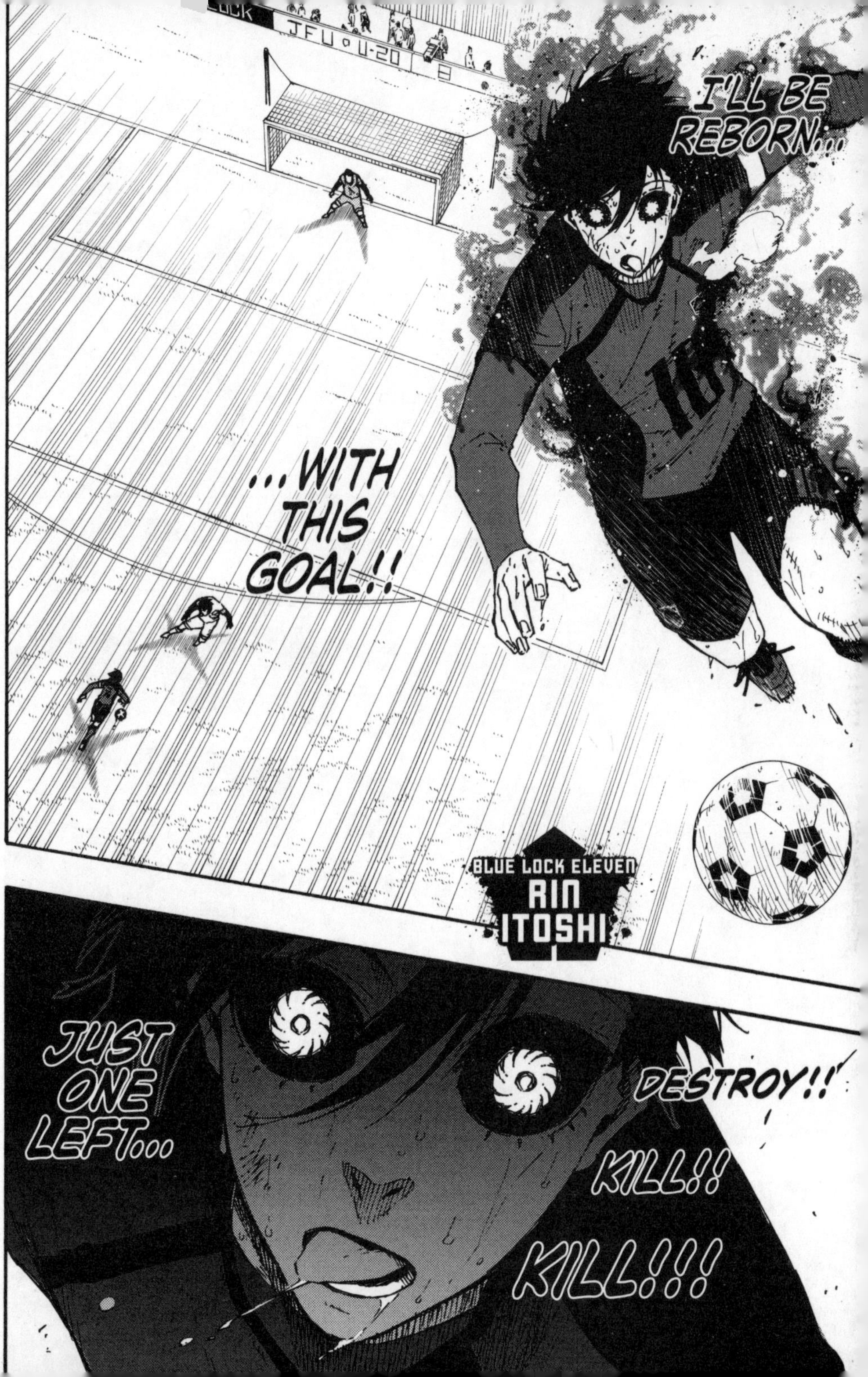
JFU U-20
I'LL BE REBORN...
...WITH THIS GOAL!!
BLUE LOCK ELEVEN
RIN ITOSHI
DESTROY!!
KILL!!
KILL!!!
JUST ONE LEFT...

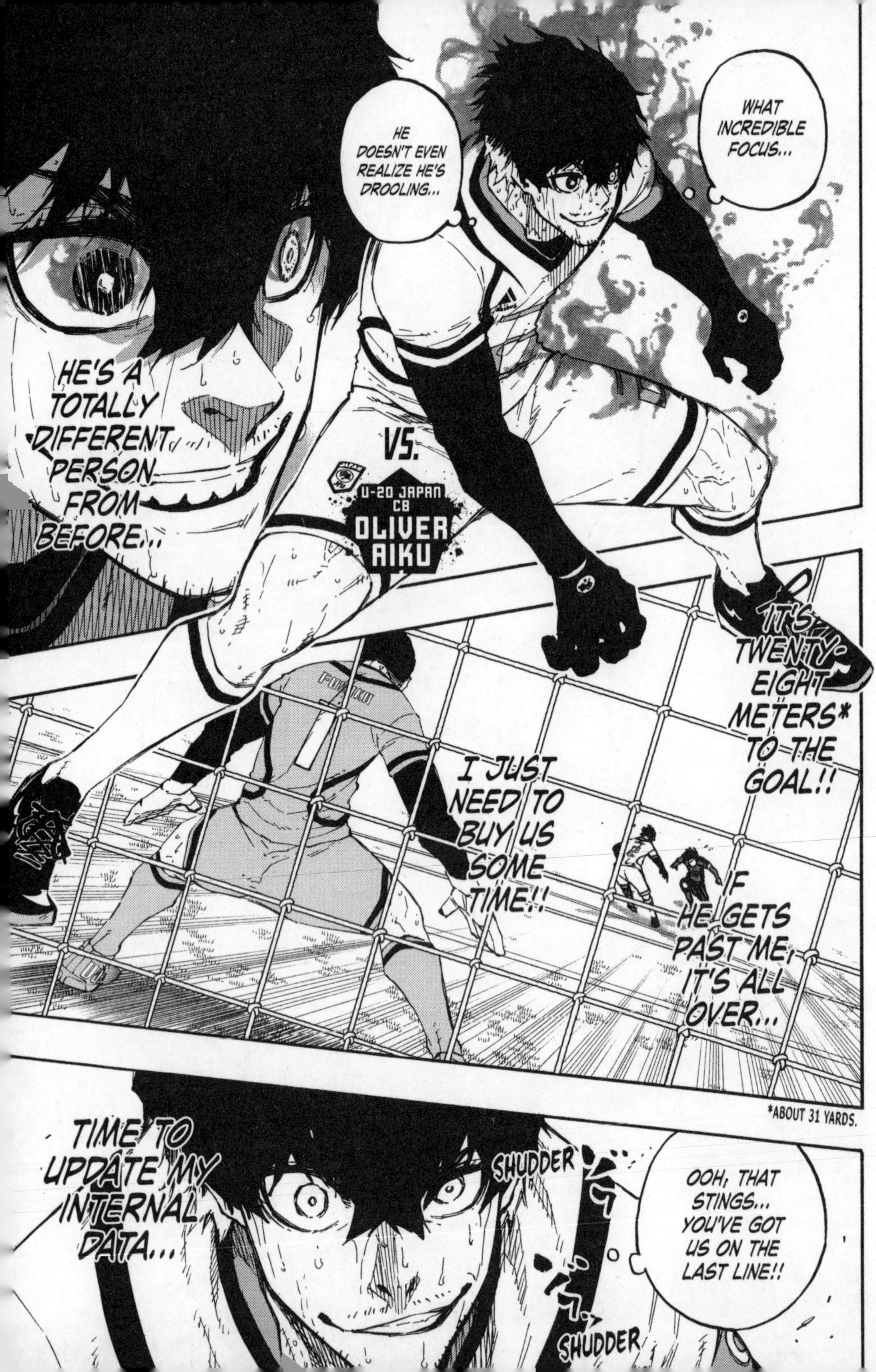
WHAT INCREDIBLE FOCUS...
HE DOESN'T EVEN REALIZE HE'S DROOLING...
HE'S A TOTALLY DIFFERENT PERSON FROM BEFORE...
VS.
U-20 JAPAN CB
OLIVER AIKU
IT'S TWENTY-EIGHT METERS* TO THE GOAL!!
I JUST NEED TO BUY US SOME TIME!!
IF HE GETS PAST ME, IT'S ALL OVER...
SHUDDER
OOH, THAT STINGS... YOU'VE GOT US ON THE LAST LINE!!
SHUDDER
TIME TO UPDATE MY INTERNAL DATA...

*ABOUT 31 YARDS.

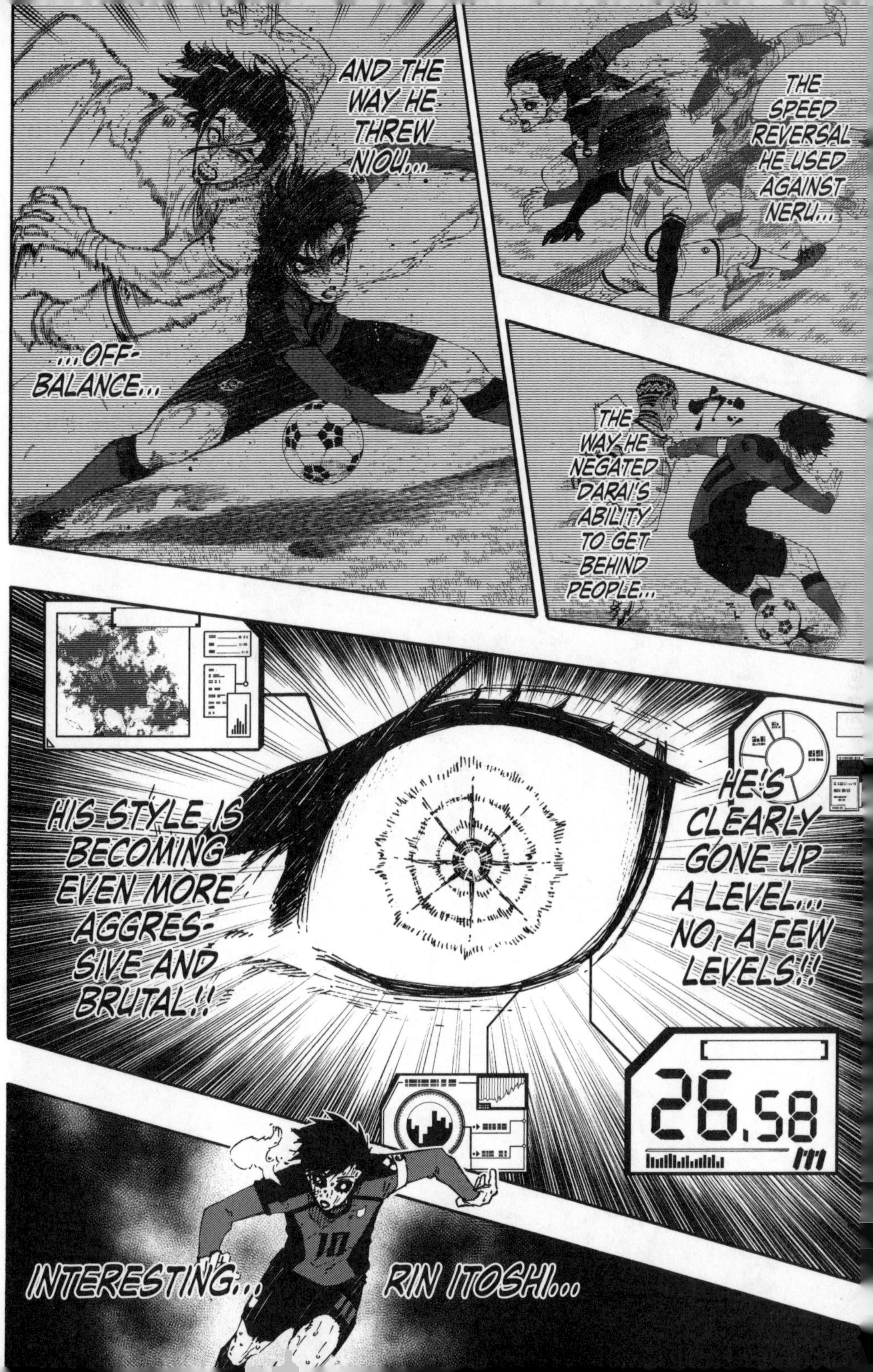
THE SPEED REVERSAL HE USED AGAINST NERU...
THE WAY HE NEGATED DARAI'S ABILITY TO GET BEHIND PEOPLE...
AND THE WAY HE THREW NIOU...
...OFF-BALANCE...
HE'S CLEARLY GONE UP A LEVEL... NO, A FEW LEVELS!!
HIS STYLE IS BECOMING EVEN MORE AGGRES-SIVE AND BRUTAL!!
26.58 m
INTERESTING...
RIN ITOSHI...

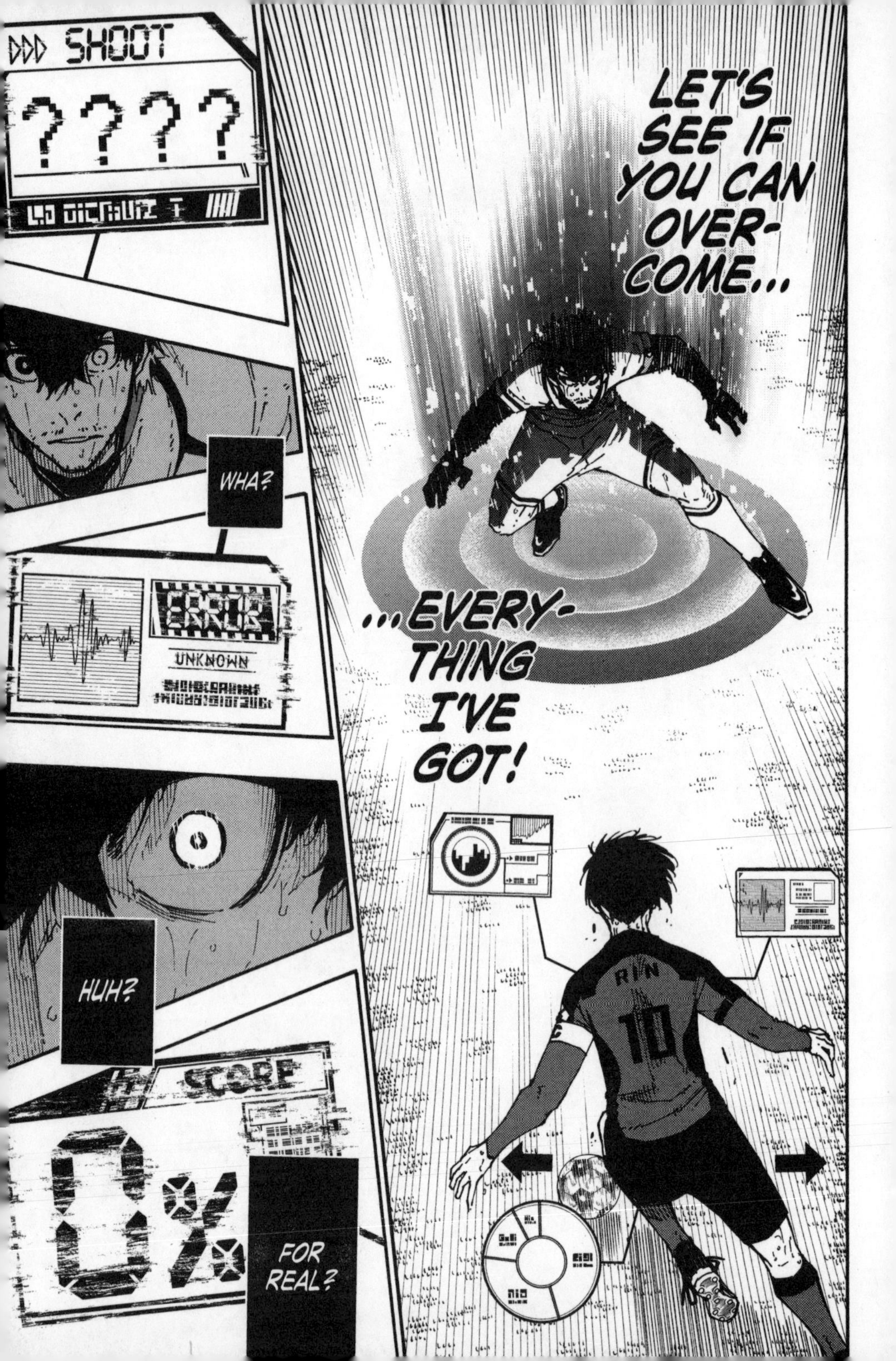
LET'S SEE IF YOU CAN OVER-COME...
...EVERY-THING I'VE GOT!
RIN
10
SHOOT
????
WHA?
ERROR
UNKNOWN
HUH?
SCORE
0%
FOR REAL?

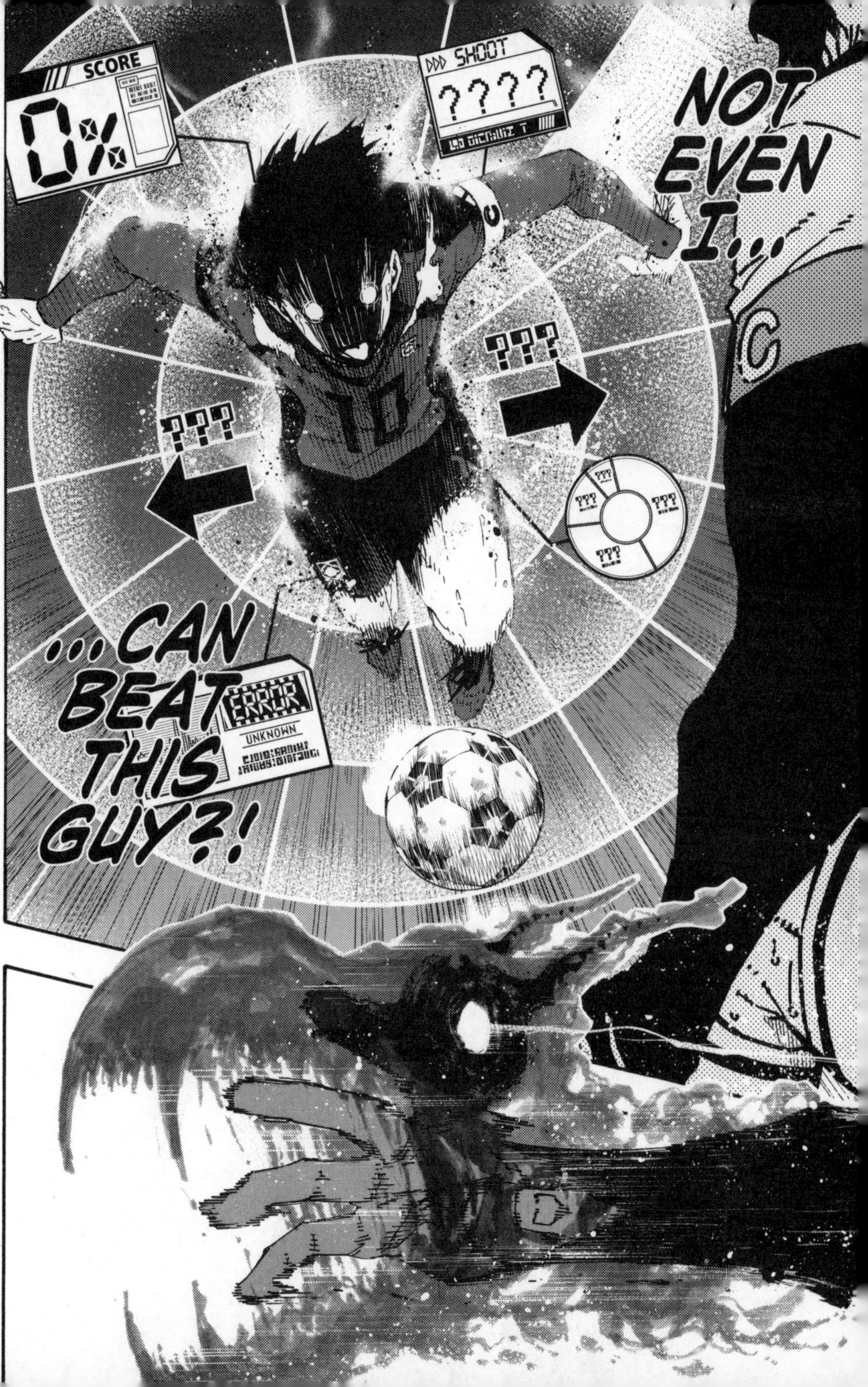
NOT EVEN I...
SHOOT
????
???
SCORE
0%
???
...CAN BEAT THIS GUY?!
ERROR
UNKNOWN

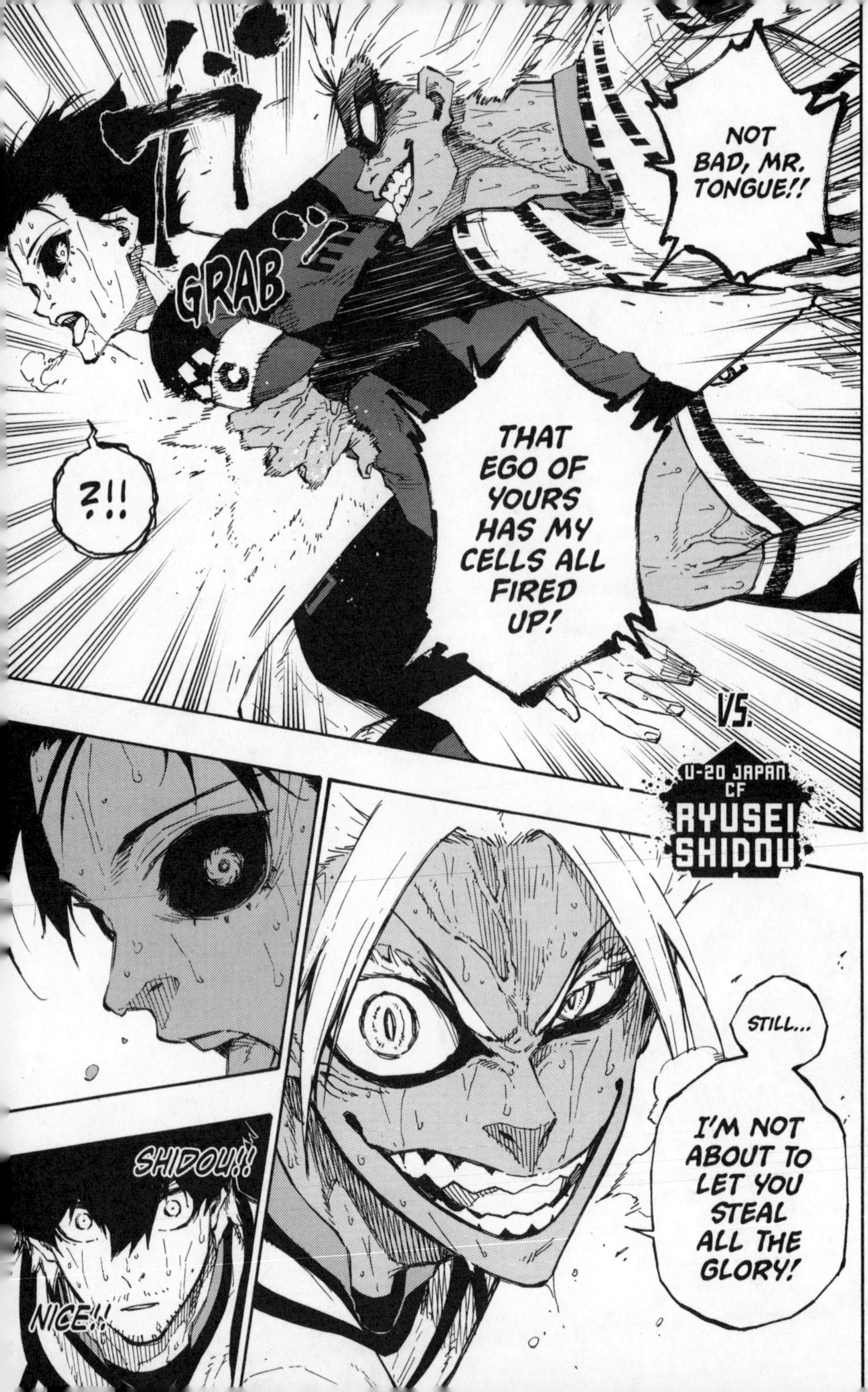
NOT BAD, MR. TONGUE!!
GRAB
THAT EGO OF YOURS HAS MY CELLS ALL FIRED UP!
?!!
VS.
U-20 JAPAN CF
RYUSEI SHIDOU
STILL...
I'M NOT ABOUT TO LET YOU STEAL ALL THE GLORY!
SHIDOU!!
NICE!!

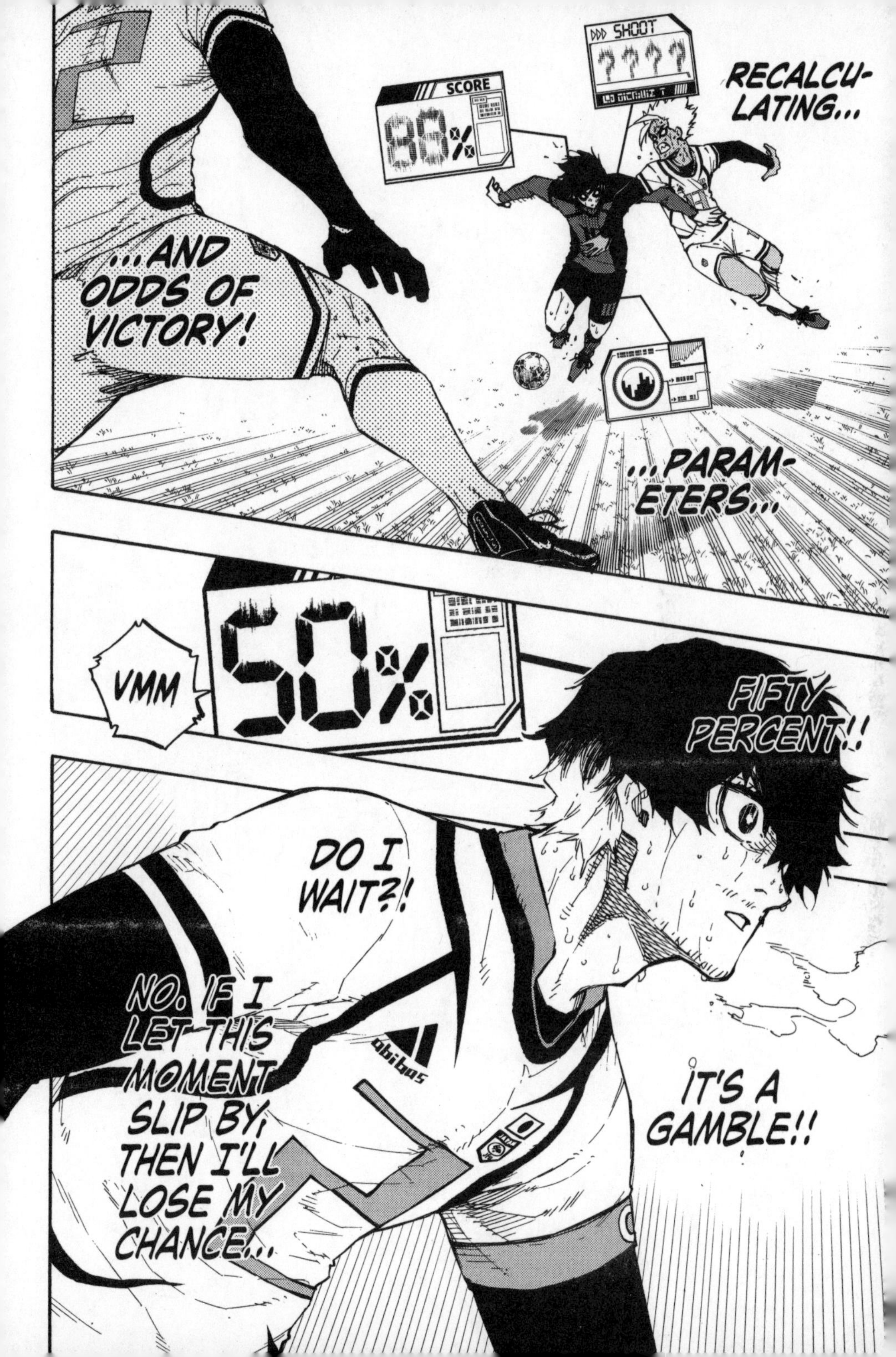
RECALCU-
LATING...
SHOOT
????
SCORE
88%
...PARAM-
ETERS...
...AND ODDS OF VICTORY!
50%
VMM
FIFTY PERCENT!!
IT'S A GAMBLE!!
DO I WAIT?!
NO. IF I LET THIS MOMENT SLIP BY, THEN I'LL LOSE MY CHANCE...

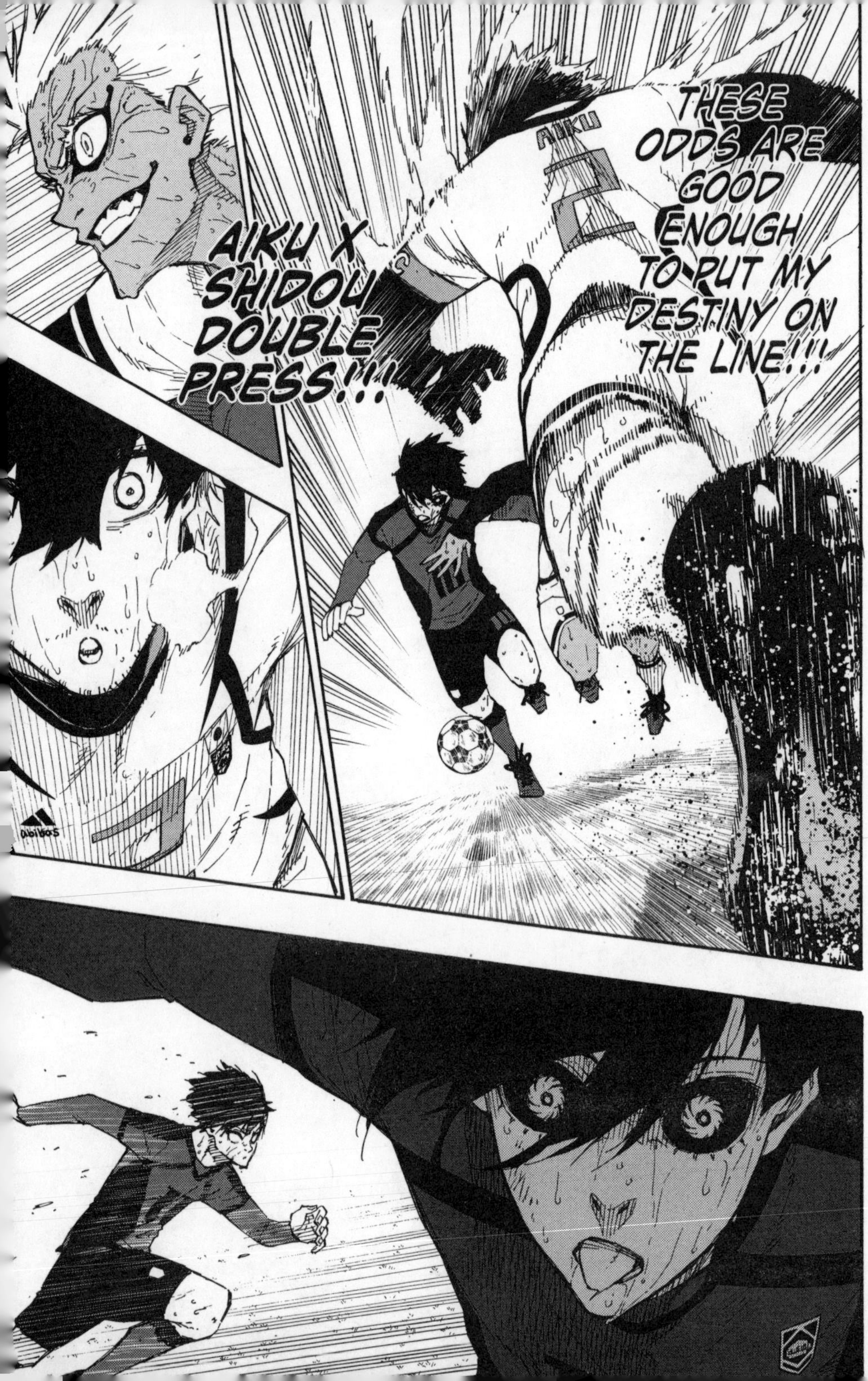
THESE ODDS ARE GOOD ENOUGH TO PUT MY DESTINY ON THE LINE!!!
AIKU X SHIDOU DOUBLE PRESS!!!

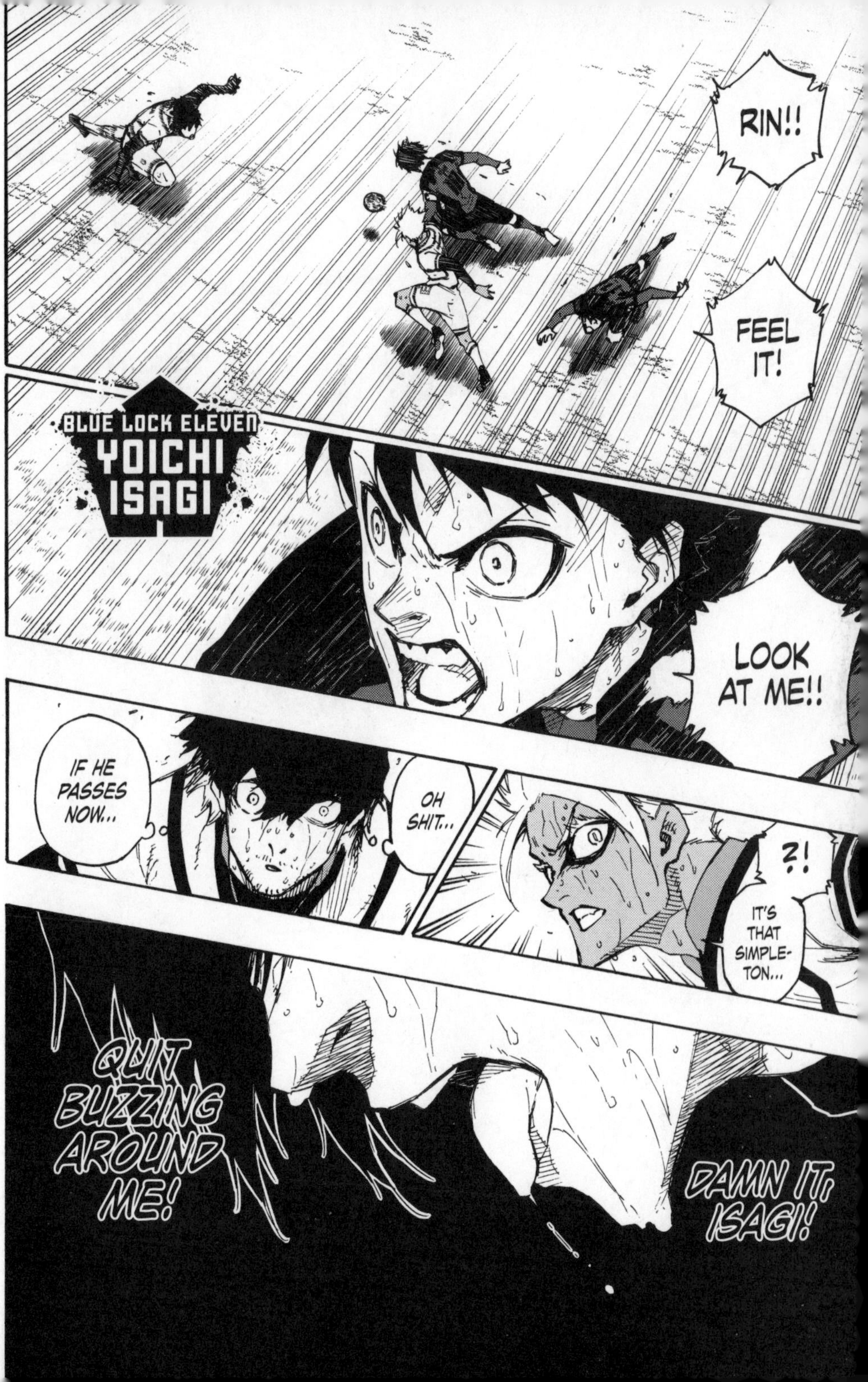
RIN!!
FEEL IT!
BLUE LOCK ELEVEN
YOICHI ISAGI
LOOK AT ME!!
?!
IT'S THAT SIMPLE-TON...
OH SHIT...
IF HE PASSES NOW...
DAMN IT, ISAGI!
QUIT BUZZING AROUND ME!

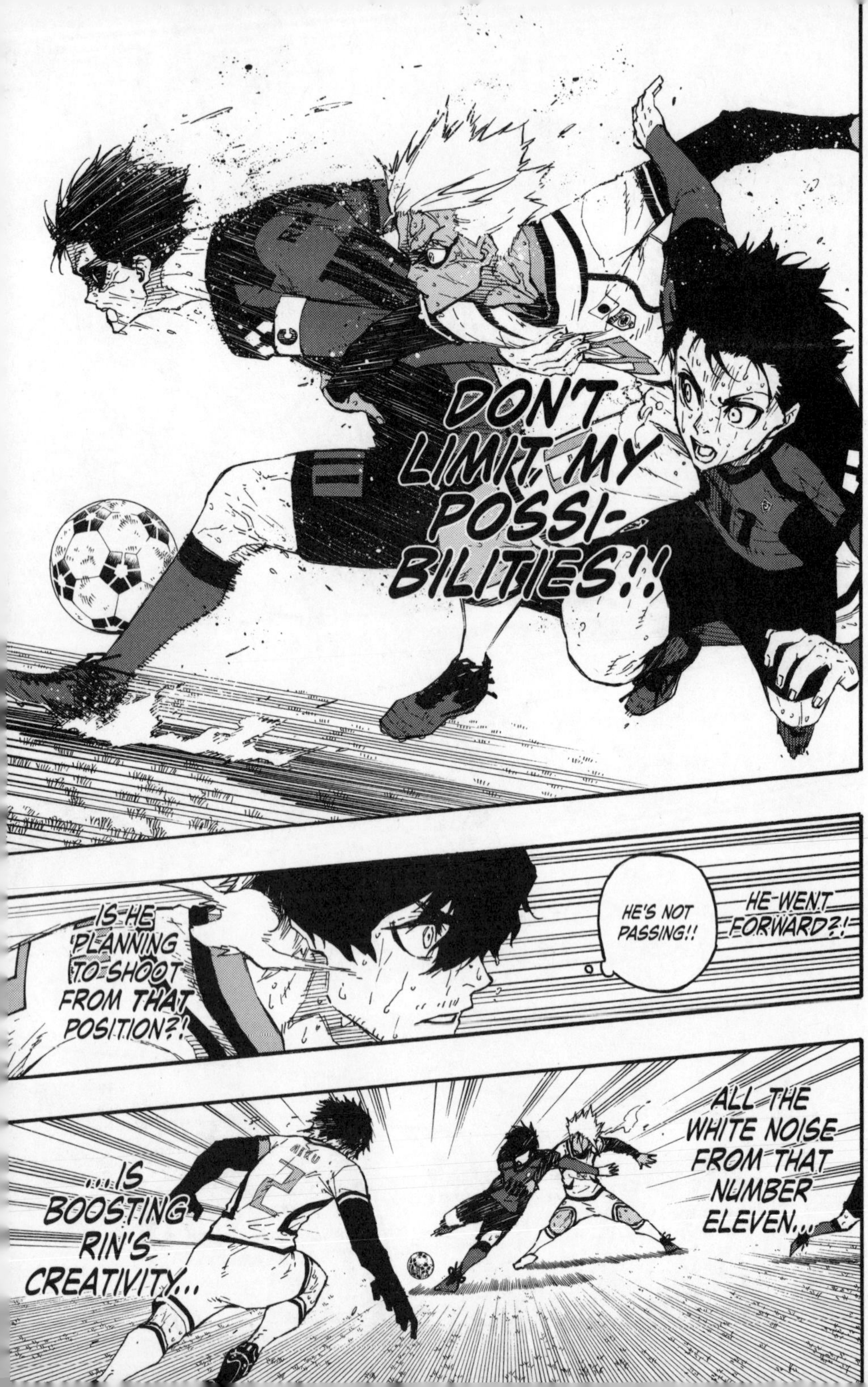
DON'T LIMIT MY POSSI-BILITIES!!
HE WENT FORWARD?!
HE'S NOT PASSING!!
IS HE PLANNING TO SHOOT FROM THAT POSITION?!
ALL THE WHITE NOISE FROM THAT NUMBER ELEVEN...
...IS BOOSTING RIN'S CREATIVITY...

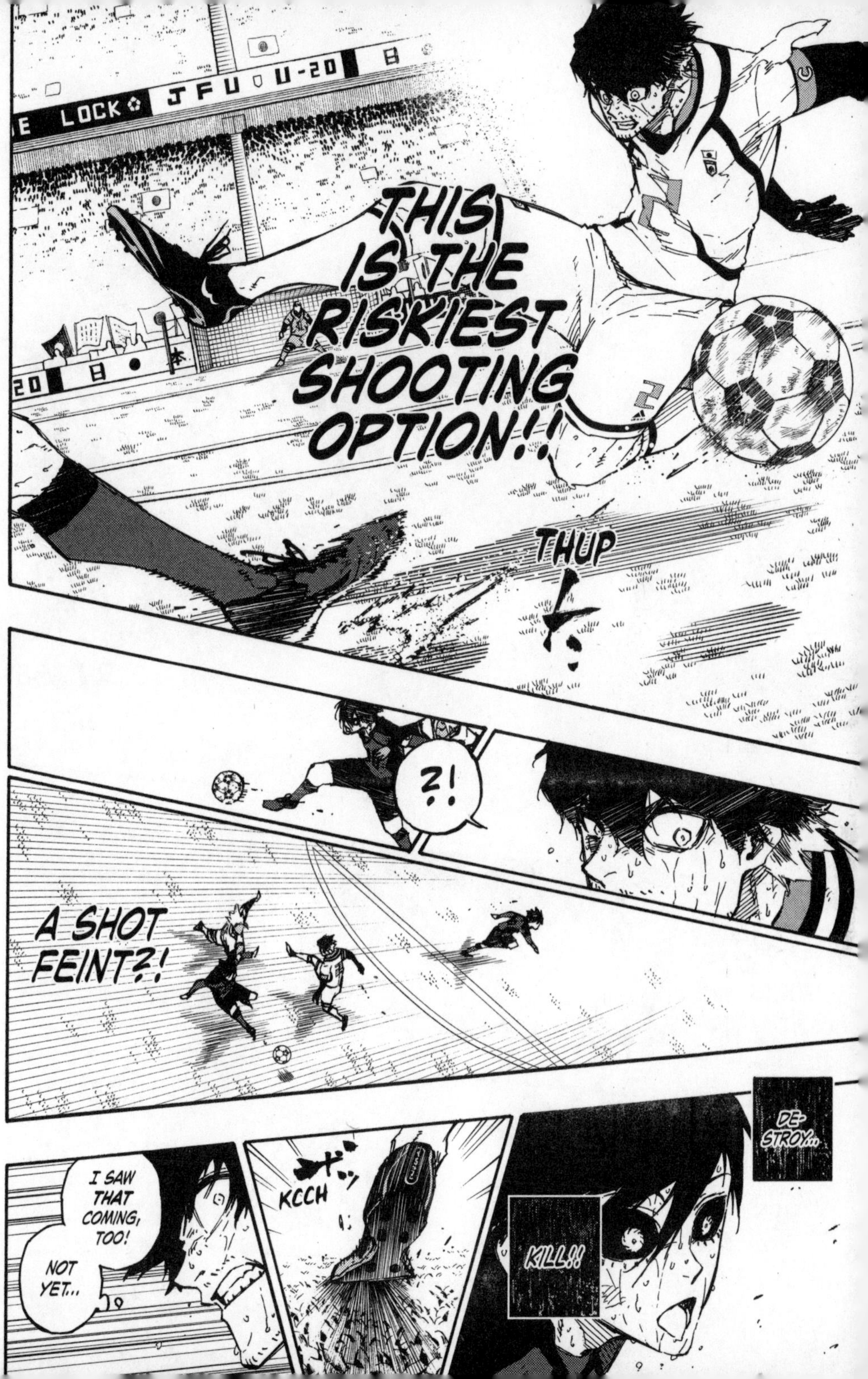

JFU U-20
LOCK
THIS IS THE RISKIEST SHOOTING OPTION!!
THUP
?!
A SHOT FEINT?!
DE-STROY...
KILL!!
KCCH
I SAW THAT COMING, TOO!
NOT YET...

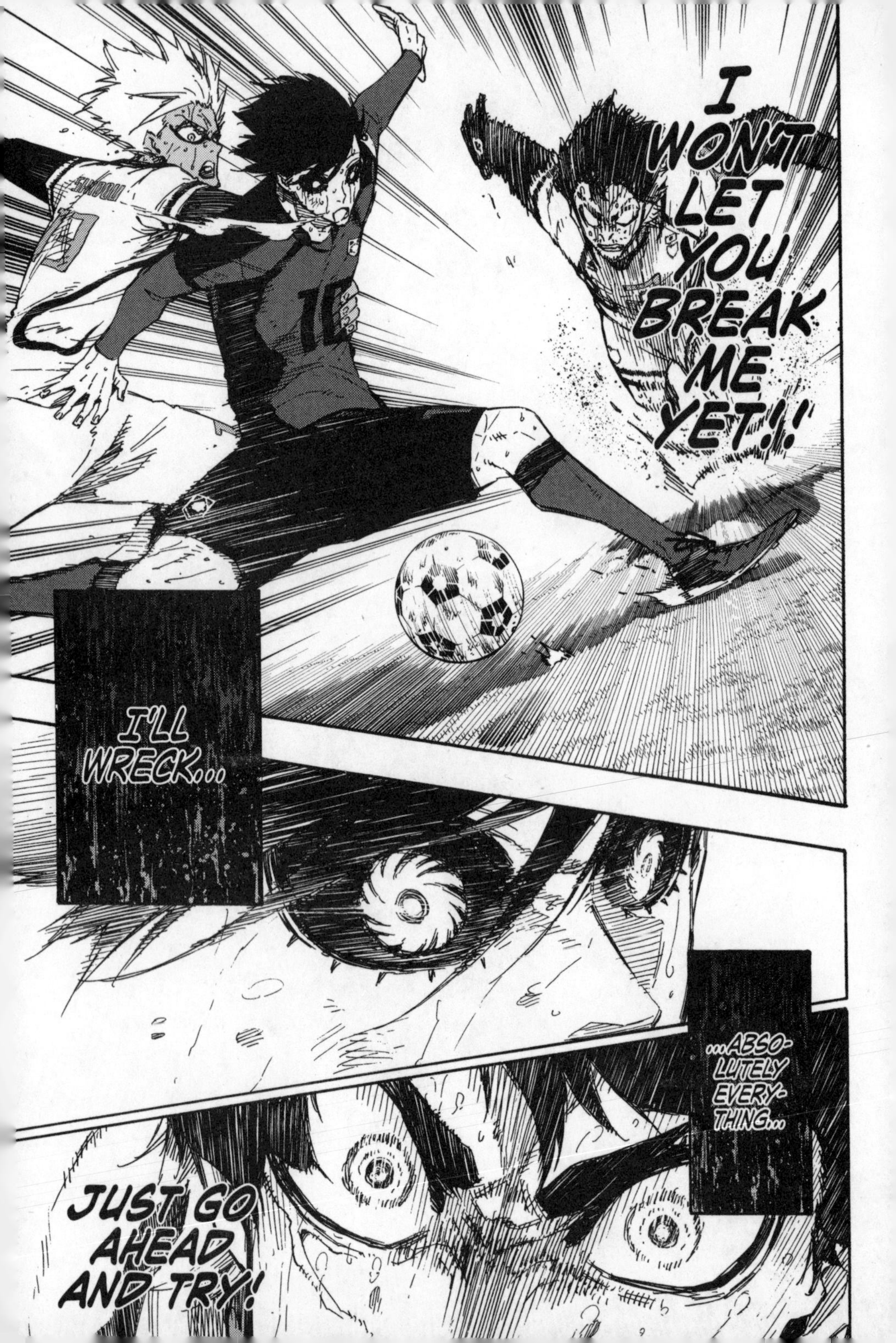
I WON'T LET YOU BREAK ME YET!!
I'LL WRECK...
...ABSOLUTELY EVERYTHING...
JUST GO AHEAD AND TRY!

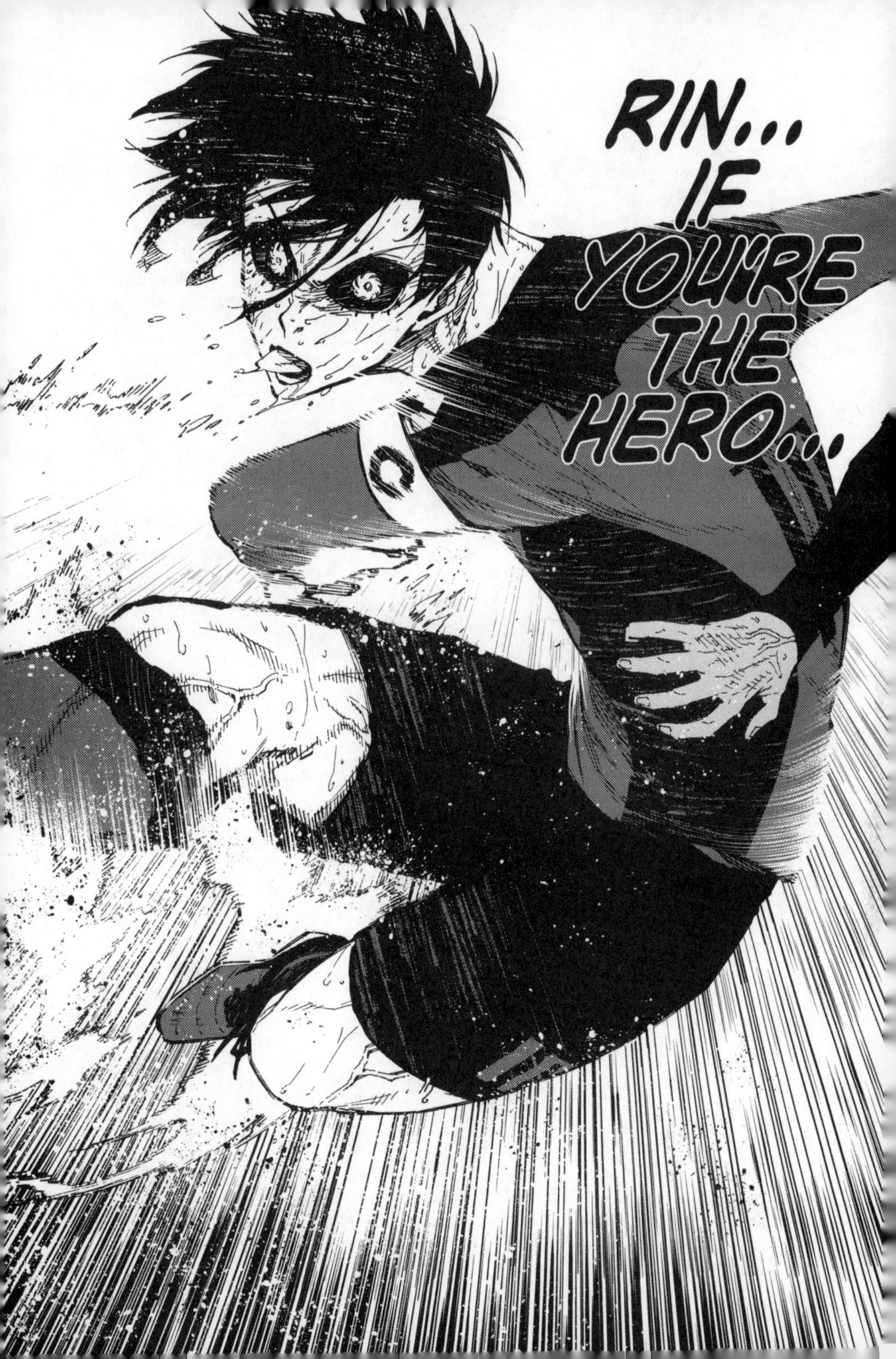
RIN... IF YOU'RE THE HERO...

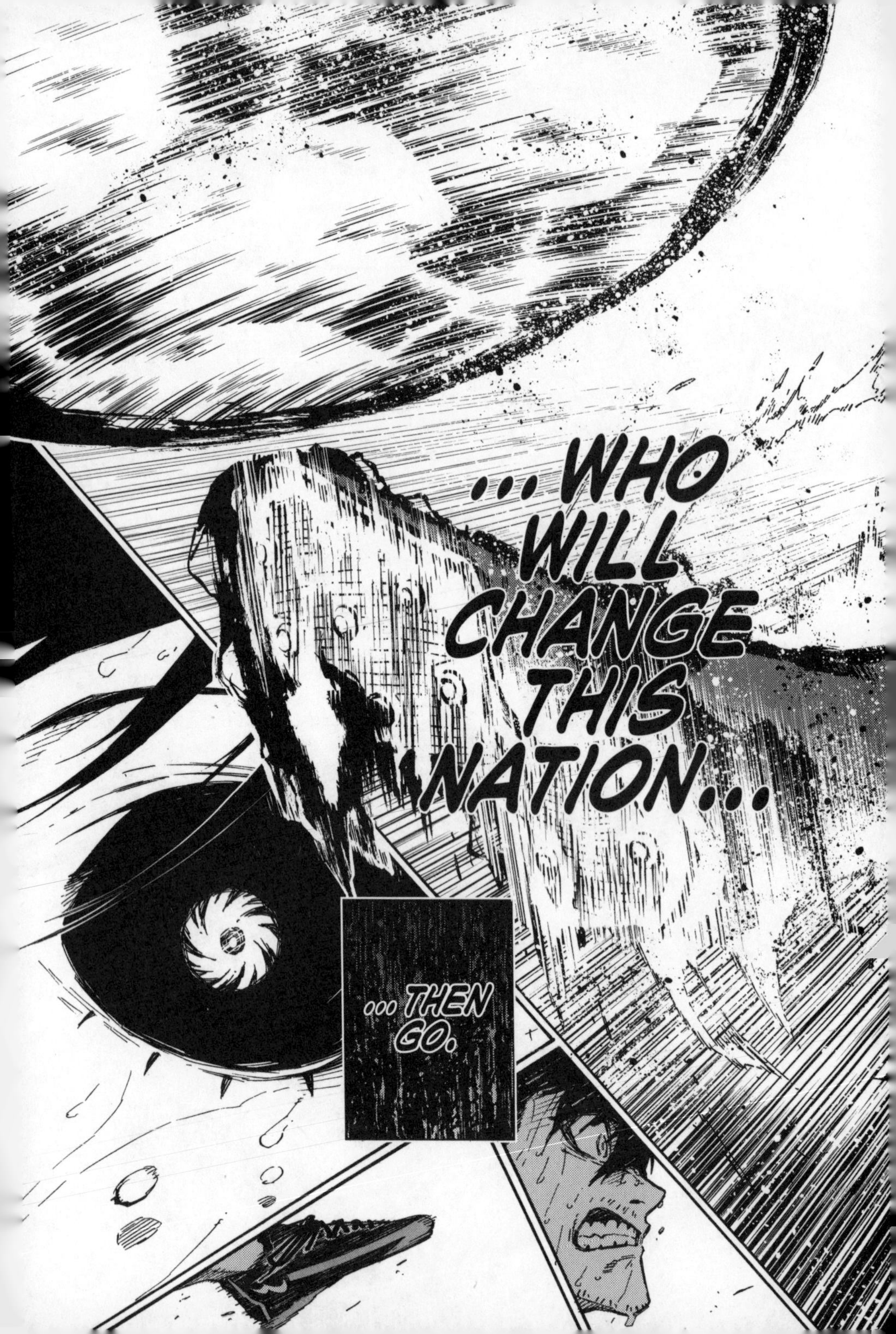
...WHO WILL CHANGE THIS NATION...
...THEN GO.

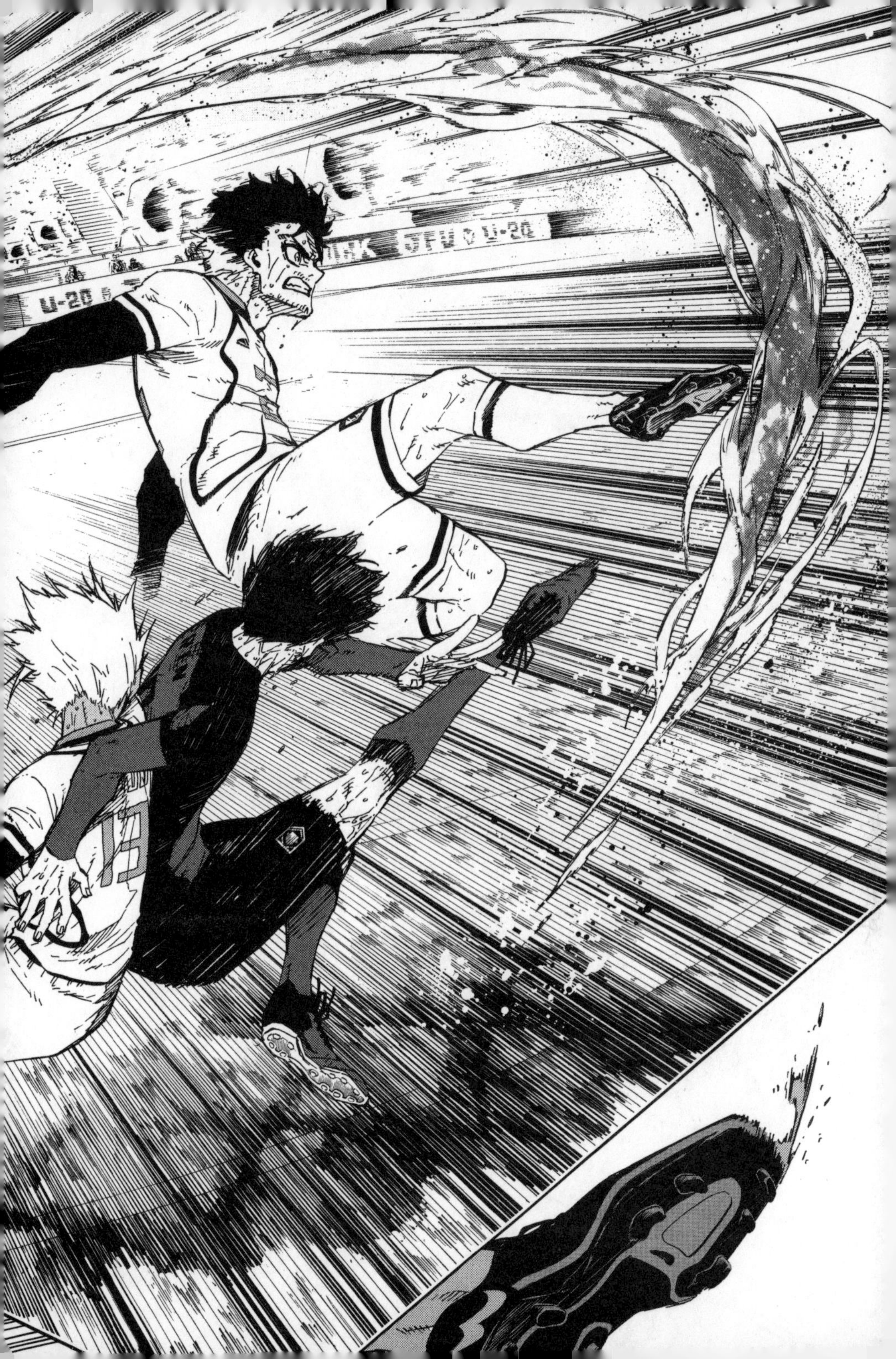
JFU U-20
U-20

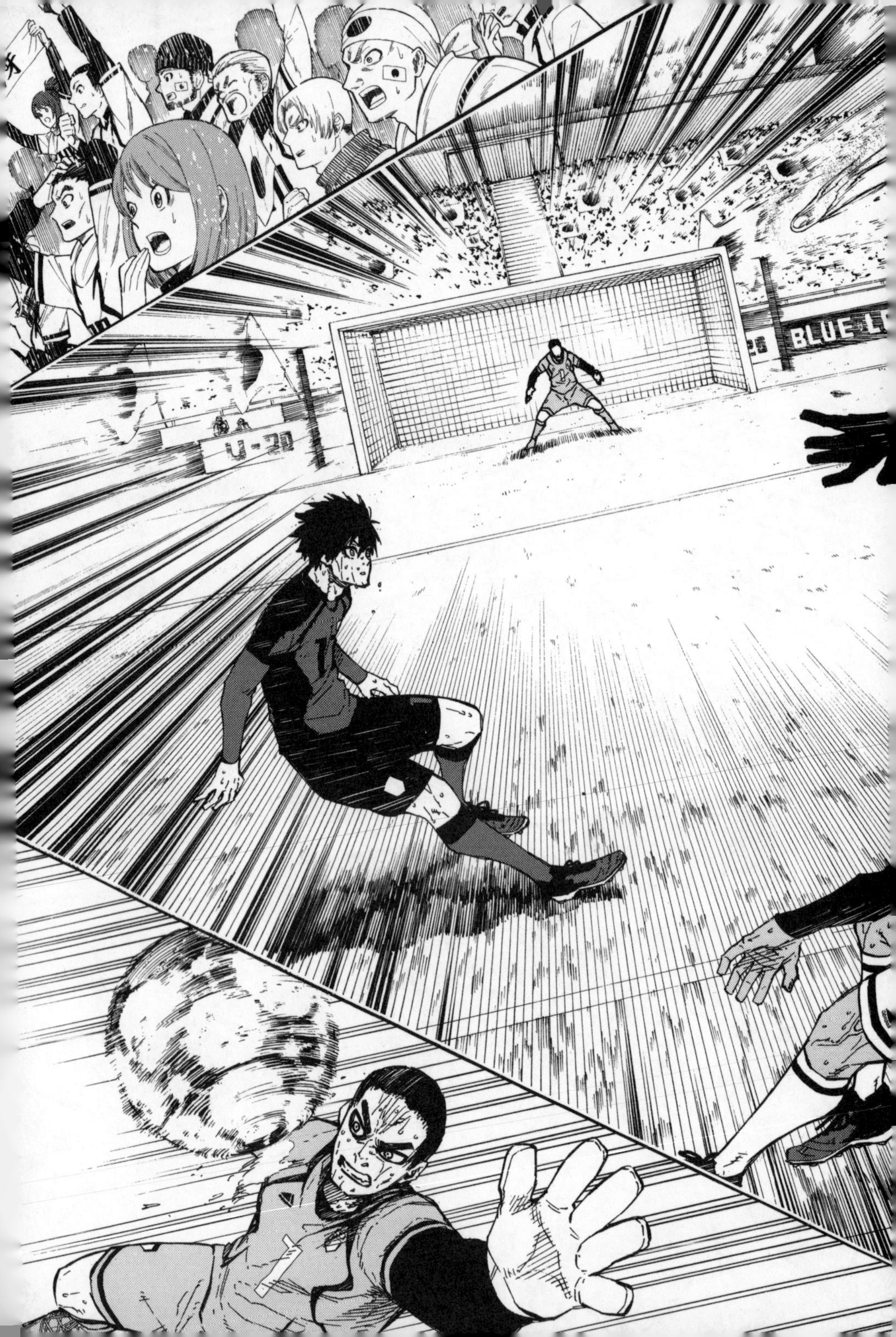
U-20

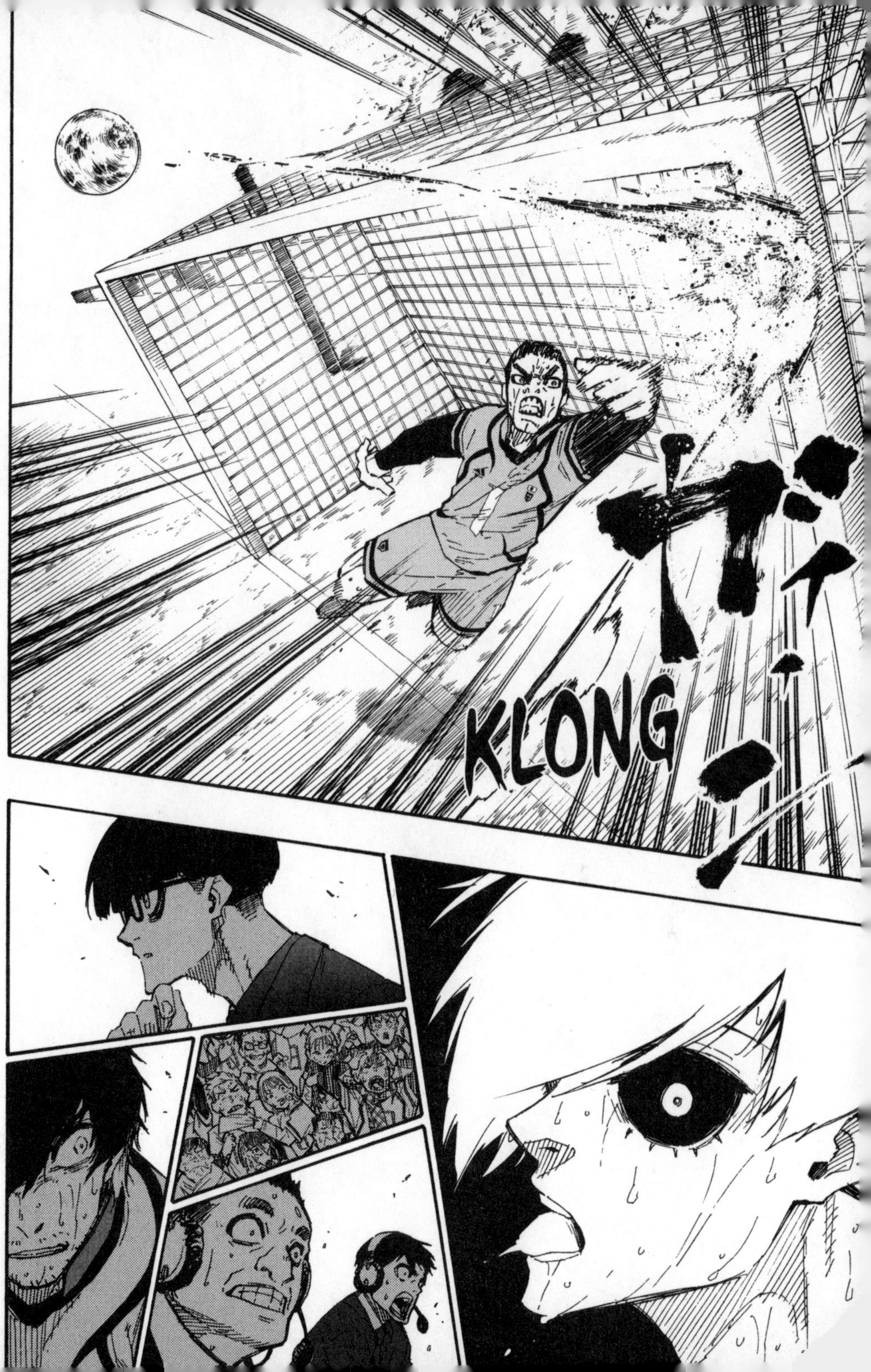
ガイーン
KLONG

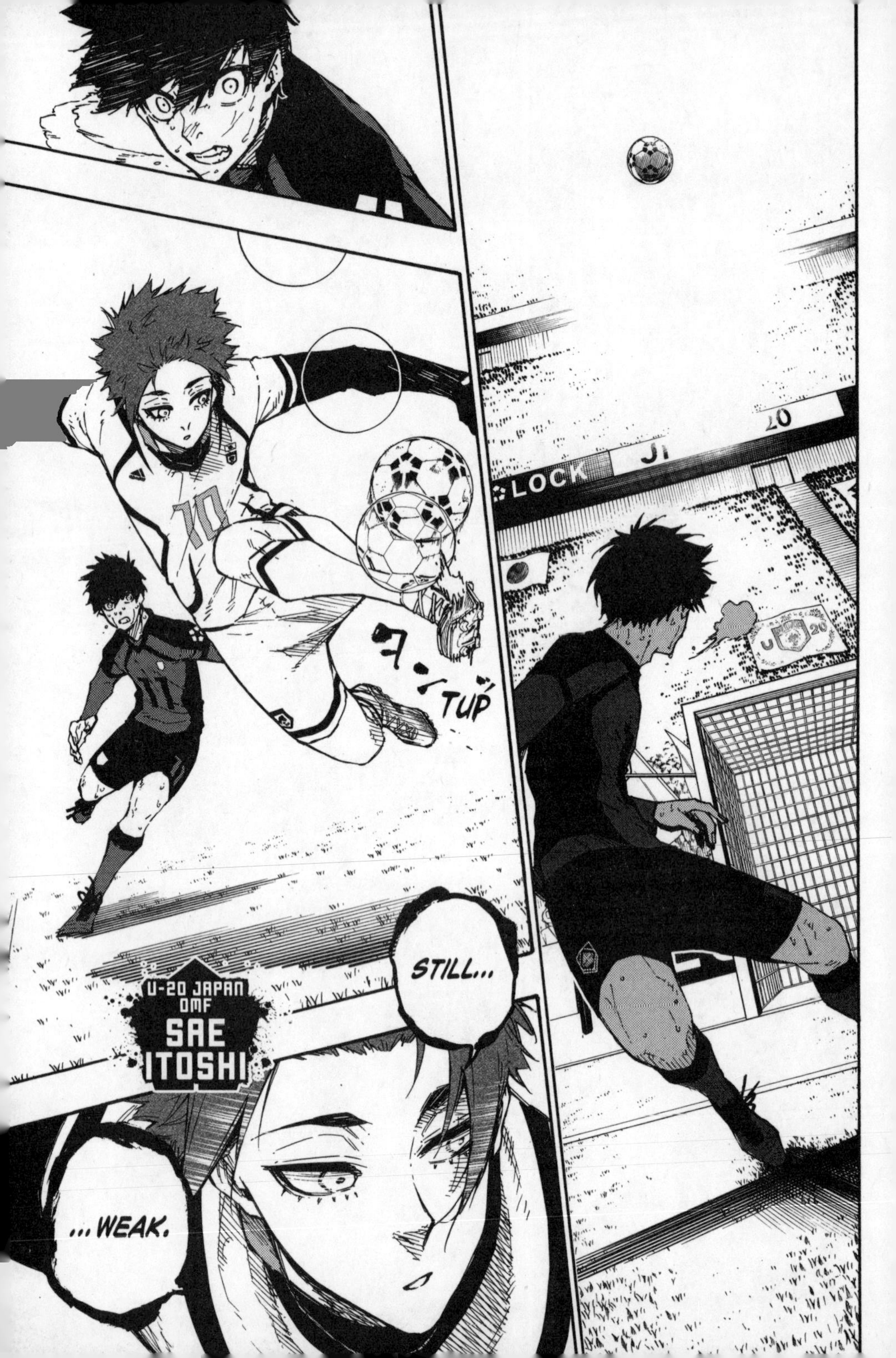
LOCK
TUP
U-20 JAPAN OMF
SAE ITOSHI
STILL...
...WEAK.

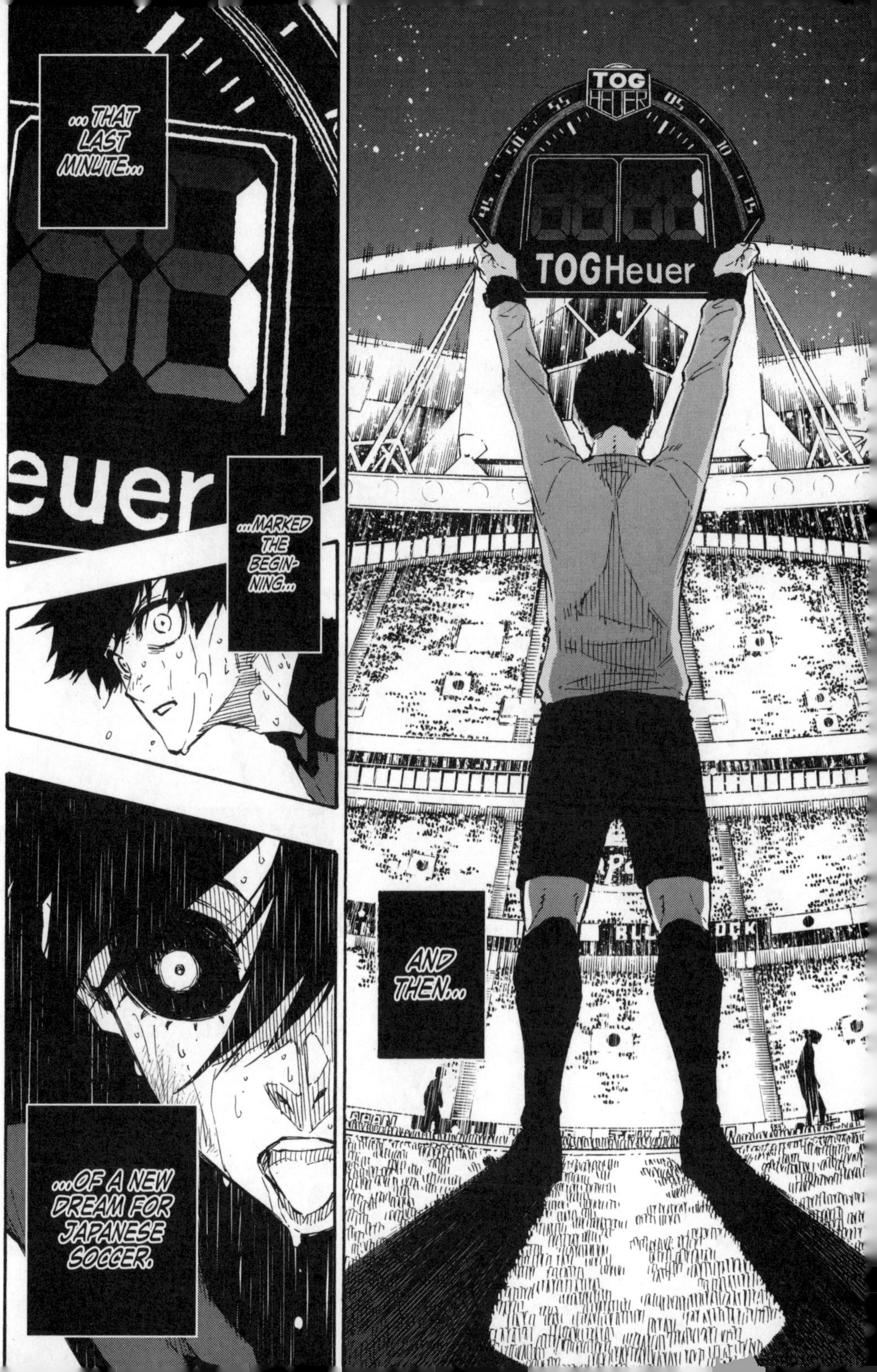
TOG HEUER
TOGHeuer
AND THEN...
...THAT LAST MINUTE...
...MARKED THE BEGIN-NING...
...OF A NEW DREAM FOR JAPANESE SOCCER.

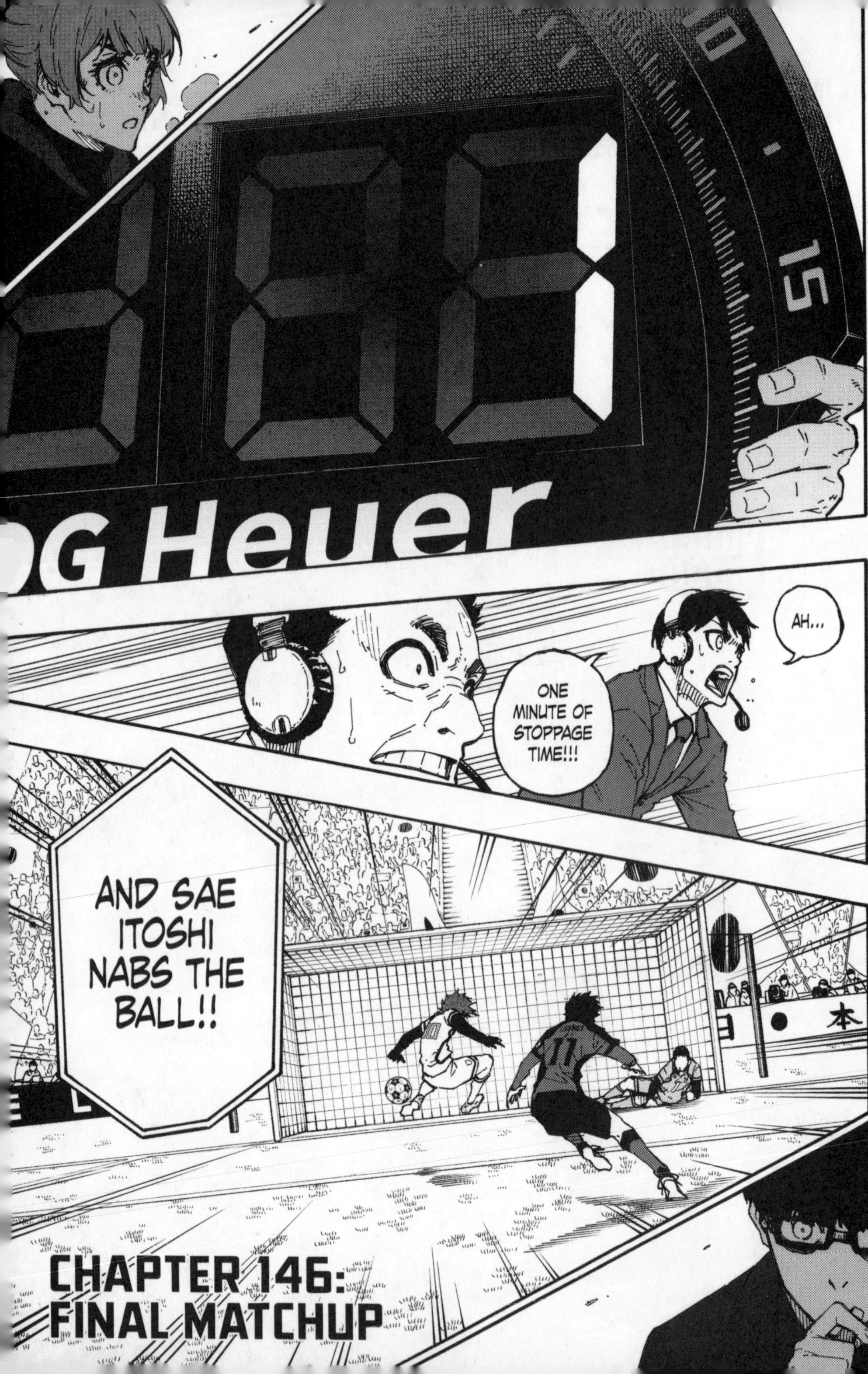
15
0G Heuer
AH...
ONE MINUTE OF STOPPAGE TIME!!!
AND SAE ITOSHI NABS THE BALL!!
CHAPTER 146: FINAL MATCHUP

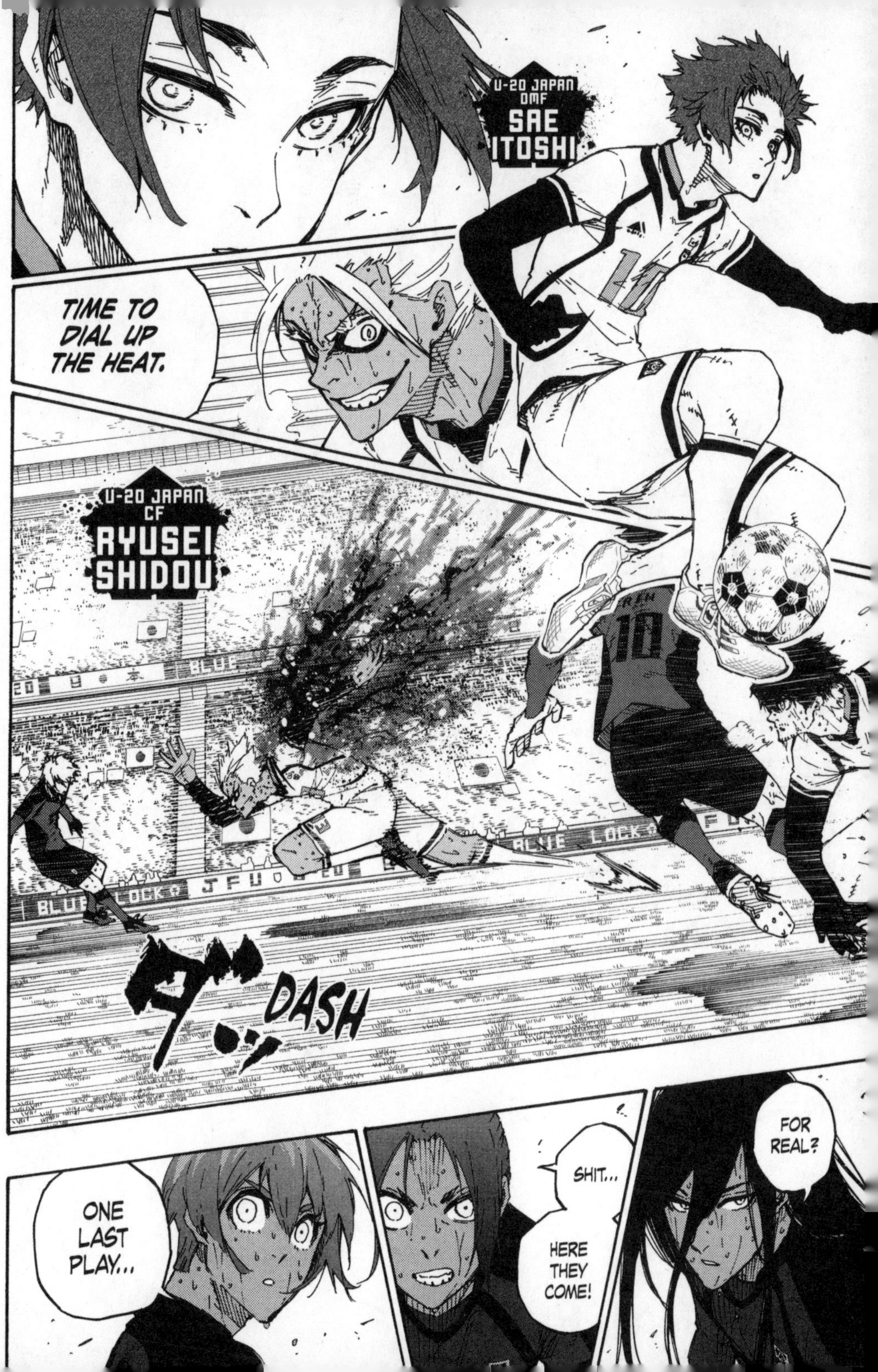
U-20 JAPAN
OMF
SAE
ITOSHI
TIME TO DIAL UP THE HEAT.
U-20 JAPAN
CF
RYUSEI
SHIDOU
DASH
FOR REAL?
SHIT...
HERE THEY COME!
ONE LAST PLAY...

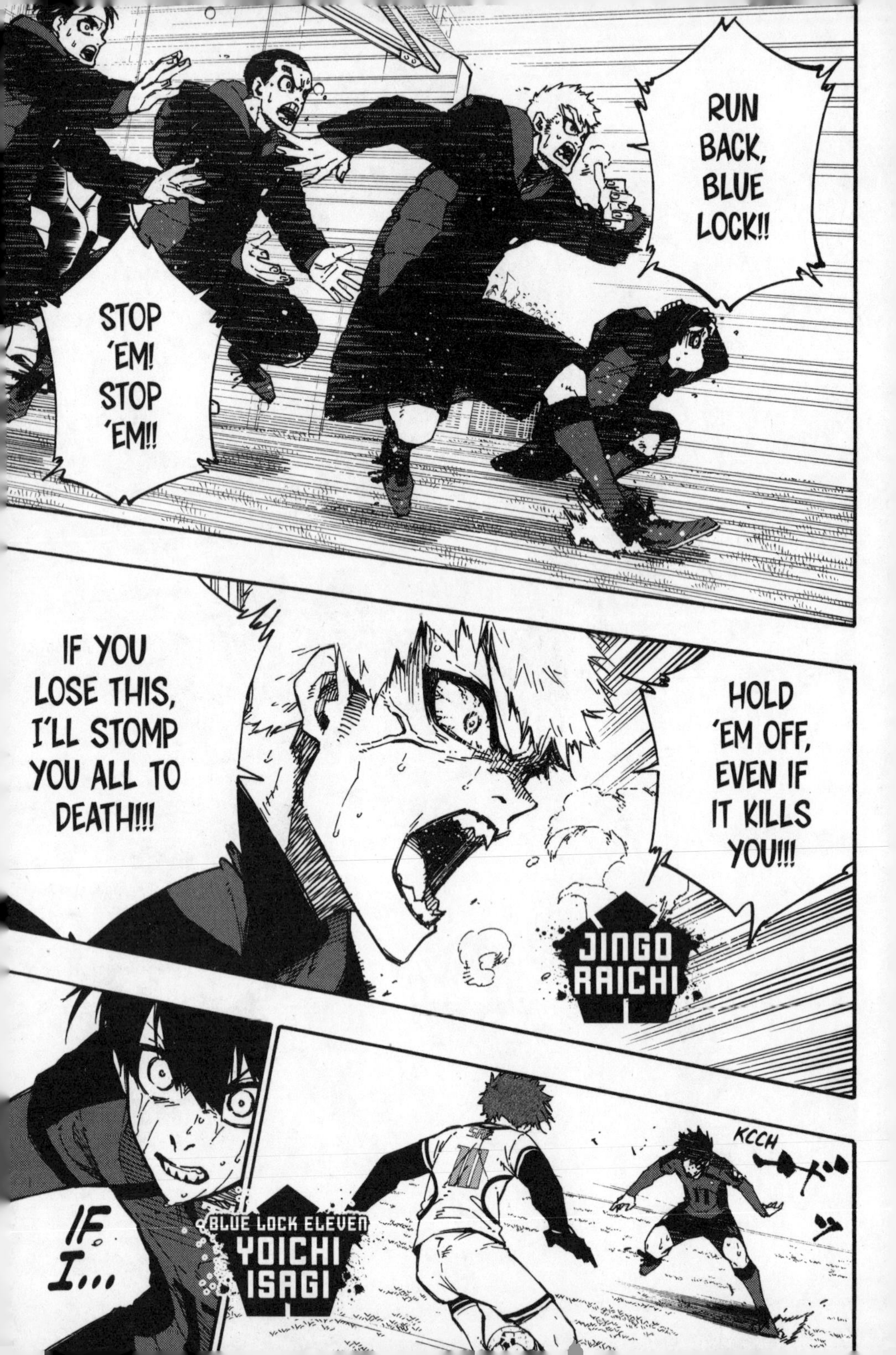
RUN BACK, BLUE LOCK!!
STOP 'EM! STOP 'EM!!
HOLD 'EM OFF, EVEN IF IT KILLS YOU!!!
IF YOU LOSE THIS, I'LL STOMP YOU ALL TO DEATH!!!
JINGO RAICHI
KCCH
BLUE LOCK ELEVEN
YOICHI ISAGI
IF. I...

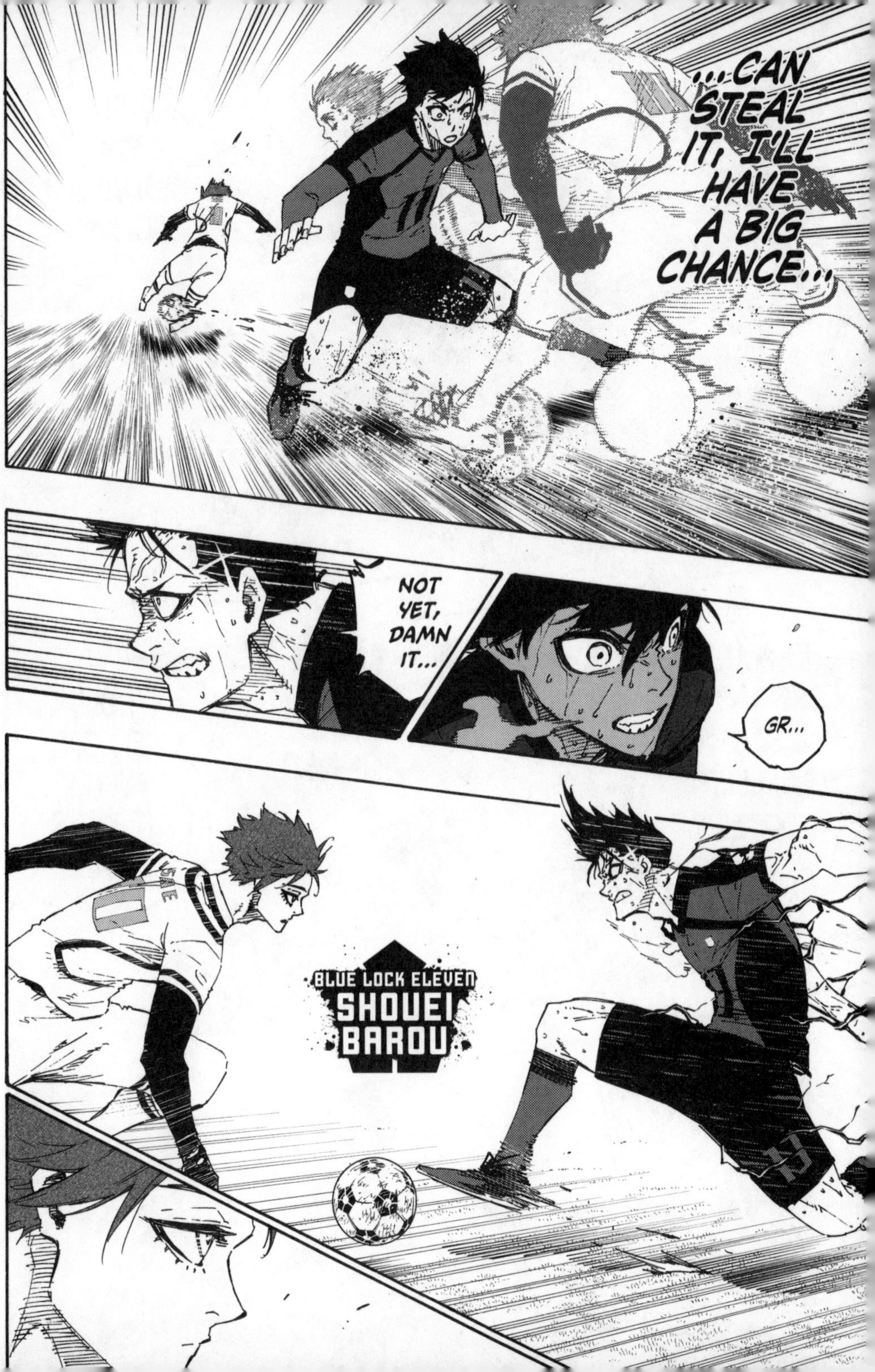
...CAN STEAL IT, I'LL HAVE A BIG CHANCE...
NOT YET, DAMN IT...
GR...
BLUE LOCK ELEVEN
SHOUEI BAROU

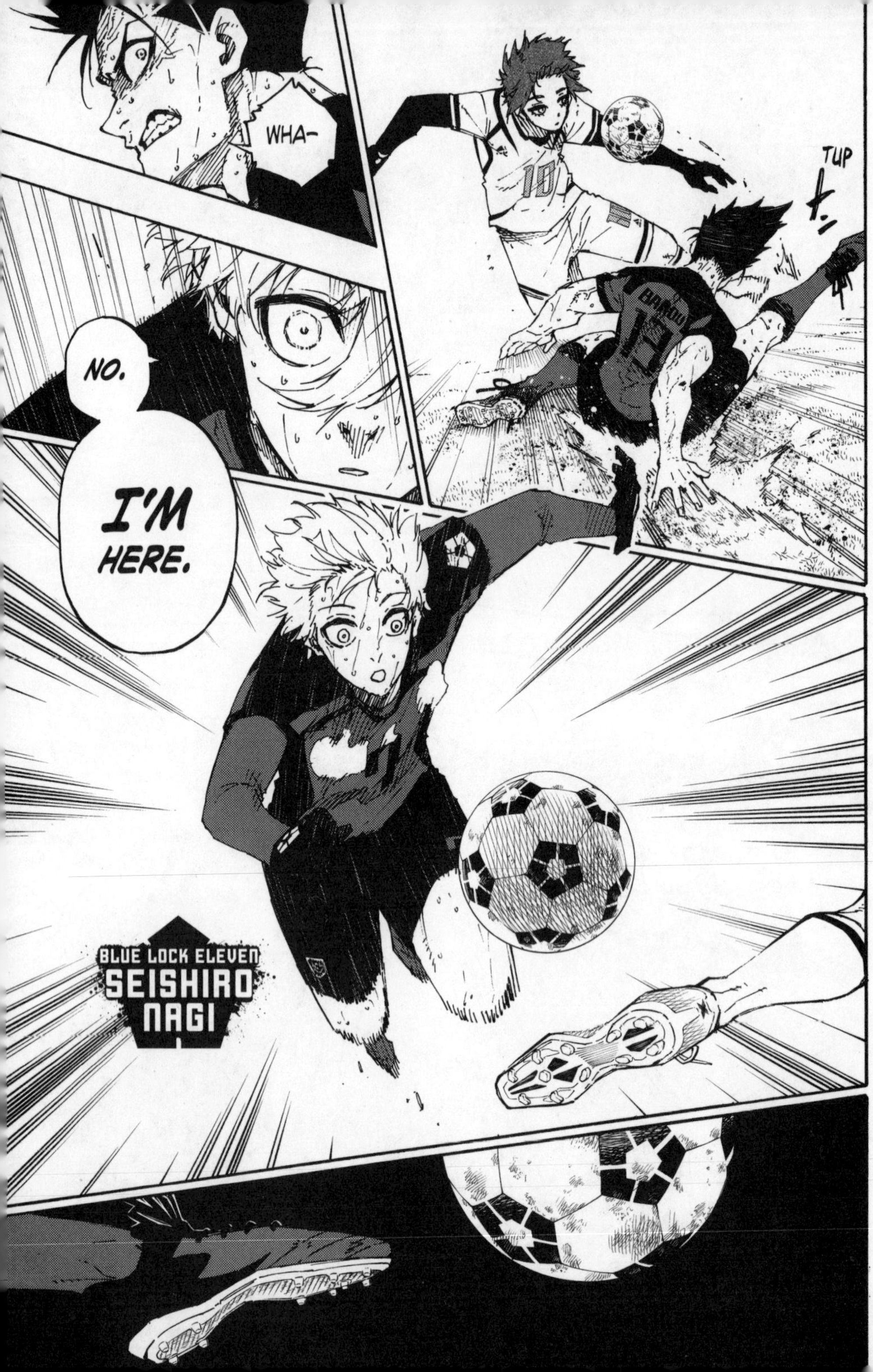
TUP
WHA-
NO.
I'M HERE.
BLUE LOCK ELEVEN
SEISHIRO NAGI

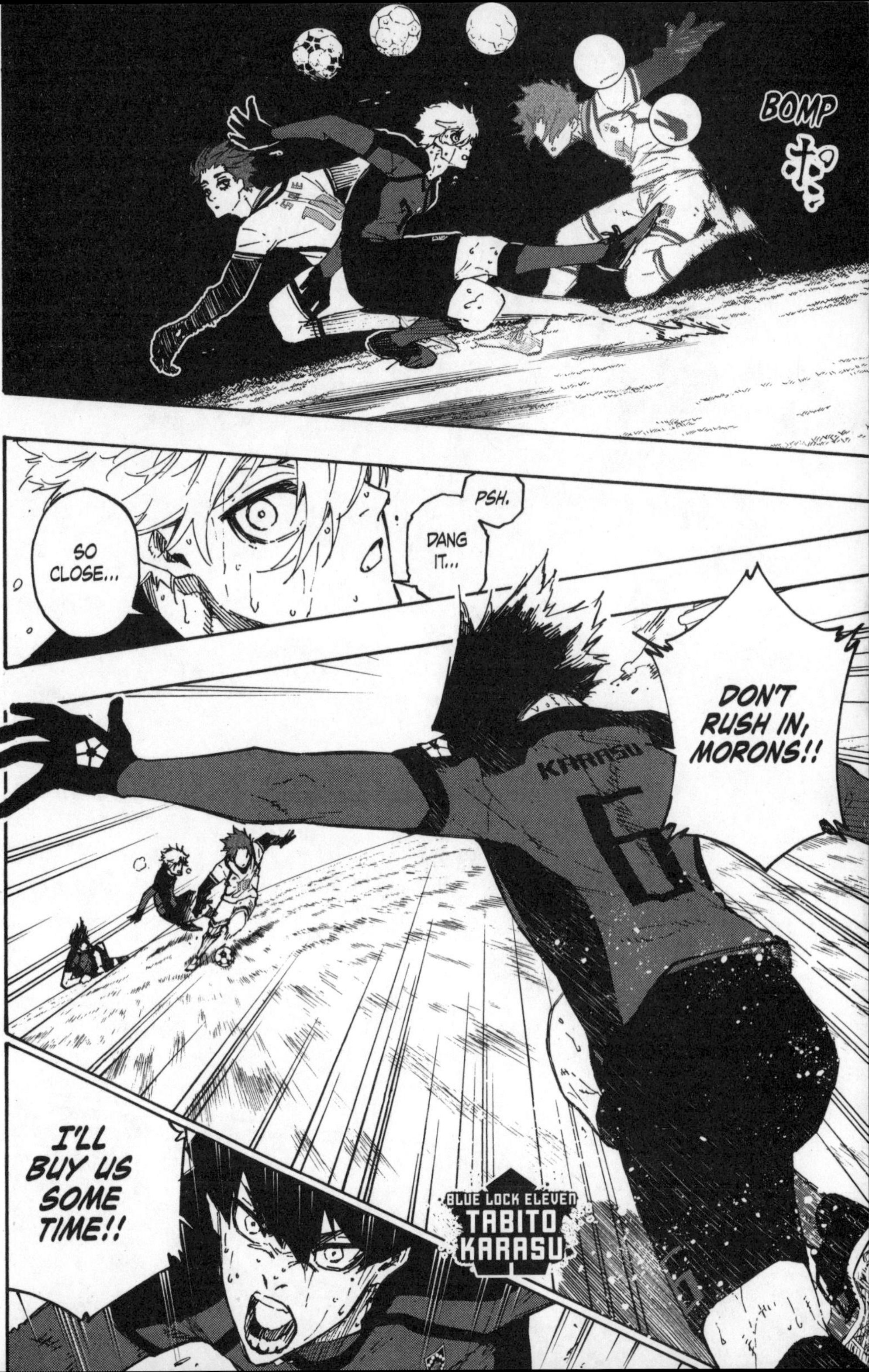
BOMP
PSH.
DANG IT...
SO CLOSE...
DON'T RUSH IN, MORONS!!
BLUE LOCK ELEVEN
TABITO KARASU
I'LL BUY US SOME TIME!!

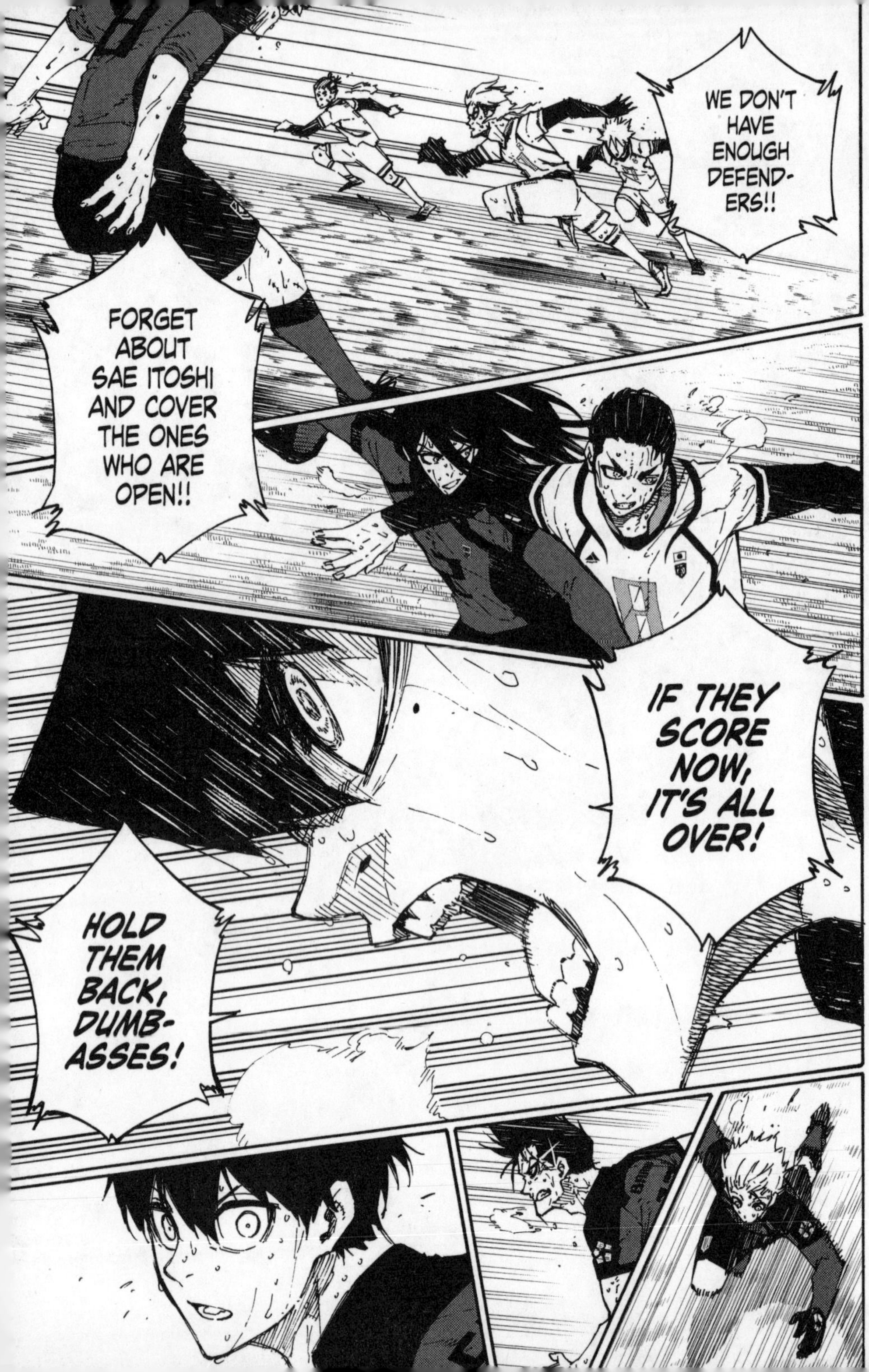
WE DON'T HAVE ENOUGH DEFEND-ERS!!
FORGET ABOUT SAE ITOSHI AND COVER THE ONES WHO ARE OPEN!!
IF THEY SCORE NOW, IT'S ALL OVER!
HOLD THEM BACK, DUMB-ASSES!

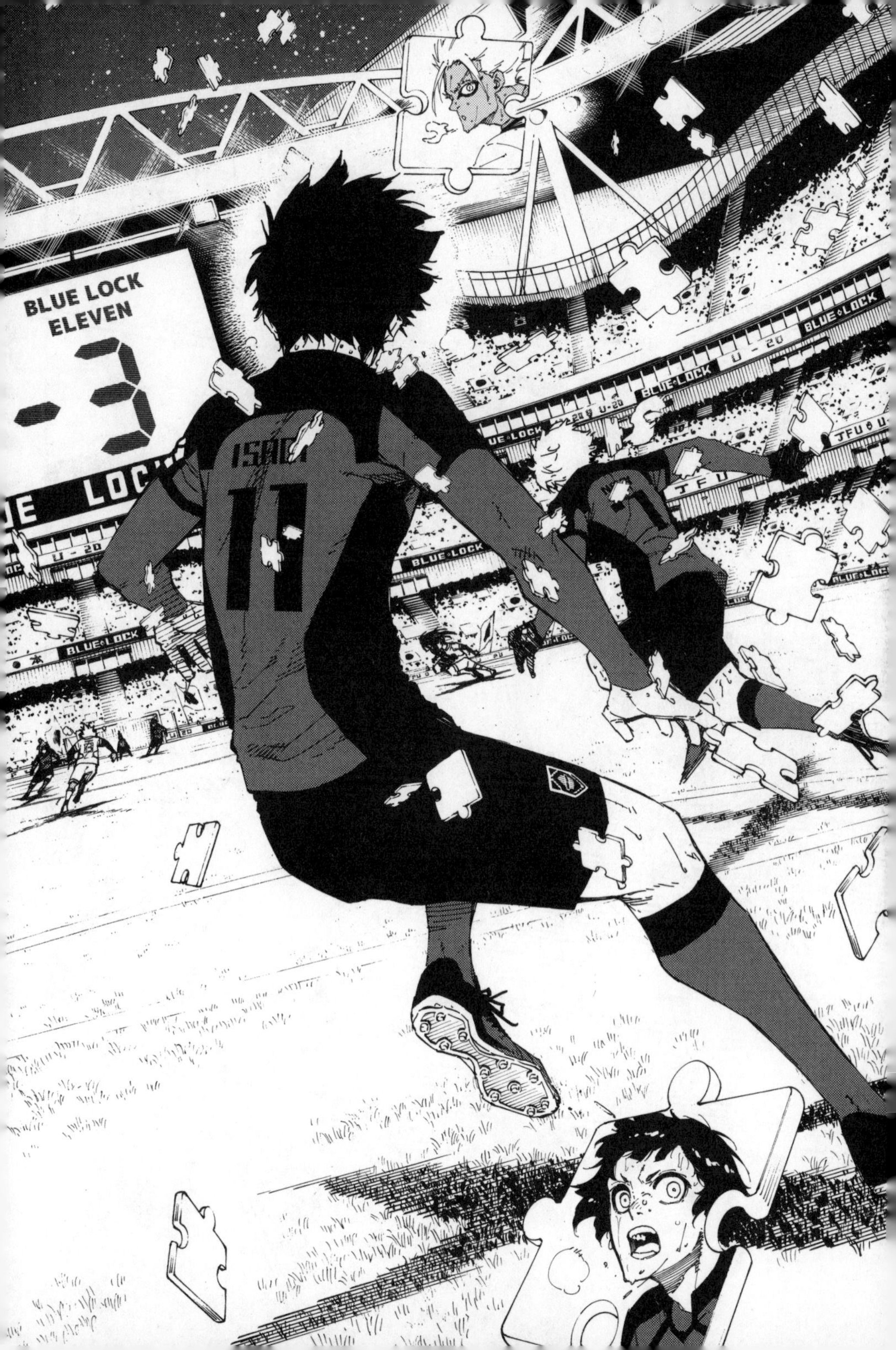
BLUE LOCK
ELEVEN
-3
ISAGI
11

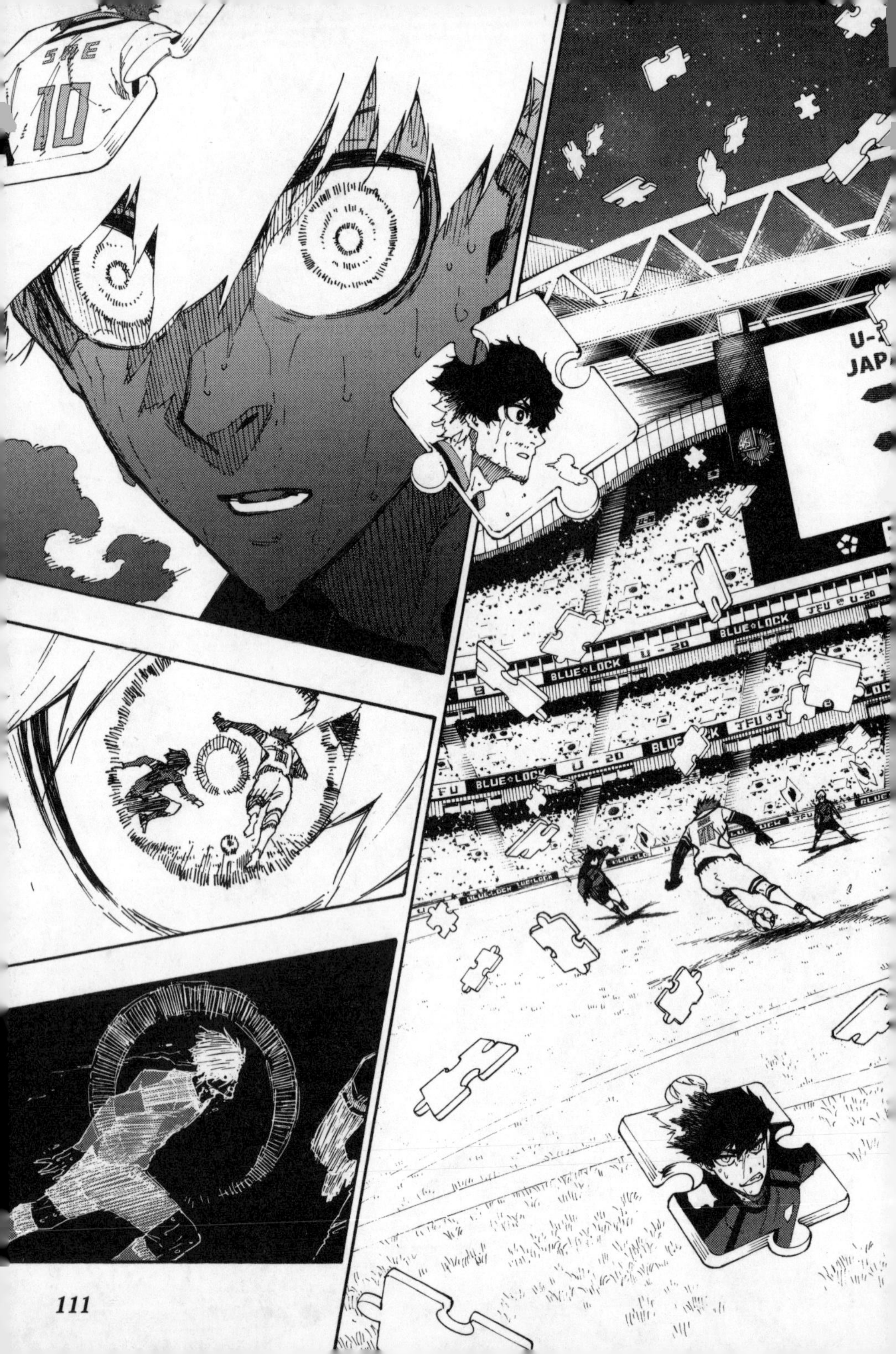
10
BLUE☆LOCK
U-20
JFU
BLUE☆LOCK
U-20
BLUE☆LOCK

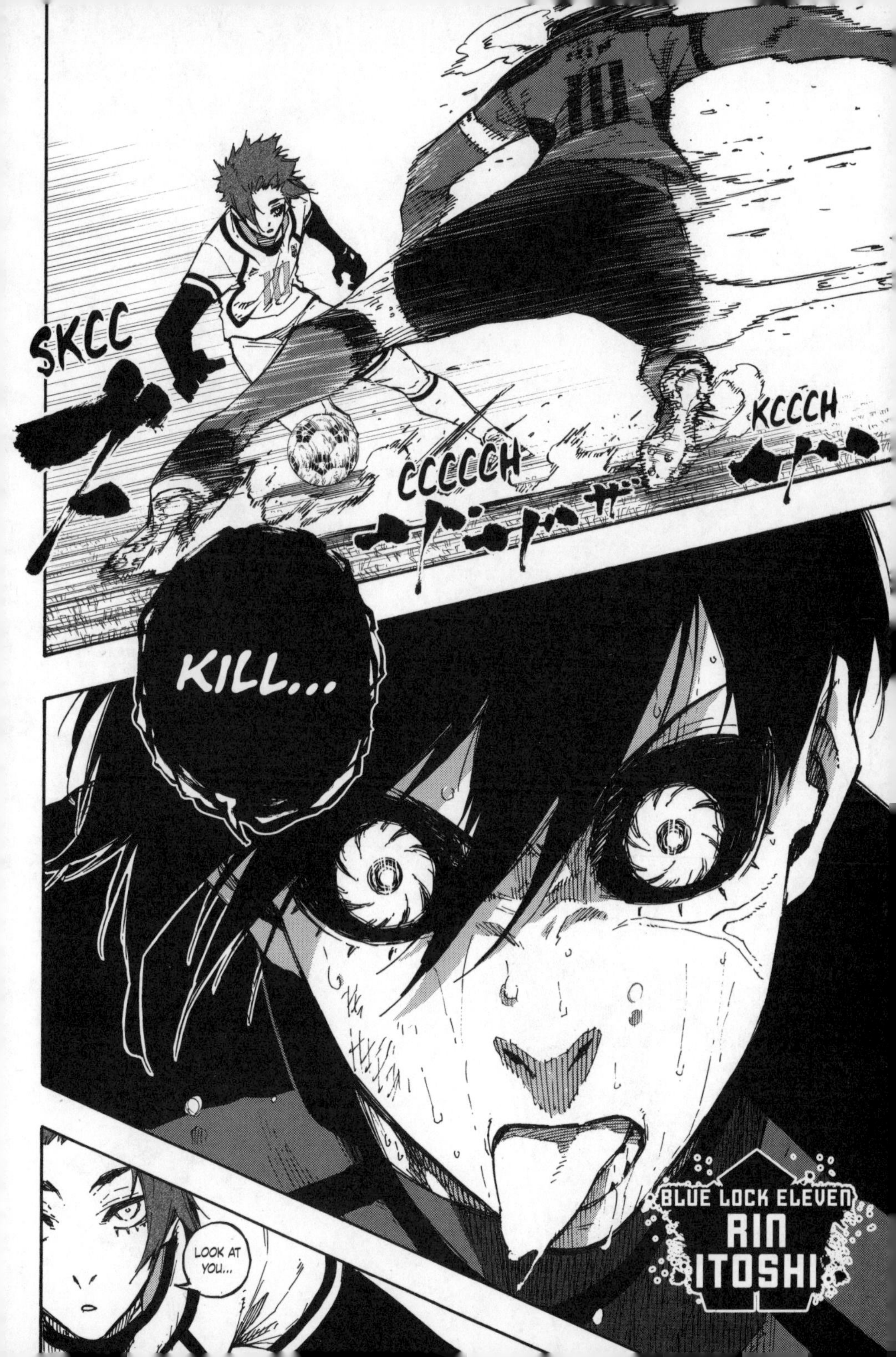
KCCCH
CCCCCH
SKCC
KILL...
BLUE LOCK ELEVEN
RIN ITOSHI
LOOK AT YOU...

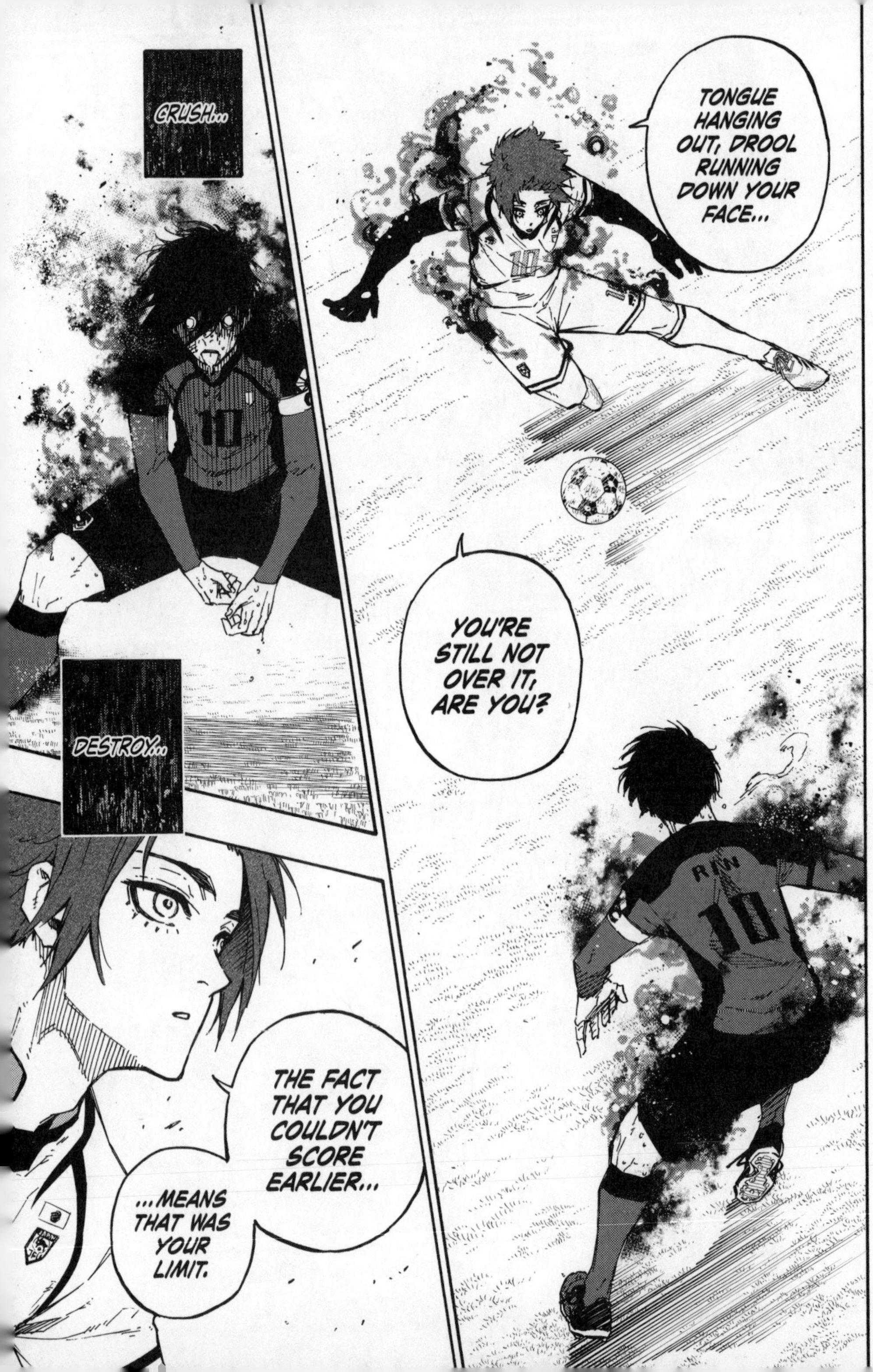
TONGUE HANGING OUT, DROOL RUNNING DOWN YOUR FACE...
YOU'RE STILL NOT OVER IT, ARE YOU?
CRUSH...
DESTROY...
THE FACT THAT YOU COULDN'T SCORE EARLIER...
...MEANS THAT WAS YOUR LIMIT.

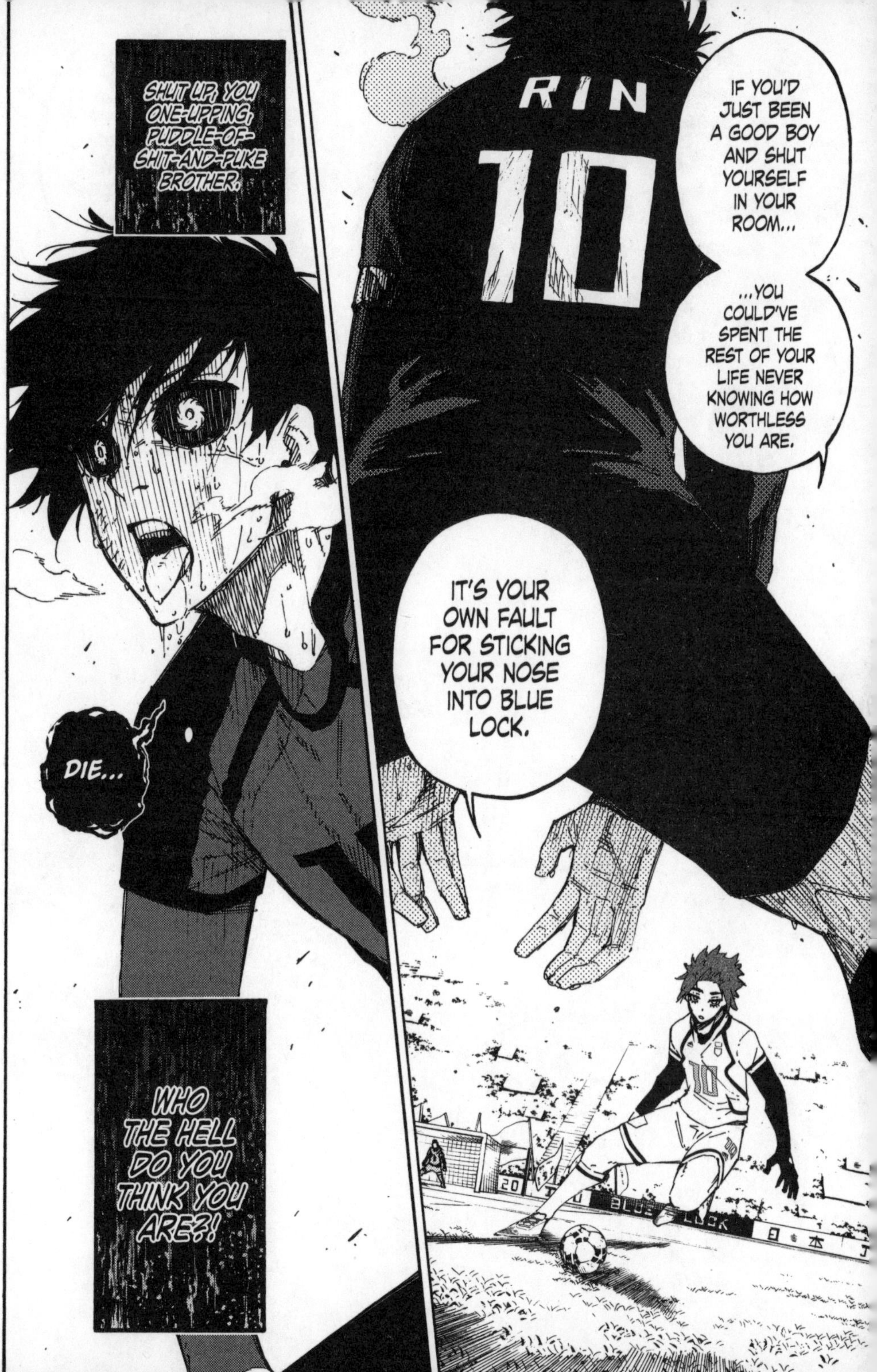
RIN
10
IF YOU'D JUST BEEN A GOOD BOY AND SHUT YOURSELF IN YOUR ROOM...
...YOU COULD'VE SPENT THE REST OF YOUR LIFE NEVER KNOWING HOW WORTHLESS YOU ARE.
IT'S YOUR OWN FAULT FOR STICKING YOUR NOSE INTO BLUE LOCK.
SHUT UP, YOU ONE-UPPING, PUDDLE-OF-SHIT-AND-PUKE BROTHER.
DIE...
WHO THE HELL DO YOU THINK YOU ARE?!

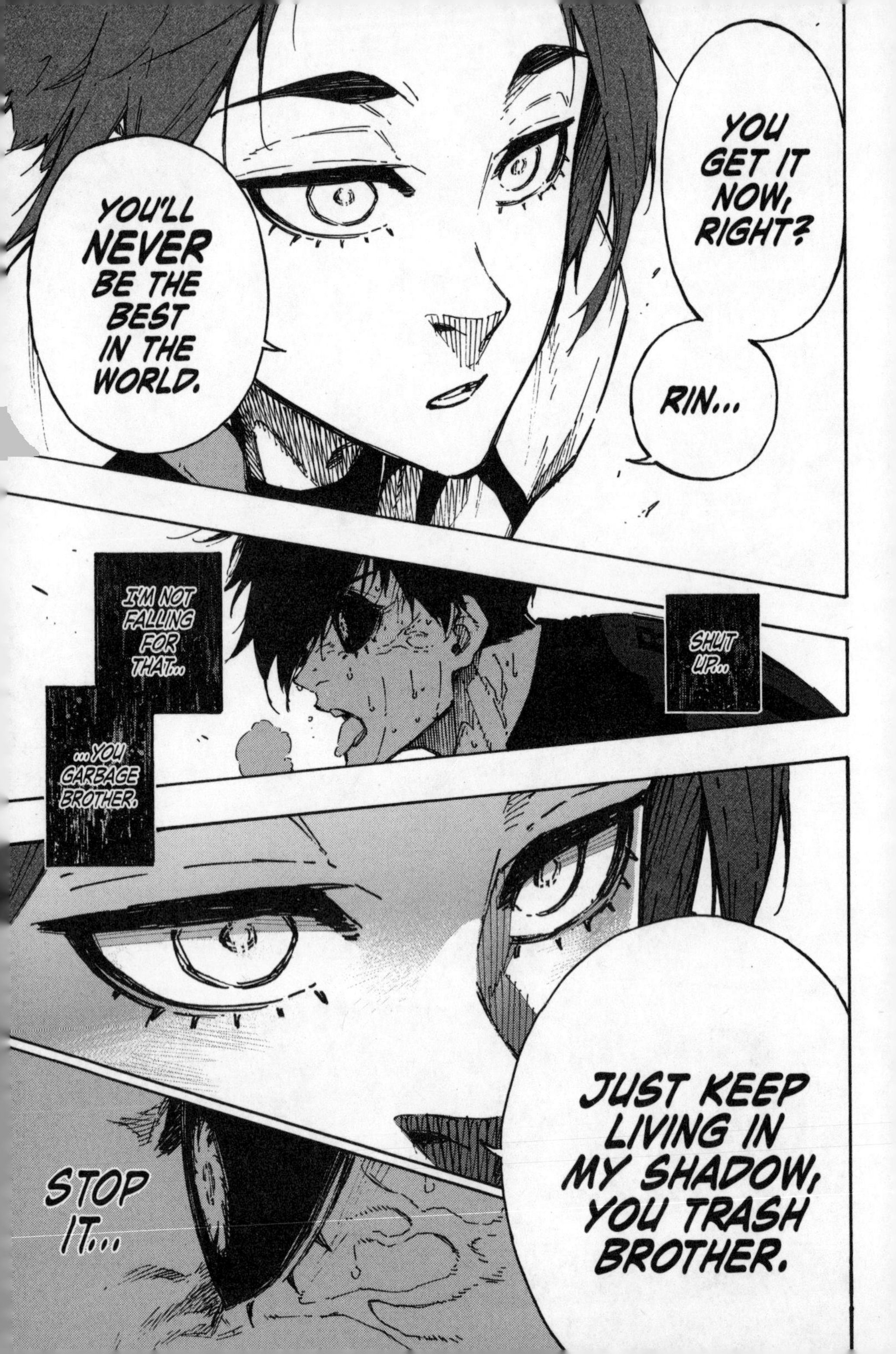
YOU GET IT NOW, RIGHT?
RIN...
YOU'LL NEVER BE THE BEST IN THE WORLD.
SHUT UP...
I'M NOT FALLING FOR THAT...
...YOU GARBAGE BROTHER.
JUST KEEP LIVING IN MY SHADOW, YOU TRASH BROTHER.
STOP IT...

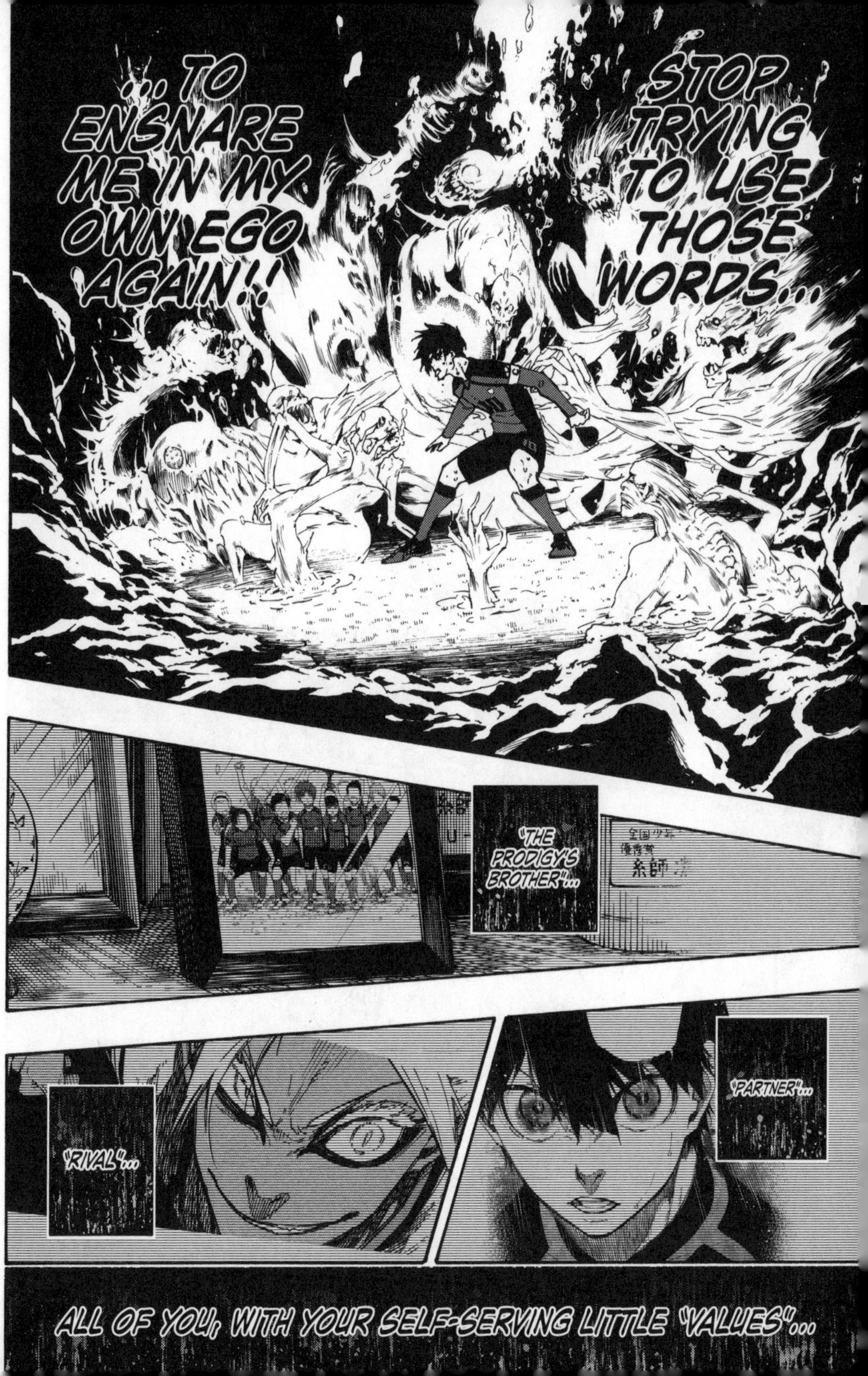
STOP TRYING TO USE THOSE WORDS...
...TO ENSNARE ME IN MY OWN EGO AGAIN!!
"THE PRODIGY'S BROTHER"...
"PARTNER"...
"RIVAL"...
ALL OF YOU, WITH YOUR SELF-SERVING LITTLE "VALUES"...

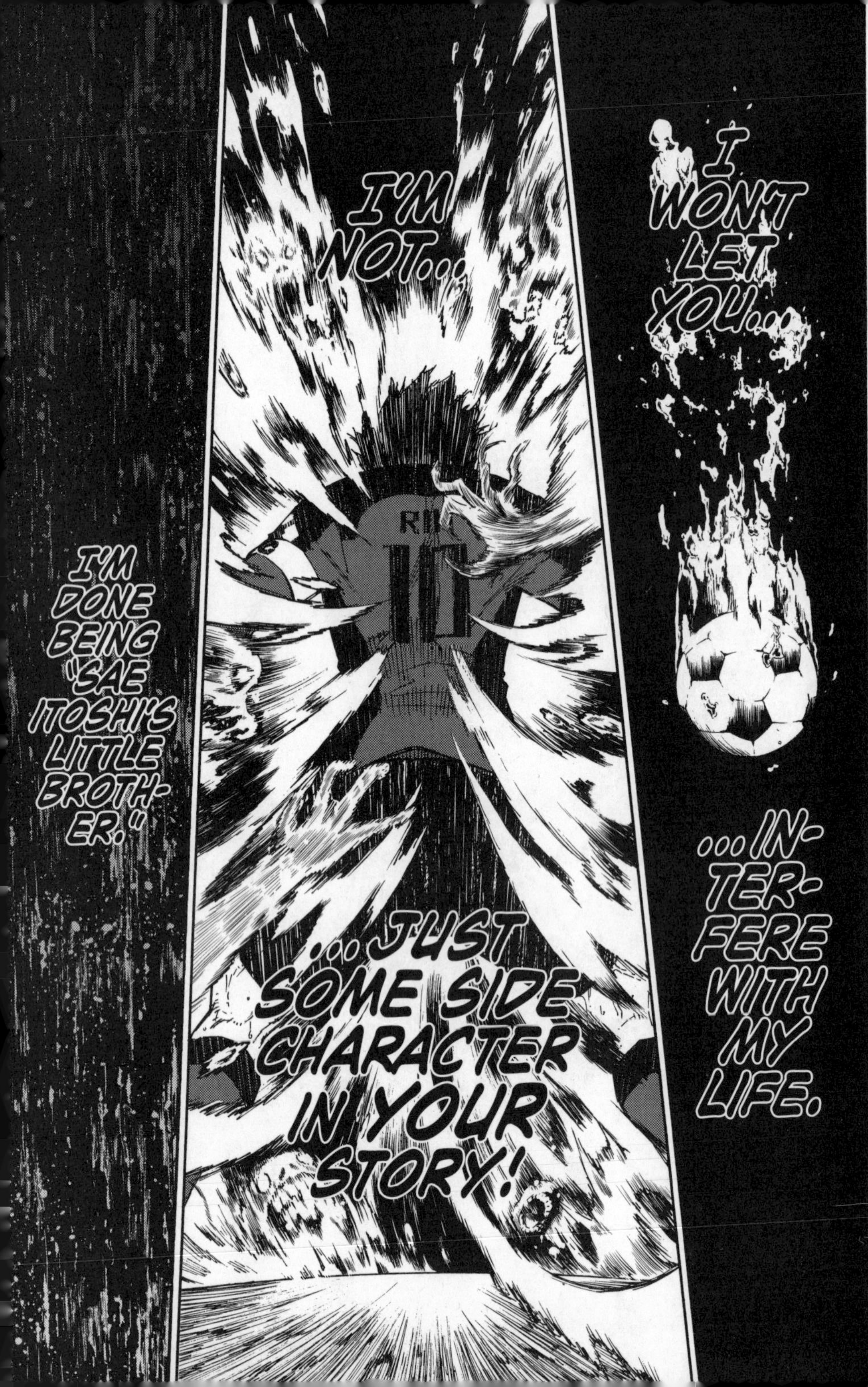
I WON'T LET YOU...
...IN-TER-FERE WITH MY LIFE.
I'M NOT...
...JUST SOME SIDE CHARACTER IN YOUR STORY!
I'M DONE BEING "SAE ITOSHI'S LITTLE BROTH-ER."

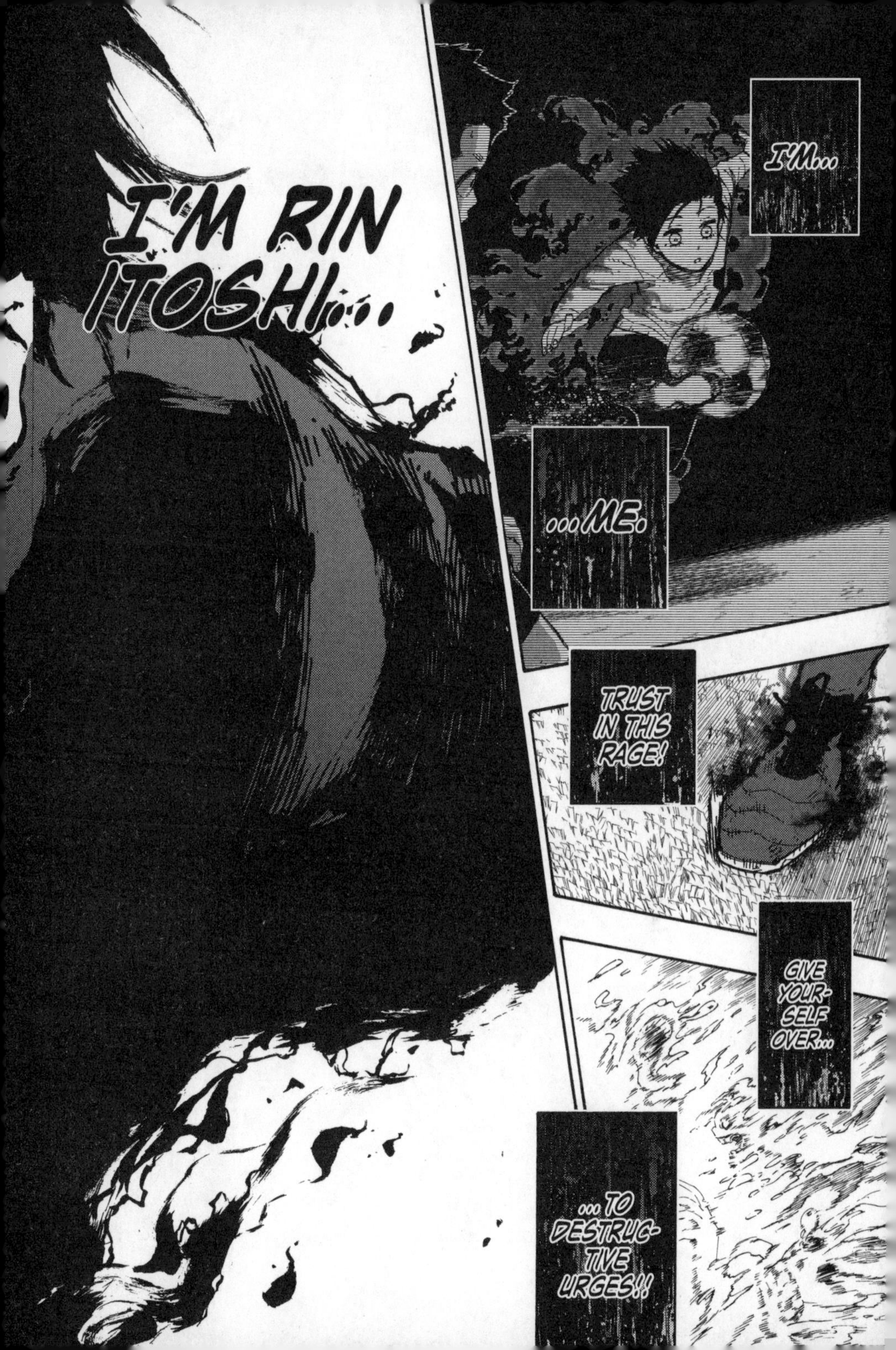
I'M...
...ME.
TRUST IN THIS RAGE!
GIVE YOUR-SELF OVER...
...TO DESTRUC-TIVE URGES!!
I'M RIN ITOSHI...

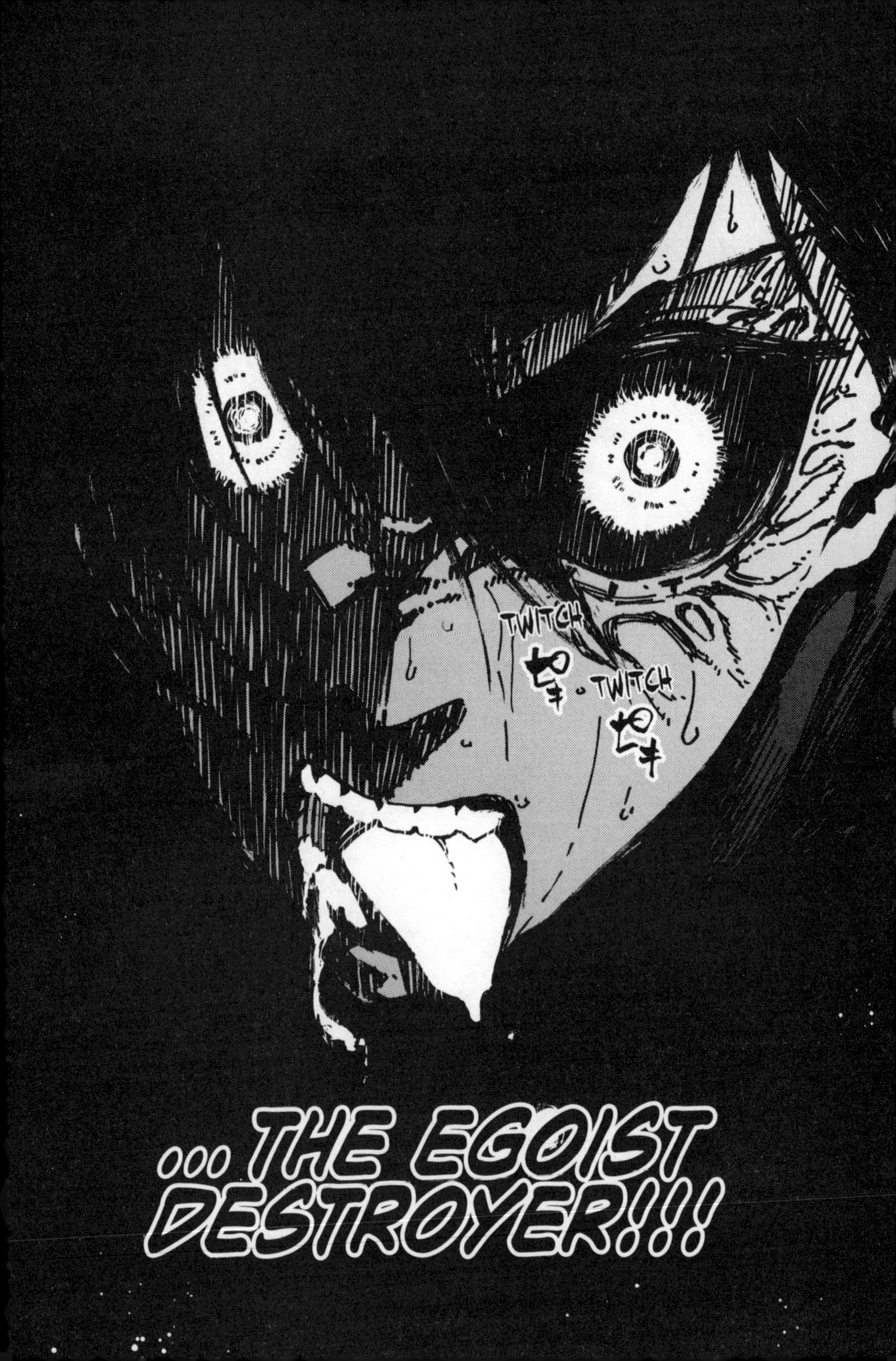
TWITCH
TWITCH
...THE EGOIST DESTROYER!!!

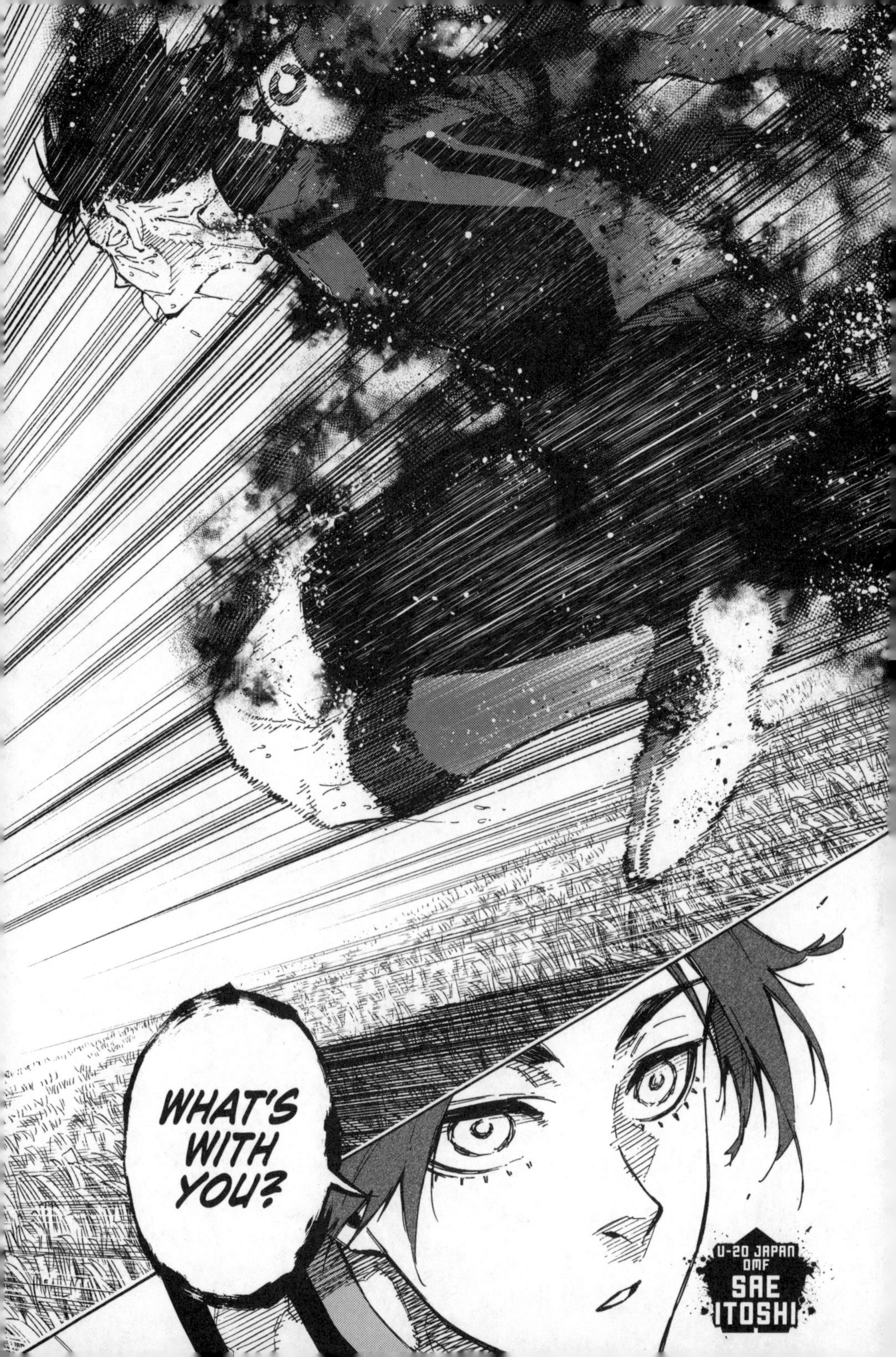
WHAT'S WITH YOU?
U-20 JAPAN OMF SAE ITOSHI

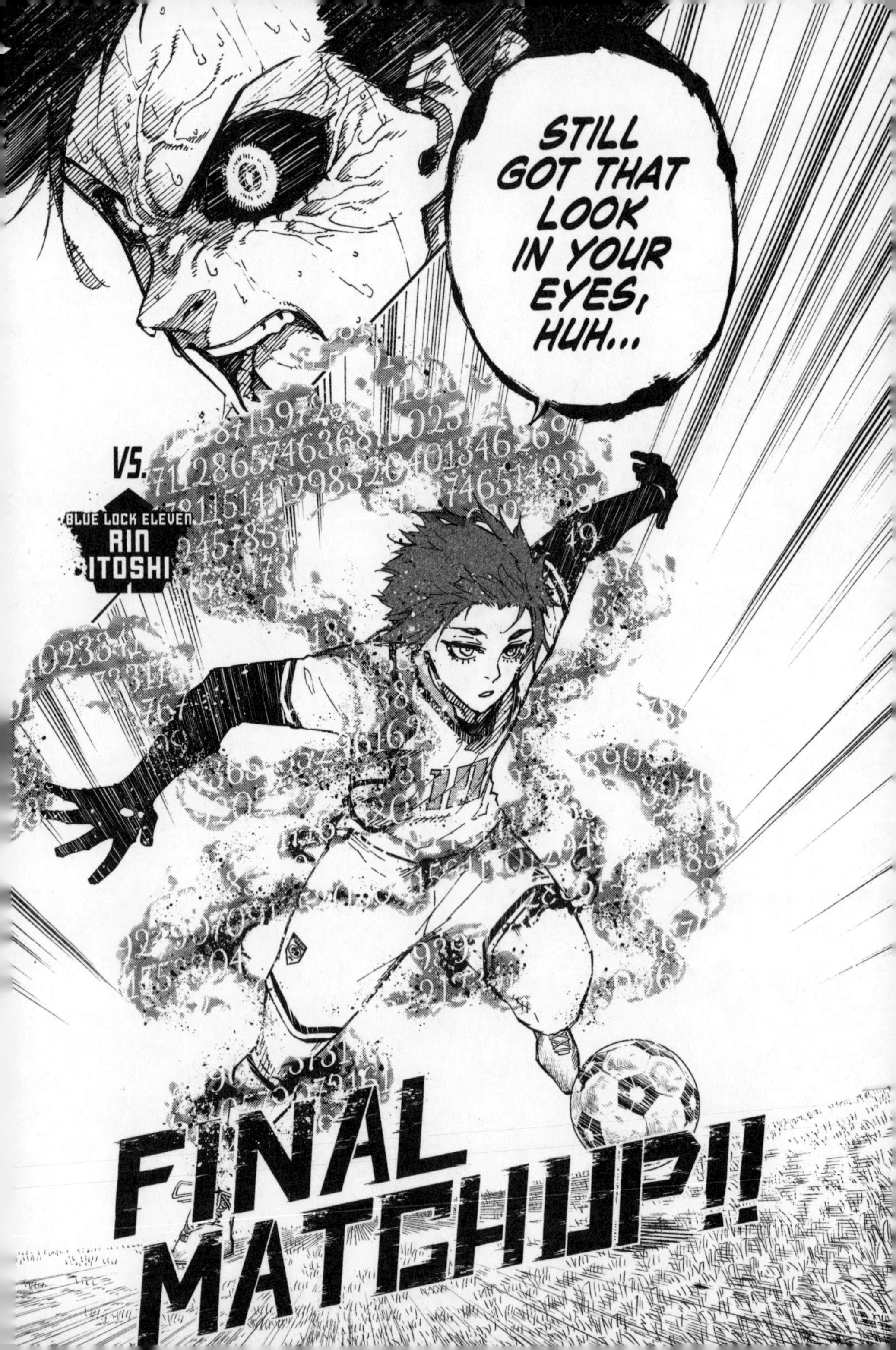
STILL GOT THAT LOOK IN YOUR EYES, HUH...
VS.
BLUE LOCK ELEVEN
RIN ITOSHI
FINAL MATCHUP!!

BLUE LOCK

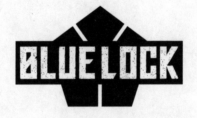

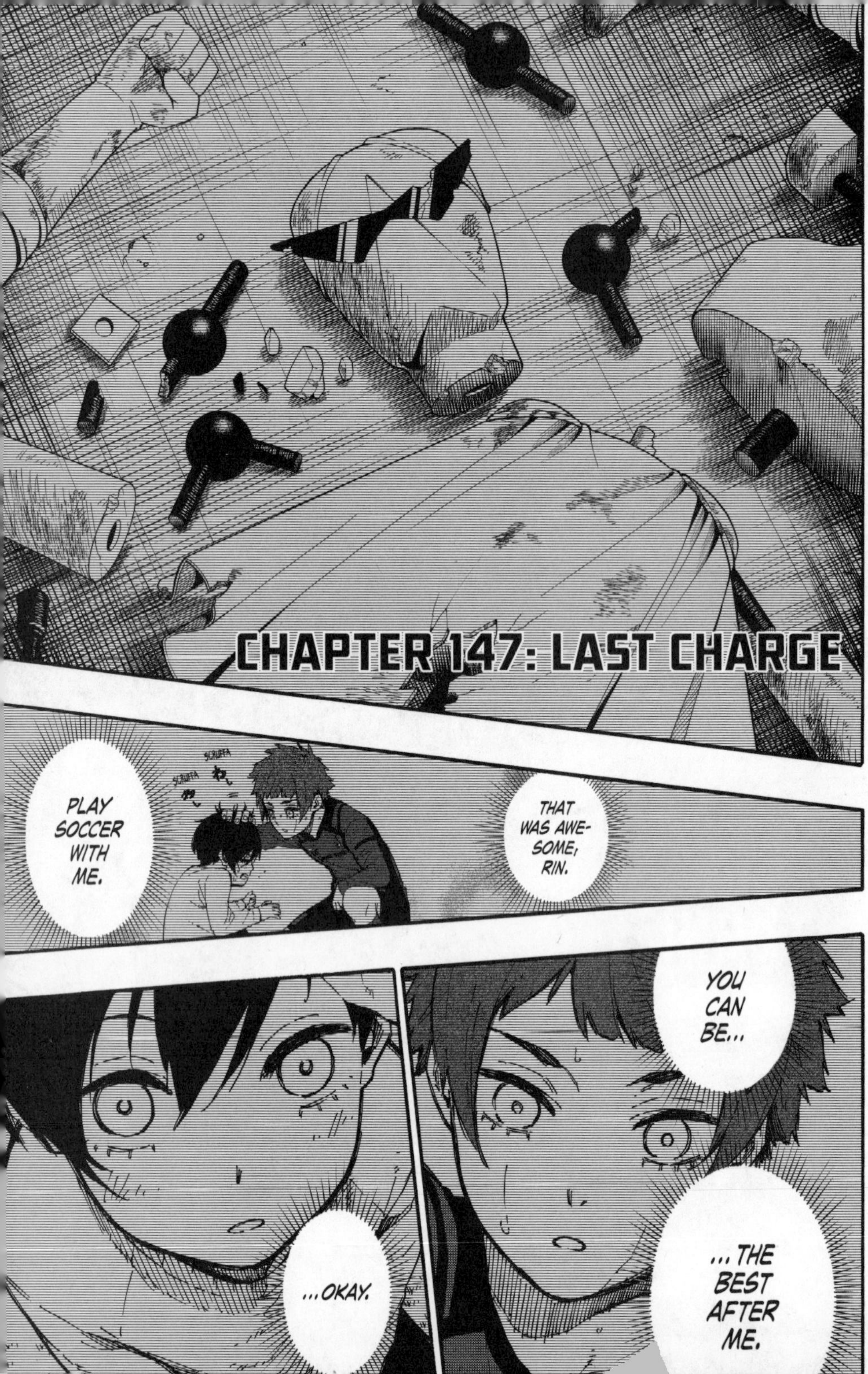
CHAPTER 147: LAST CHARGE
THAT WAS AWE-SOME, RIN.
PLAY SOCCER WITH ME.
YOU CAN BE...
...THE BEST AFTER ME.
...OKAY.

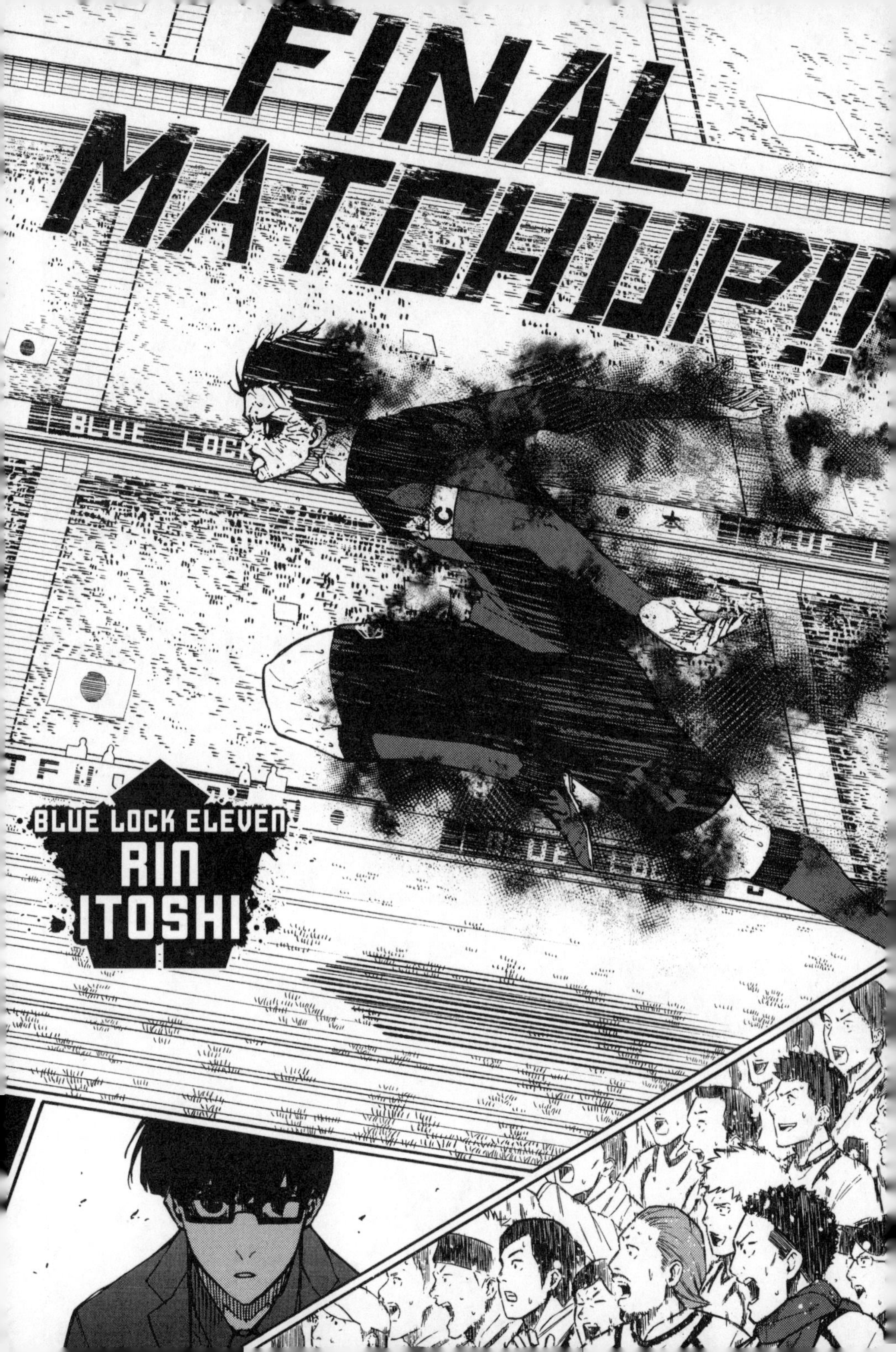
FINAL MATCHUP!!
BLUE LOCK ELEVEN
RIN ITOSHI

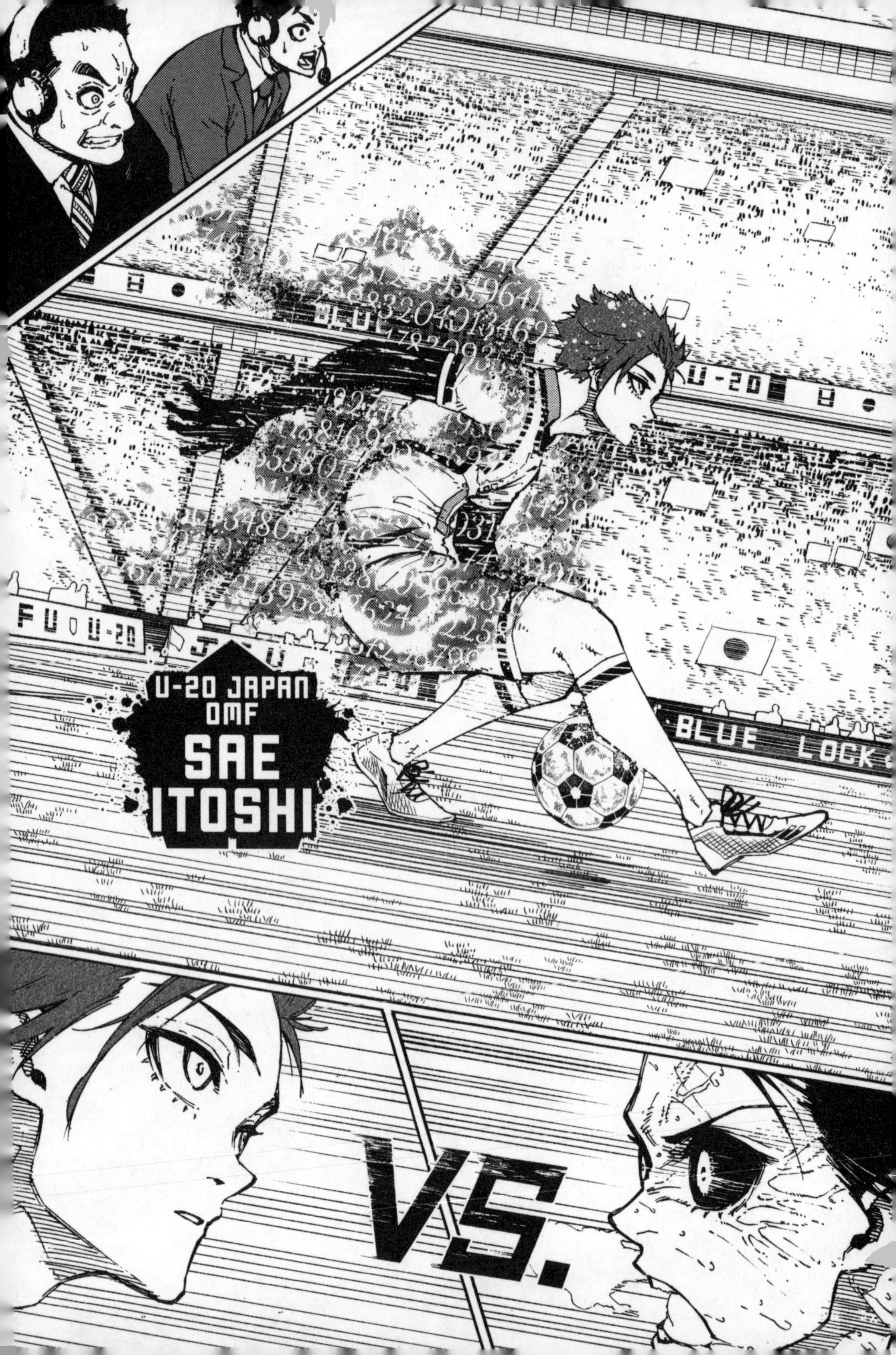
U-20
BLUE LOCK
FU U-20
U-20 JAPAN
OMF
SAE
ITOSHI
VS.

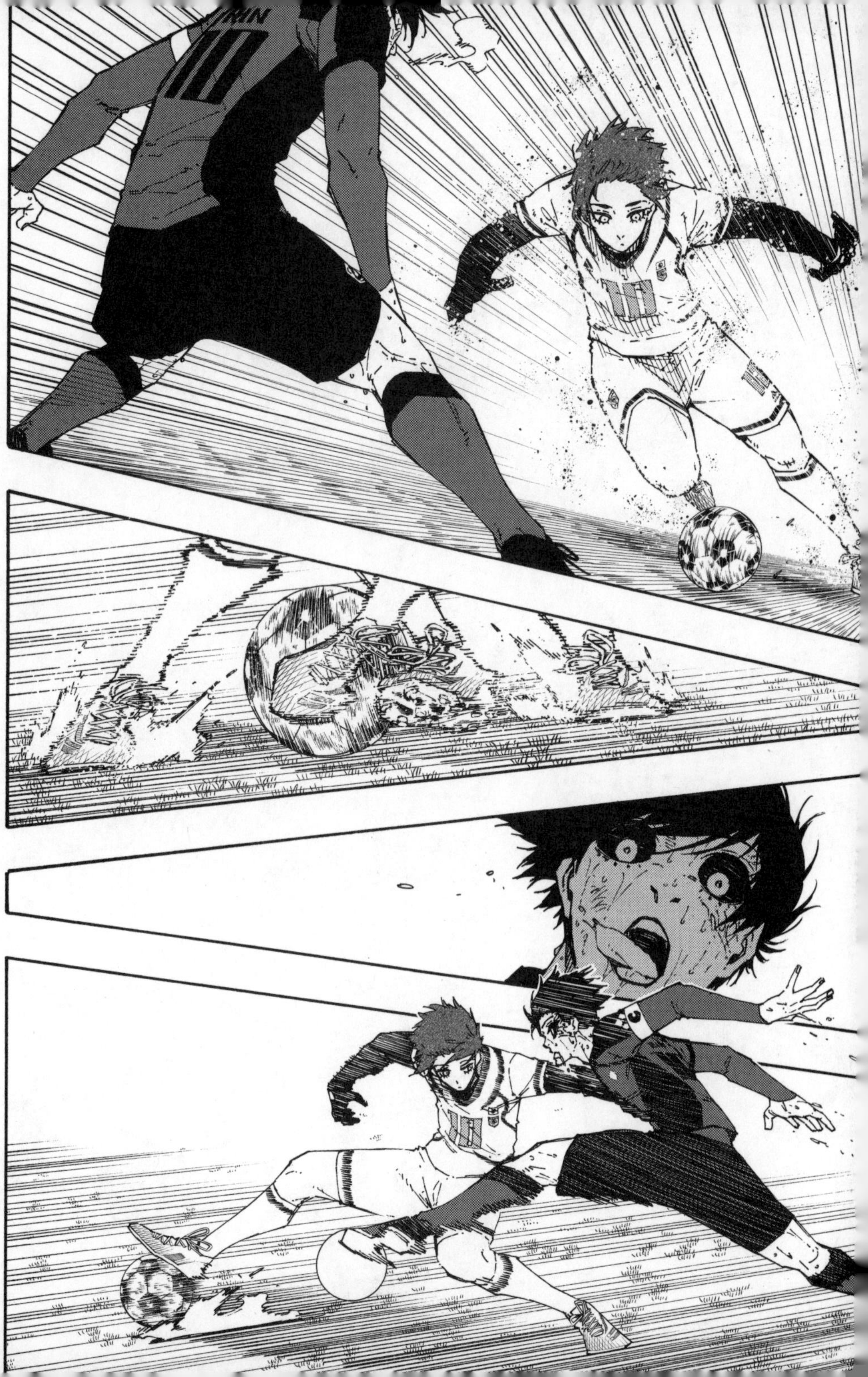

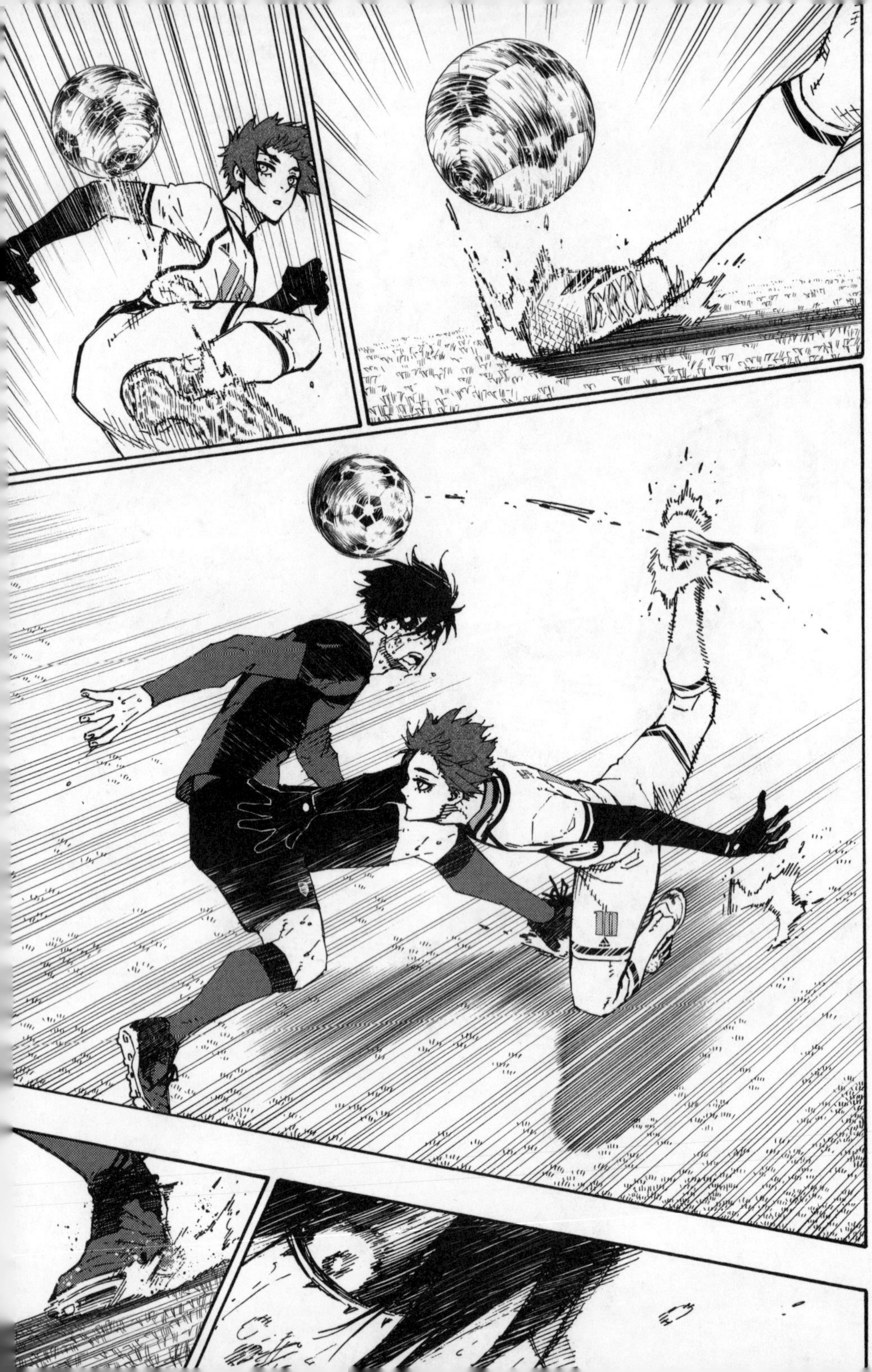

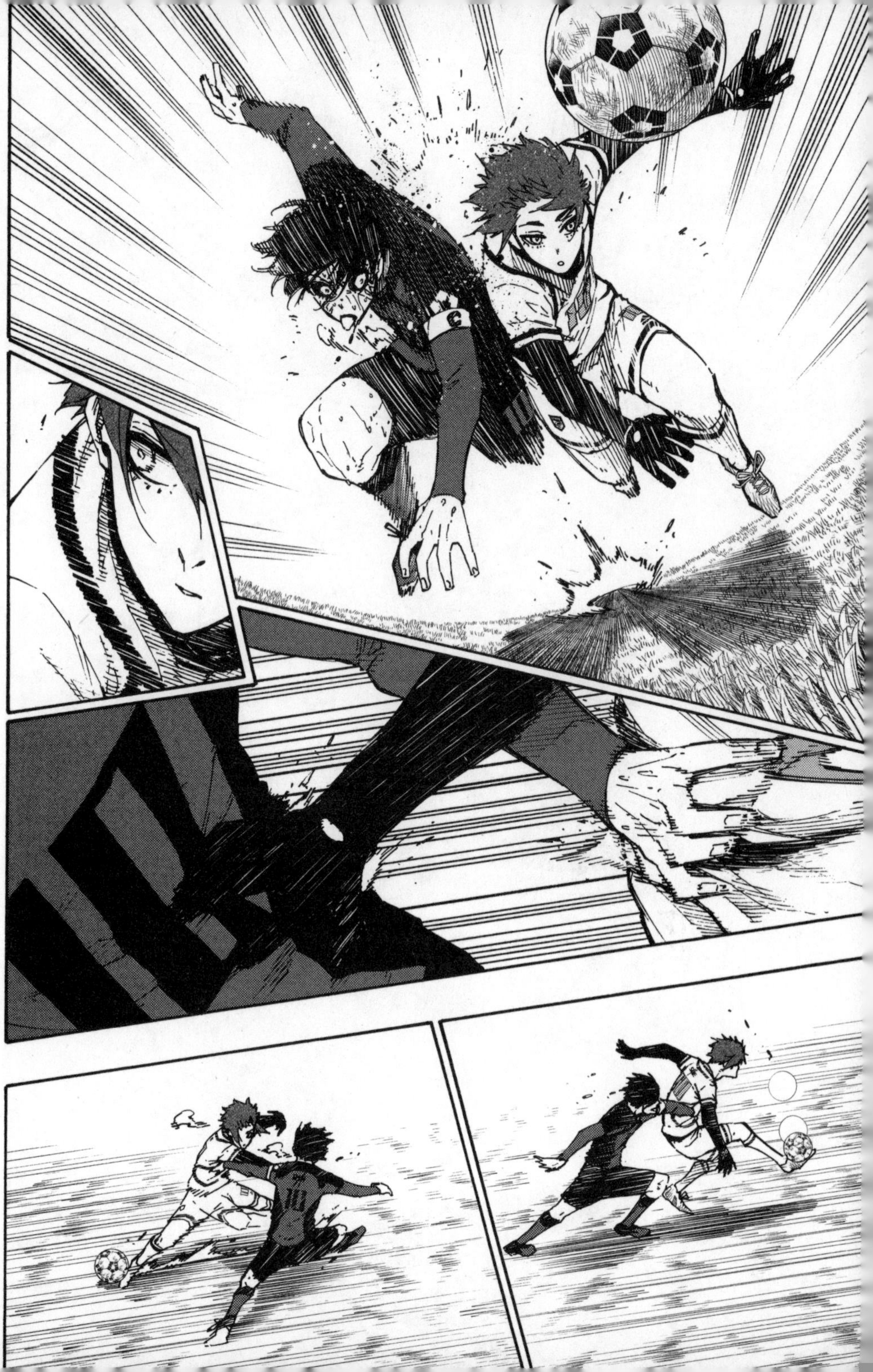

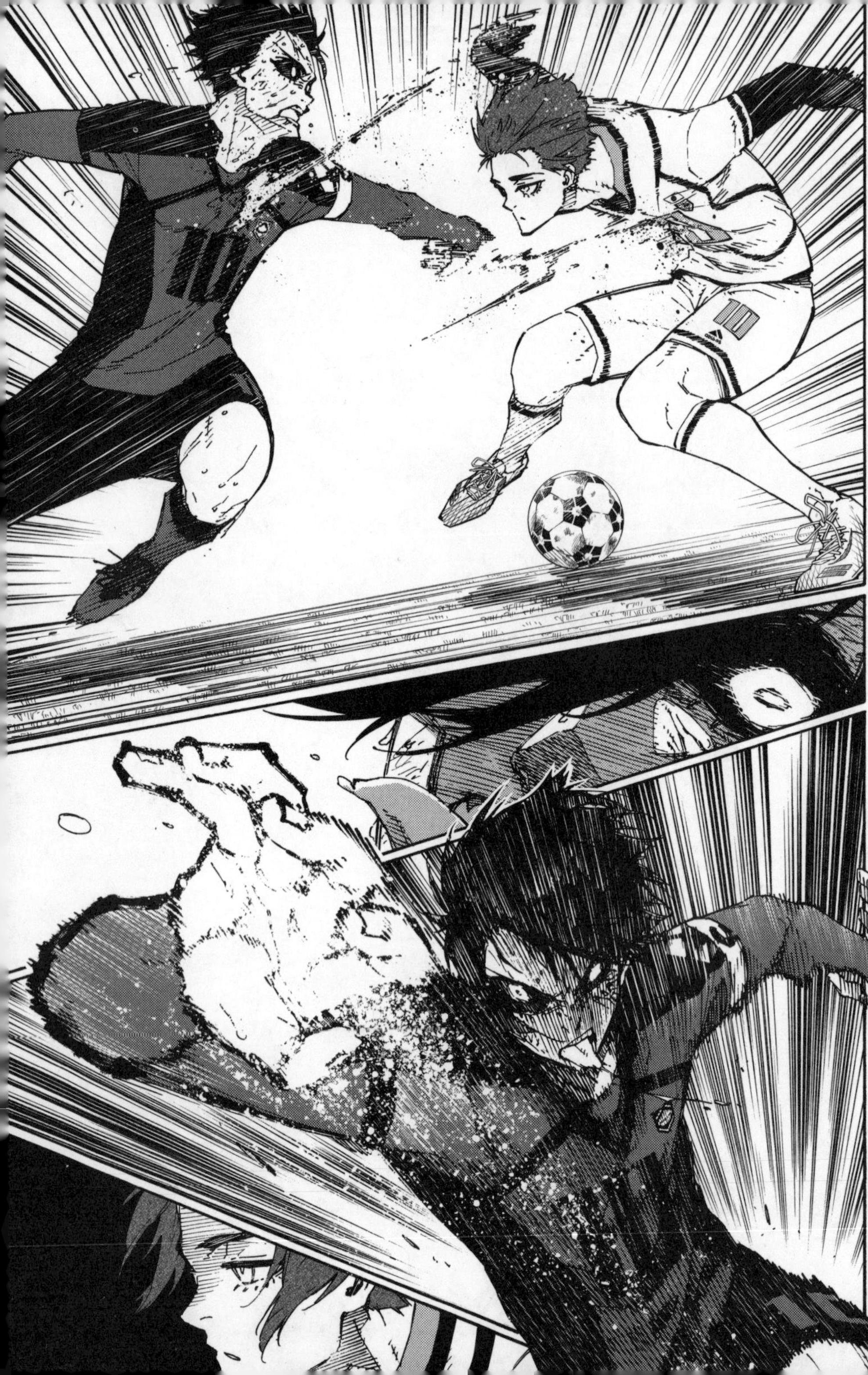

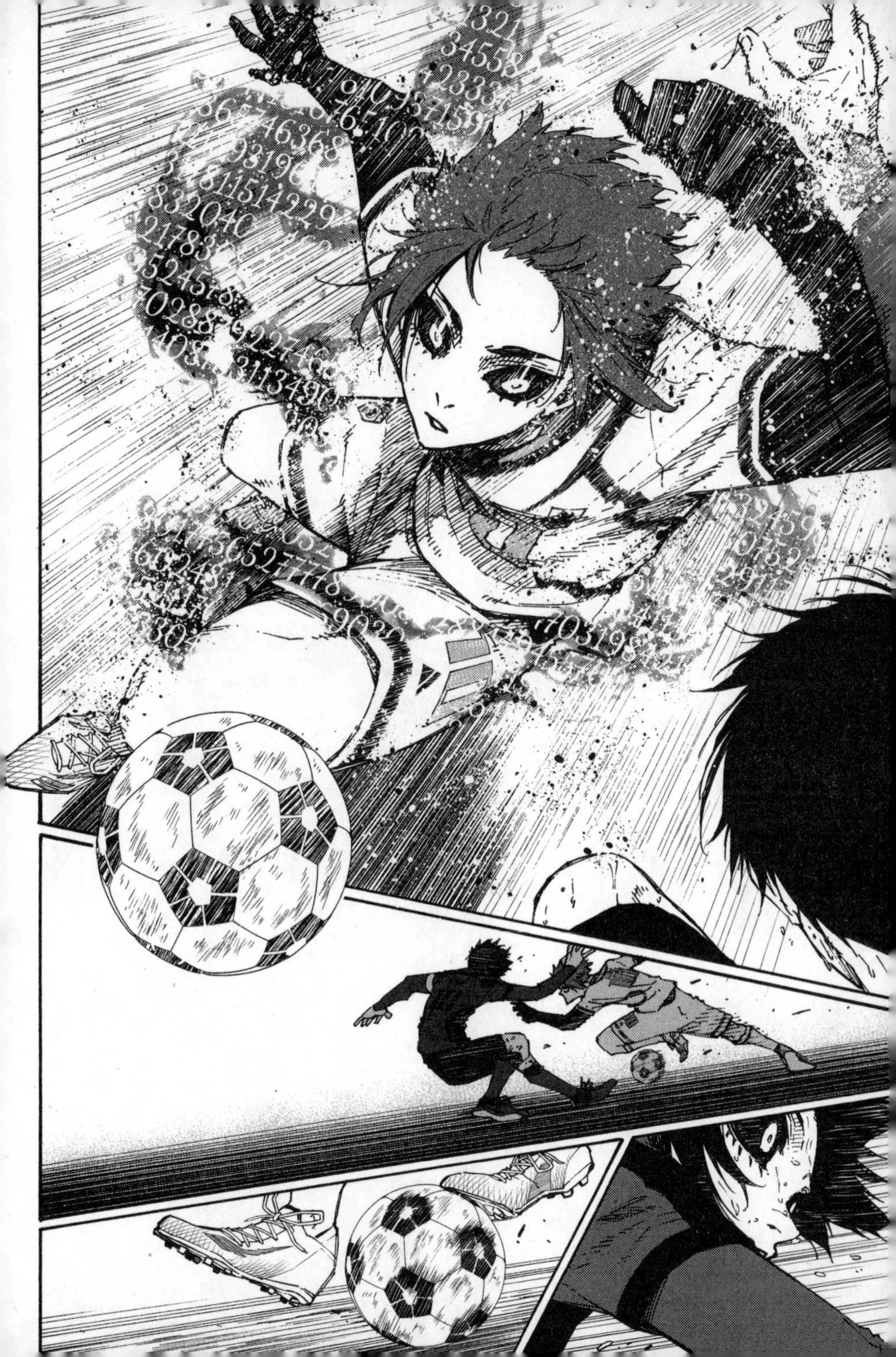

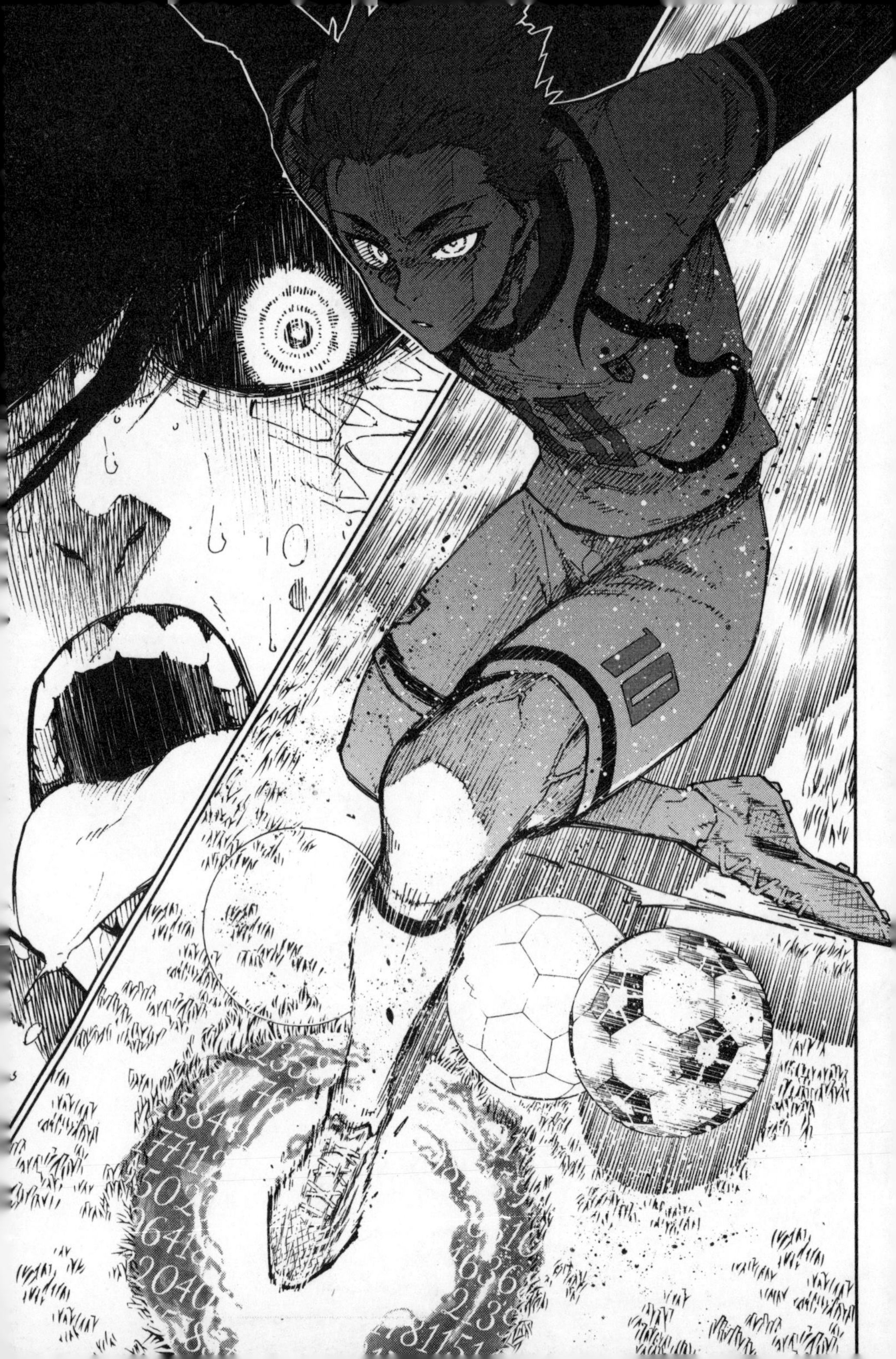

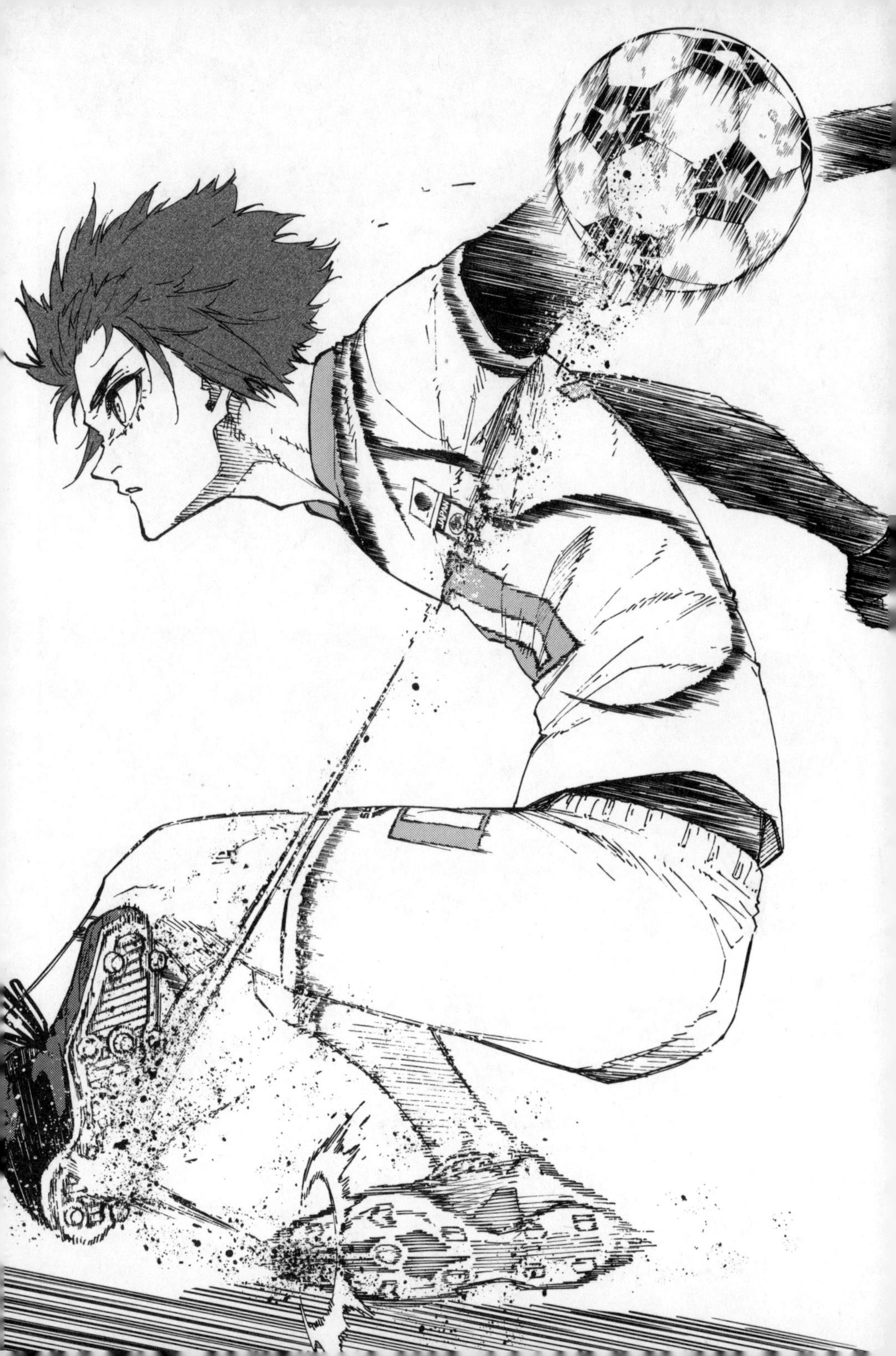

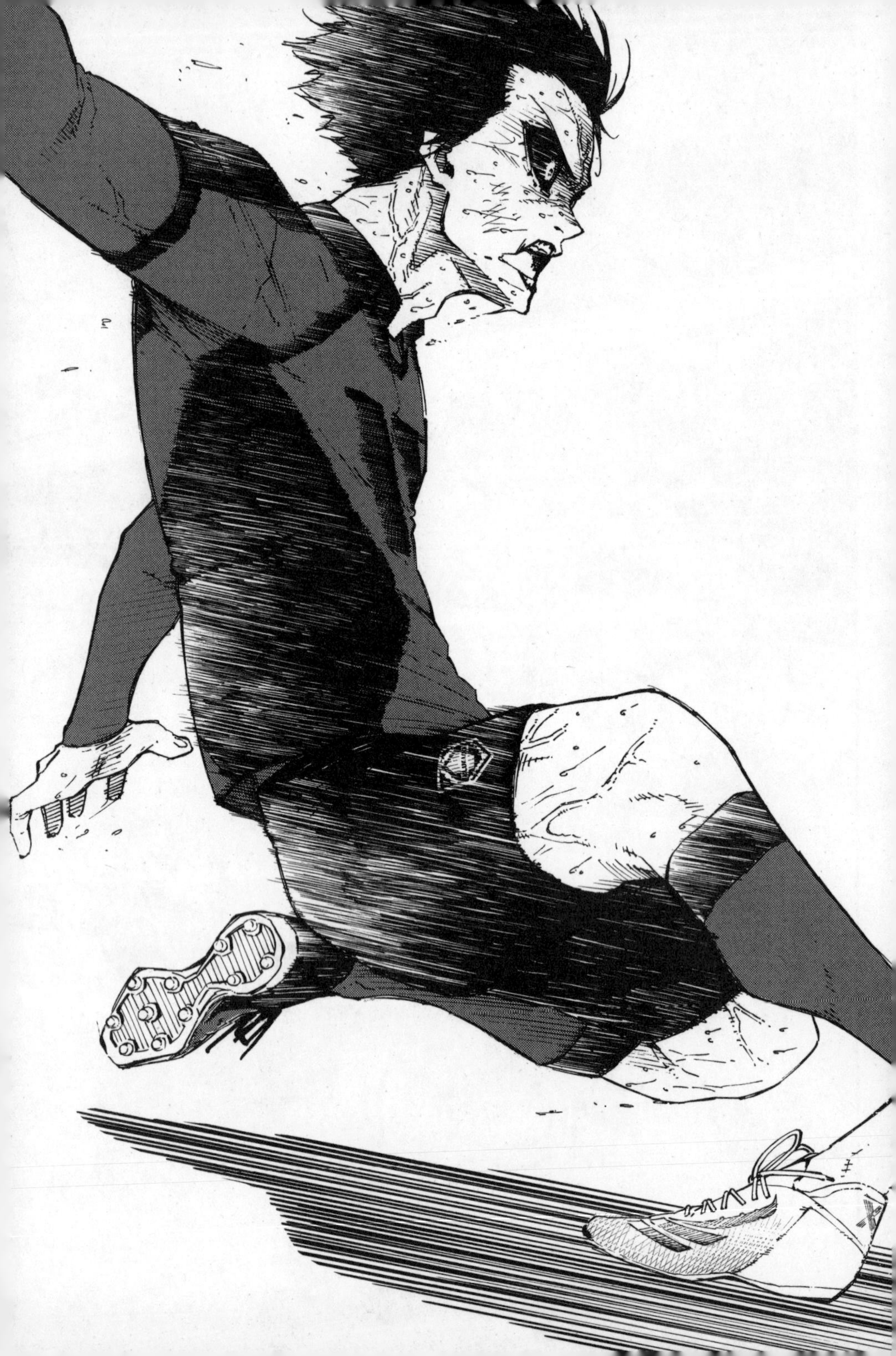

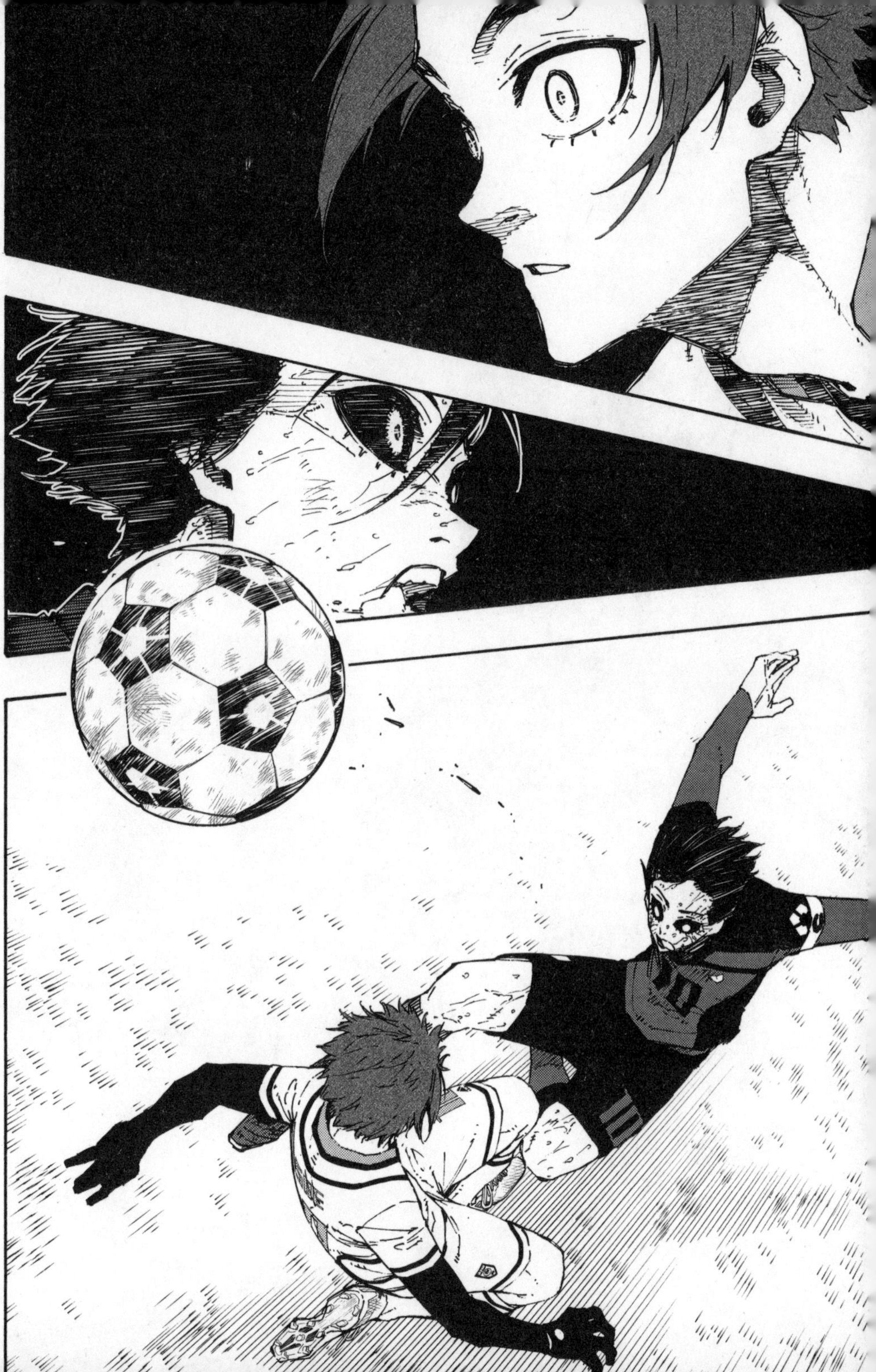

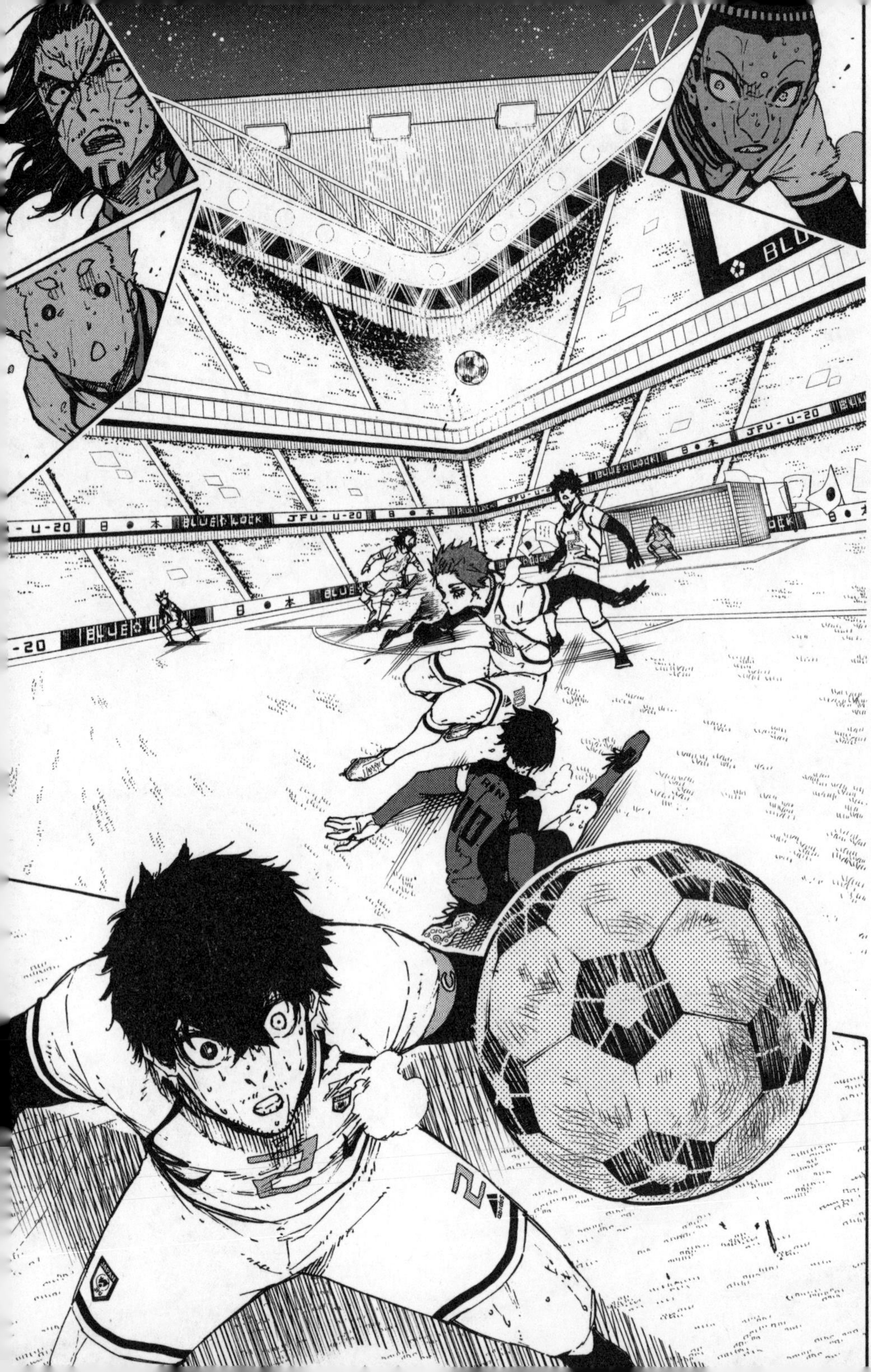
JFU-U-20
日 本
BLUE LOCK

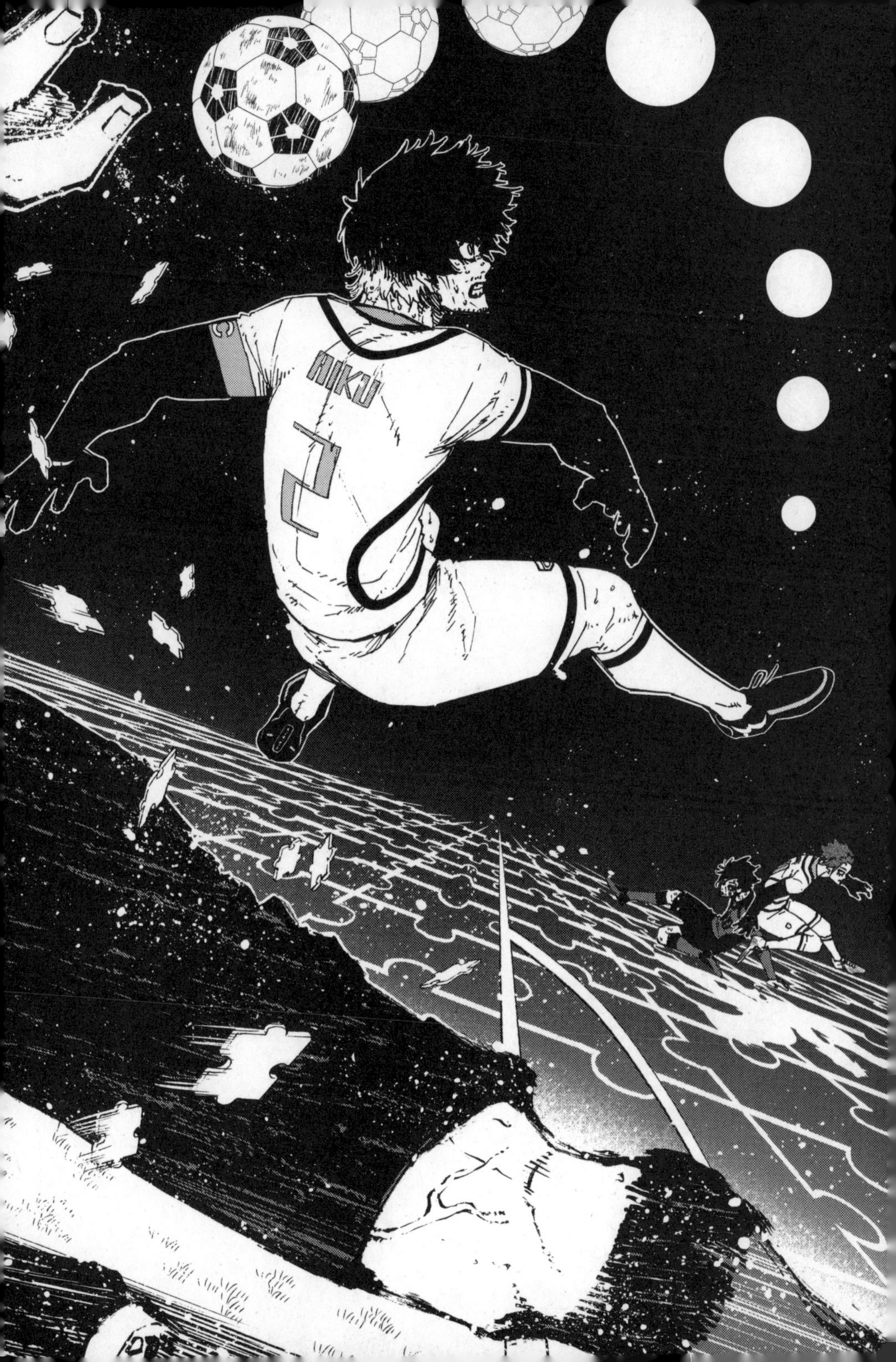

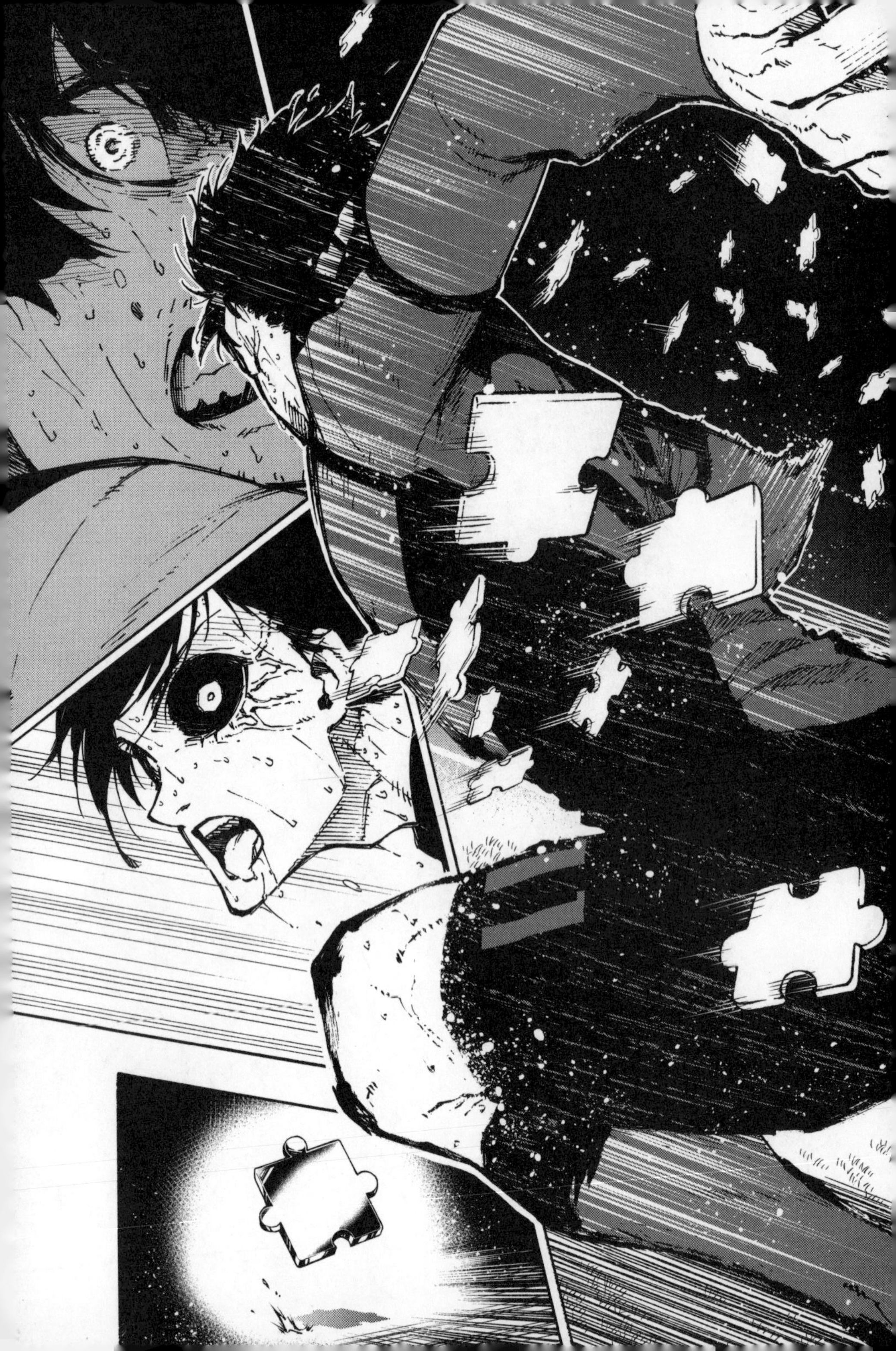

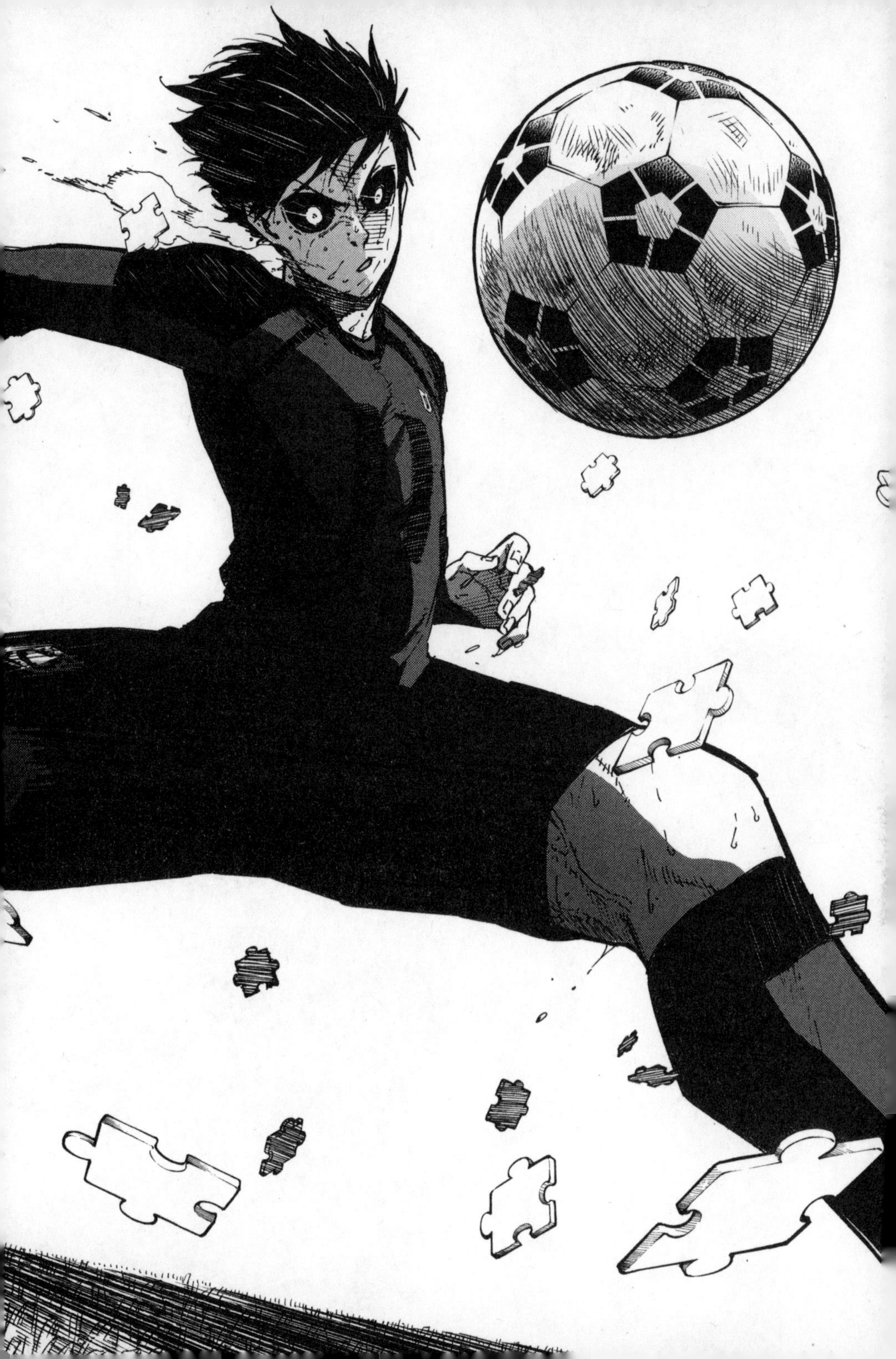

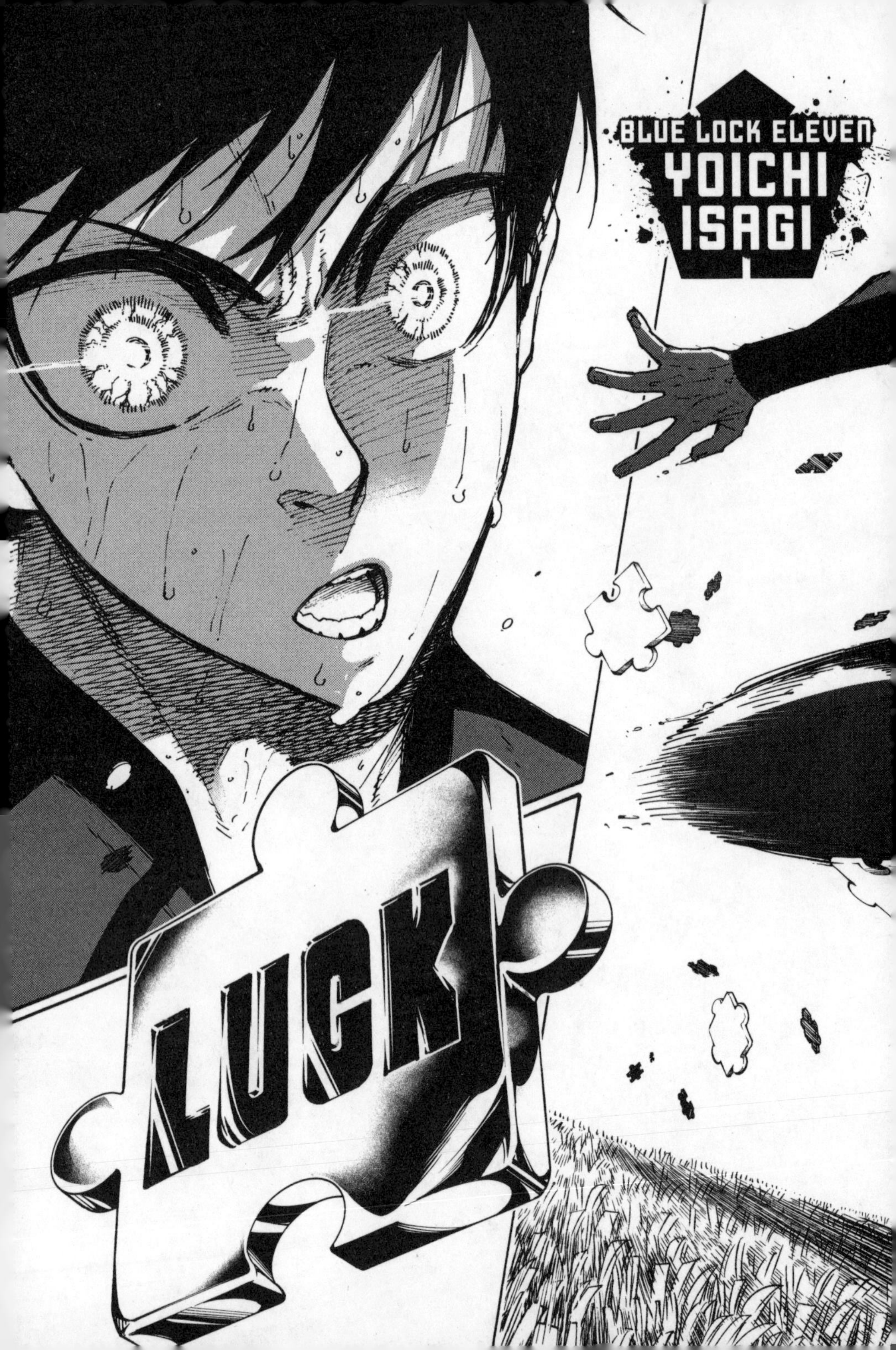
BLUE LOCK ELEVEN
YOICHI ISAGI
LUCK

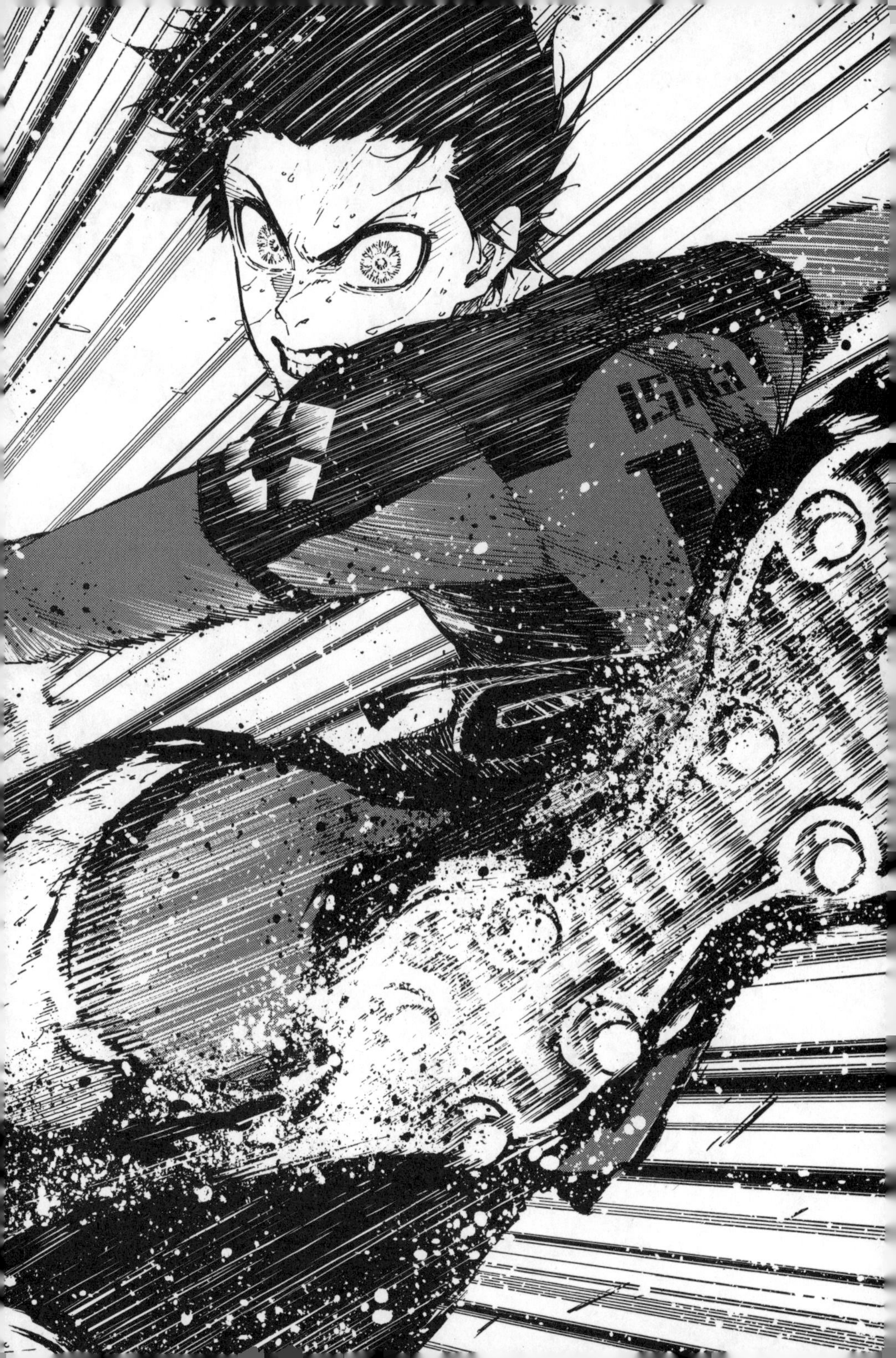

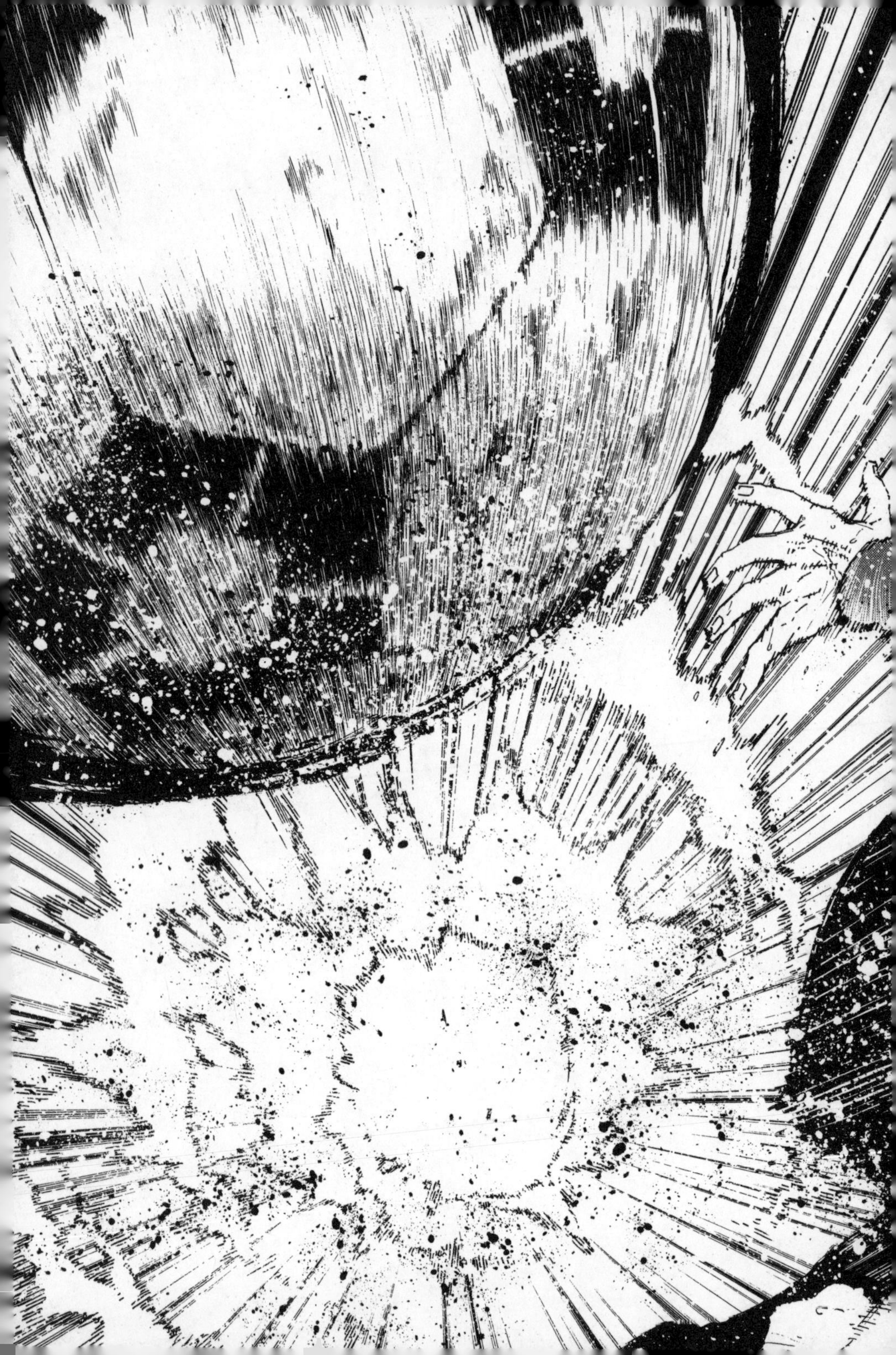

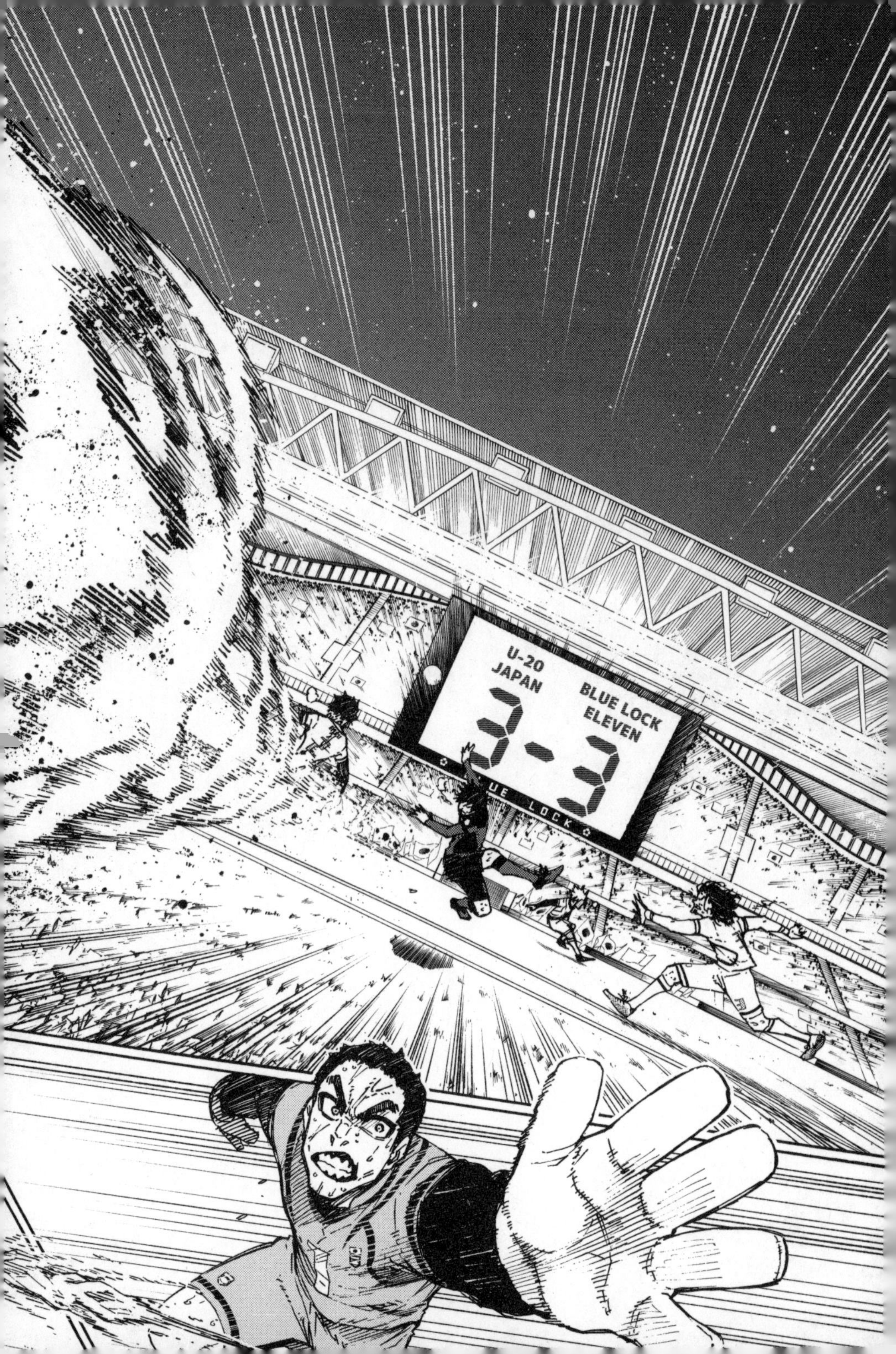
U-20
JAPAN
BLUE LOCK
ELEVEN
3 - 3
BLUE LOCK

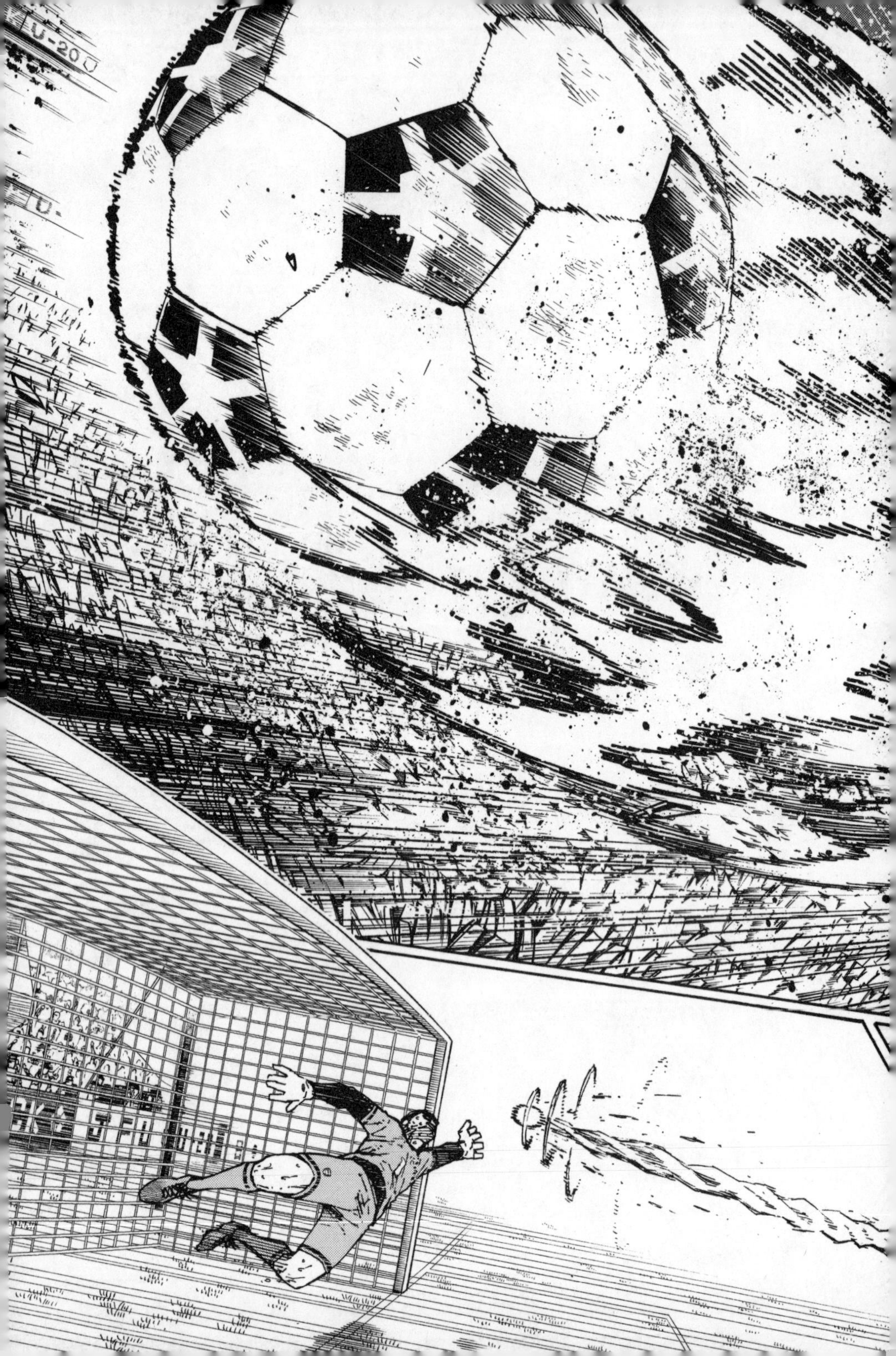
U-20

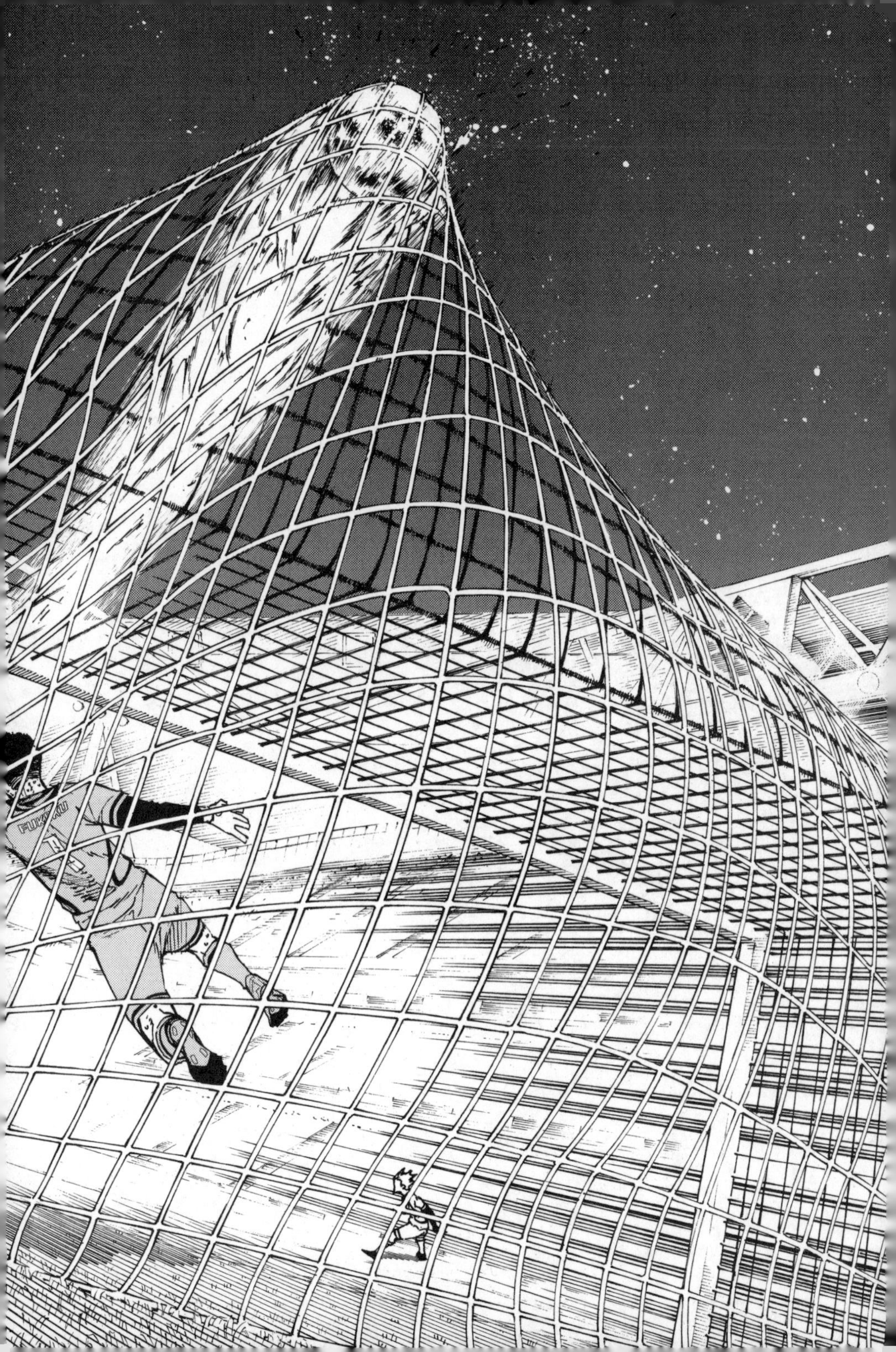

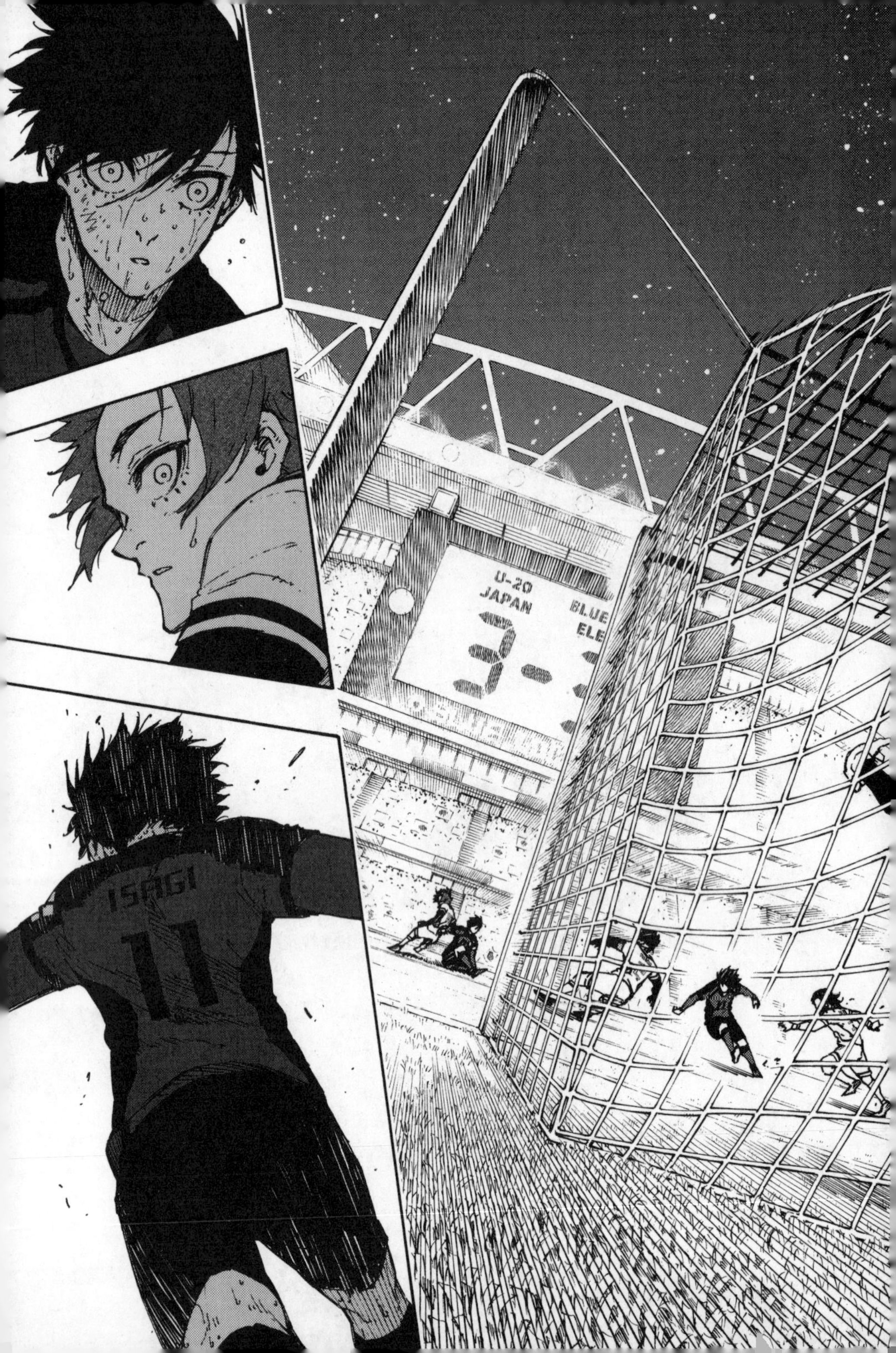
U-20
JAPAN
BLUE
ISAGI
11

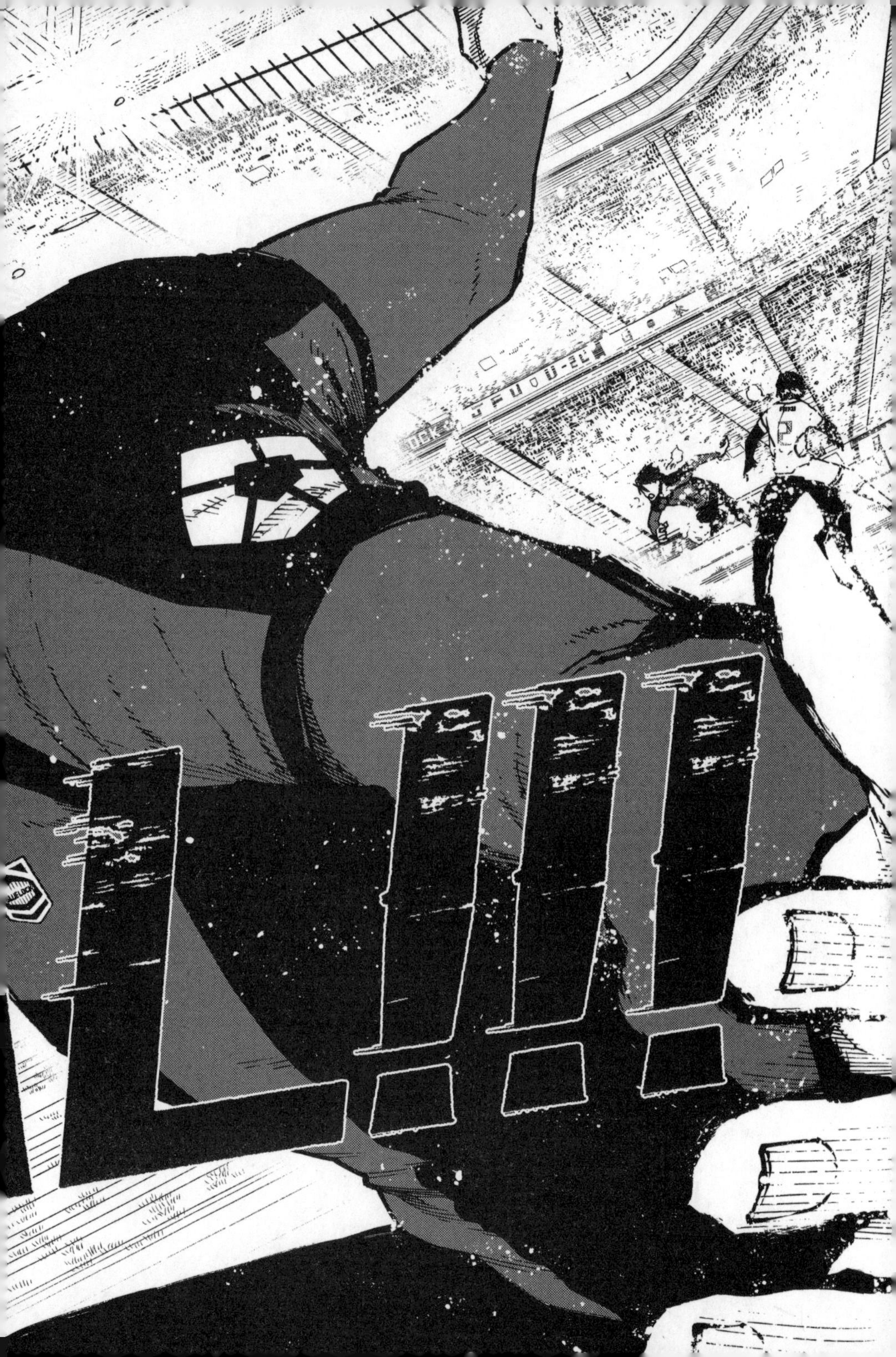

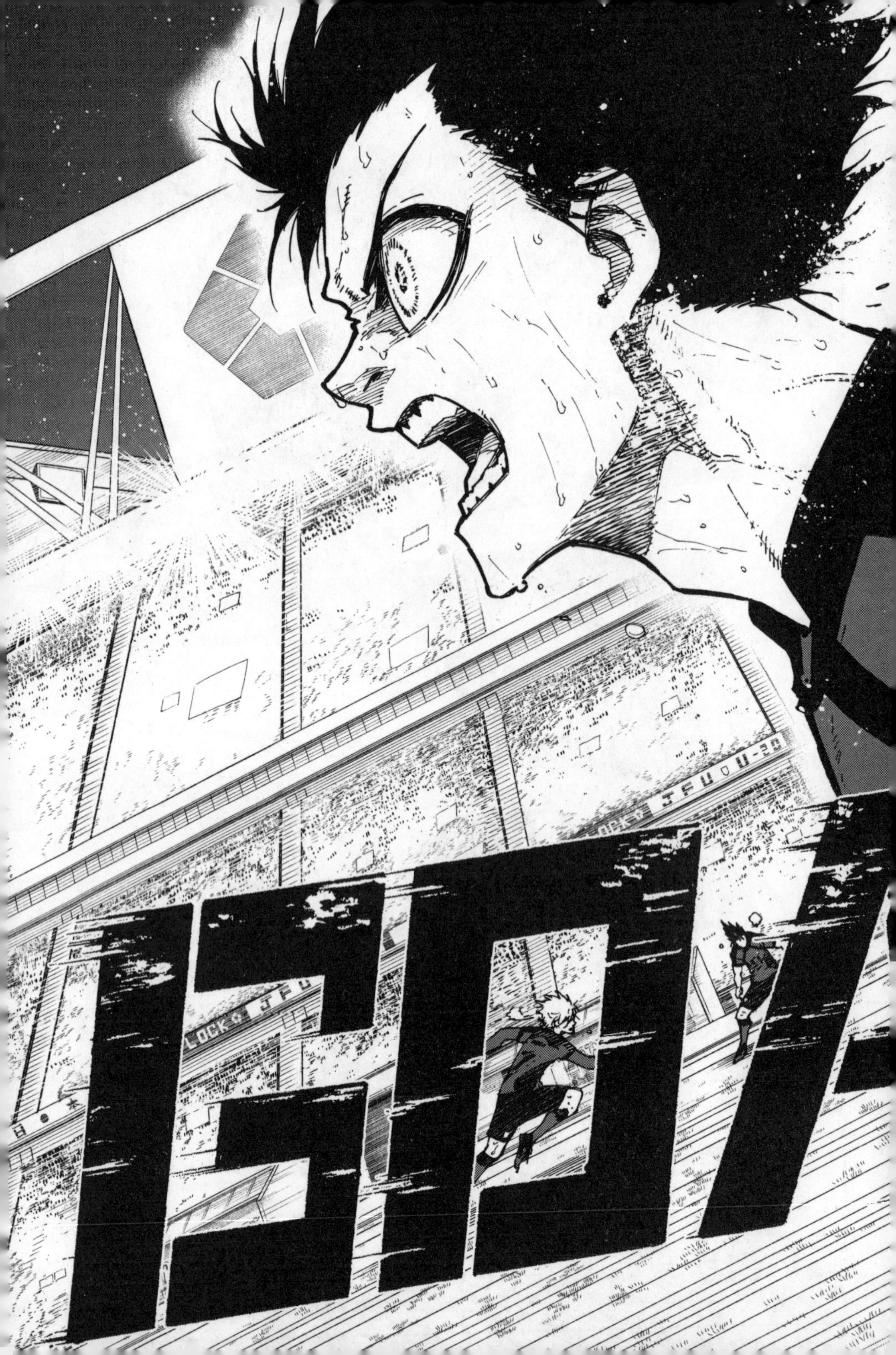
LOCK
JFU
U-20

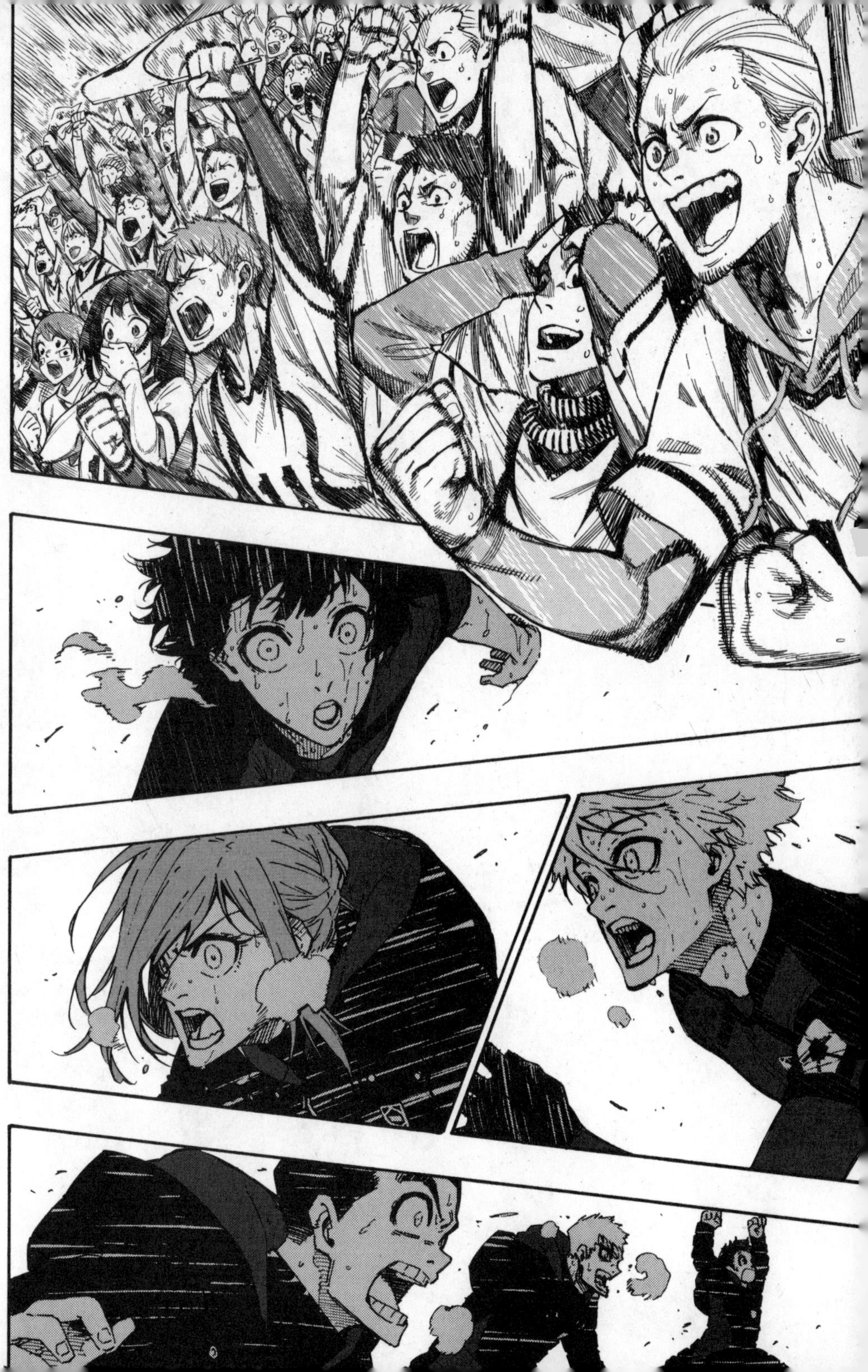

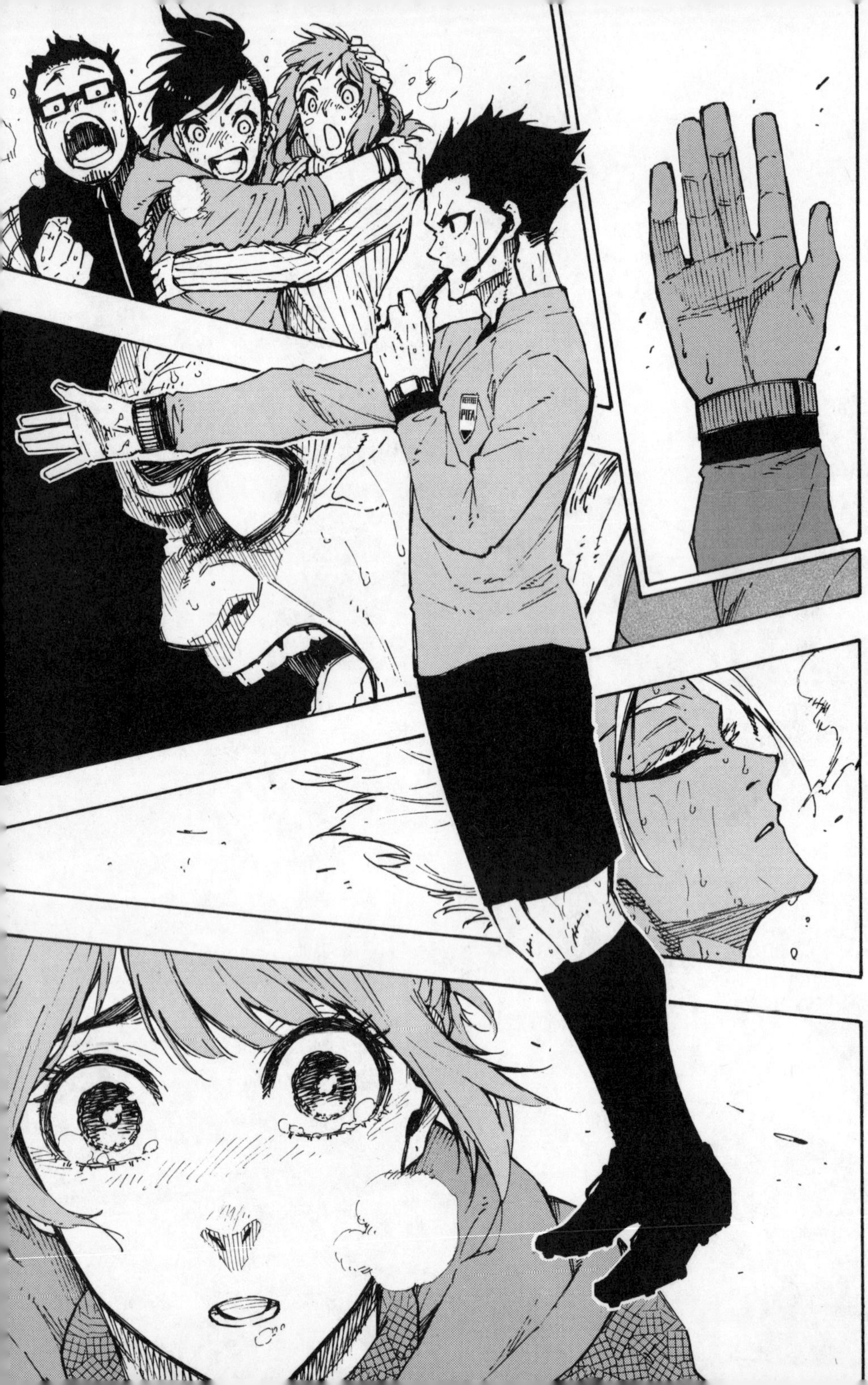
REFEREE
PIFA

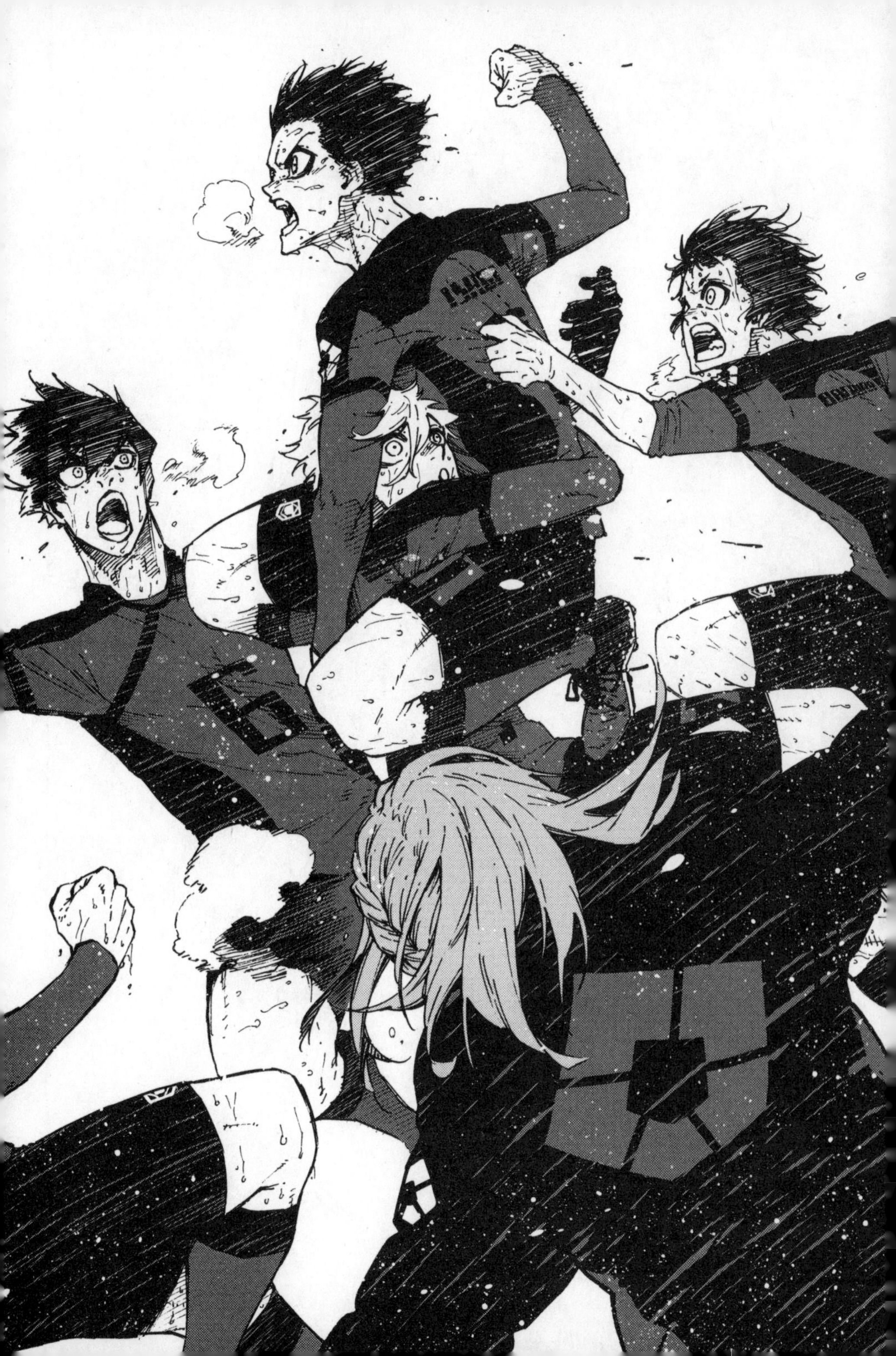

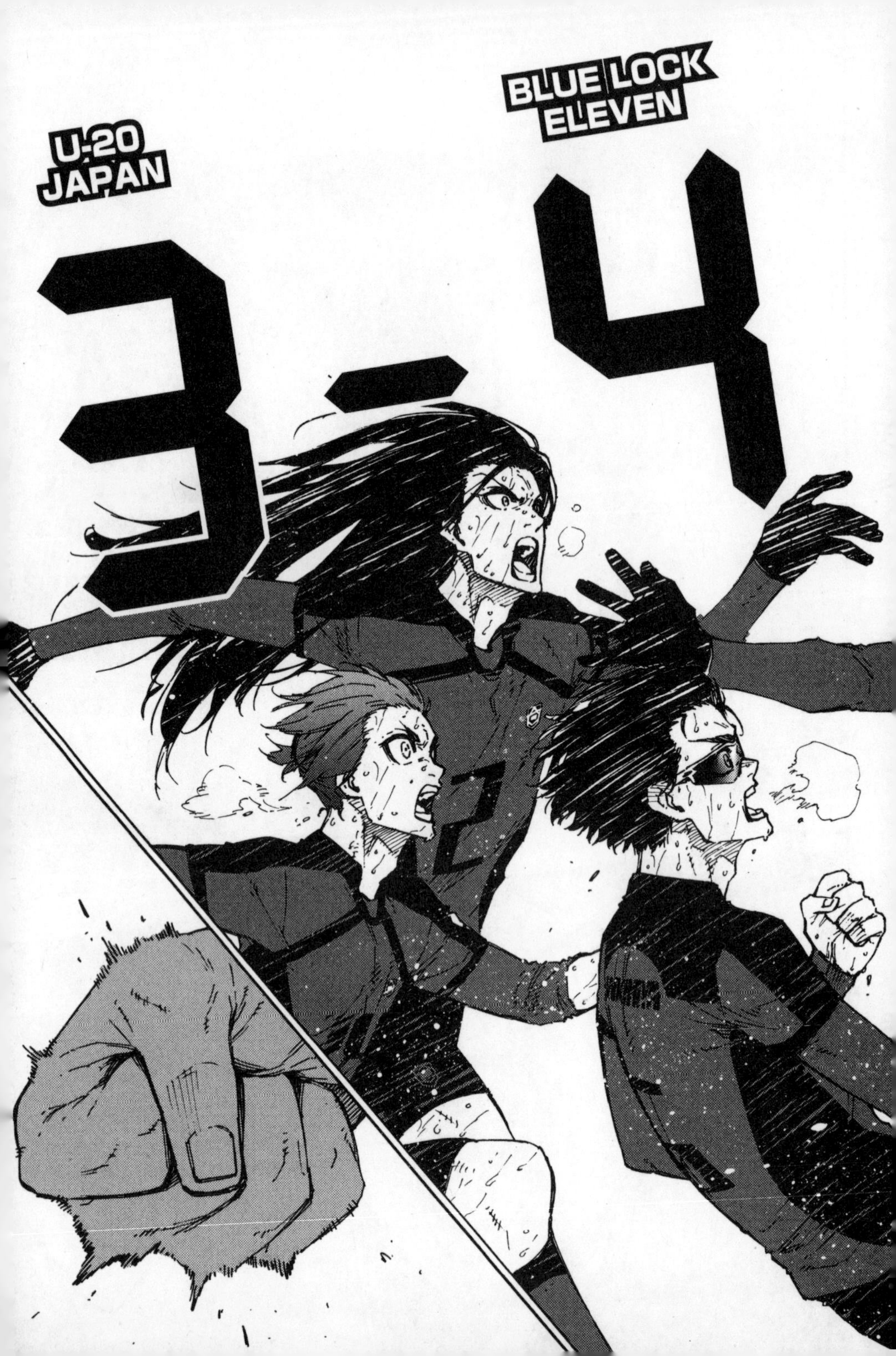
BLUE LOCK ELEVEN
U-20 JAPAN
3 - 4

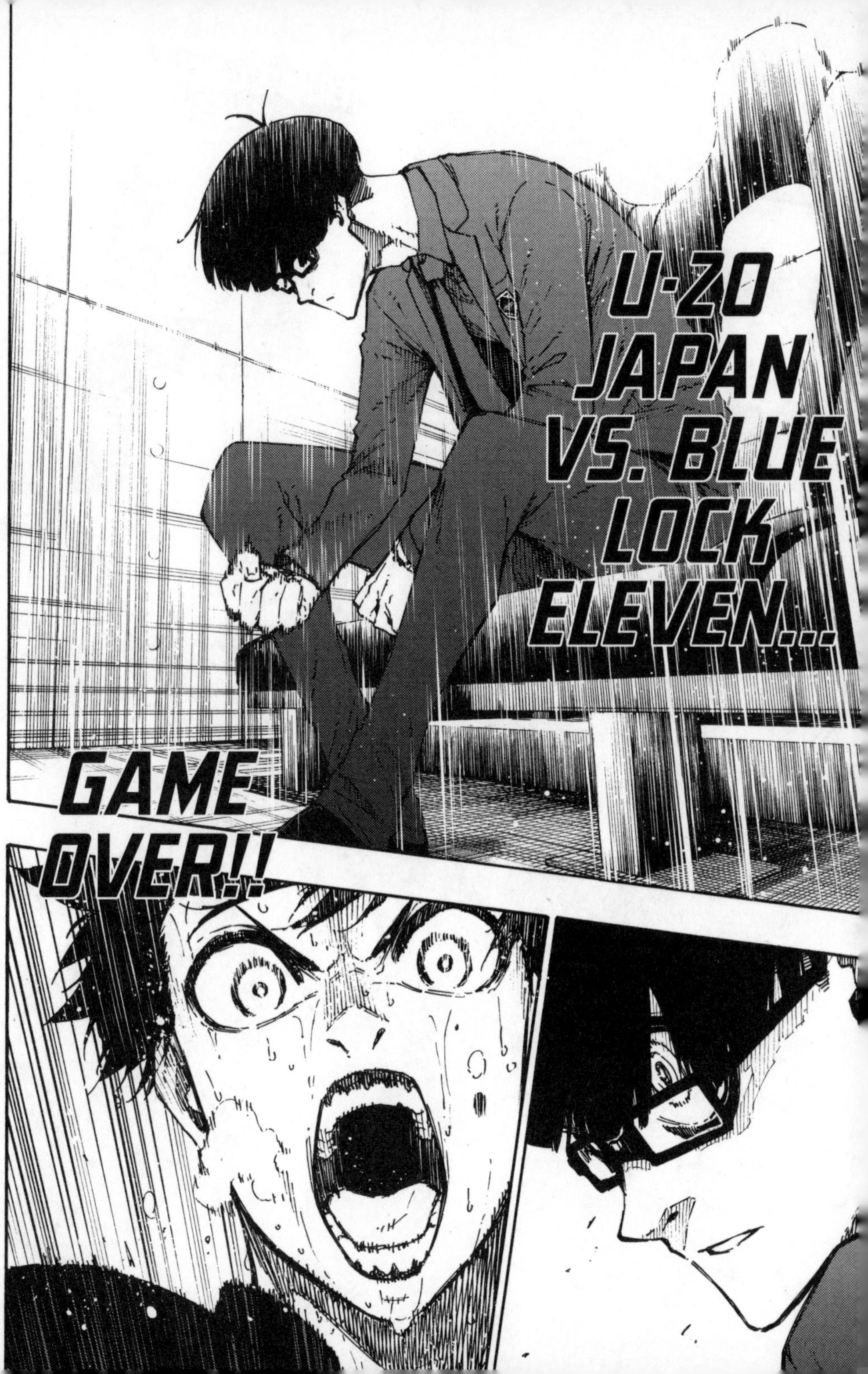
U-20 JAPAN VS. BLUE LOCK ELEVEN...
GAME OVER!!

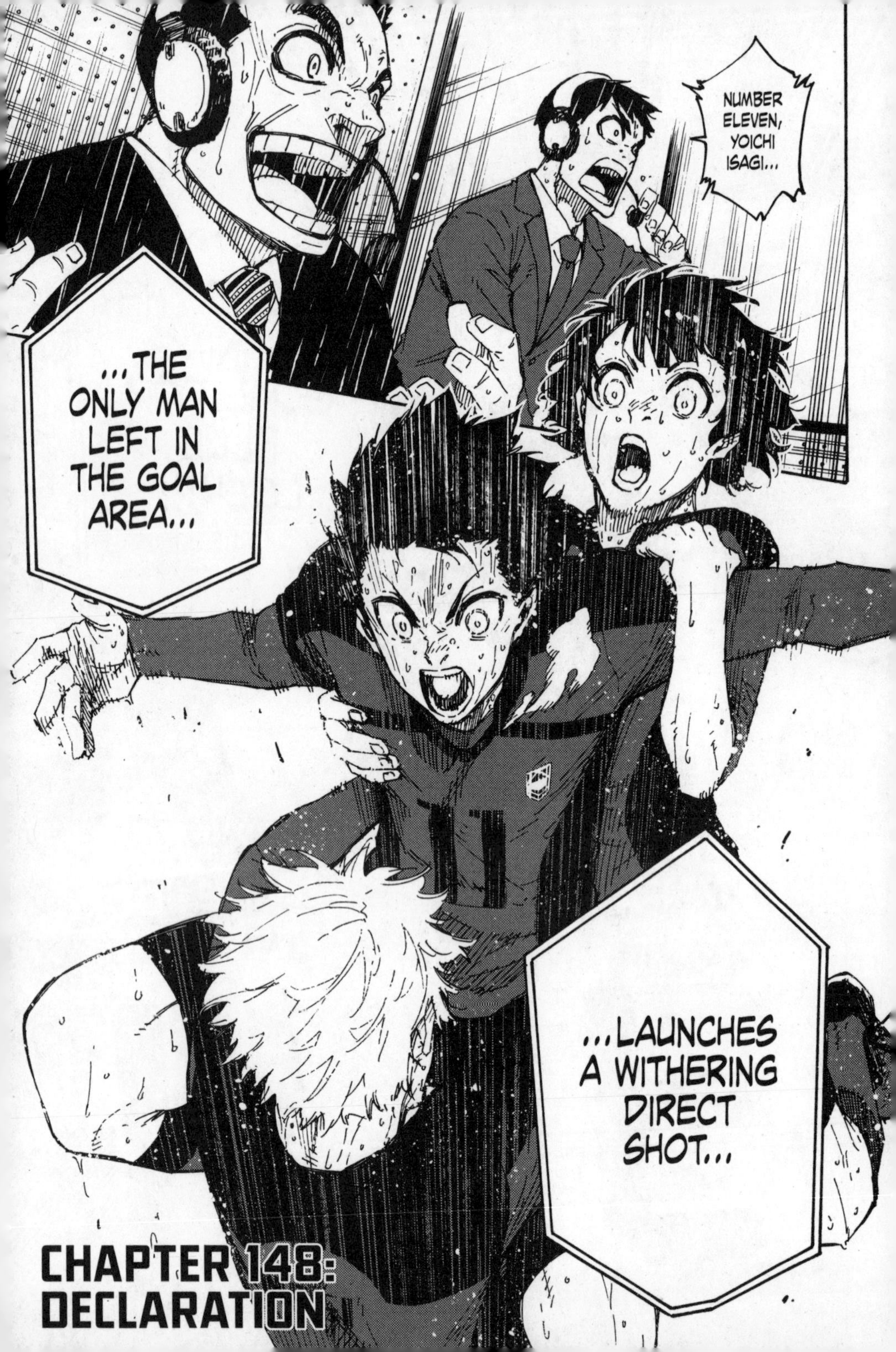
NUMBER ELEVEN, YOICHI ISAGI...
...THE ONLY MAN LEFT IN THE GOAL AREA...
...LAUNCHES A WITHERING DIRECT SHOT...
CHAPTER 148: DECLARATION

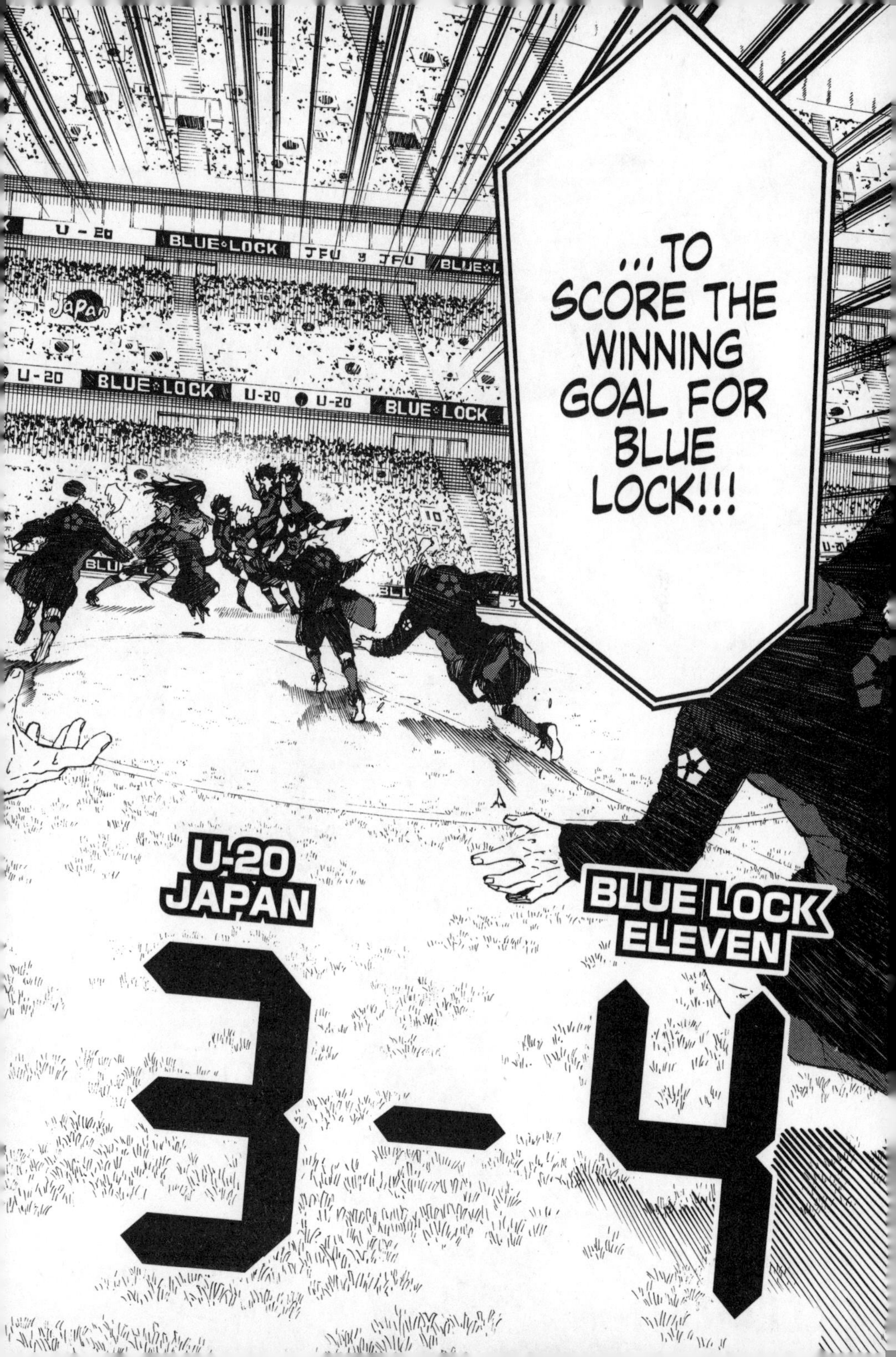
...TO SCORE THE WINNING GOAL FOR BLUE LOCK!!!
U-20 JAPAN
BLUE LOCK ELEVEN
3-4

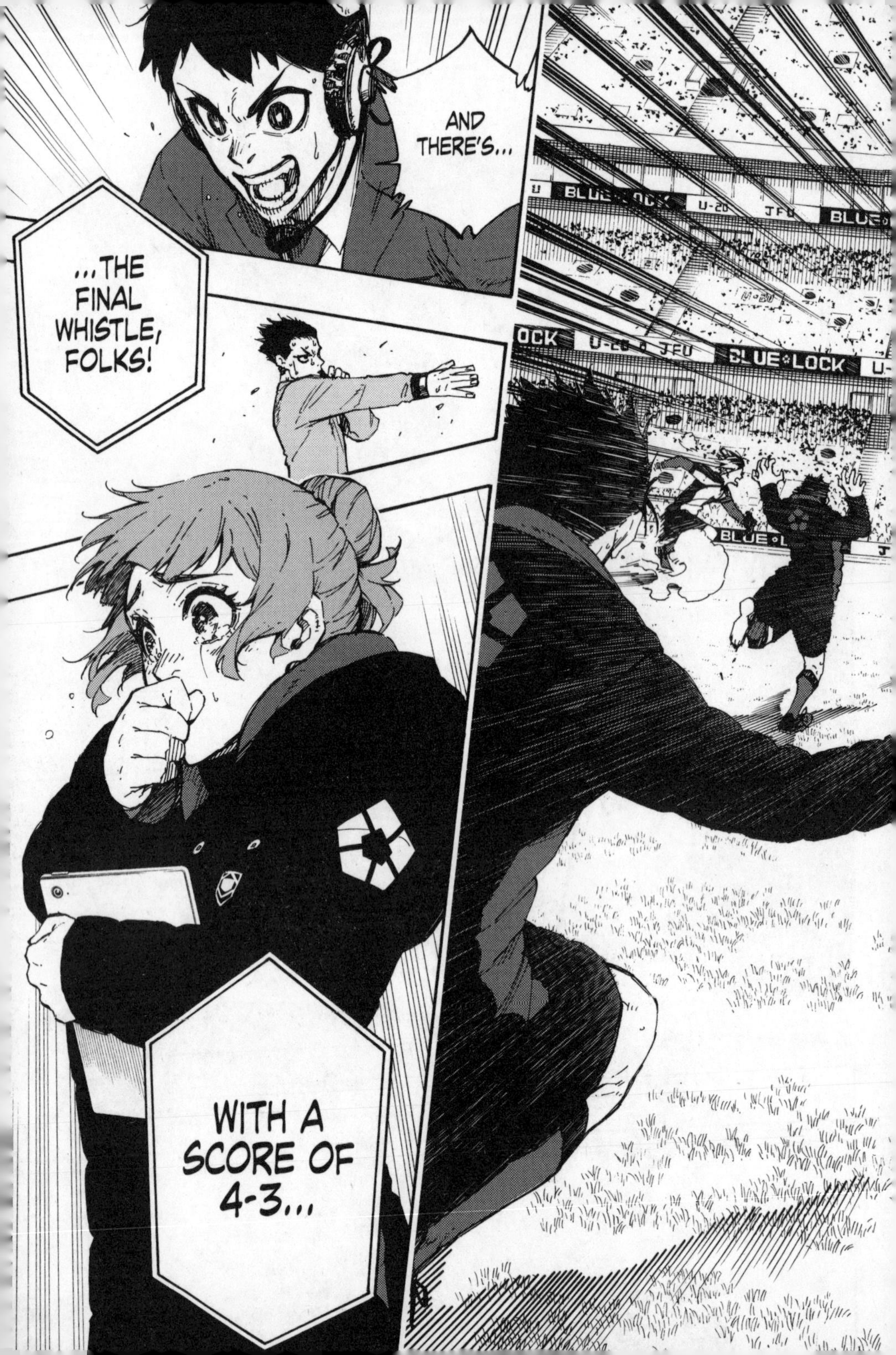

BLUE LOCK
U-20
JFU
AND THERE'S...
...THE FINAL WHISTLE, FOLKS!
WITH A SCORE OF 4-3...

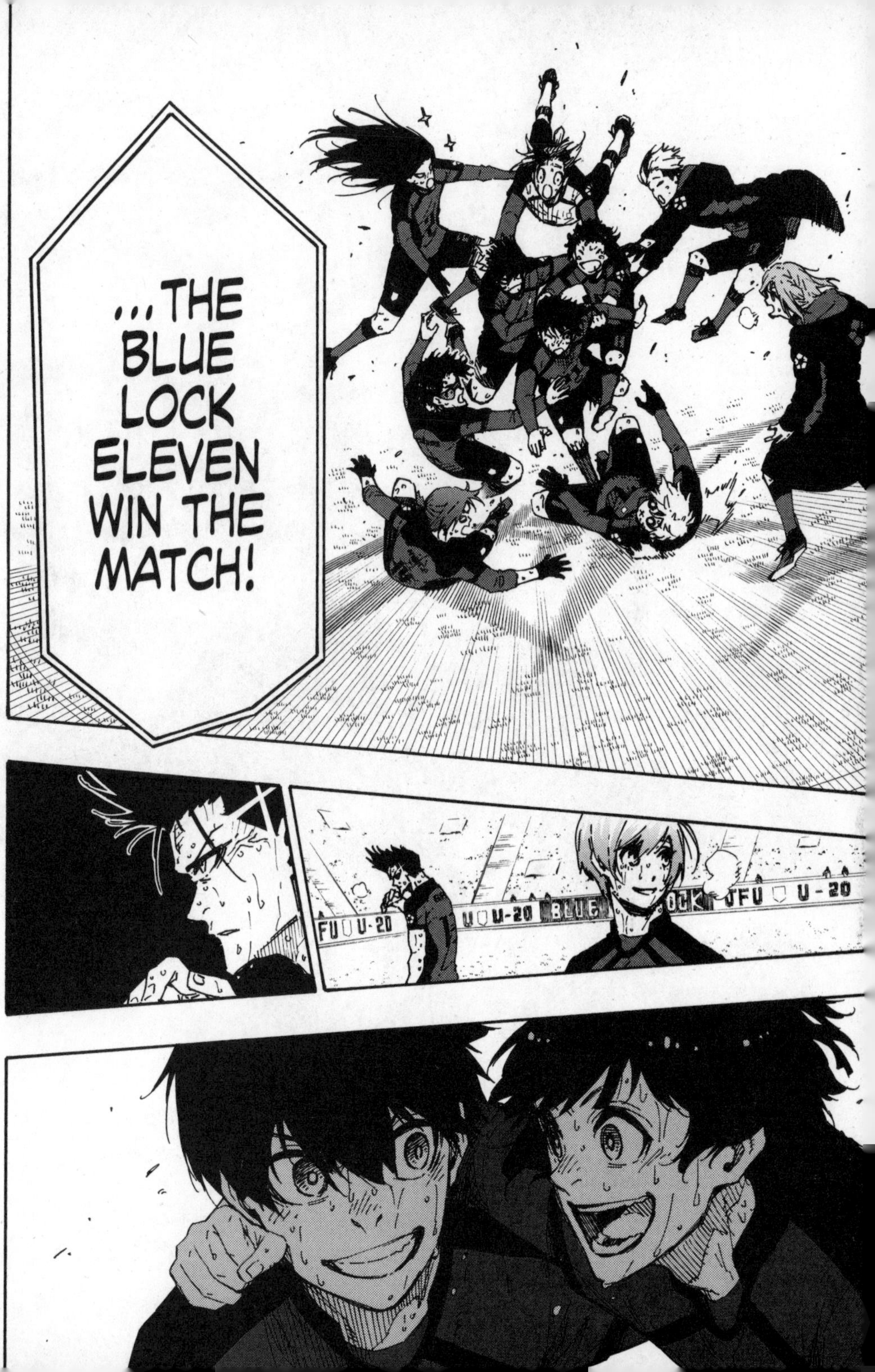
...THE BLUE LOCK ELEVEN WIN THE MATCH!

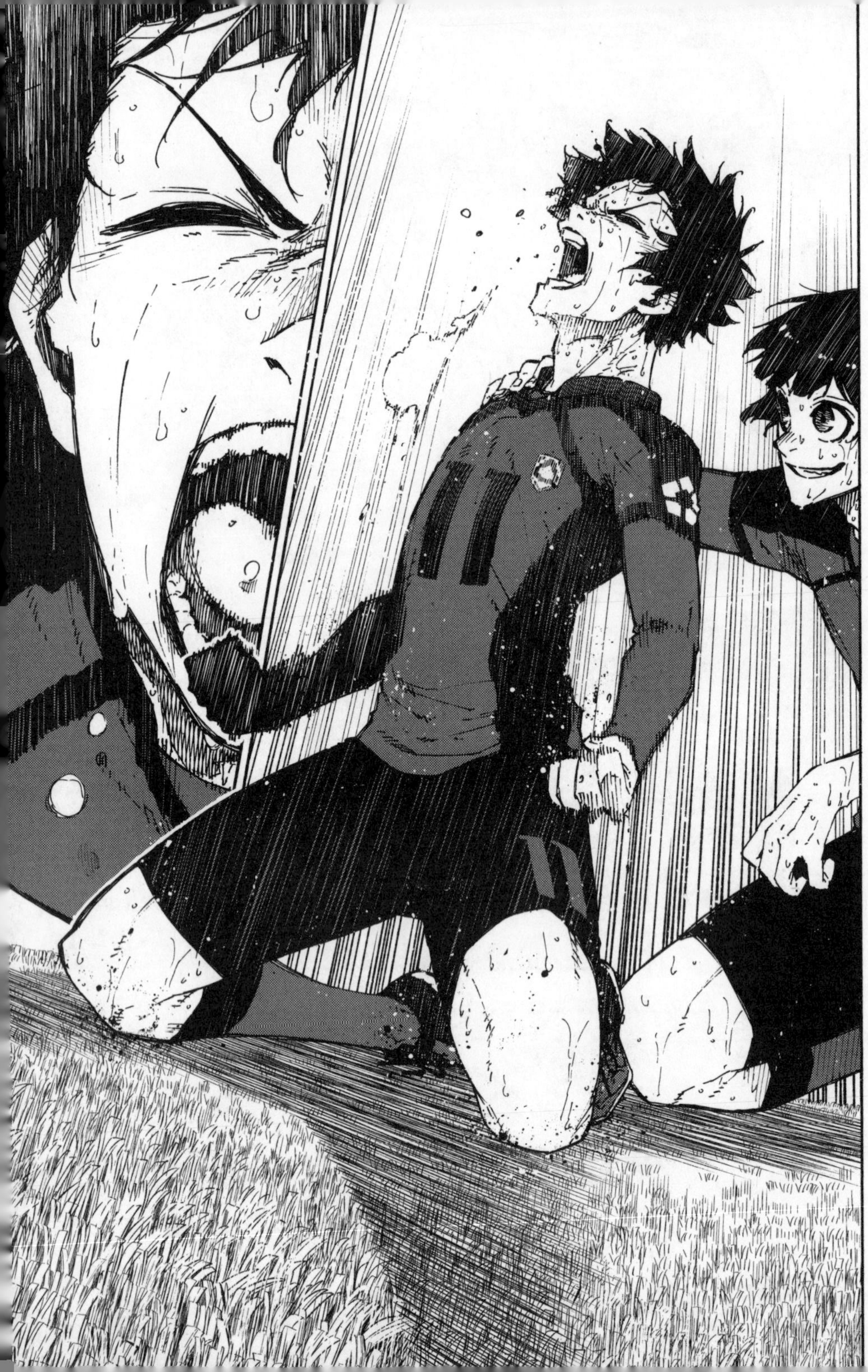

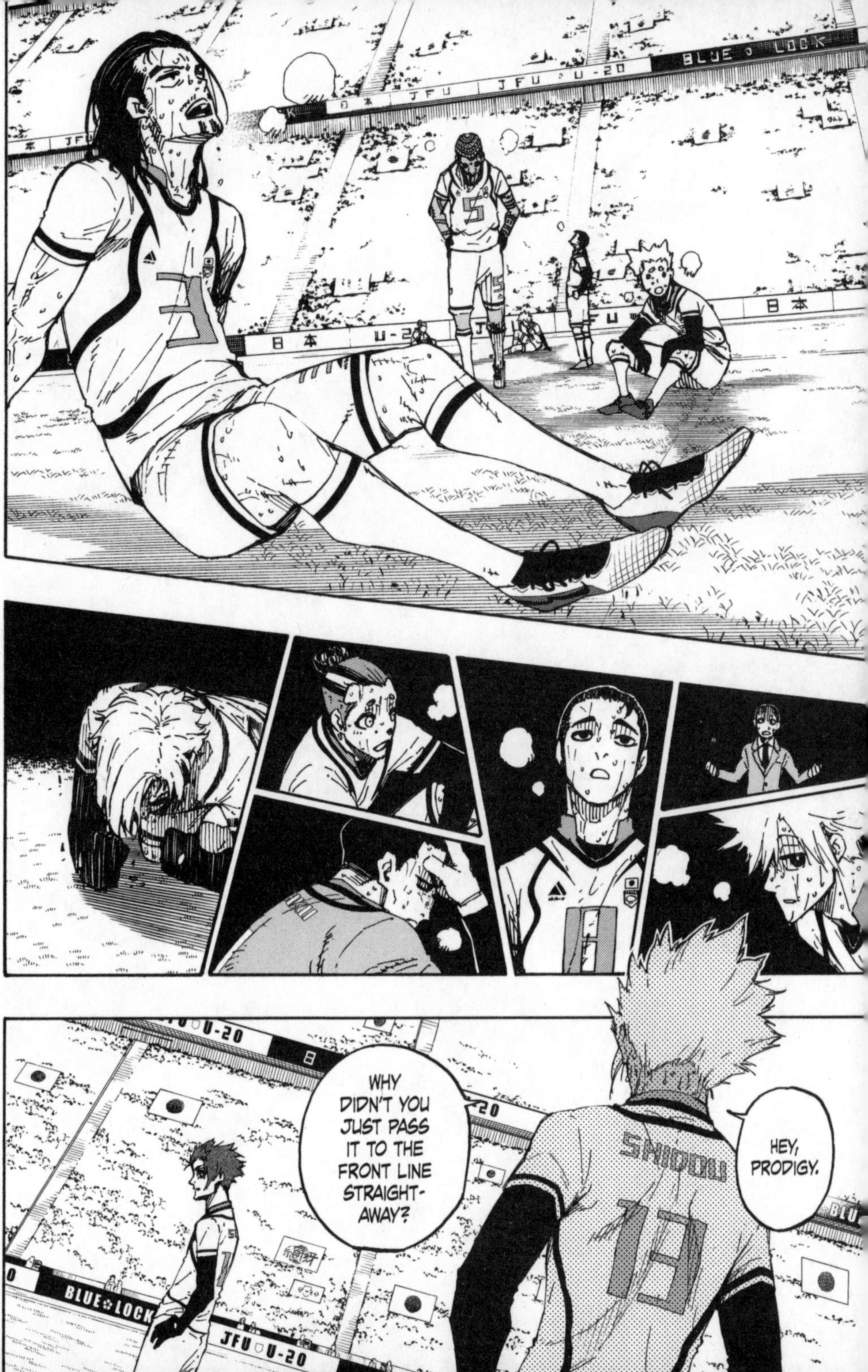
HEY, PRODIGY.
WHY DIDN'T YOU JUST PASS IT TO THE FRONT LINE STRAIGHT-AWAY?

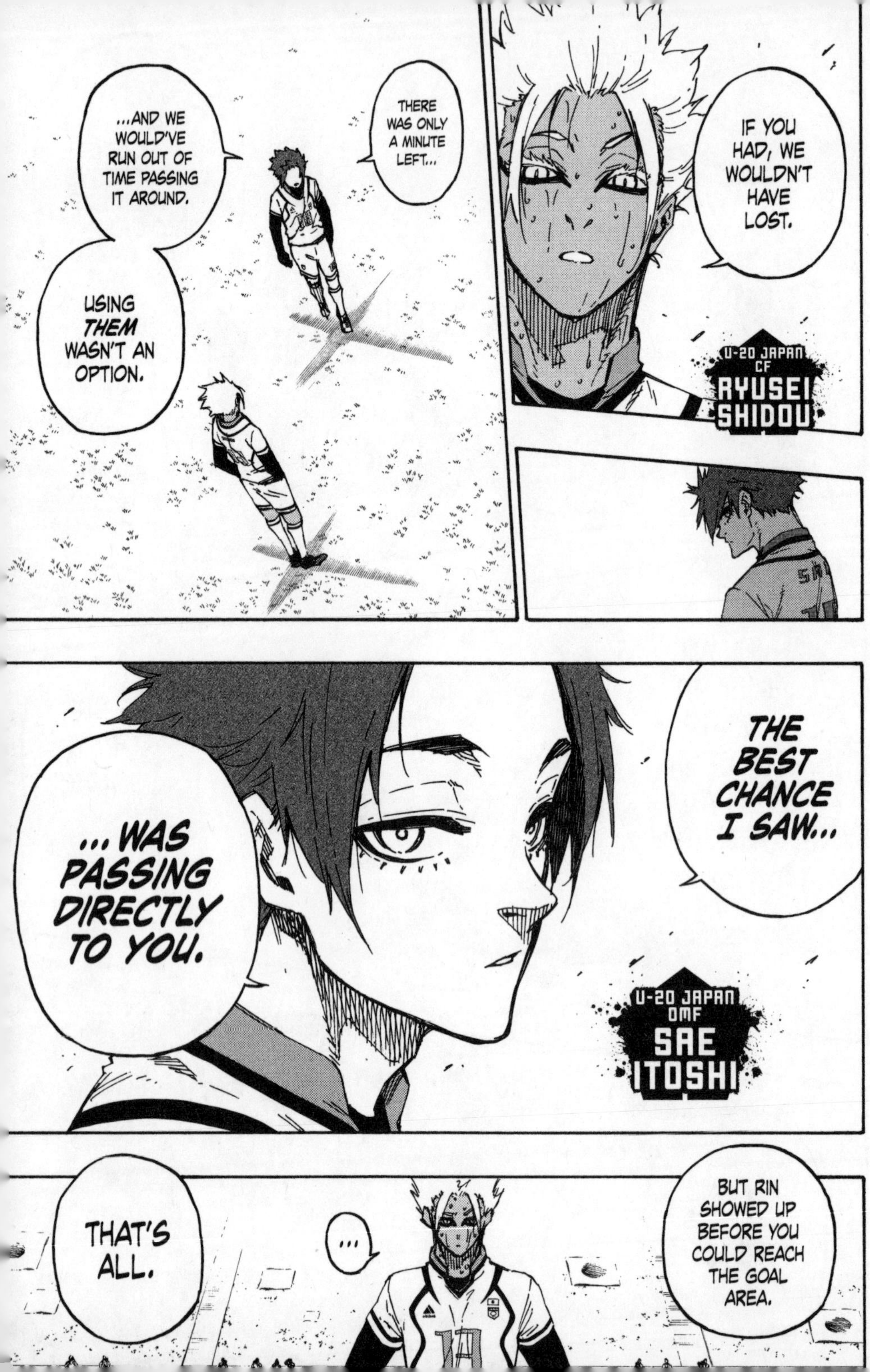
IF YOU HAD, WE WOULDN'T HAVE LOST.
U-20 JAPAN CF
RYUSEI SHIDOU
THERE WAS ONLY A MINUTE LEFT...
...AND WE WOULD'VE RUN OUT OF TIME PASSING IT AROUND.
USING *THEM* WASN'T AN OPTION.
THE BEST CHANCE I SAW...
...WAS PASSING DIRECTLY TO YOU.
U-20 JAPAN OMF
SAE ITOSHI
BUT RIN SHOWED UP BEFORE YOU COULD REACH THE GOAL AREA.
...
THAT'S ALL.

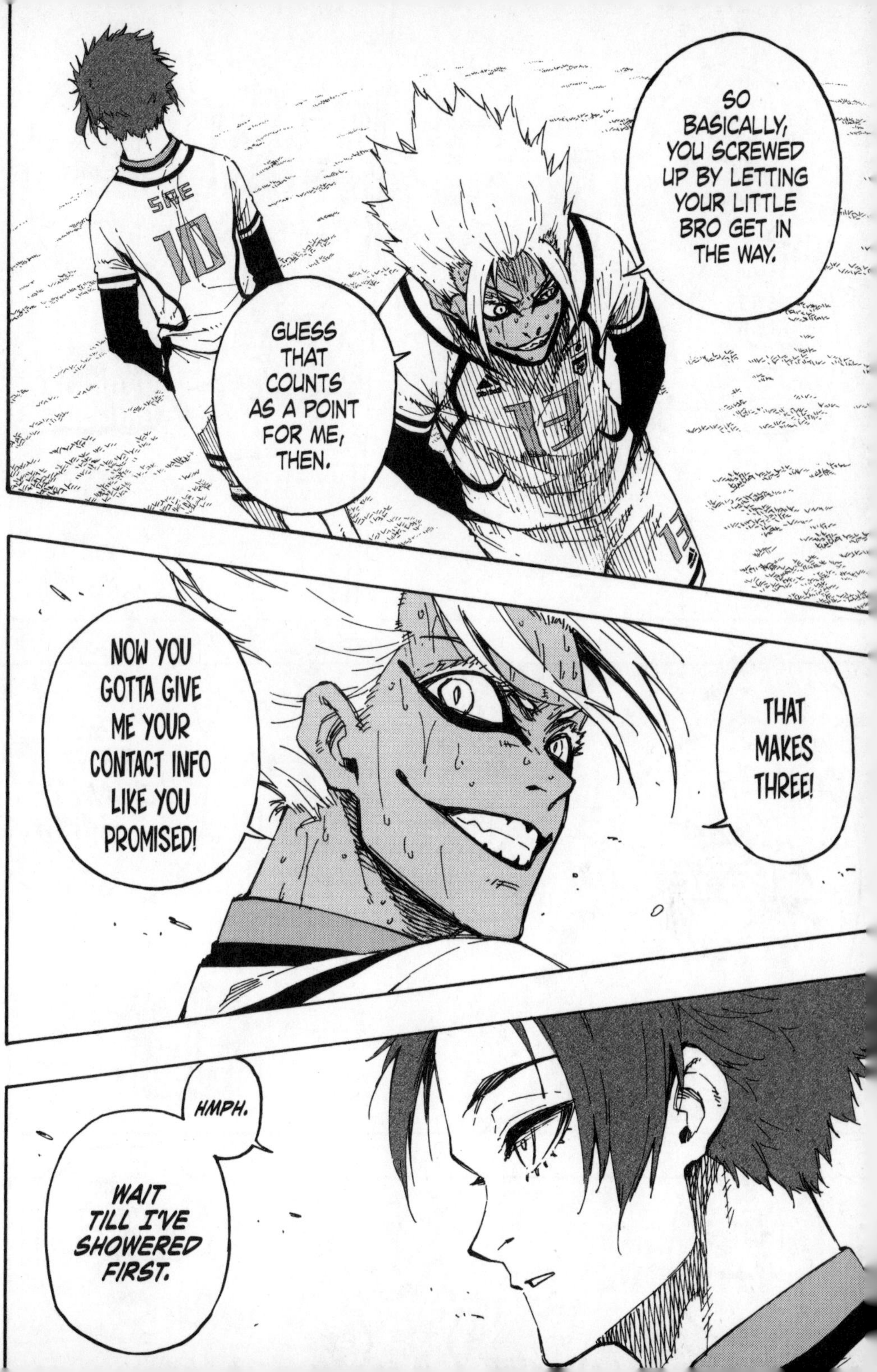
SO BASICALLY, YOU SCREWED UP BY LETTING YOUR LITTLE BRO GET IN THE WAY.
GUESS THAT COUNTS AS A POINT FOR ME, THEN.
THAT MAKES THREE!
NOW YOU GOTTA GIVE ME YOUR CONTACT INFO LIKE YOU PROMISED!
HMPH.
WAIT TILL I'VE SHOWERED FIRST.

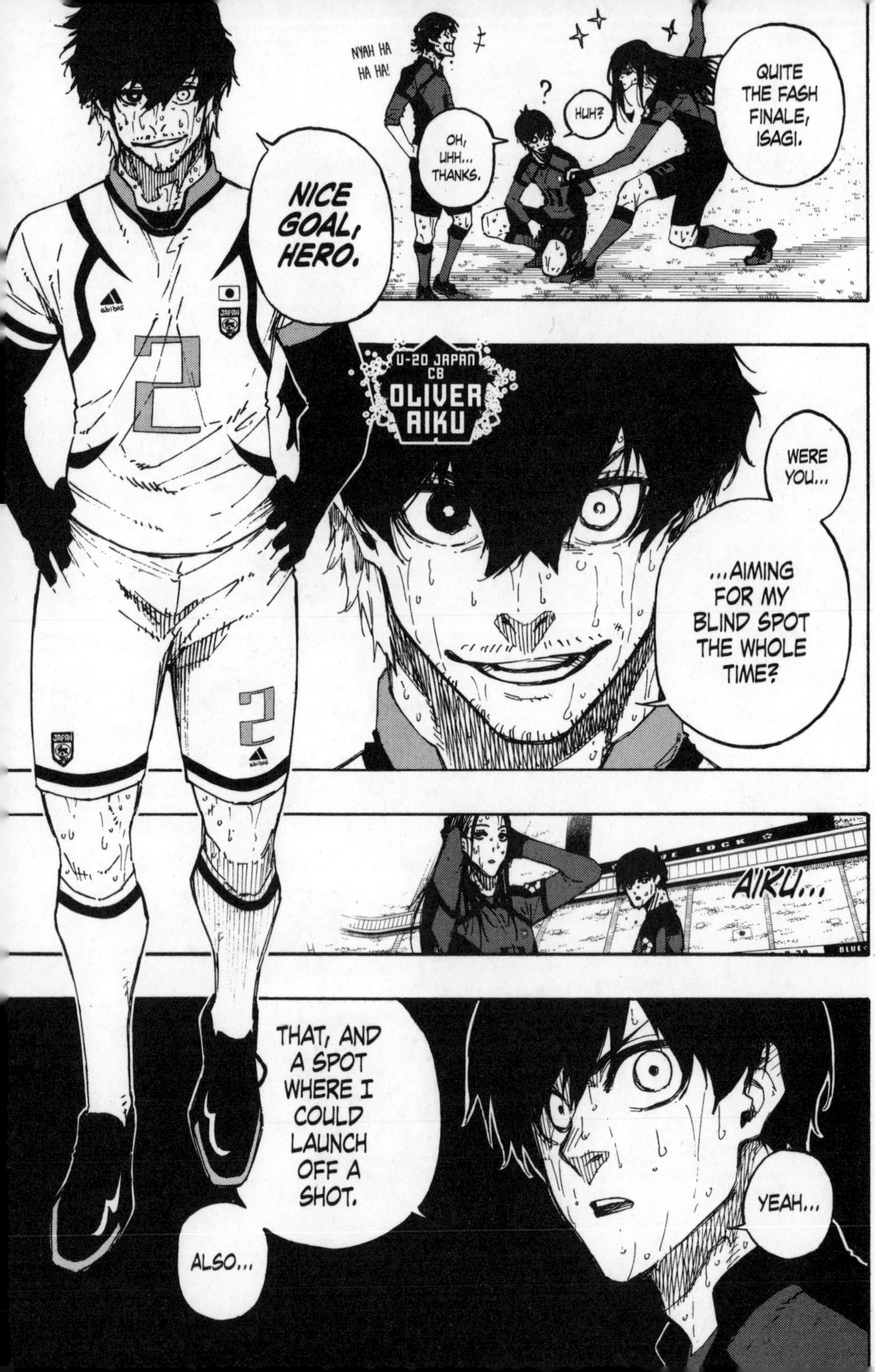
QUITE THE FASH FINALE, ISAGI.
HUH?
OH, UHH... THANKS.
NYAH HA HA HA!
NICE GOAL, HERO.
U-20 JAPAN CB OLIVER AIKU
WERE YOU...
...AIMING FOR MY BLIND SPOT THE WHOLE TIME?
AIKU...
YEAH...
THAT, AND A SPOT WHERE I COULD LAUNCH OFF A SHOT.
ALSO...

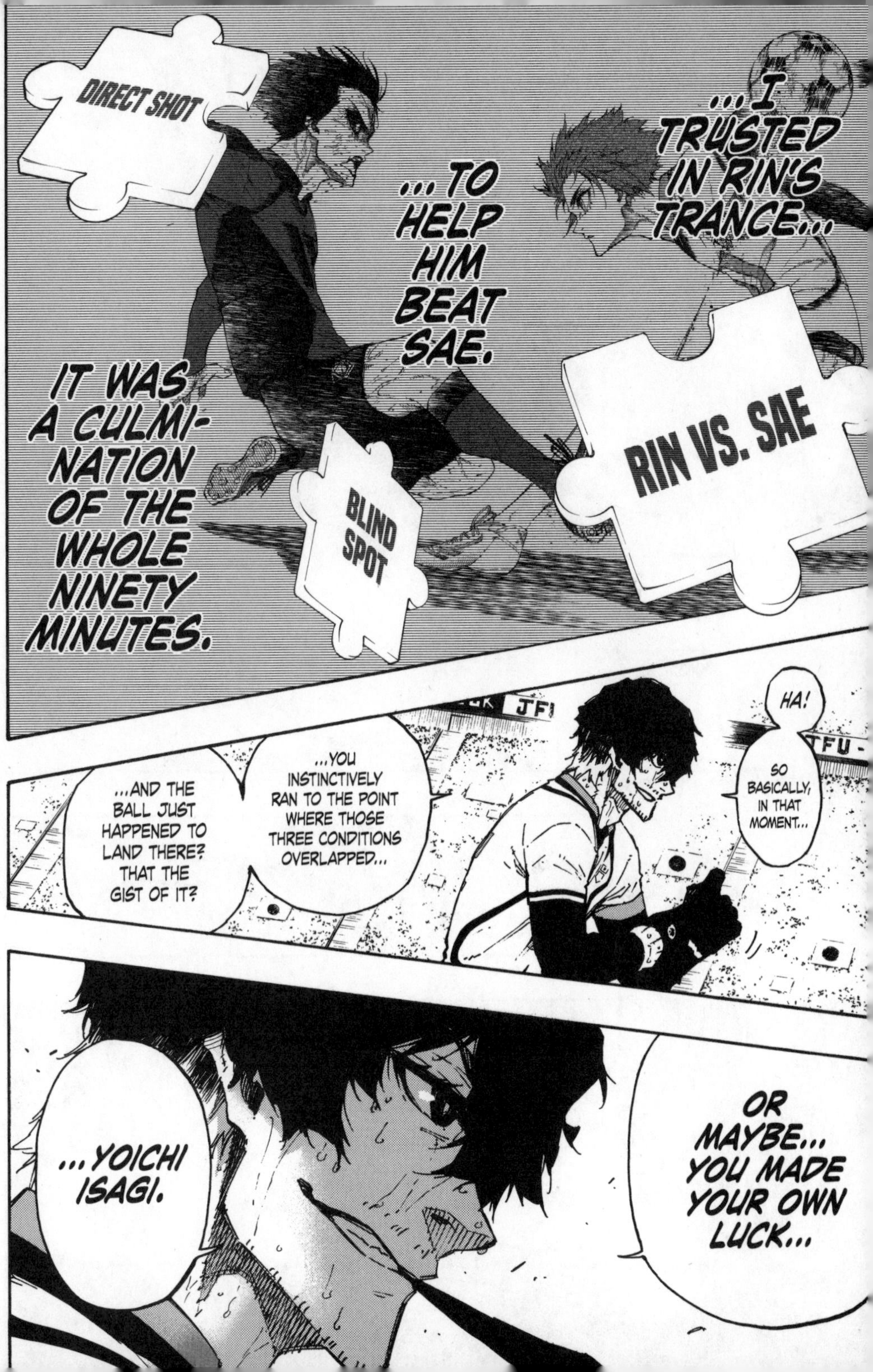
...I TRUSTED IN RIN'S TRANCE...
...TO HELP HIM BEAT SAE.
DIRECT SHOT
RIN VS. SAE
BLIND SPOT
IT WAS A CULMINATION OF THE WHOLE NINETY MINUTES.
HA!
SO BASICALLY, IN THAT MOMENT...
...YOU INSTINCTIVELY RAN TO THE POINT WHERE THOSE THREE CONDITIONS OVERLAPPED...
...AND THE BALL JUST HAPPENED TO LAND THERE? THAT THE GIST OF IT?
OR MAYBE... YOU MADE YOUR OWN LUCK...
...YOICHI ISAGI.

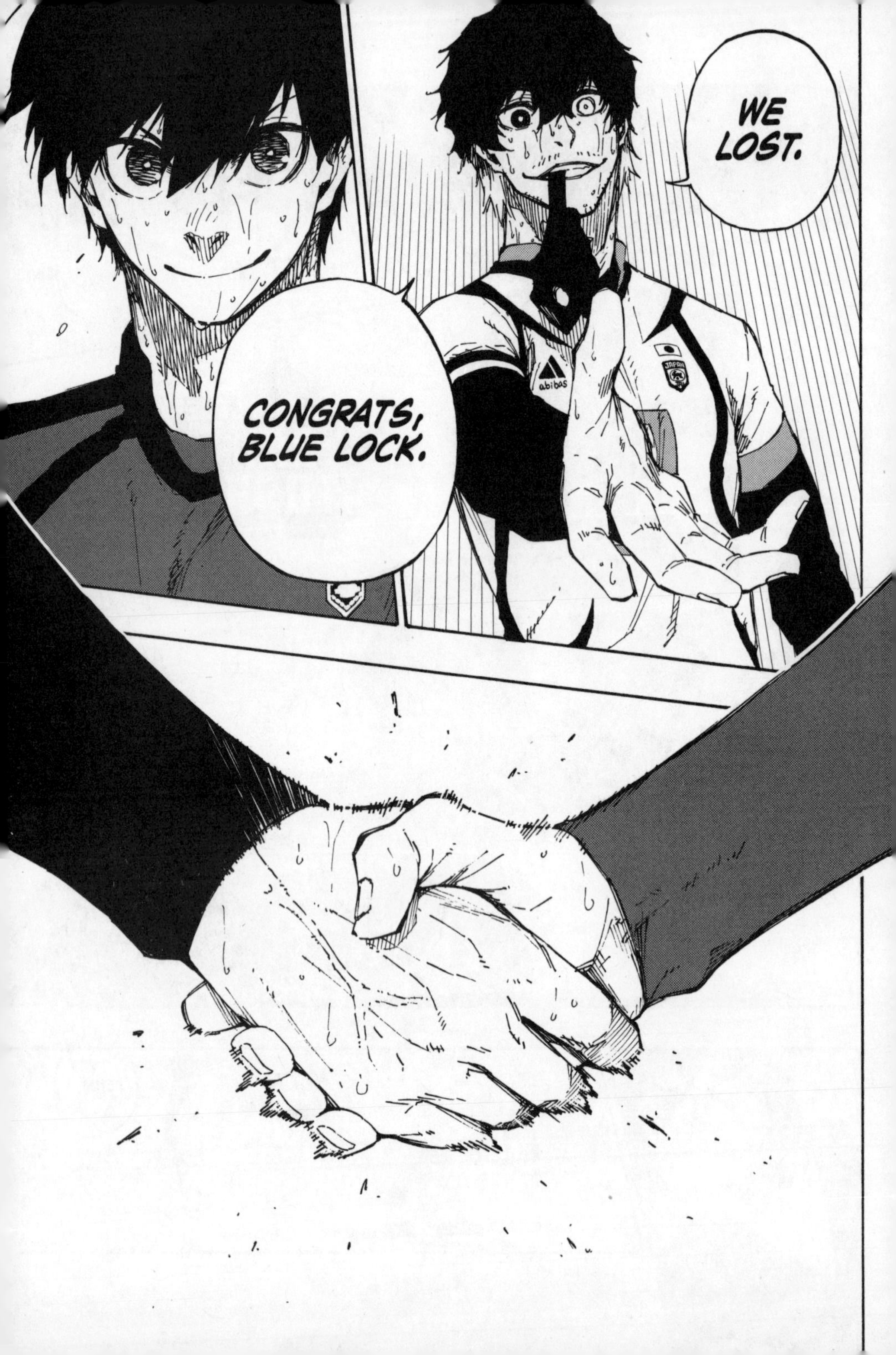
WE LOST.
CONGRATS, BLUE LOCK.

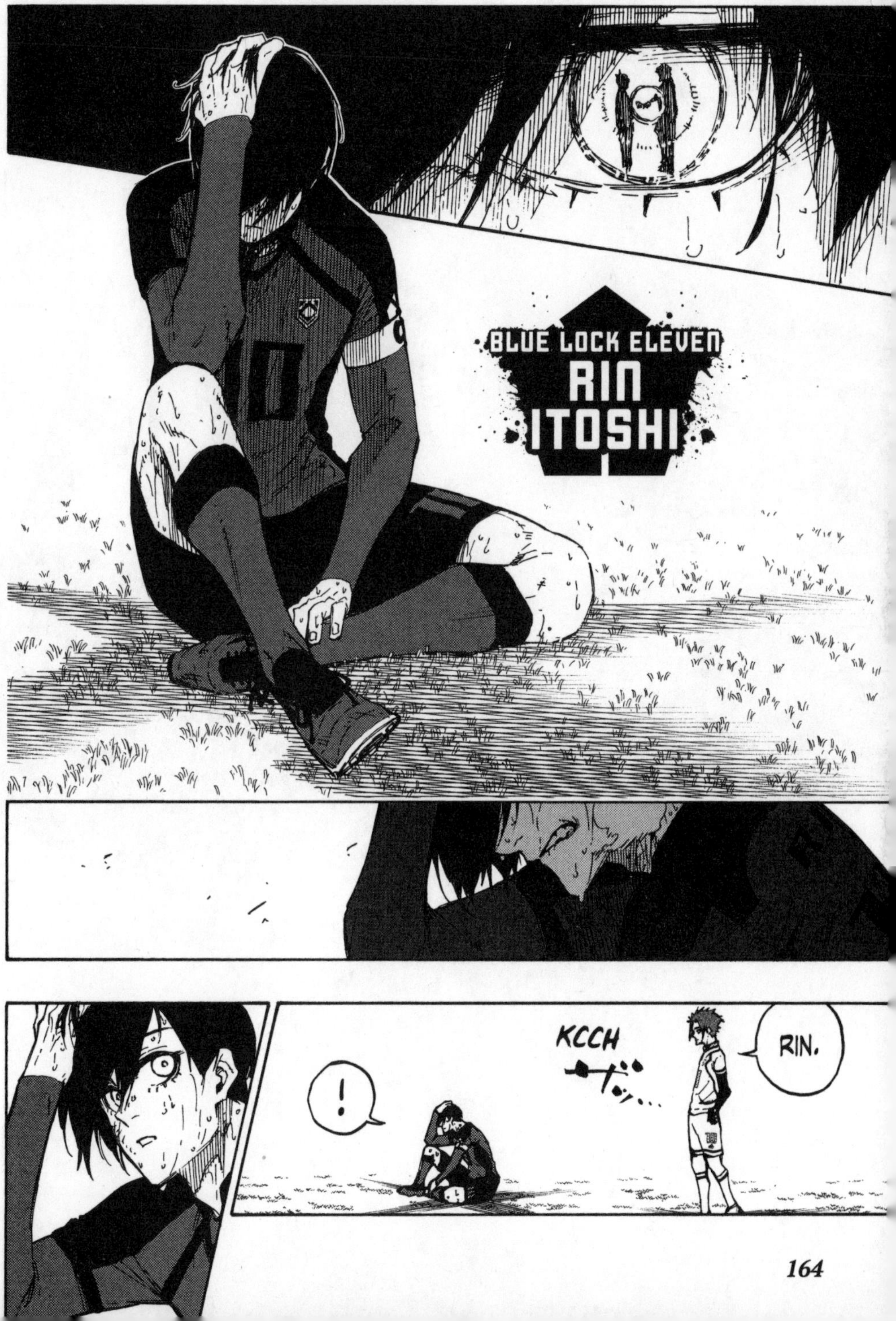
BLUE LOCK ELEVEN
RIN
ITOSHI
RIN.
KCCH
!

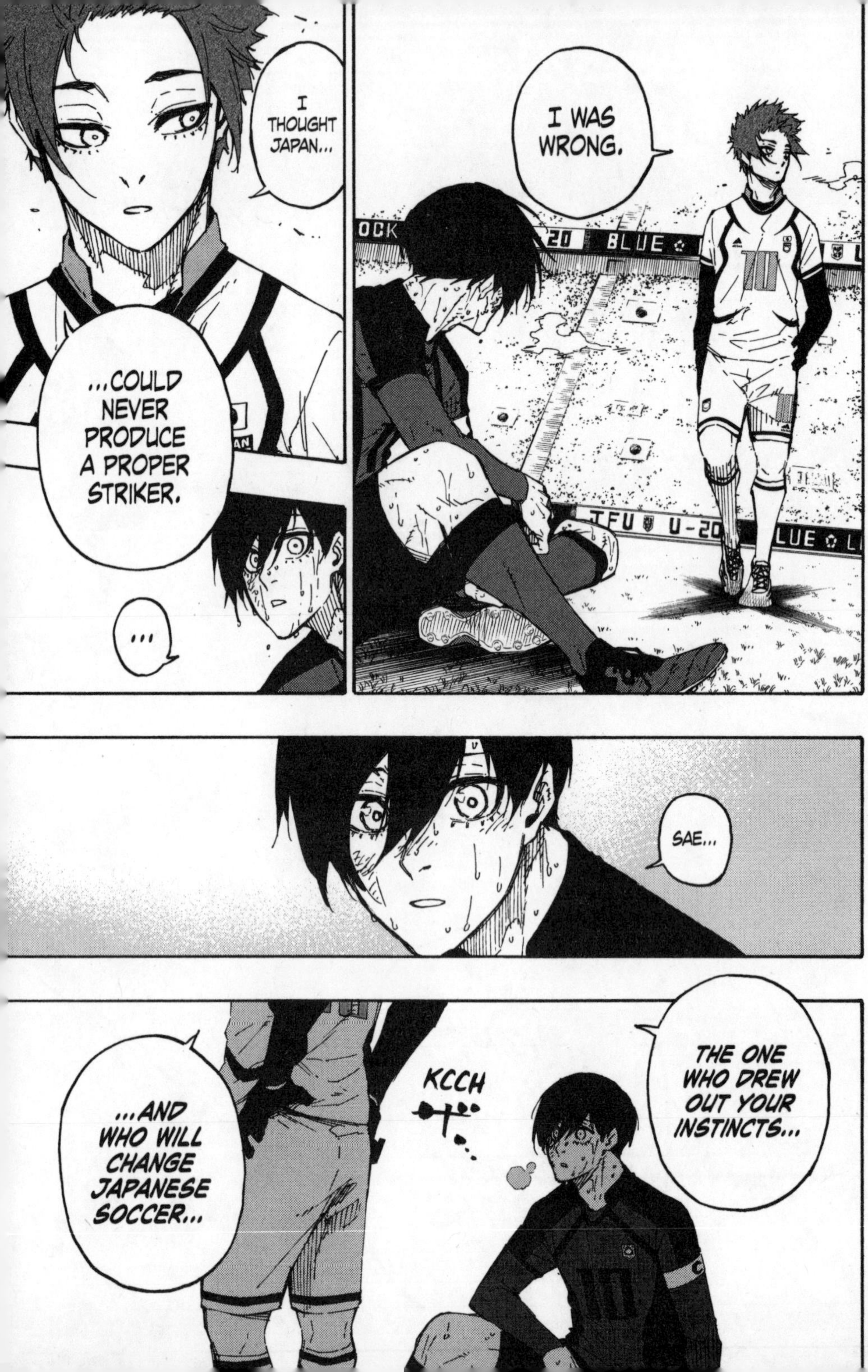
I WAS WRONG.
I THOUGHT JAPAN...
...COULD NEVER PRODUCE A PROPER STRIKER.
...
SAE...
THE ONE WHO DREW OUT YOUR INSTINCTS...
KCCH
...AND WHO WILL CHANGE JAPANESE SOCCER...

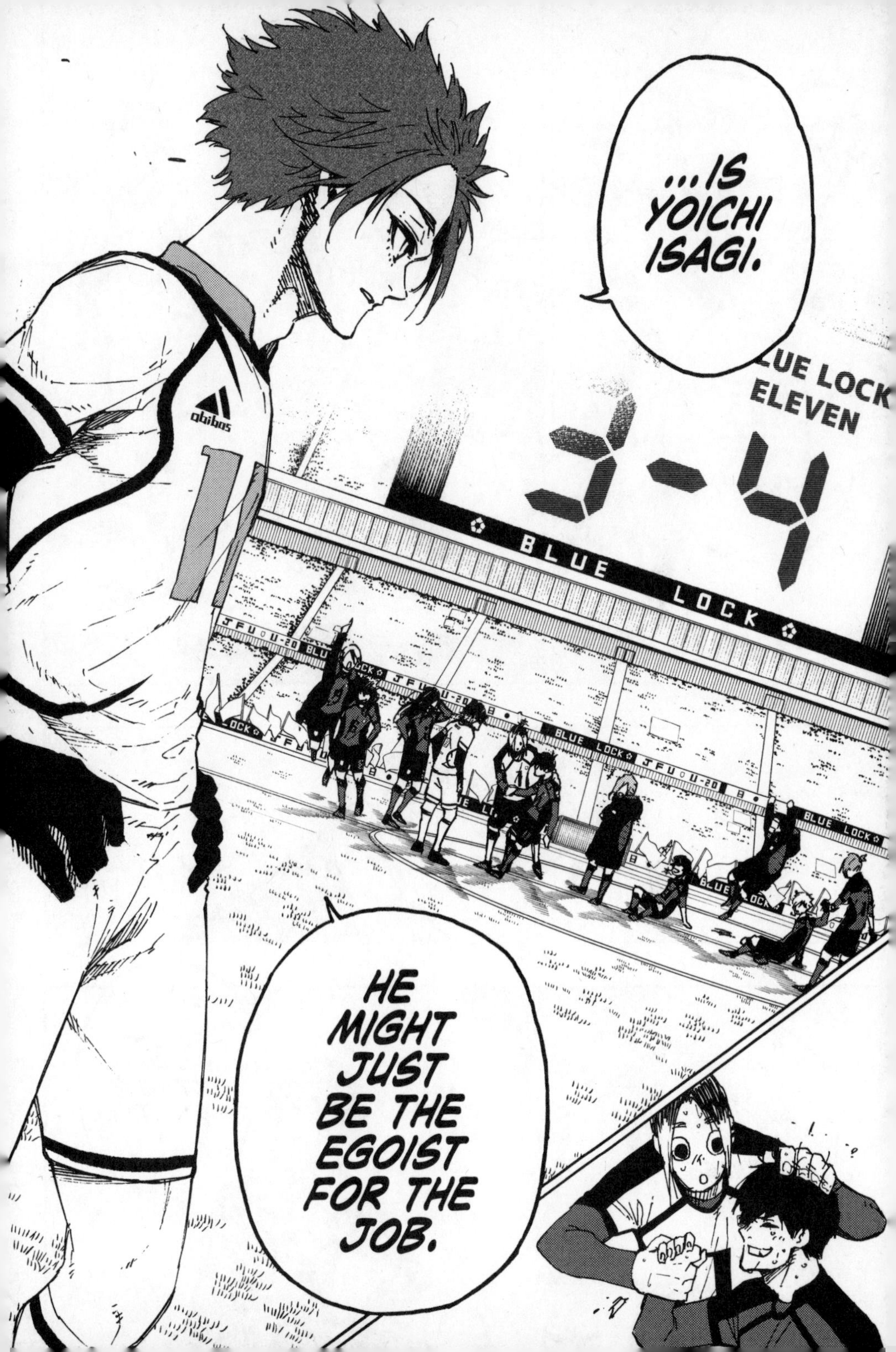
...IS YOICHI ISAGI.
LUE LOCK ELEVEN
BLUE LOCK
HE MIGHT JUST BE THE EGOIST FOR THE JOB.

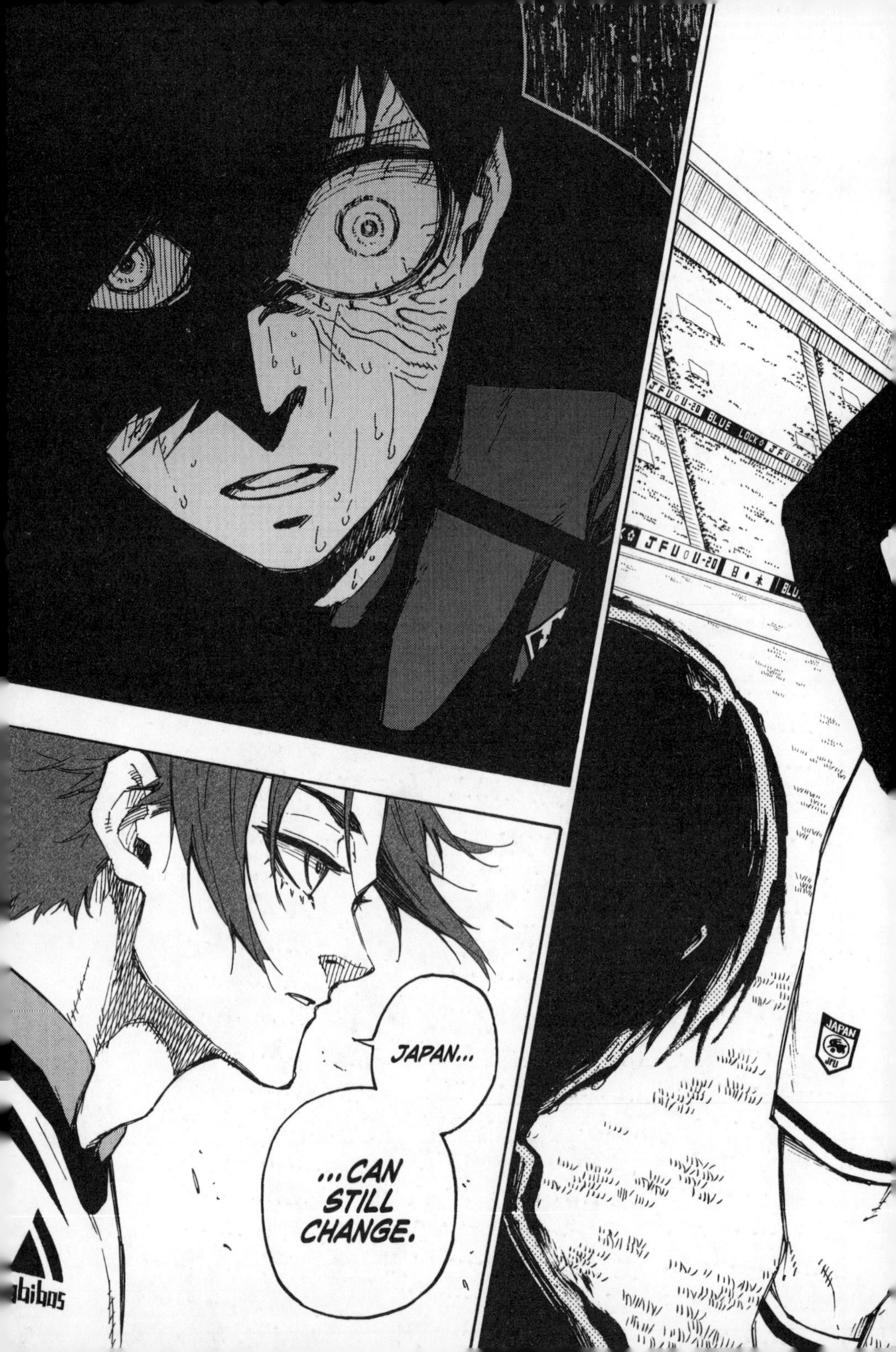
JFU U-20 BLUE LOCK JFU
JFU U-20
JAPAN JFU
JAPAN...
...CAN STILL CHANGE.

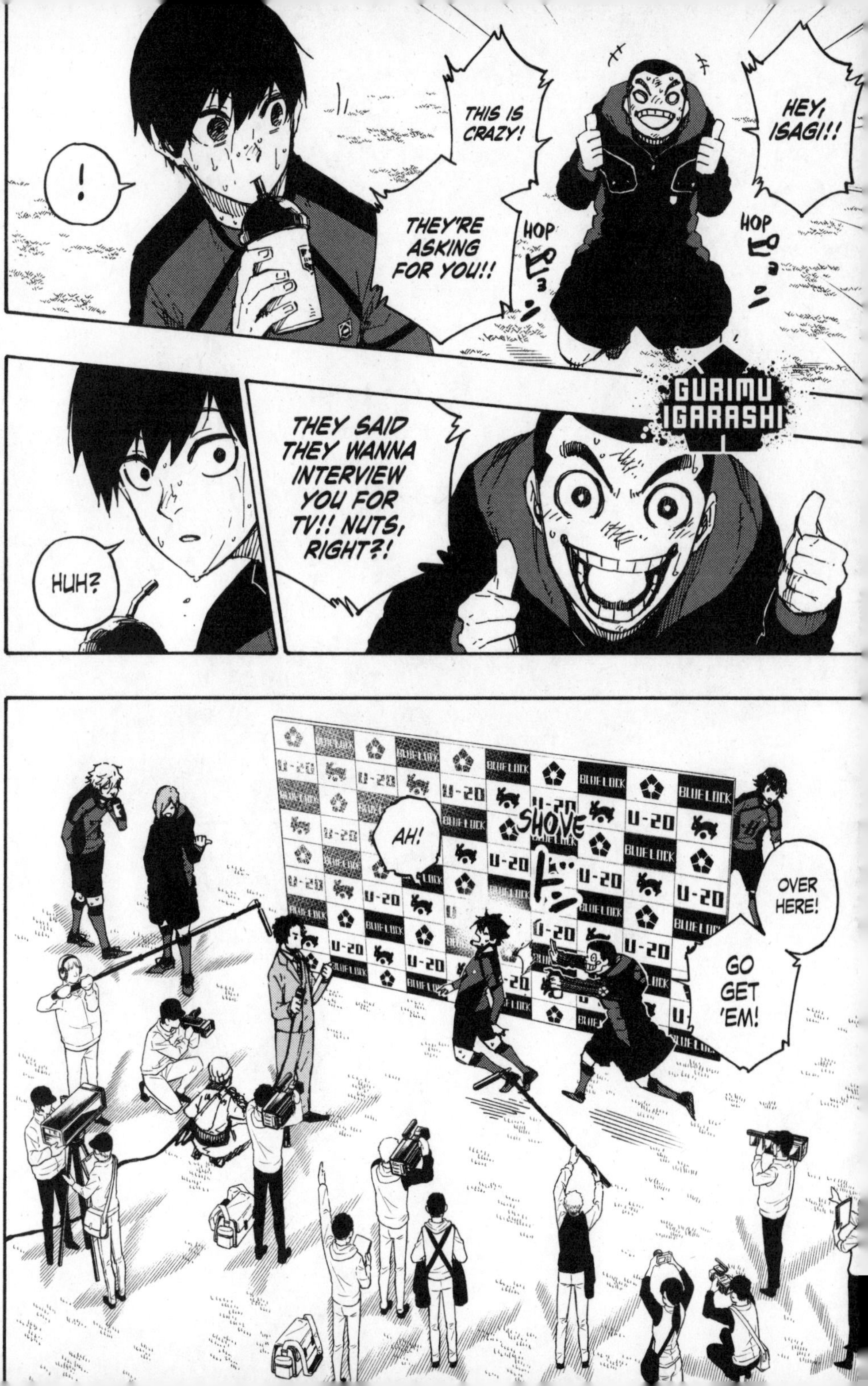
HEY, ISAGI!!
HOP
HOP
THIS IS CRAZY!
THEY'RE ASKING FOR YOU!!
!
GURIMU IGARASHI
THEY SAID THEY WANNA INTERVIEW YOU FOR TV!! NUTS, RIGHT?!
HUH?
OVER HERE!
GO GET 'EM!
SHOVE
AH!

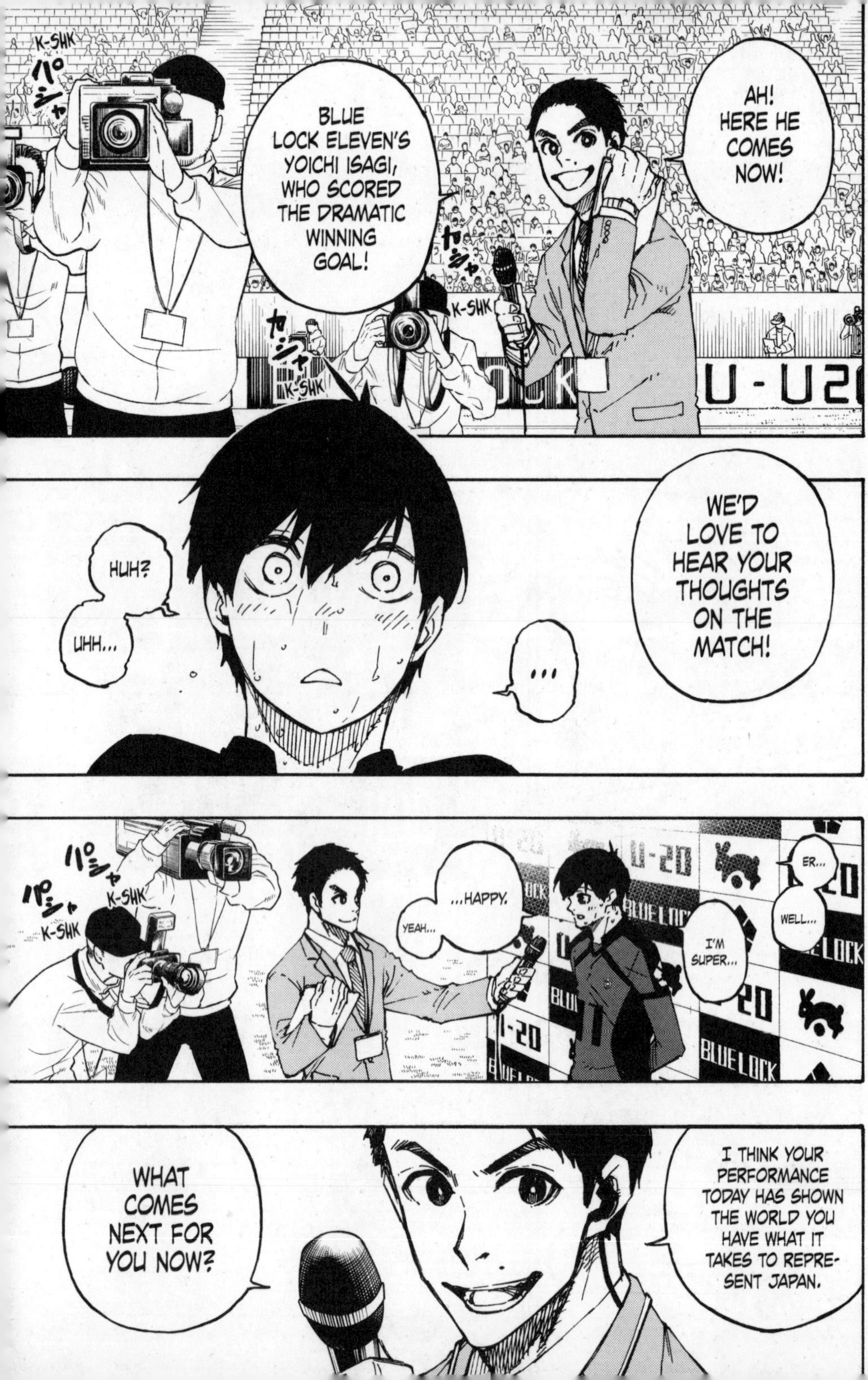
AH! HERE HE COMES NOW!
BLUE LOCK ELEVEN'S YOICHI ISAGI, WHO SCORED THE DRAMATIC WINNING GOAL!
K-SHK
パシャ
カシャ
K-SHK
カシャ
K-SHK
WE'D LOVE TO HEAR YOUR THOUGHTS ON THE MATCH!
...
HUH?
UHH...
ER...
WELL...
I'M SUPER...
...HAPPY.
YEAH...
パシャ
K-SHK
パシャ
K-SHK
I THINK YOUR PERFORMANCE TODAY HAS SHOWN THE WORLD YOU HAVE WHAT IT TAKES TO REPRE- SENT JAPAN.
WHAT COMES NEXT FOR YOU NOW?

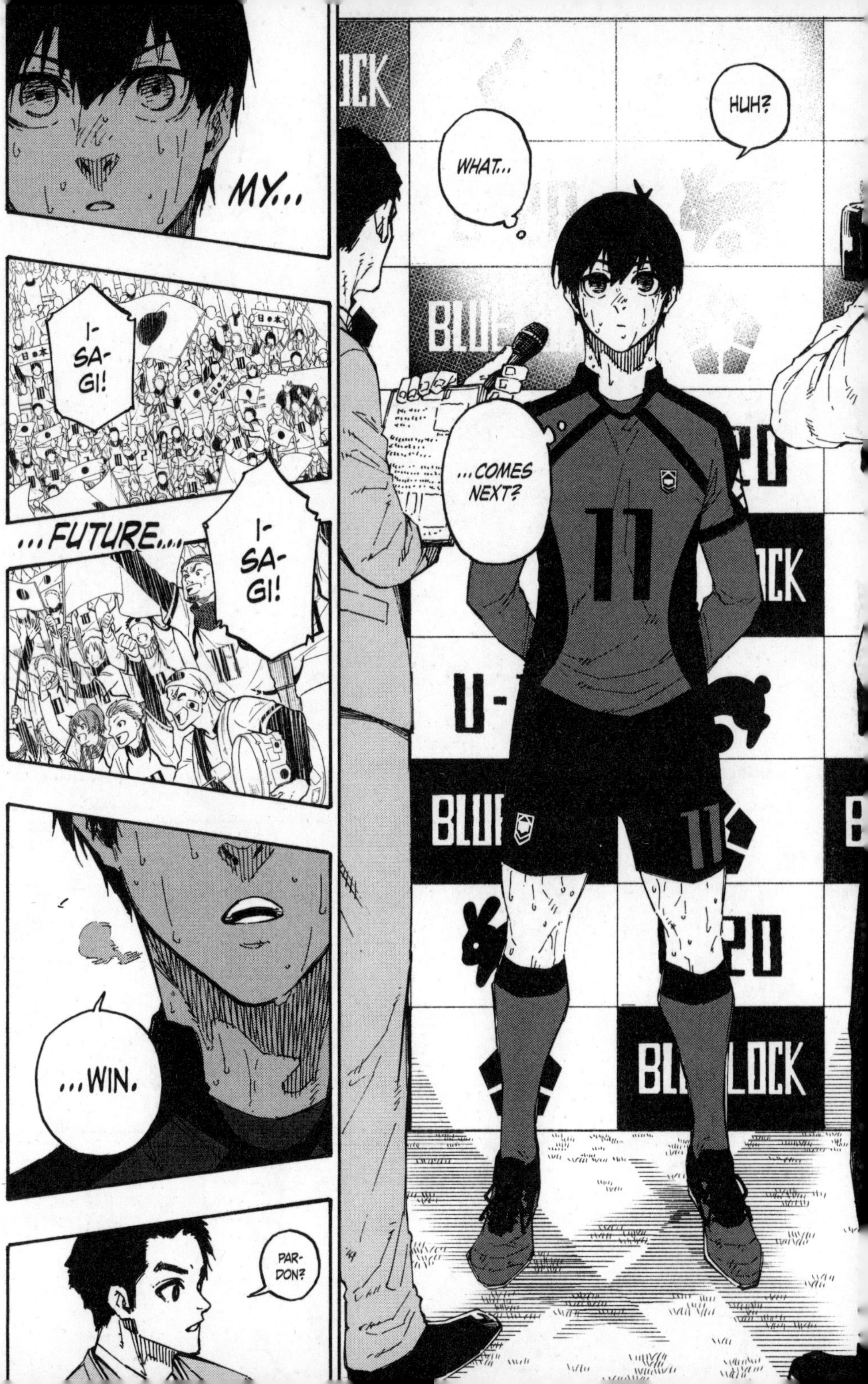

HUH?
WHAT...
...COMES NEXT?
MY...
I-SA-GI!
...FUTURE...
I-SA-GI!
...WIN.
PAR-DON?

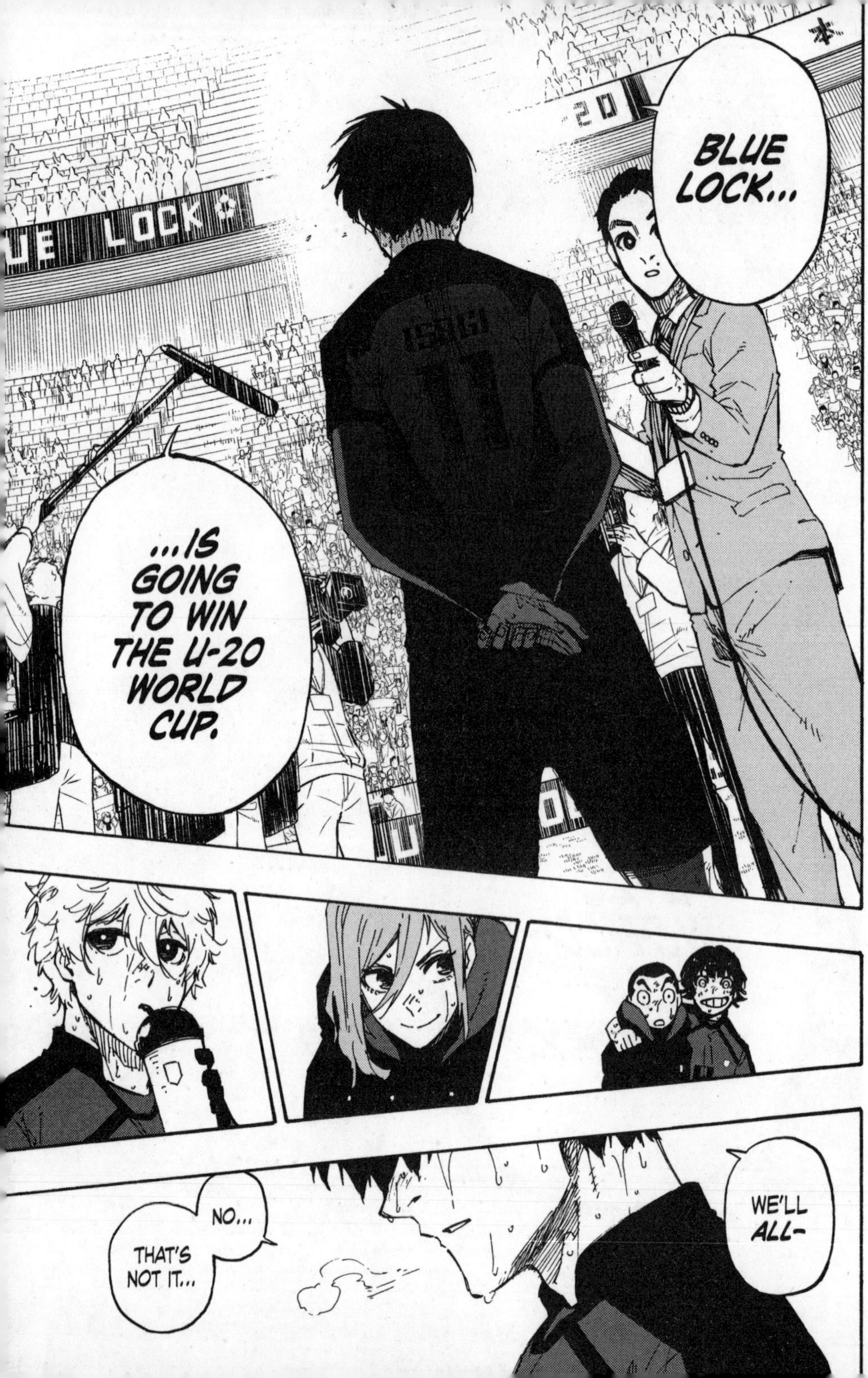
BLUE LOCK...
...IS GOING TO WIN THE U-20 WORLD CUP.
WE'LL ALL-
NO...
THAT'S NOT IT...

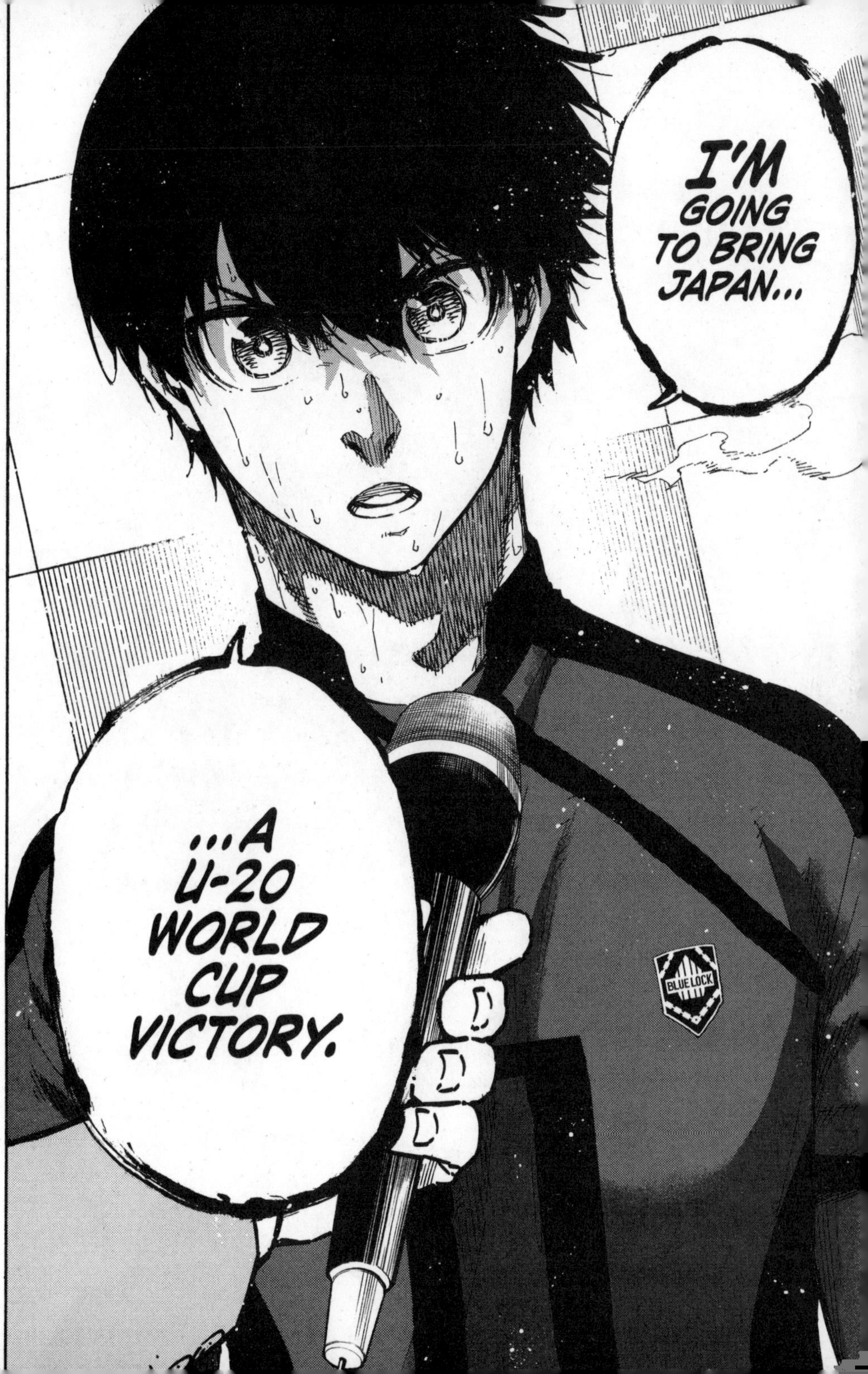
I'M GOING TO BRING JAPAN...
...A U-20 WORLD CUP VICTORY.
BLUE LOCK

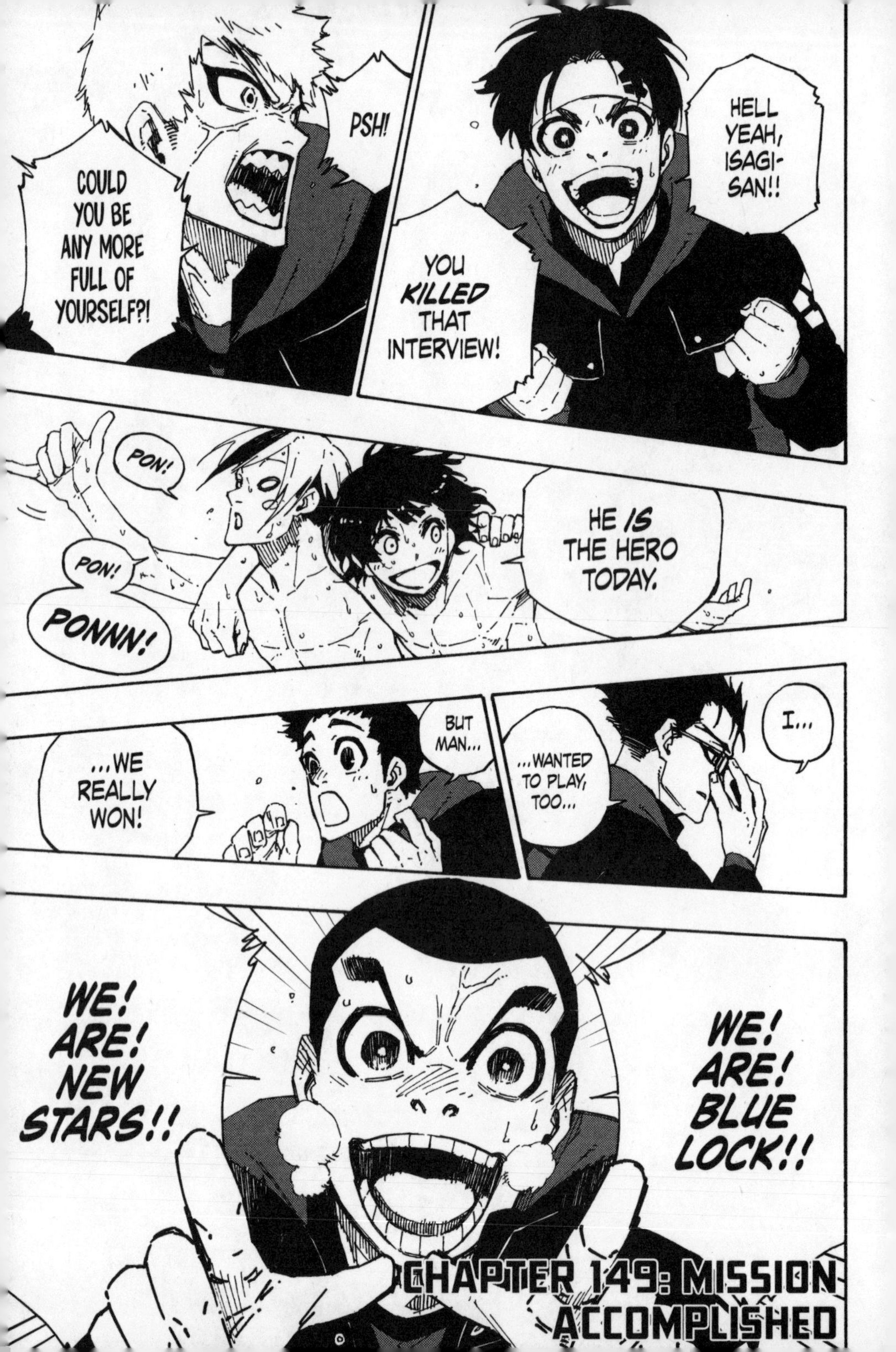
HELL YEAH, ISAGI-SAN!!
YOU *KILLED* THAT INTERVIEW!
PSH!
COULD YOU BE ANY MORE FULL OF YOURSELF?!
HE *IS* THE HERO TODAY.
PON!
PON!
PONNN!
I...
...WANTED TO PLAY, TOO...
BUT MAN...
...WE REALLY WON!
WE! ARE! BLUE LOCK!!
WE! ARE! NEW STARS!!
CHAPTER 149: MISSION ACCOMPLISHED

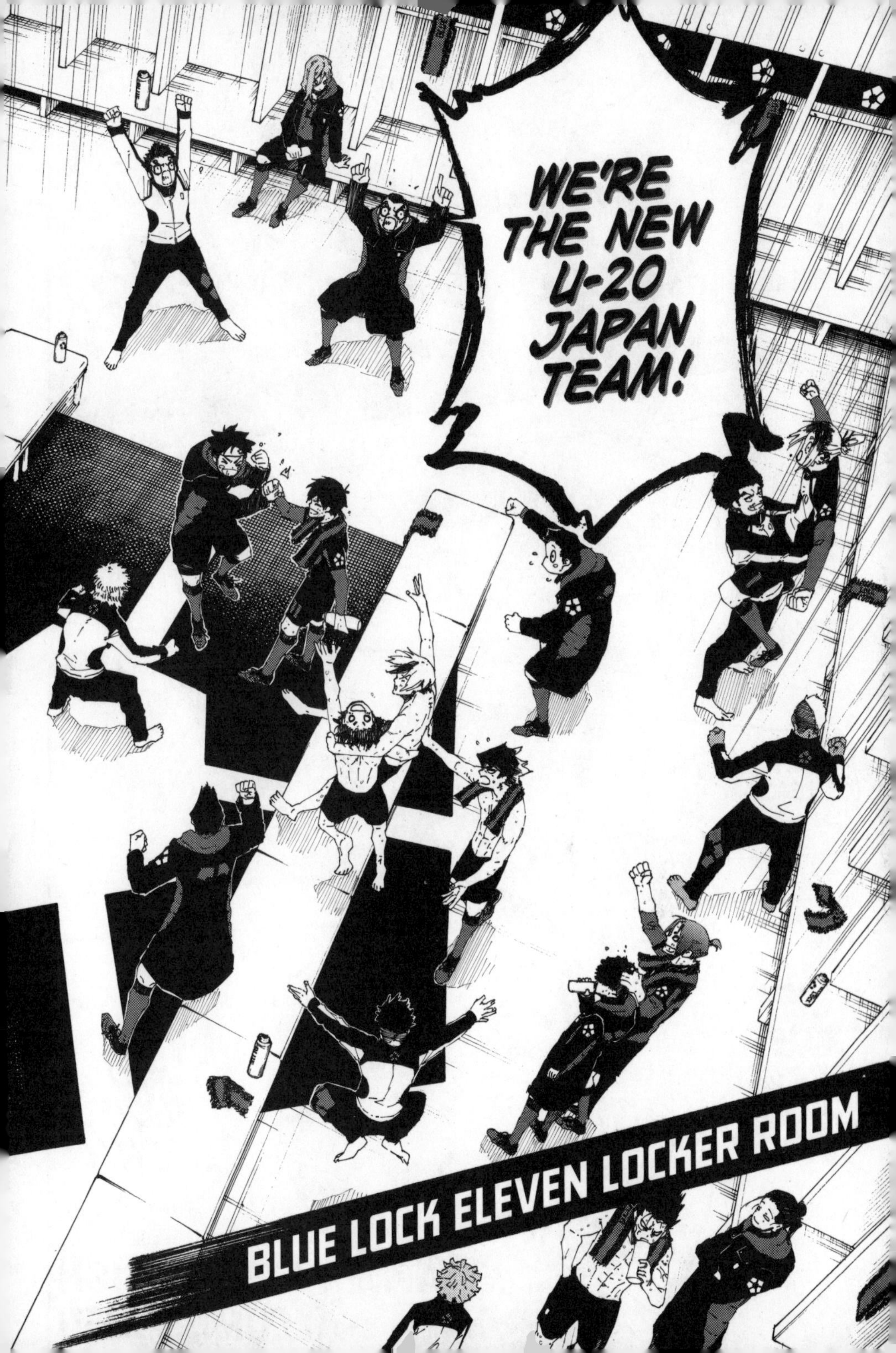
WE'RE THE NEW U-20 JAPAN TEAM!
BLUE LOCK ELEVEN LOCKER ROOM

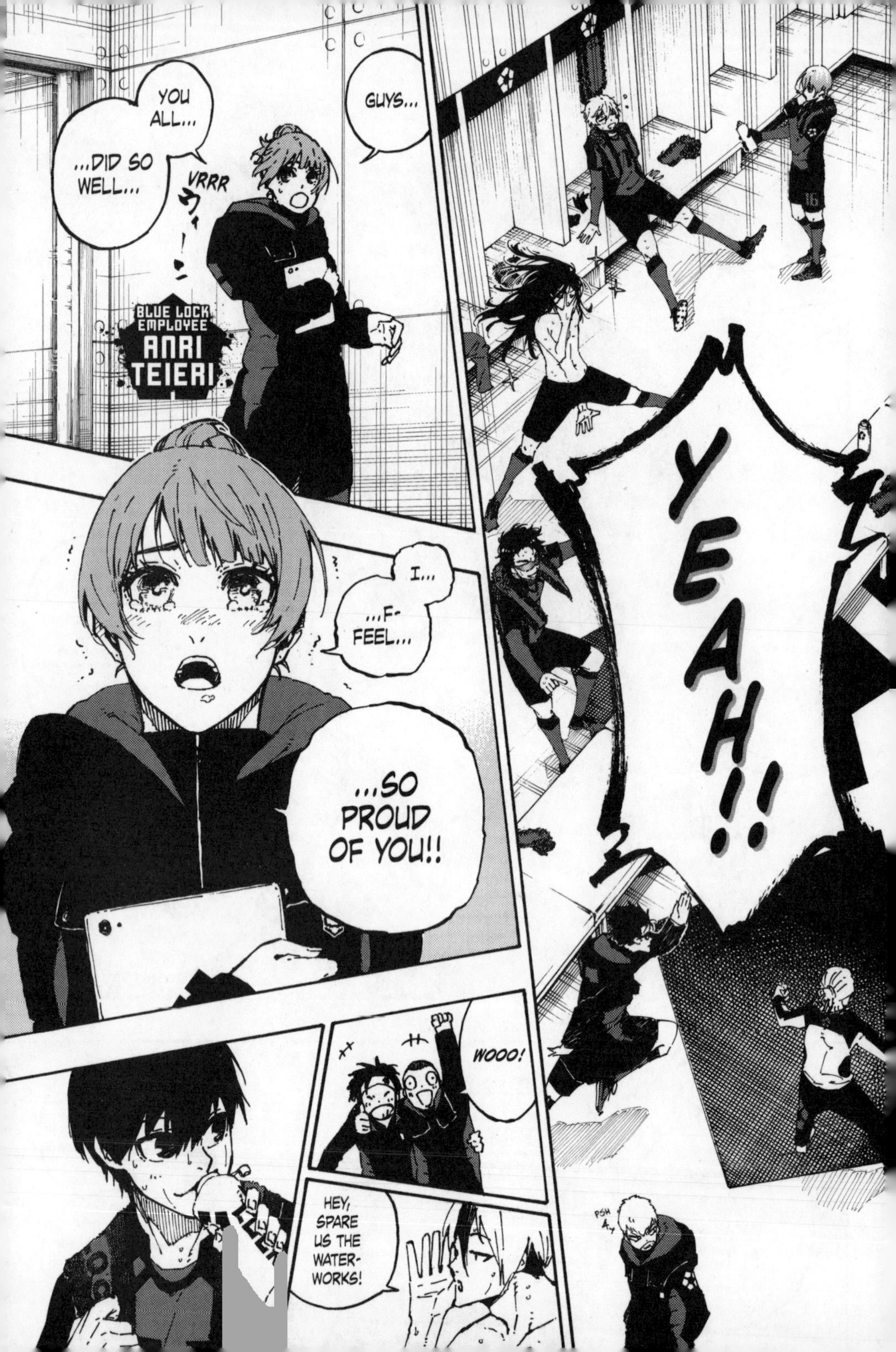
YEAH!!
PSH
GUYS...
YOU ALL...
...DID SO WELL...
VRRR
BLUE LOCK EMPLOYEE
ANRI TEIERI
I...
...F-FEEL...
...SO PROUD OF YOU!!
WOOO!
HEY, SPARE US THE WATER-WORKS!

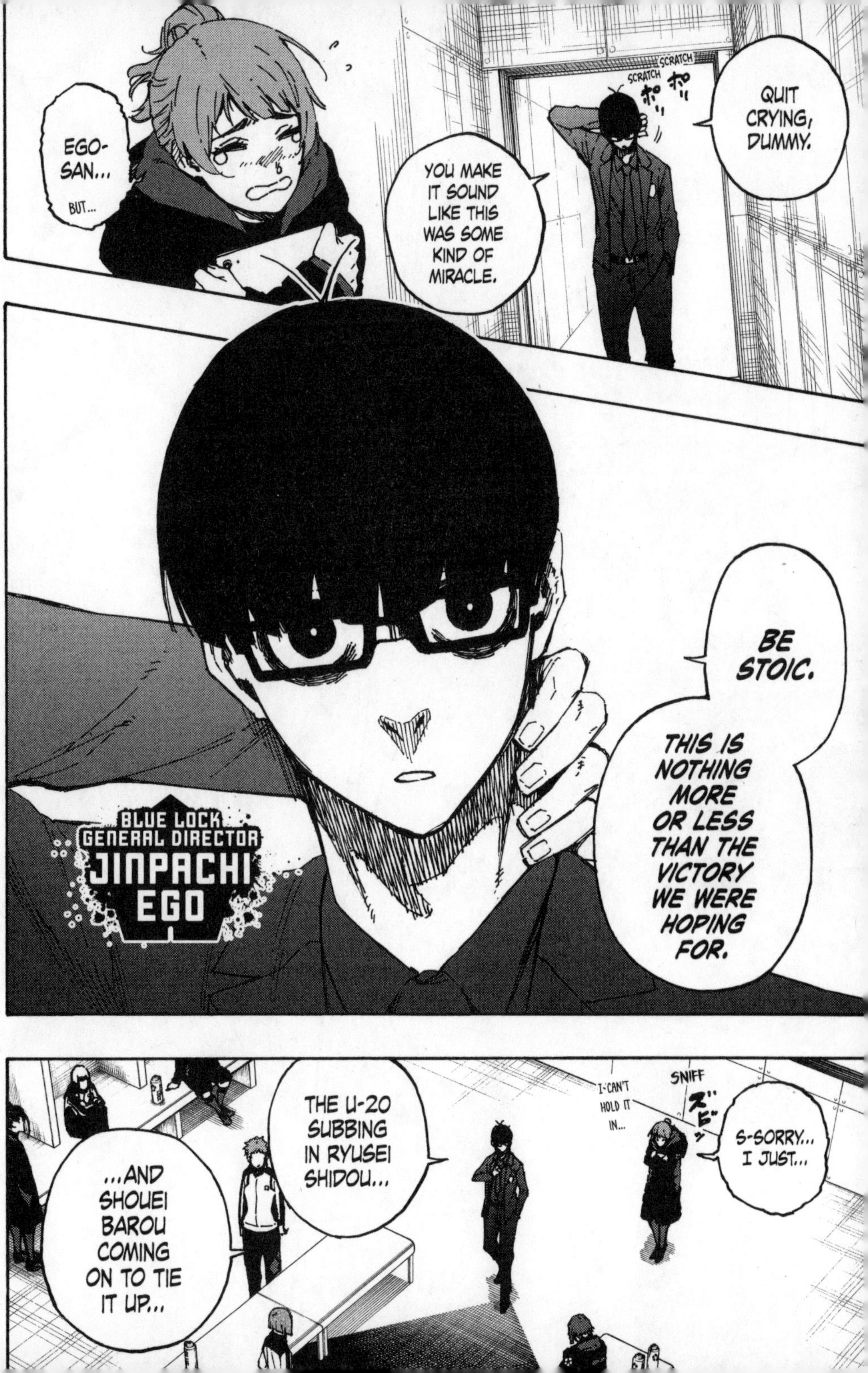
SCRATCH SCRATCH
QUIT CRYING, DUMMY.
EGO-SAN...
BUT...
YOU MAKE IT SOUND LIKE THIS WAS SOME KIND OF MIRACLE.
BE STOIC.
THIS IS NOTHING MORE OR LESS THAN THE VICTORY WE WERE HOPING FOR.
BLUE LOCK GENERAL DIRECTOR JINPACHI EGO
S-SORRY... I JUST...
SNIFF
I-CAN'T HOLD IT IN...
THE U-20 SUBBING IN RYUSEI SHIDOU...
...AND SHOUEI BAROU COMING ON TO TIE IT UP...

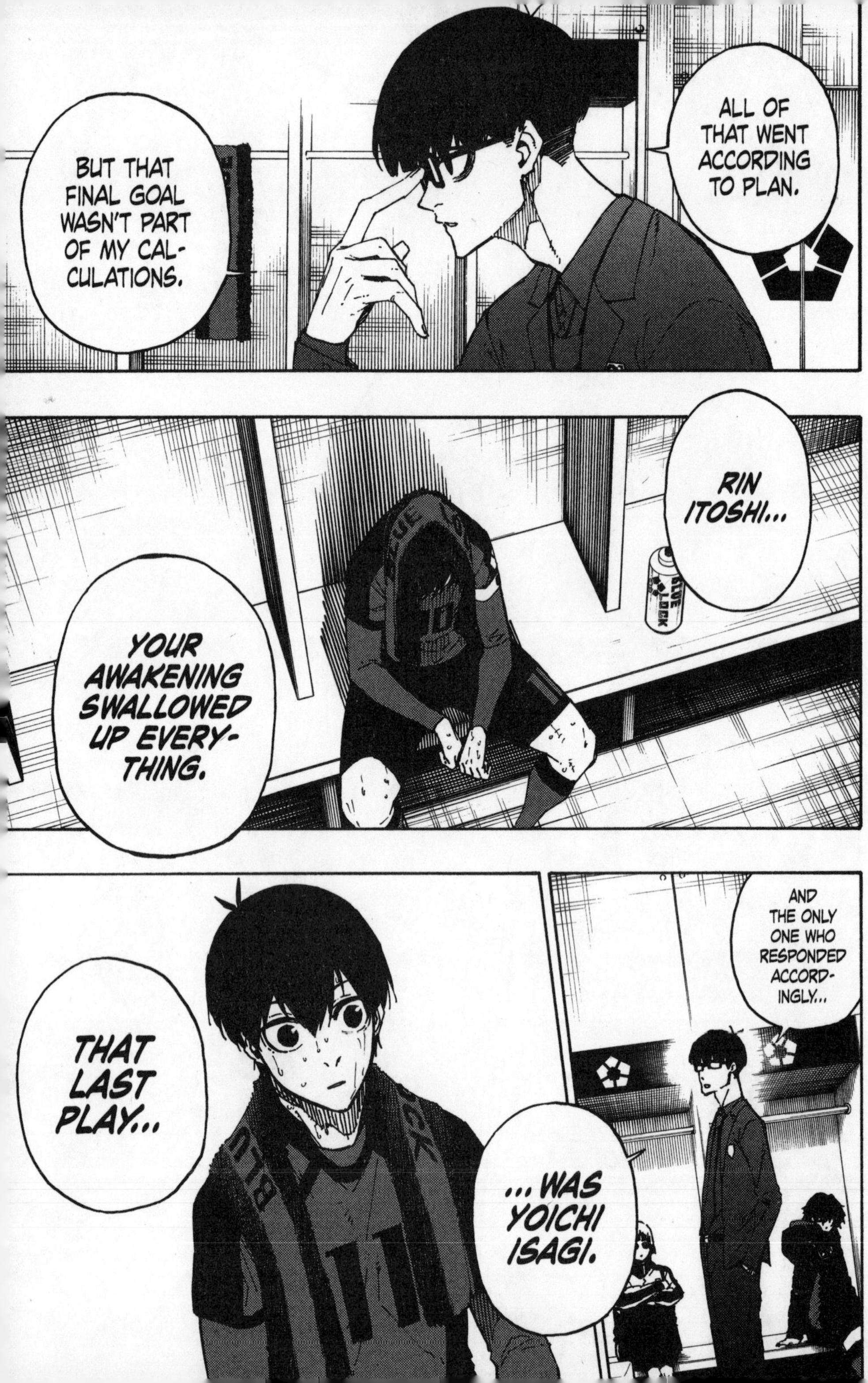
ALL OF THAT WENT ACCORDING TO PLAN.
BUT THAT FINAL GOAL WASN'T PART OF MY CAL-CULATIONS.
RIN ITOSHI...
YOUR AWAKENING SWALLOWED UP EVERY-THING.
AND THE ONLY ONE WHO RESPONDED ACCORD-INGLY...
...WAS YOICHI ISAGI.
THAT LAST PLAY...

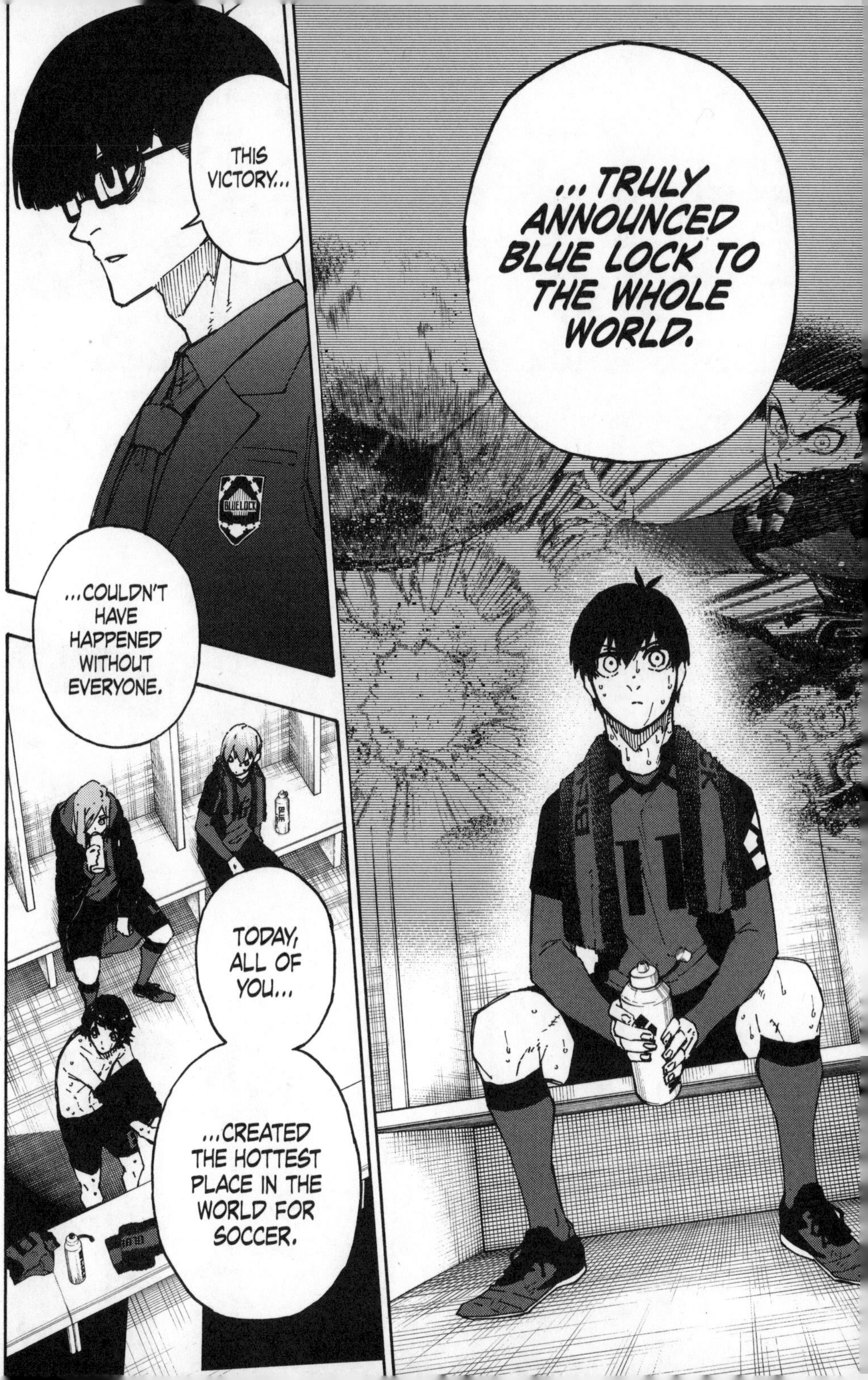
THIS VICTORY...
...COULDN'T HAVE HAPPENED WITHOUT EVERYONE.
TODAY, ALL OF YOU...
...CREATED THE HOTTEST PLACE IN THE WORLD FOR SOCCER.
...TRULY ANNOUNCED BLUE LOCK TO THE WHOLE WORLD.

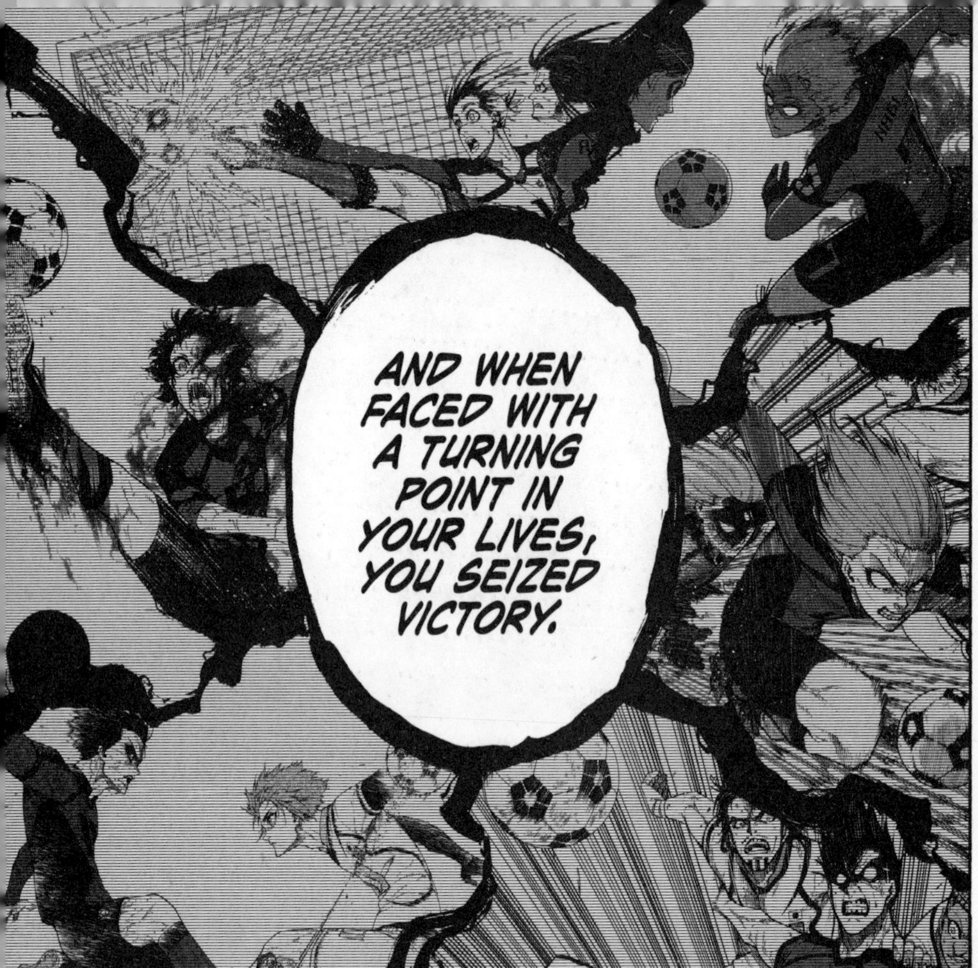
AND WHEN FACED WITH A TURNING POINT IN YOUR LIVES, YOU SEIZED VICTORY.
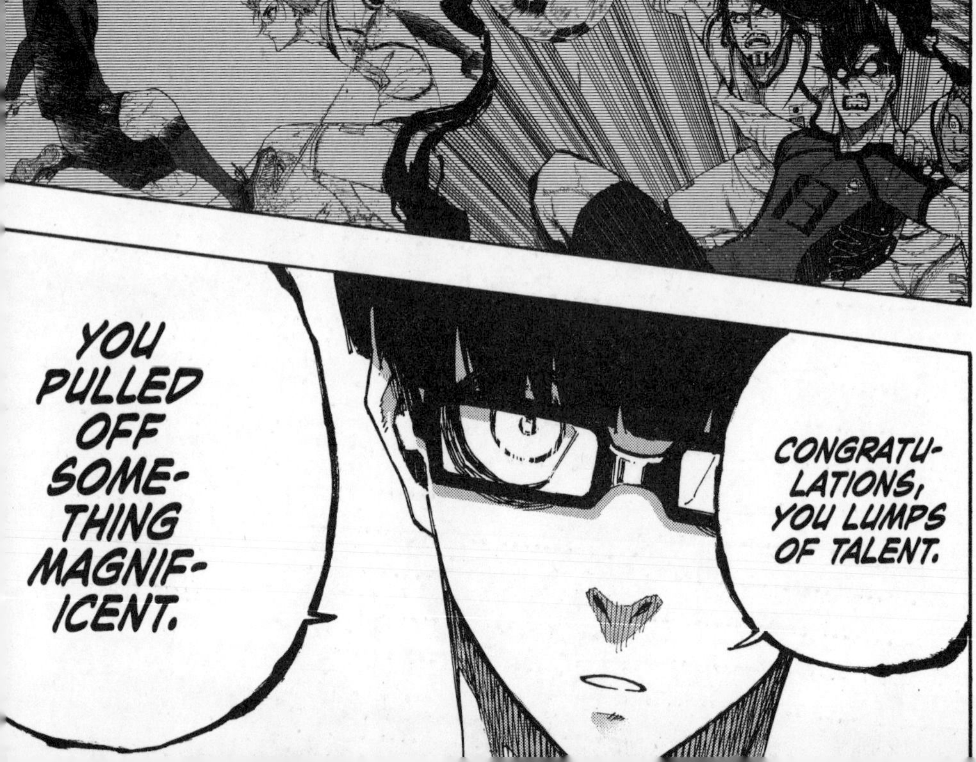
CONGRATU-LATIONS, YOU LUMPS OF TALENT.
YOU PULLED OFF SOME-THING MAGNIF-ICENT.

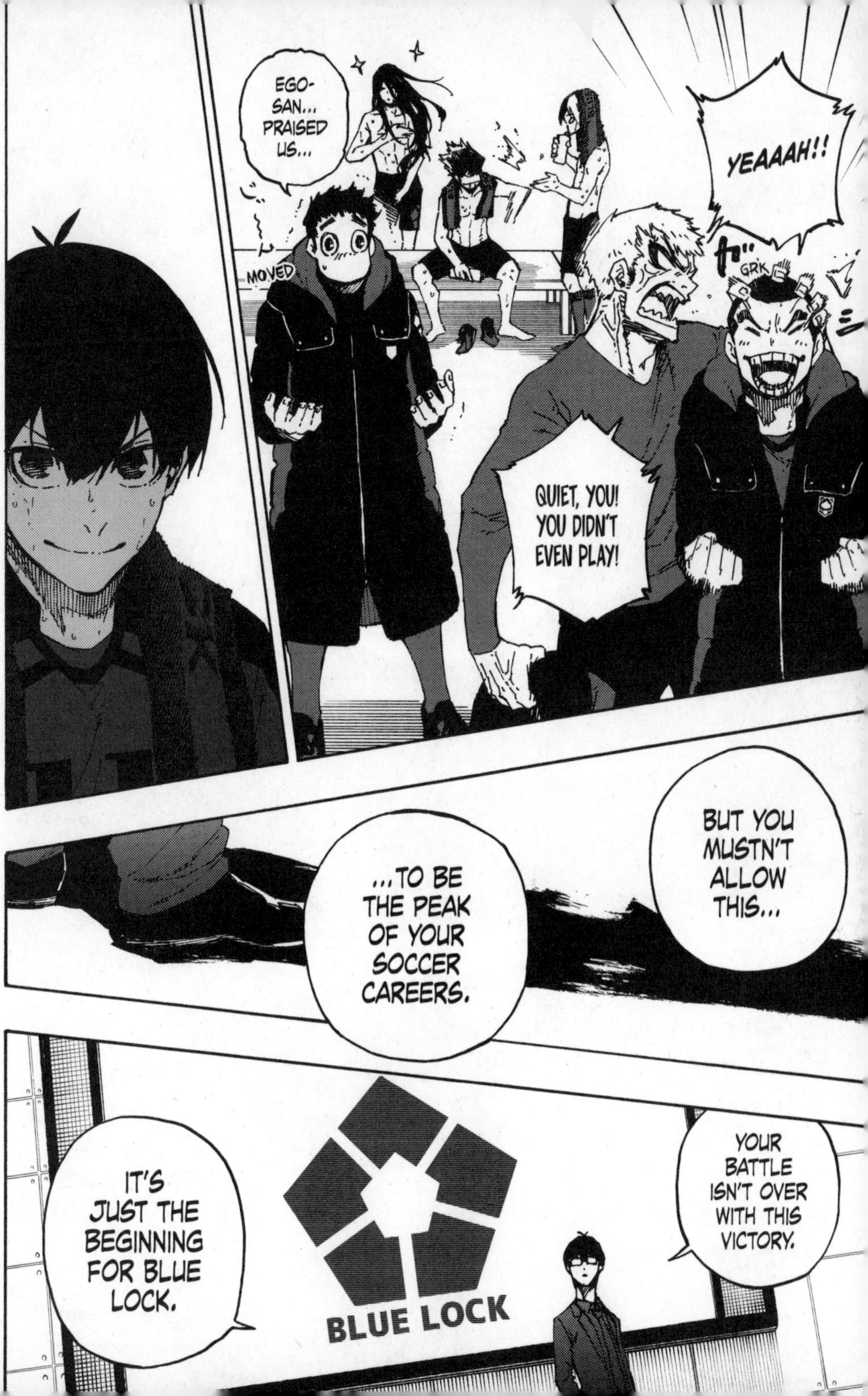
YEAAAH!!
GRK
EGO-SAN... PRAISED US...
MOVED
QUIET, YOU! YOU DIDN'T EVEN PLAY!
BUT YOU MUSTN'T ALLOW THIS...
...TO BE THE PEAK OF YOUR SOCCER CAREERS.
YOUR BATTLE ISN'T OVER WITH THIS VICTORY.
BLUE LOCK
IT'S JUST THE BEGINNING FOR BLUE LOCK.

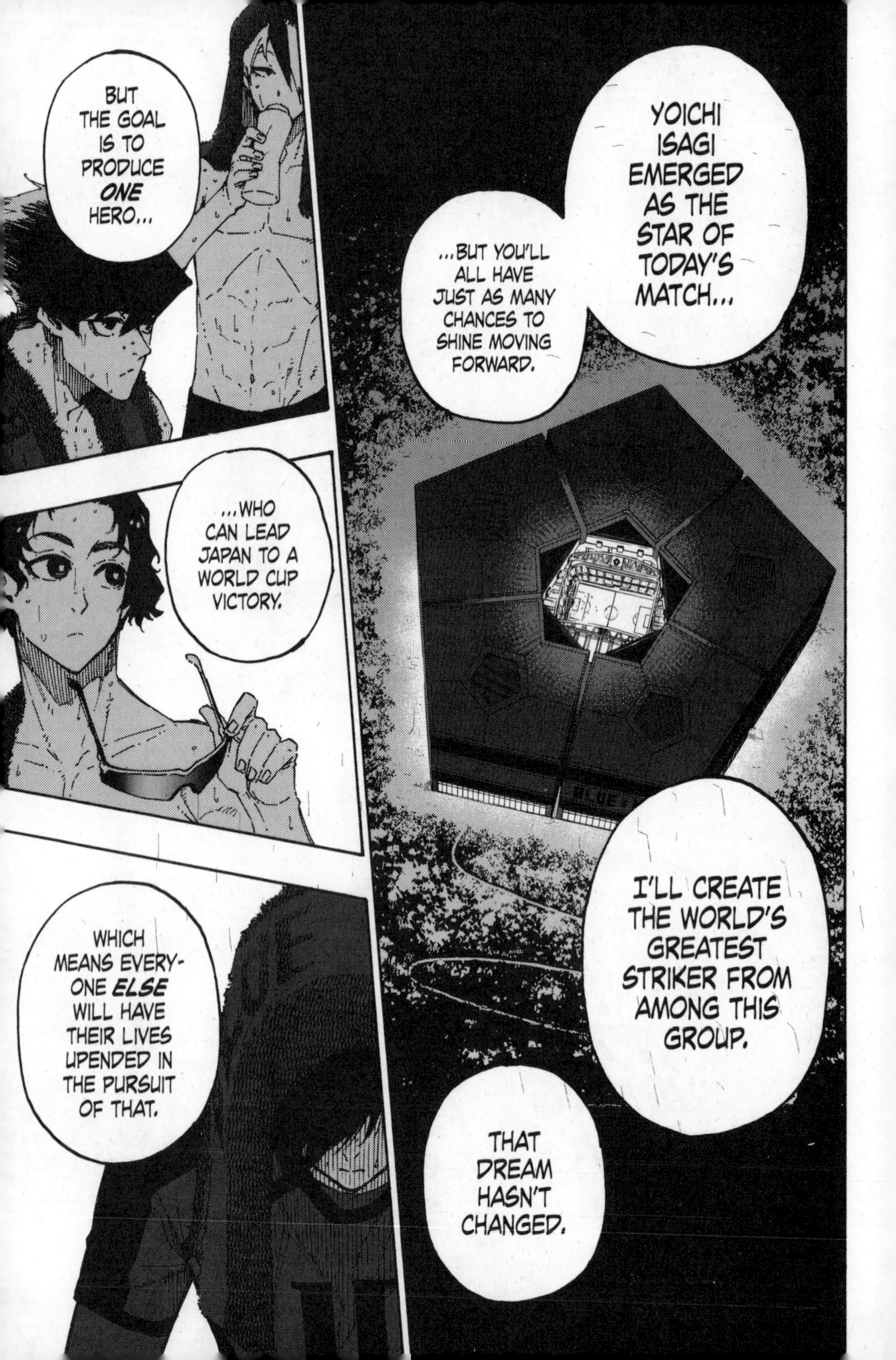
YOICHI ISAGI EMERGED AS THE STAR OF TODAY'S MATCH...
...BUT YOU'LL ALL HAVE JUST AS MANY CHANCES TO SHINE MOVING FORWARD.
I'LL CREATE THE WORLD'S GREATEST STRIKER FROM AMONG THIS GROUP.
THAT DREAM HASN'T CHANGED.
BUT THE GOAL IS TO PRODUCE *ONE* HERO...
...WHO CAN LEAD JAPAN TO A WORLD CUP VICTORY.
WHICH MEANS EVERY-ONE *ELSE* WILL HAVE THEIR LIVES UPENDED IN THE PURSUIT OF THAT.

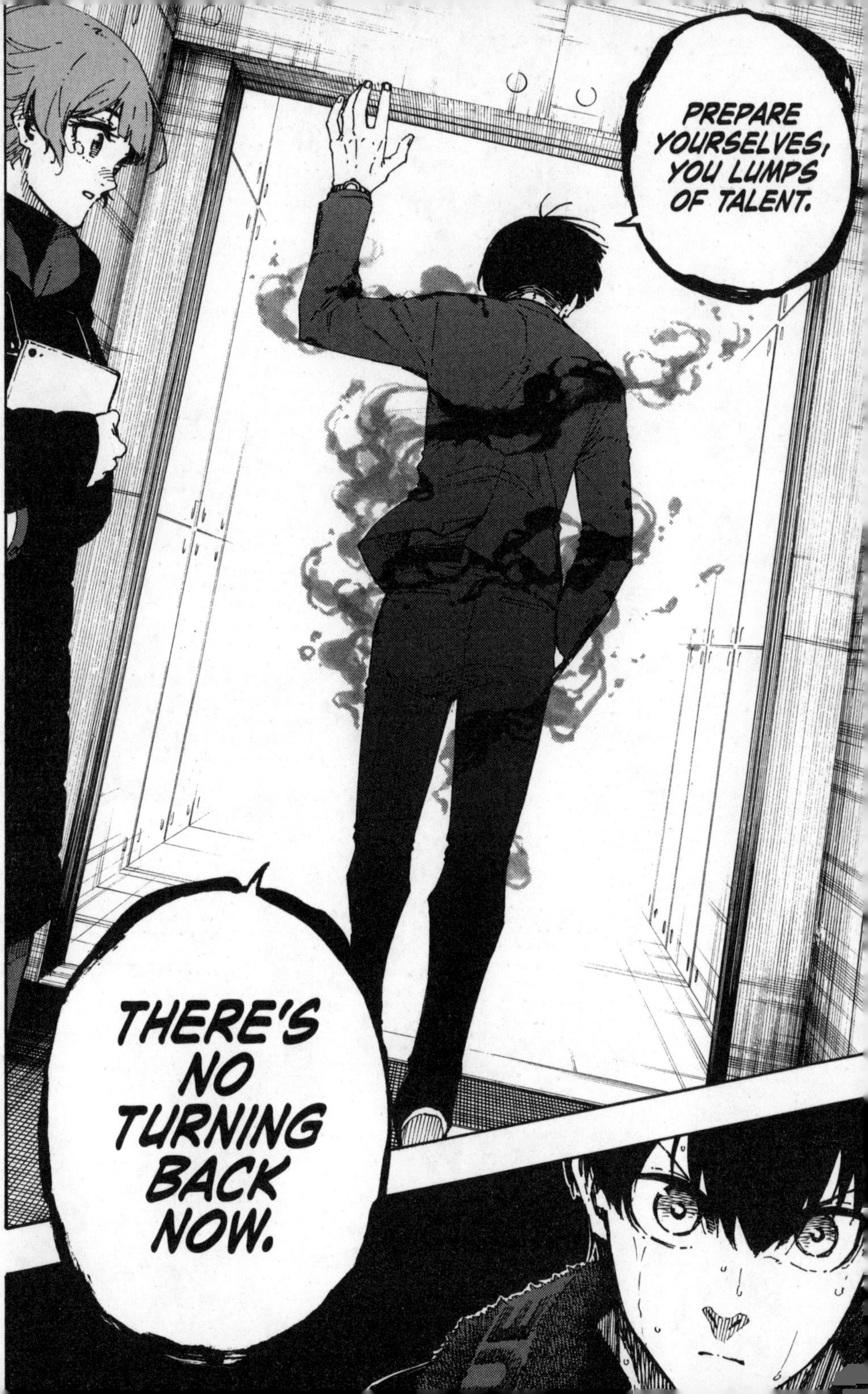
PREPARE YOURSELVES, YOU LUMPS OF TALENT.
THERE'S NO TURNING BACK NOW.

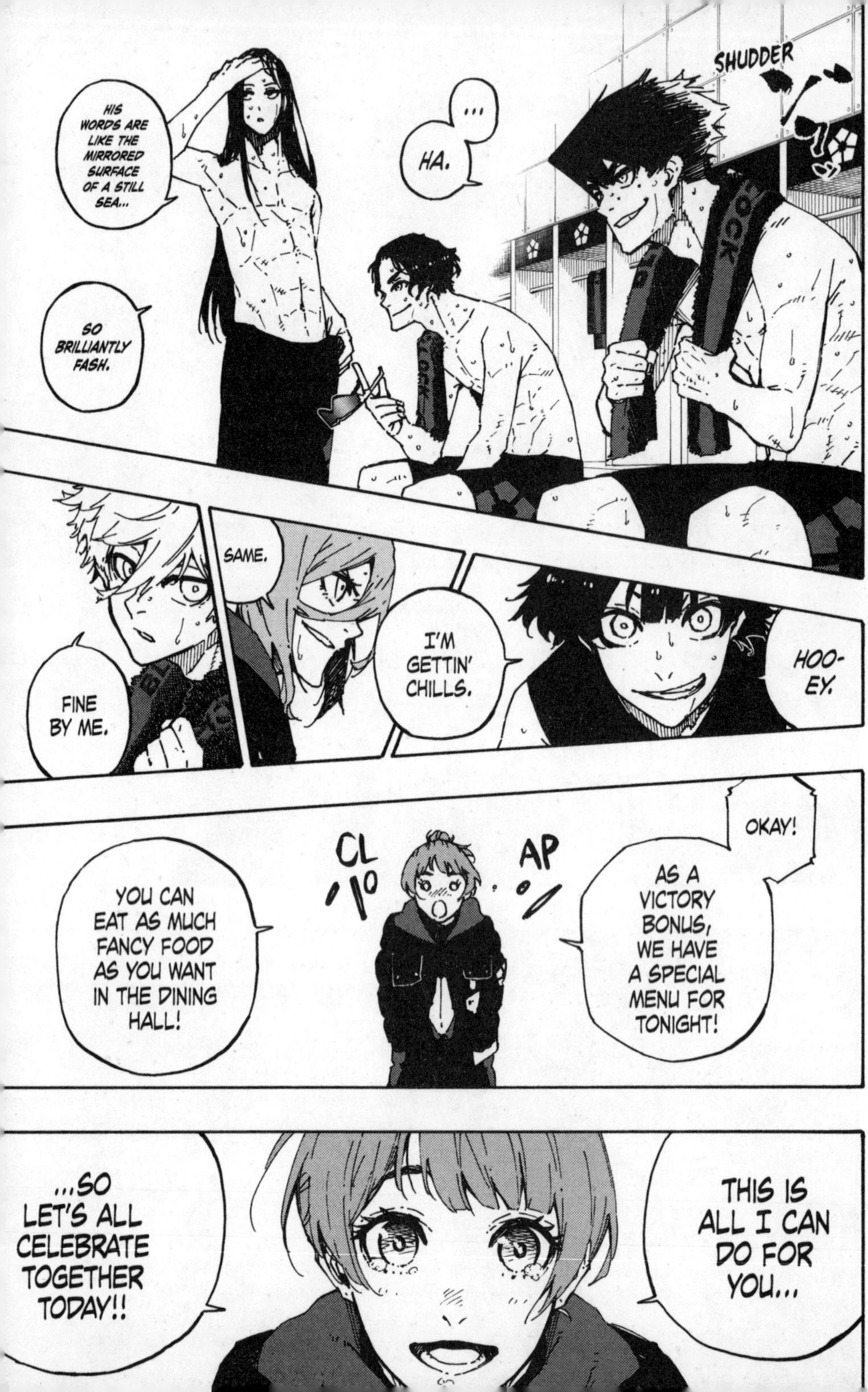

SHUDDER
... HA.
HIS WORDS ARE LIKE THE MIRRORED SURFACE OF A STILL SEA...
SO BRILLIANTLY FASH.
HOO-EY.
I'M GETTIN' CHILLS.
SAME.
FINE BY ME.
OKAY!
AS A VICTORY BONUS, WE HAVE A SPECIAL MENU FOR TONIGHT!
CL AP
YOU CAN EAT AS MUCH FANCY FOOD AS YOU WANT IN THE DINING HALL!
THIS IS ALL I CAN DO FOR YOU...
...SO LET'S ALL CELEBRATE TOGETHER TODAY!!

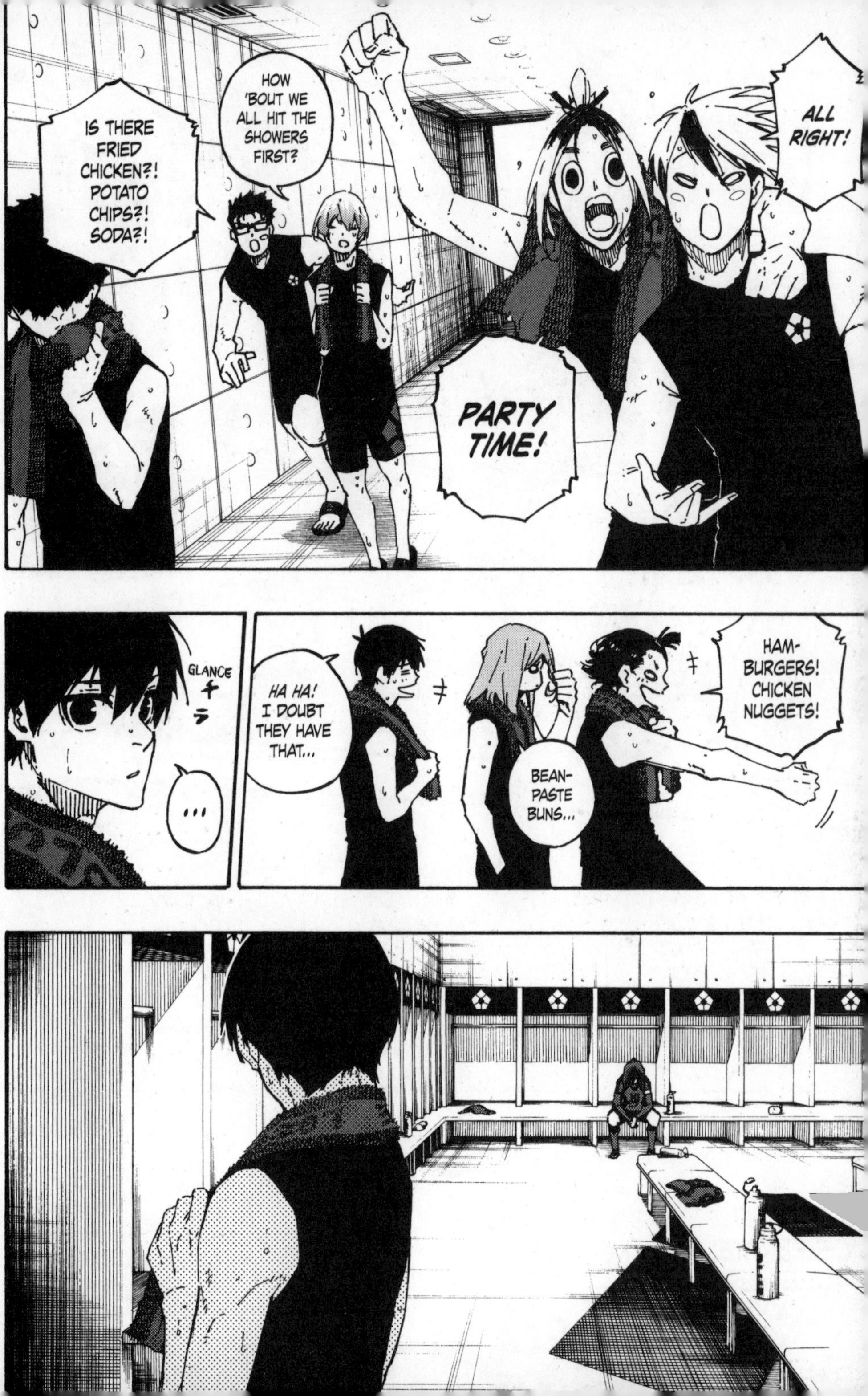
ALL RIGHT!
PARTY TIME!
HOW 'BOUT WE ALL HIT THE SHOWERS FIRST?
IS THERE FRIED CHICKEN?! POTATO CHIPS?! SODA?!
HAM-BURGERS! CHICKEN NUGGETS!
BEAN-PASTE BUNS...
HA HA! I DOUBT THEY HAVE THAT...
GLANCE
...

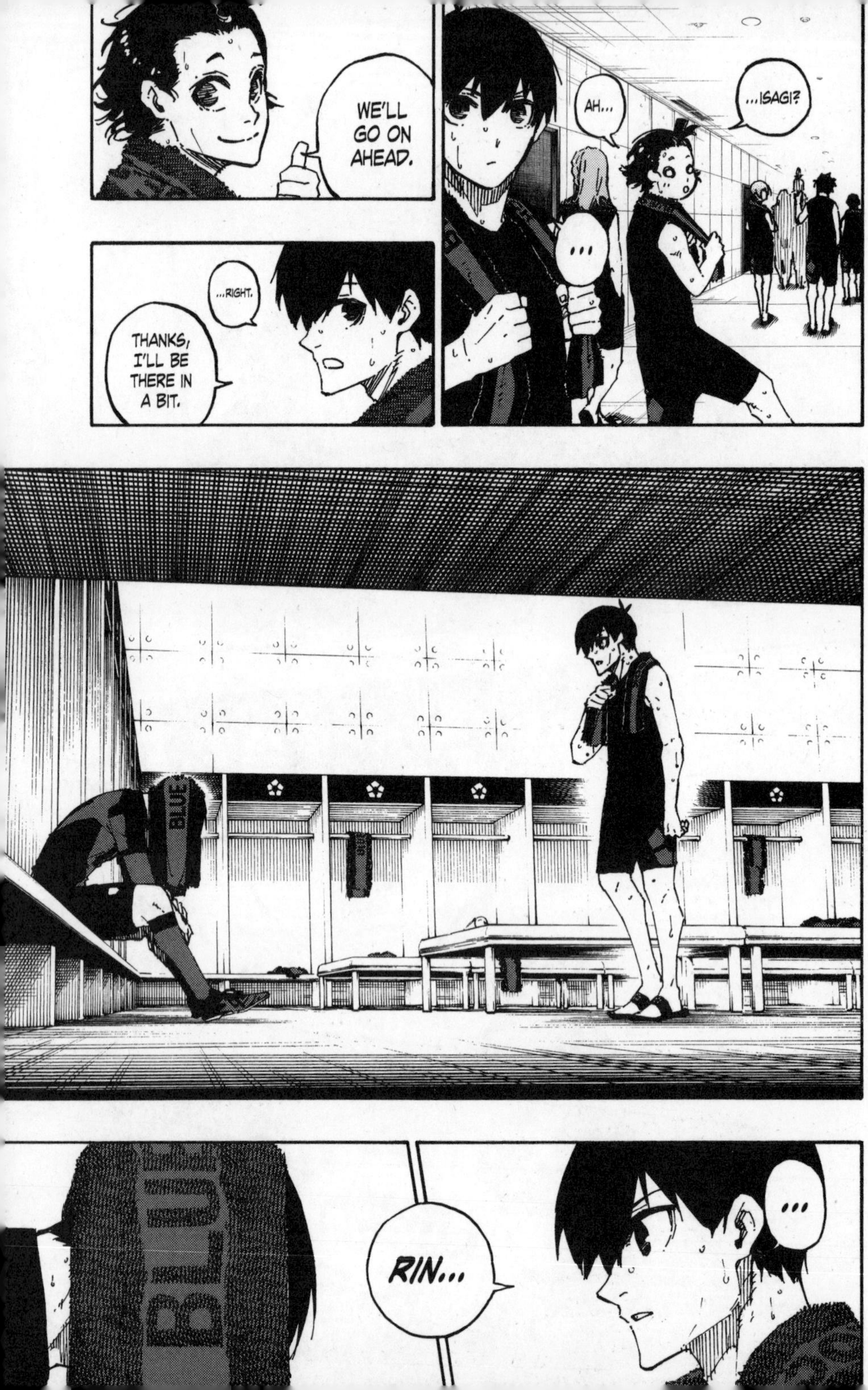

...ISAGI?
AH...
...
WE'LL GO ON AHEAD.
...RIGHT.
THANKS, I'LL BE THERE IN A BIT.
BLUE
...
RIN...
BLUE

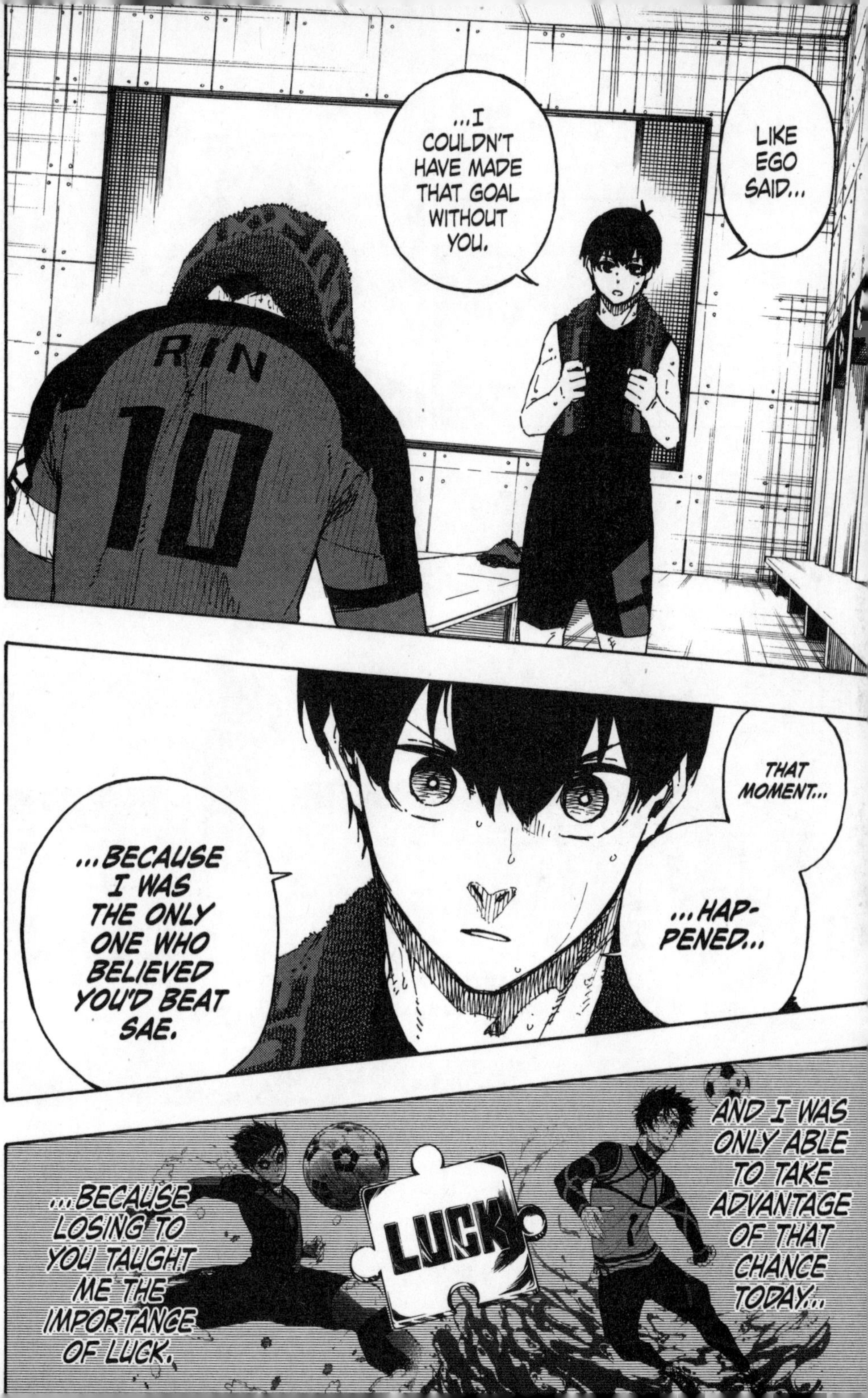
LIKE EGO SAID...
...I COULDN'T HAVE MADE THAT GOAL WITHOUT YOU.
RIN
10
THAT MOMENT...
...HAP-PENED...
...BECAUSE I WAS THE ONLY ONE WHO BELIEVED YOU'D BEAT SAE.
AND I WAS ONLY ABLE TO TAKE ADVANTAGE OF THAT CHANCE TODAY...
LUCK
...BECAUSE LOSING TO YOU TAUGHT ME THE IMPORTANCE OF LUCK.

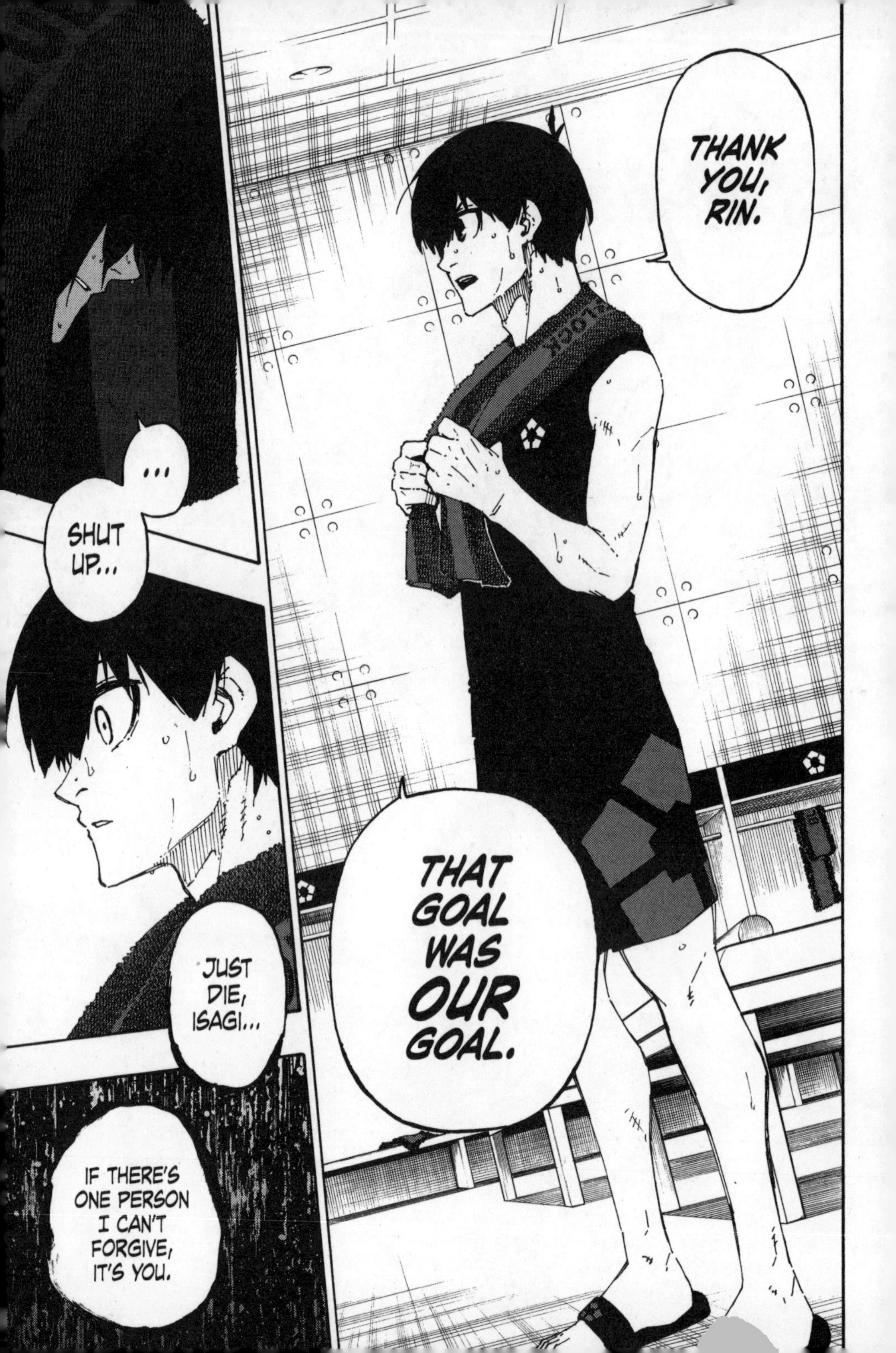
THANK YOU, RIN.
THAT GOAL WAS OUR GOAL.
...
SHUT UP...
JUST DIE, ISAGI...
IF THERE'S ONE PERSON I CAN'T FORGIVE, IT'S YOU.

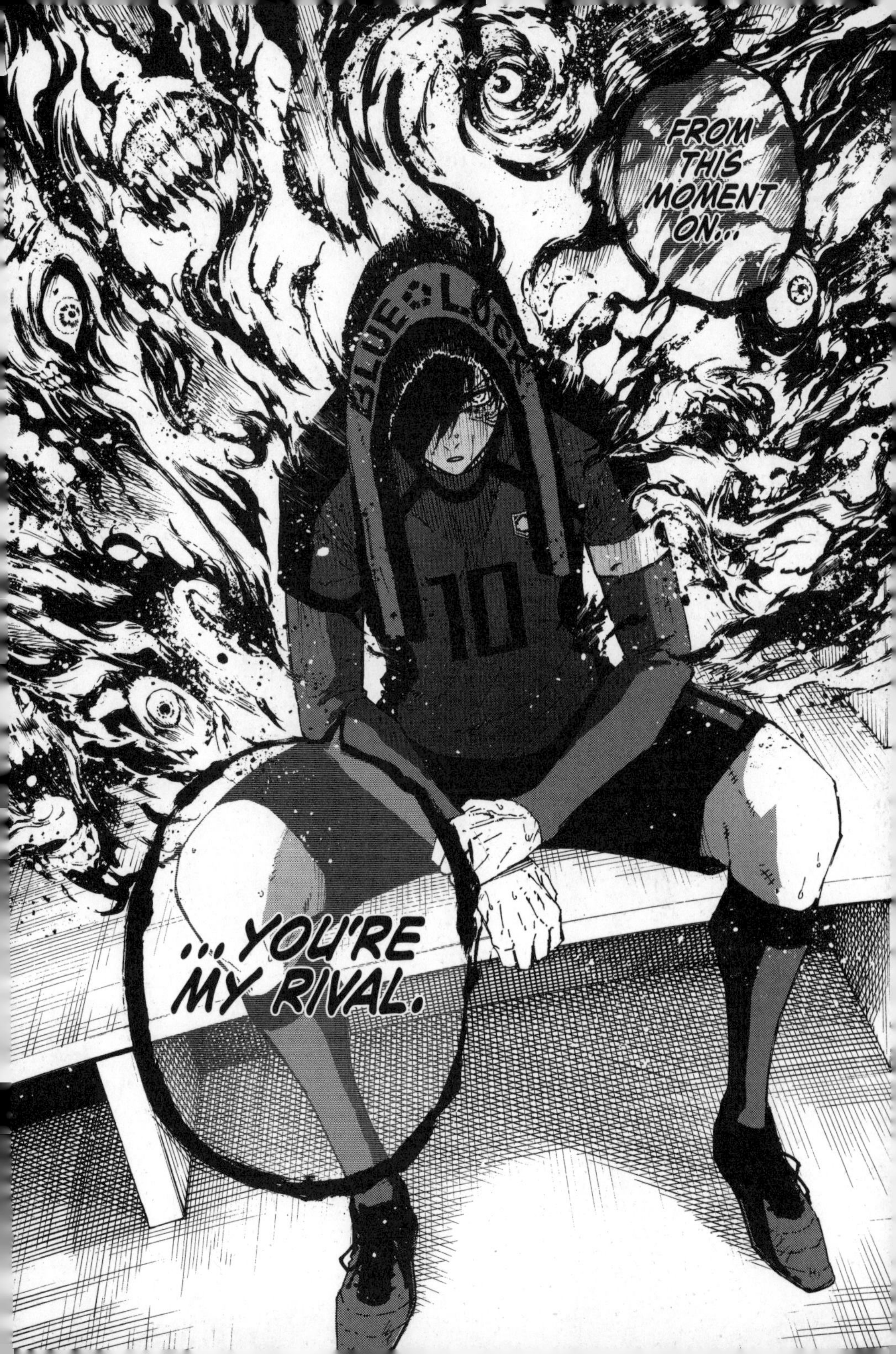
FROM THIS MOMENT ON...
...YOU'RE MY RIVAL.

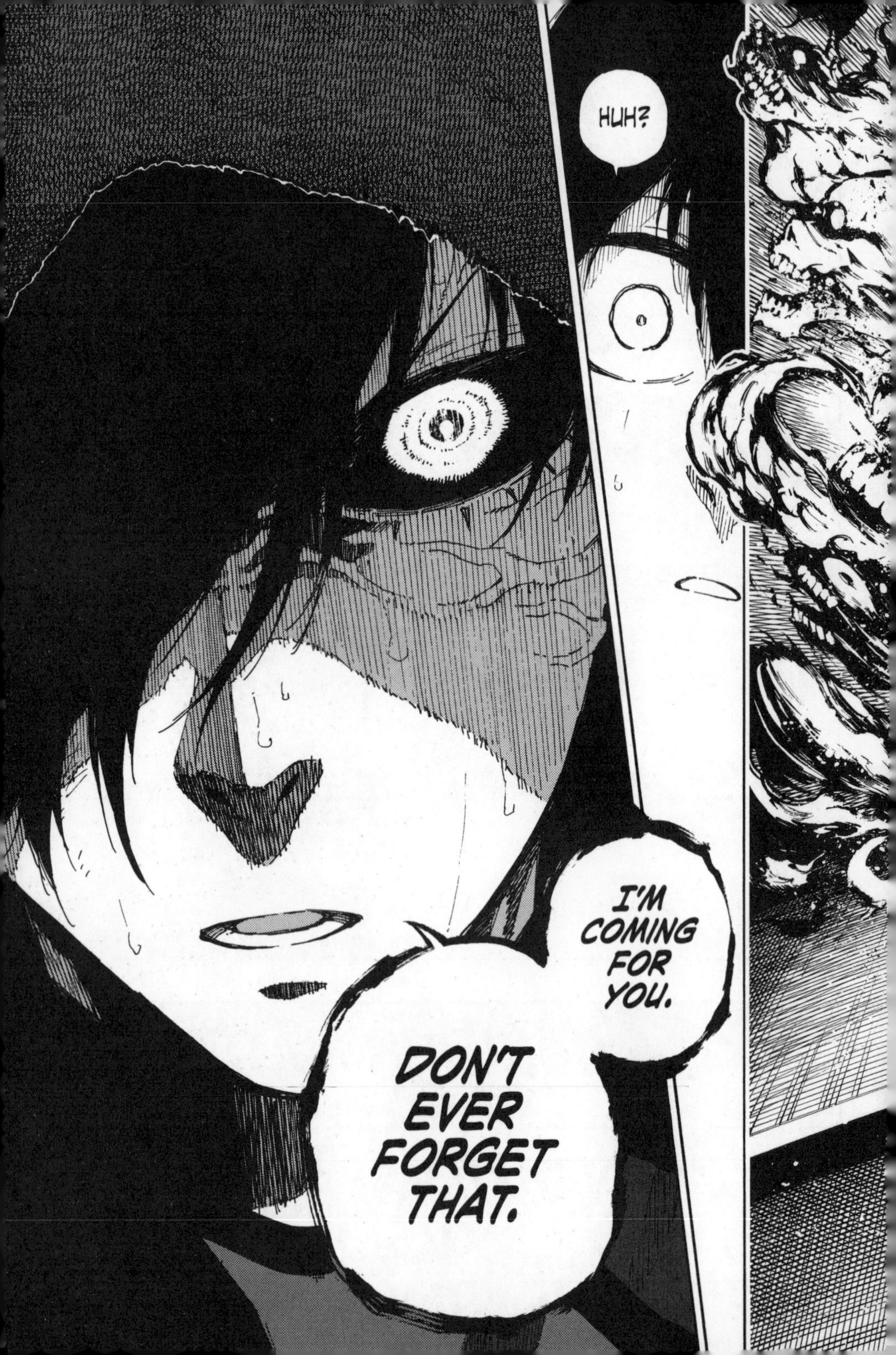
HUH?
I'M COMING FOR YOU.
DON'T EVER FORGET THAT.

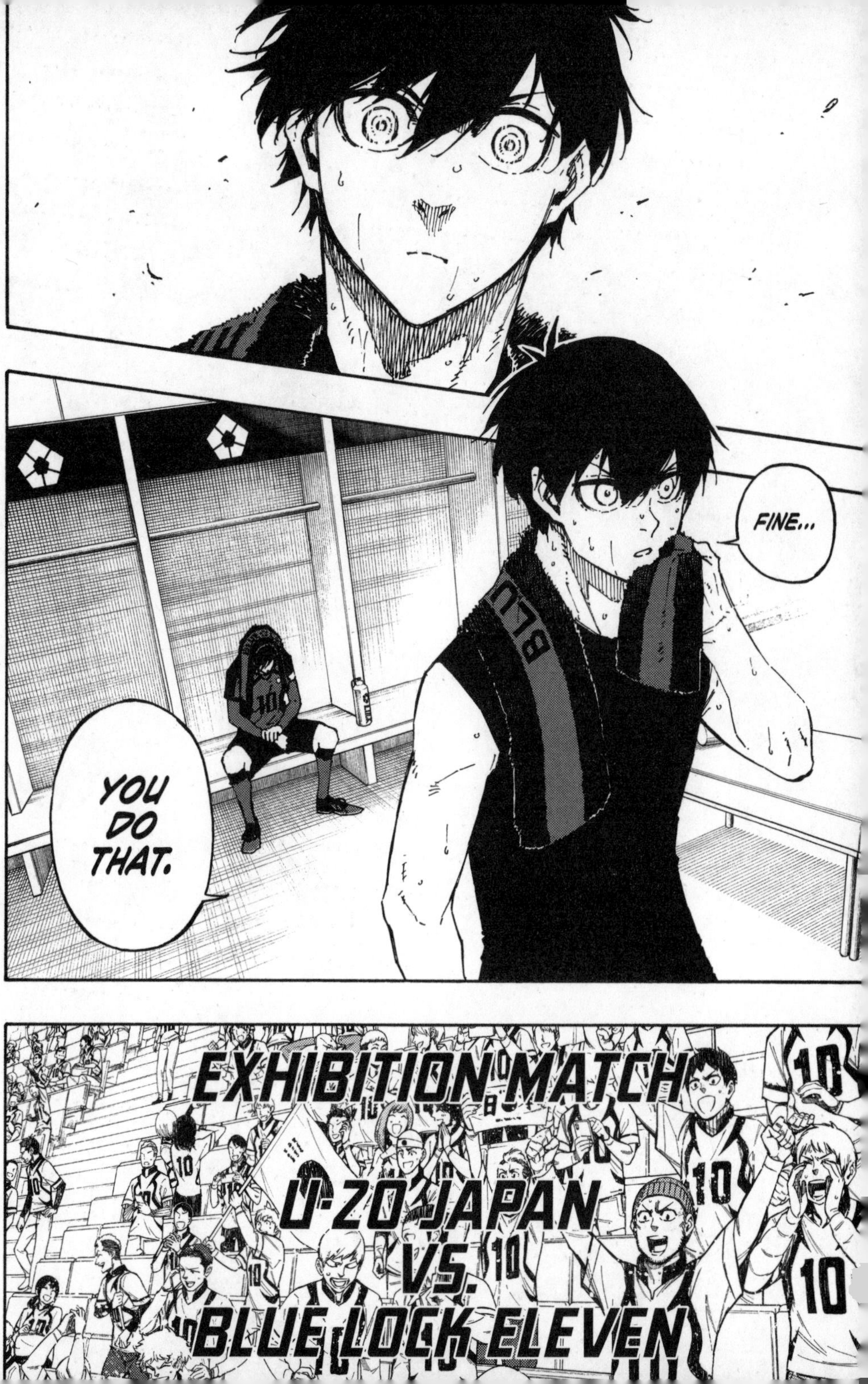
FINE...
YOU DO THAT.
EXHIBITION MATCH
U-20 JAPAN
V.S.
BLUE LOCK ELEVEN

SCORE

U-20 JAPAN 3 - 4 **BLUE LOCK ELEVEN**

U-20 JAPAN | BLUE LOCK ELEVEN
3 - 4
BLUE LOCK

GOAL

7'	SAE ITOSHI	30'	SEISHIRO NAGI
		41'	RIN ITOSHI
53'	RYUSEI SHIDOU		
58'	RYUSEI SHIDOU		
		74'	SHOUEI BAROU
		90+1'	YOICHI ISAGI

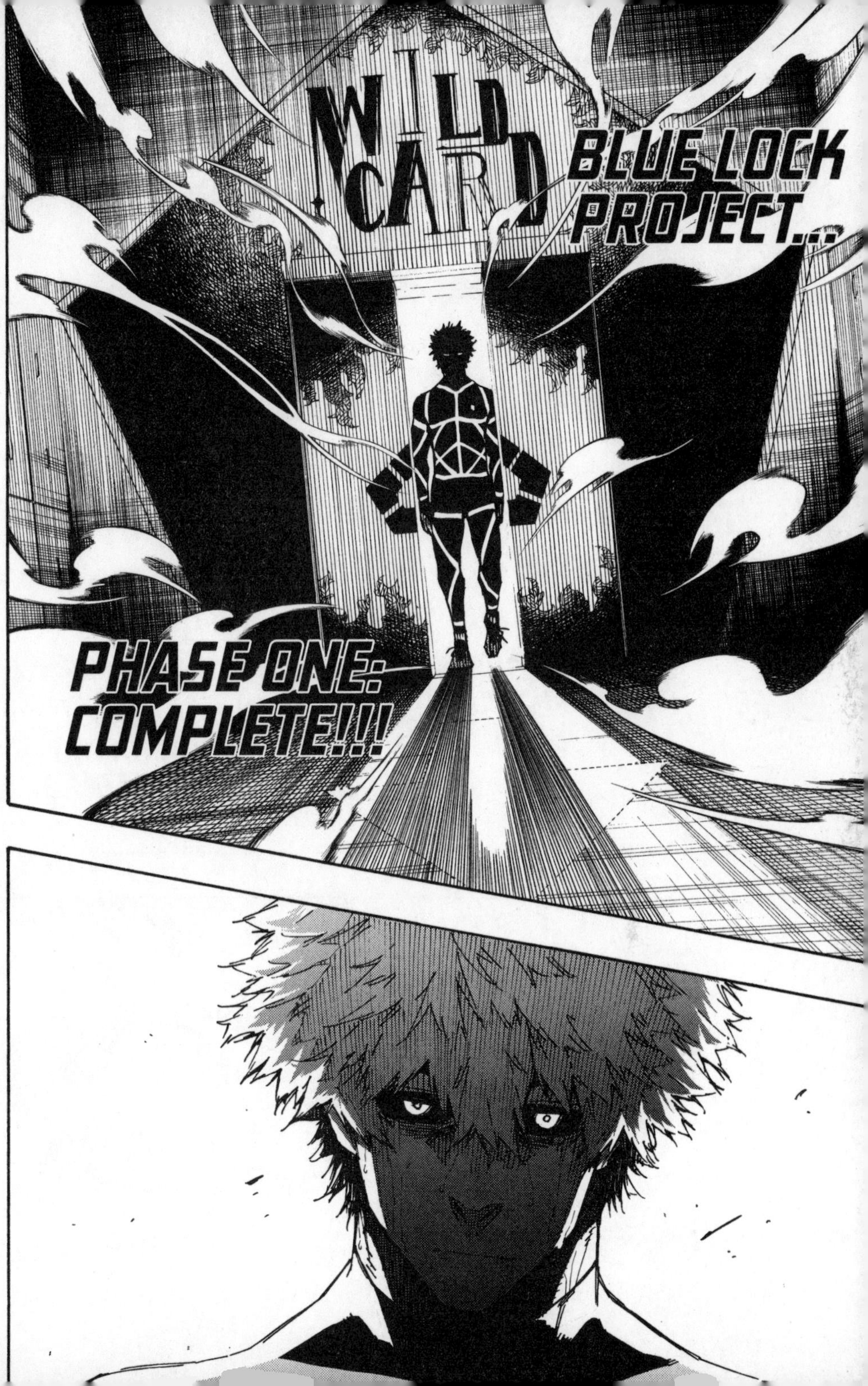
WILD CARD
BLUE LOCK PROJECT...
PHASE ONE: COMPLETE!!!

BLUE LOCK

CONTINUED IN VOL. 18

STORY — MUNEYUKI KANESHIRO

ART — YUSUKE NOMURA

ART ASSISTANTS

TAKANIWA-SAN
MUTO-SAN
OTAKE-SAN
SATO-SAN
KAWAI-SAN
SUEHIRO-SAN
AYATSUKA-SAN
FUKAYA-SAN
HARA-SAN
EBISAWA-SAN
(LISTED RANDOMLY)

DESIGN

HISAMOCHI-SAN
OSOKO-SAN
(HIVE)

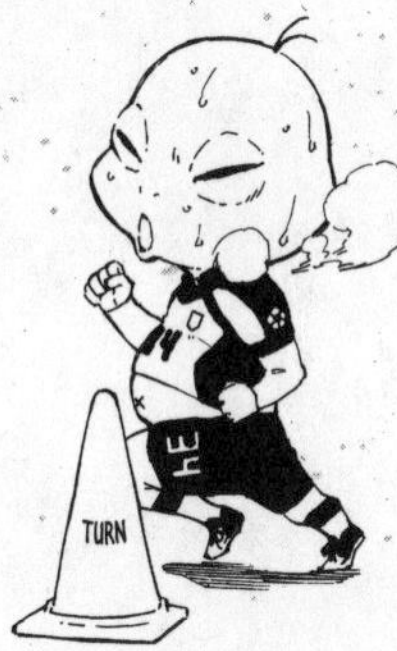
TURN

THANK YOU FOR BUYING VOLUME 17!

I'M THRILLED TO SAY THAT I RECENTLY HELD AN EXHIBITION OF ORIGINAL *BLUE LOCK* ART! I'M SO LUCKY I WAS ABLE TO DO THAT BEFORE THE ANIME STARTED. BETWEEN THE ANIME AND THE EXHIBITION, I FEEL LIKE IT REALLY DOESN'T GET BETTER THAN THIS...

BUT *BLUE LOCK* IS STILL FULL OF TWISTS AND TURNS!! I'LL GIVE IT EVERYTHING I'VE GOT IN 2022 AND SHOW YOU ALL MY GRATITUDE BY BRINGING YOU MORE AND MORE EXCITING SCENES!!

BLUE LOCK UNIFORM COLLECTION 6

BONUS SECTION

SEISHIRO NAGI & REO MIKAGE / HAKUHO H.S. [TOKYO]

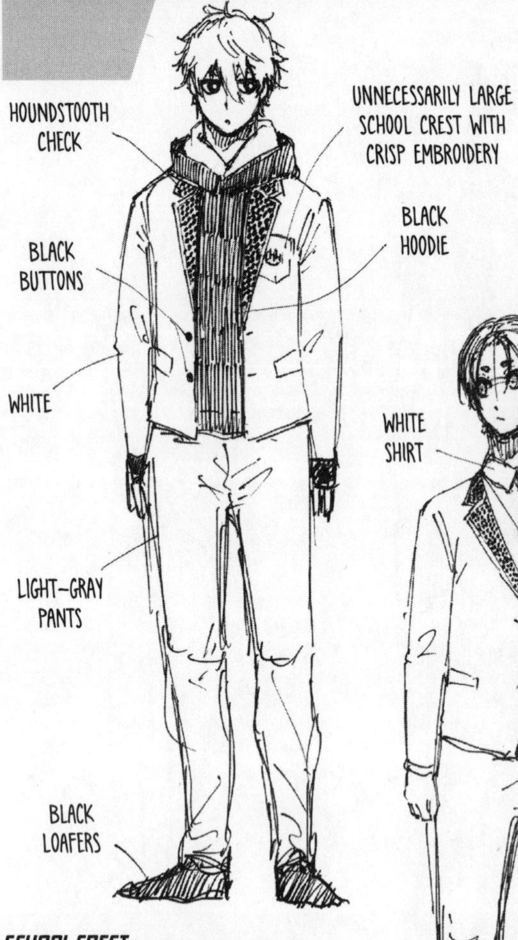
HOUNDSTOOTH CHECK
UNNECESSARILY LARGE SCHOOL CREST WITH CRISP EMBROIDERY
BLACK HOODIE
BLACK BUTTONS
WHITE
LIGHT-GRAY PANTS
BLACK LOAFERS

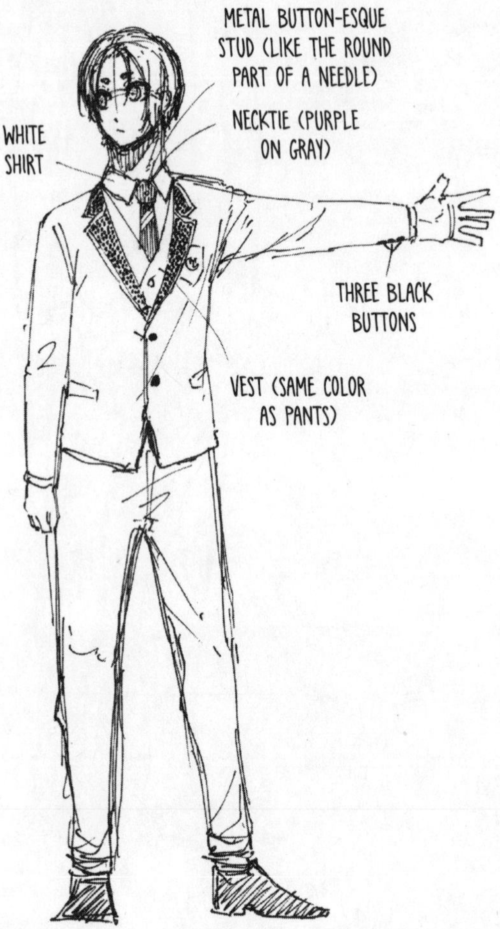
METAL BUTTON-ESQUE STUD (LIKE THE ROUND PART OF A NEEDLE)
NECKTIE (PURPLE ON GRAY)
WHITE SHIRT
THREE BLACK BUTTONS
VEST (SAME COLOR AS PANTS)

SCHOOL CREST

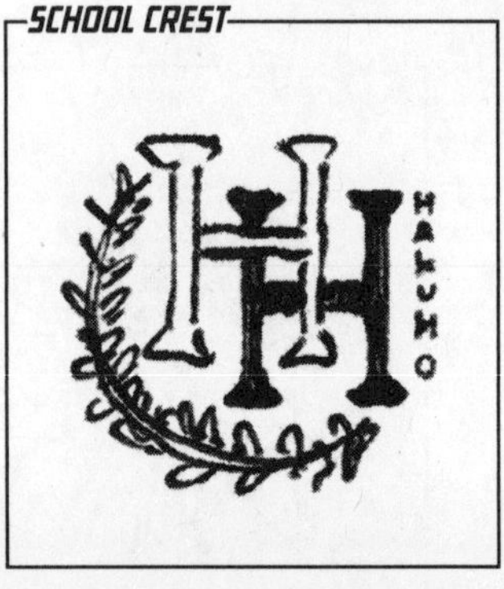
HAKUHO

BLUE LOCK UNIFORM COLLECTION 7

JYUBEI ARYU / GOKO H.S.

[TOCHIGI PREFECTURE]

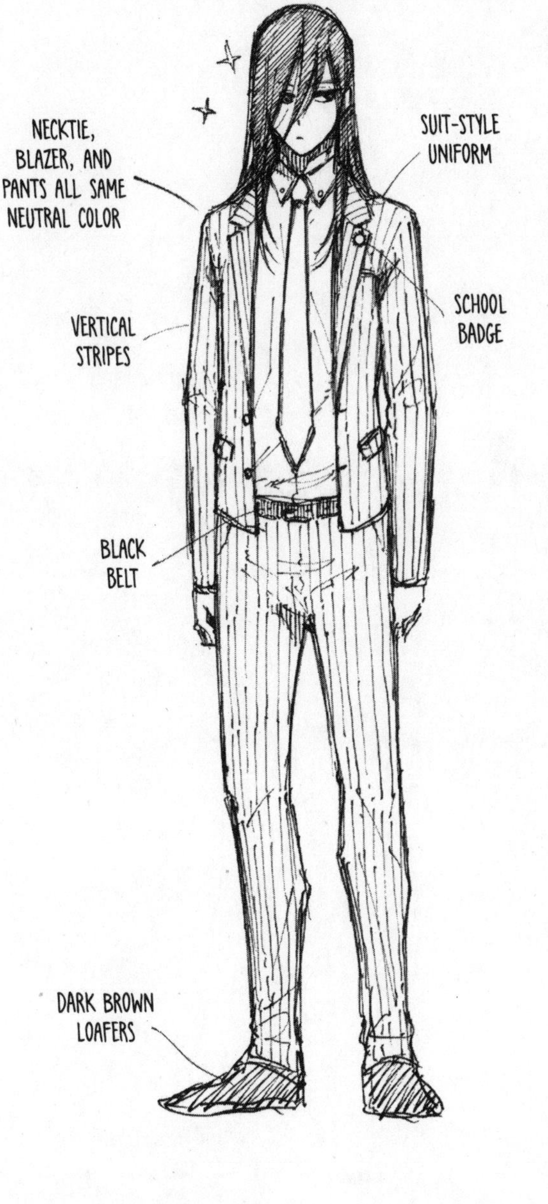
NECKTIE, BLAZER, AND PANTS ALL SAME NEUTRAL COLOR
SUIT-STYLE UNIFORM
VERTICAL STRIPES
SCHOOL BADGE
BLACK BELT
DARK BROWN LOAFERS

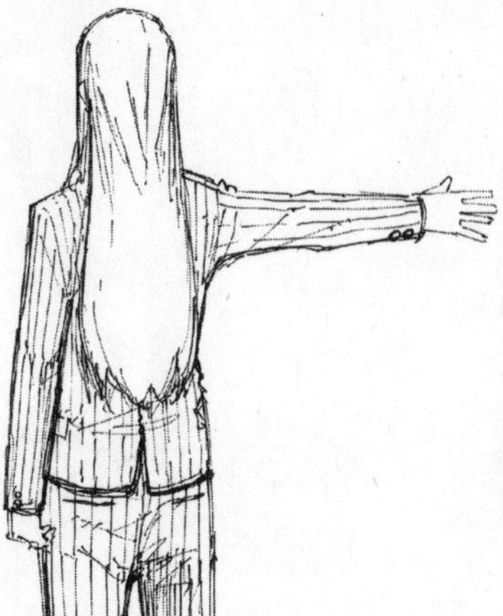

SCHOOL CREST

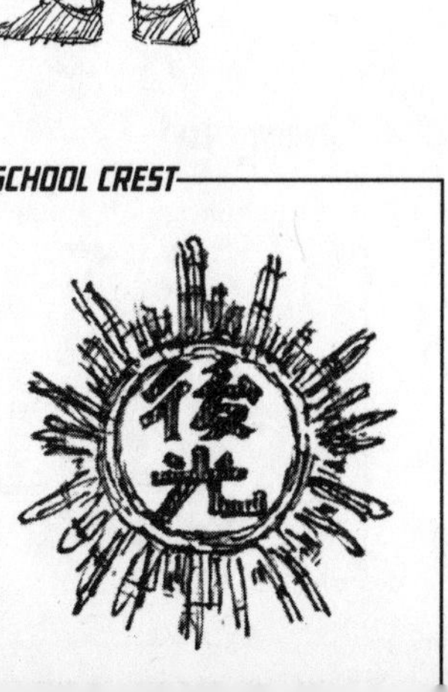
後光

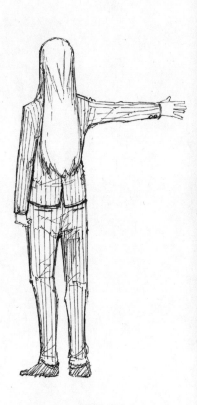

BLUE LOCK UNIFORM COLLECTION 8
AOSHI TOKIMITSU / DARUMA HIGASHI H.S. [NIIGATA PREFECTURE]

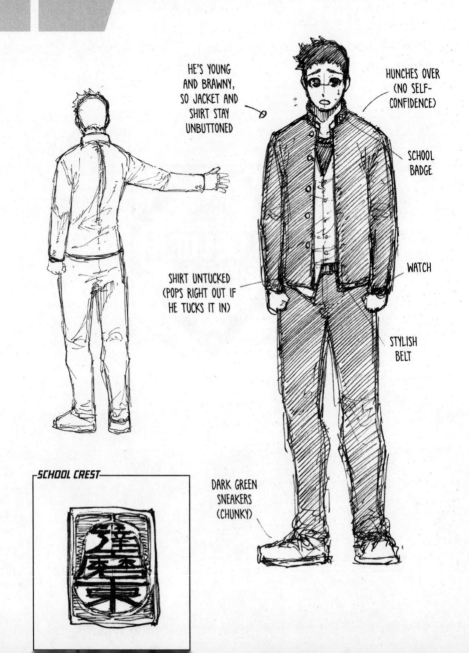

HE'S YOUNG AND BRAWNY, SO JACKET AND SHIRT STAY UNBUTTONED

HUNCHES OVER (NO SELF-CONFIDENCE)

SCHOOL BADGE

WATCH

SHIRT UNTUCKED (POPS RIGHT OUT IF HE TUCKS IT IN)

STYLISH BELT

SCHOOL CREST

DARK GREEN SNEAKERS (CHUNKY)

BLUE LOCK

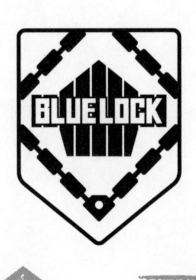

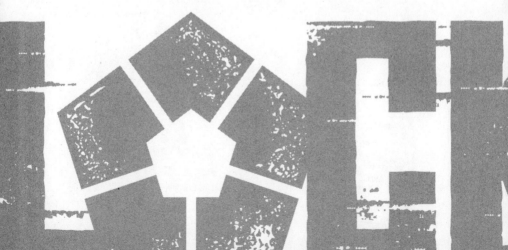

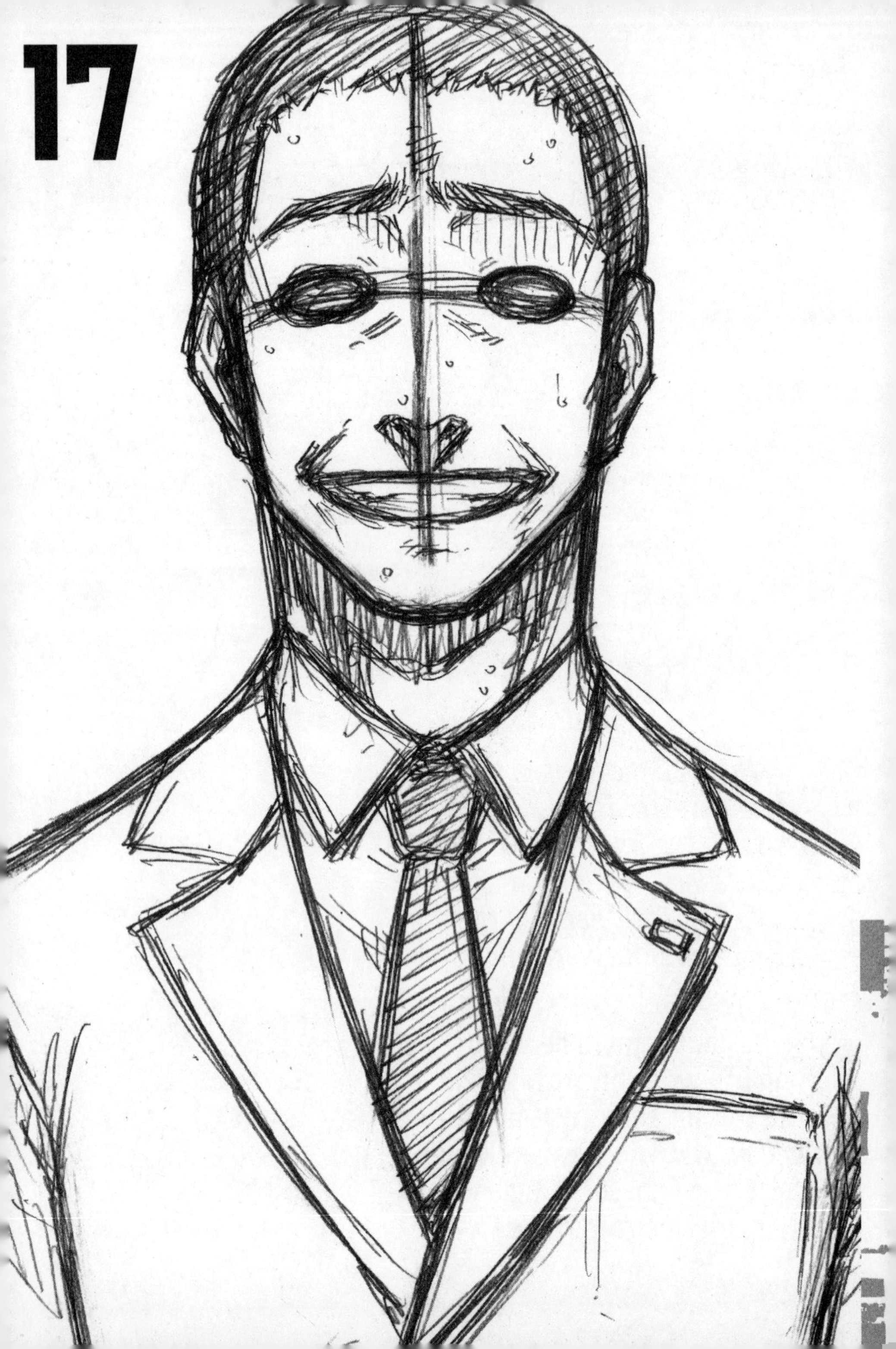
17

Yusuke Nomura

"The U-20 match is in the final stretch! I feel like I'm crossing the finish line with all the readers who have made it this far. Let's keep up the pace until the very end!"

Yusuke Nomura debuted in 2014 with the grotesquely cute cult hit alien invasion story *Dolly Kill Kill*, which was released digitally in English by Kodansha. Nomura illustrates *Blue Lock*.

Muneyuki Kaneshiro

"I did my best! I hope you enjoy volume 17!"

Muneyuki Kaneshiro broke out as the creator of 2011's *As the Gods Will*, a death game story that spawned two sequels and a film adaptation directed by the legendary Takashi Miike. Kaneshiro writes the story of *Blue Lock*.

Fire Force Omnibus

Created by
Atsushi Ohkubo

600 pages each—blaze past the anime!

In the year 198 of the Solar Era, the city of Tokyo is plagued by a deadly phenomenon: spontaneous human combustion! The only ones who can stop it are the Fire Force!

RATED: 16+

KODANSHA

Tsugumi Project

Created by
ippatu

A gritty, post-apocalyptic action manga!
A French soldier named Leon is sent on
a suicide mission to recover an ancient
weapon from Old Japan...a place ruled
by huge, mutated monsters that may
challenge what it means to be human.

RATED: 16+

 KODANSHA

The Seven Deadly Sins: Four Knights of the Apocalypse

Created by
Nakaba Suzuki

End of the world of the Sins?!

Return to the magical and thrilling world of Britannia with this new adventure from the creator of *The Seven Deadly Sins*, the manga that inspired the No. 1 hit Netflix Original Anime!

RATED: 16+

Noragami: Stray God Omnibus

Created by
Adachitoka

Revisit the Far Shore in this 3-in-1!

Yato is a homeless god without a shrine who
serves those in need. Hiyori is stuck between
two worlds after an accident. Will they both
be able to help each other...?

RATED: 16+

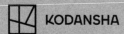

Quality Assurance in Another World

Created by
Masamichi Sato

Bugs abound in this imperfect world!

Nikola's world is filled with anomalies and Haga,
a "Seeker," comes to "debug" the situation.
Can it be that your life is nothing like what you
thought? Nobody's getting reincarnated here!

RATED: 13+

 **KODANSHA**

Wistoria: Wand and Sword

Story by Fujino Omori
Art by Toshi Aoi

The new fantasy series from manga royalty!

In a world where magic means might, one young swordsman chases an impossible dream of making it to the top.

RATED: 13+

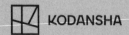
KODANSHA

A Kodansha Trade Paperback Original

Published in the United States by
Kodansha USA Publishing, LLC, New York.

Publication rights for this English edition arranged through
Kodansha Ltd., Tokyo.

First published in Japan in 2021 by Kodansha Ltd., Tokyo
as *Buruu rokku*, volume 17.

ISBN 978-1-64651-674-2

Printed in the United States of America.

9 8 7 6 5 4 3 2 1

Original Digital Edition Translator: Nate Derr
Original Digital Edition Letterer: Chris Burgener
Original Digital Edition Editor: Thalia Sutton
YKS Services LLC/SKY JAPAN, Inc.
Print Edition Letterer: Scott O. Brown
Print Edition Editor: Andres Oliver
Managing Editor: Dasia Payne
Production Manager: Angela Zurlo

Kodansha USA Publishing edition cover design by Matthew Akuginow

Publisher: Toshihiro Tsuchiya

Director of Publishing Services: Ben Applegate
Director of Publishing Operations: Dave Barrett

KODANSHA.US